EMMA HART AND THE WEREWOLVES

A.L. Stephens

Rock Creek Press

Rock Creek Press

Books in the Emma Hart Series:

Book 1 - Emma Hart and the Demi-gods

Book 2 - Emma Hart and the Werewolves

CONTENTS

CHAPTER 1 -
TY CAN'T FORGET

When Emma came into my life, I didn't think my life could have changed so drastically. I knew when we took her from the Rifts, we'd be changing her life, saving her, but I didn't know she'd be saving and changing my life completely. The moment I touched her, I knew my life had changed.

Even with her as injured as she was, so close to death, our connection was still strong enough to send a shock through my system. I had only known her for three weeks before the battle at the Elders. Now, three months have passed since the battle and that day will be a day that I will never forget.

I tried to ignore it, but the more I got to know Emma, the more I knew she was special, and not in the way we, all Demi-gods, had hoped she would be. Hoping she was The One for the better of our people was definitely something I had hoped for, but finding out that she was *my* one, was not something I expected.

When we went to the Elders, I was confident

in Emma's Talents to keep her safe. She had already shown she was capable of so many amazing things, but I didn't realize I needed to worry about protecting her from herself. I should have known because I had come to see how selfless and caring she was for people she had only just met.

Seeing Shae lying in Charlie's arms, dead, will be something stuck in my memory for a very long time. Seeing Charlie completely devastated from the loss of his Anima Gemella will be something I'll never forget, also.

Watching Emma work her Talent or whatever it was, was something to see. She saw something none of us saw and she did something I've never seen. She brought Shae back to life. I could Sense her heart weakening and then stop, but then Emma did her thing and Shae's heart was stronger than ever, but her body was weak.

Then time stood still. One minute, everyone was ecstatic about Shae being saved and the next, we were frantic about Emma. Libby couldn't handle all the emotions and passed out. Max took her back to the jet. Charlie Jumped Shae back to the Estate. Malory, Alysa, and Clay helped me with Emma.

It's so hard to think about how she laid motionless in my arms. I kept thinking she couldn't be dead, she just couldn't. After all that she'd done, there was no way she was dead, but I could tell she wasn't there with us. I searched for her heartbeat, she had one, but it was extremely weak. She was just a shell, I could tell what made her Emma, had left. I was frantic to get her back to the Estate, to have Doc there to help, and Meredith's wisdom to think of what to do.

I punched the punching bag hanging in front of me to bring me back to present day. I don't like thinking about that day, but it always creeps into my mind. I punch harder as the memory of her warmth had started to leave her body. Then Vanessa's face comes to mind and I punch the bag so hard that a hole rips through it.

Vanessa has always been at fault for everything. But now, I have a personal reason to want her caught, and admittedly, dead. I've never wished that about anyone, but I have never felt like this before now.

As I move over to a new bag, Alysa walks into the gym.

"Hi Ty," she says more shyly than I've ever heard her sound.

"Hey," is all I say back. I'm trying really hard not to blame her, and Charlie, for what happened to Emma. But I can't help think that if they hadn't run away, and just faced the punishments they had coming to them, that day wouldn't have happened.

When we got back, the Leaders were still missing, and even right now, nobody has heard from them. I know that is what I need to be focusing on, but I just can't get my head on straight. When we got back, the guys and I discussed what should happen to Charlie and Alysa because there had to be consequences for their actions. A decision was made that they would spend two months in a cell, I didn't feel like it was long enough, but I was out voted. Max said that I couldn't be objective because of how I was feeling. He may have been right.

"How are you?" Alysa asks, pulling me out of my thoughts.

"I'm fine," I answer shortly.

"That's good. Can I get you anything?" she asks.

"No, Alysa, I'm fine. I just want to work out," I say in a way that I hope she takes as me telling her to leave.

She nods and then leaves. Well, she got the message. As she walks by, out of the corner of my eye, I see her wipe something from her face.

Crap, is she crying? I think to myself. Ugh, now I feel bad but not bad enough to go after her to talk to her. I'll let someone else comfort her. She needs to understand how stupid she's been.

I start punching the bag again, trying not to break this one. The door opens again and sunlight shines through, silhouetting someone. A smile spreads across my face.

"You still mad?" she asks.

"Just upset. I can't get that image out of my head," I say.

She walks into the room and wraps her arms around my waist. I brush the hair out of her face and bend down and kiss her. When I open my eyes, I'm staring into the most beautiful blue eyes I have ever seen. Emma's beaming smile fills me with warmth and washes all memory from that day away, at least for a moment.

CHAPTER 2

- AFTERMATH

"Hi," I say after a minute of kissing Ty.

"You should be resting," Ty says but squeezes me into a tighter hug.

"I am rested," I can see the 'v' between his eyes is back. A sign he's been thinking about something stressful and this time I know what. "Thinking about that day again?"

"It's hard to forget," he says, shrugging. I reach up and try to smooth the 'v' away.

"It all worked out well enough. I'm fine. Shae is fine. The only thing I regret is that Vanessa and Chris got away," I say the last bit with gritted teeth.

"We'll Track them down and they'll get what they deserve," Ty says, bending down and kissing me again, this time deepening the kiss.

The all too familiar fire in the pit of my stomach ignites. I run my hands up his chest and around his neck, up through his hair, and link my fingers together once they touch each other. I hold his face even closer to mine, I wouldn't have thought it was possible. Ty steps closer to me so that our bodies are all but one. I can feel his heart hammering against his chest, beating into mine. It's going almost as fast as my heart.

Our kissing slows. As Ty kisses my nose, he takes a step back, putting a little space between us.

"I keep expecting for these feelings to simmer down but they just continue to get more intense," he says with a small laugh.

"I know, same for me," I say, my cheeks turning a little pink. I take another step away. I can feel the pull from our electrical pulse is causing havoc on my body. "I'm going to go get some lunch, you want to join me?"

"I'll catch up with you in a few, I need to finish this workout. Maybe even more so now," he says with a smirk and a wink.

Heart fluttering, I leave Ty beating the stuffing out of another punching bag. Thinking about the little 'v' in between his eyes, has me thinking back about that day.

I didn't quite die, I don't think, but I did have an out-of-body experience. I was standing beside my body, and I could see and hear everything going on around me, but nobody could hear or see me. I couldn't feel anything, either. I was watching Ty shaking my shoulders, trying to wake me but I couldn't feel it. I could see Libby collapse, but they couldn't hear me telling them I was okay, that I was right there. Thinking back about it, I feel like I'm there, experiencing it all over again.

A bright white light, an unnaturally bright light, comes from the doorway leading outside. The door that Max had just walked out of, carrying Libby. I walk towards it but instead of stepping outside of the mountain mansion, I'm suddenly standing on top of a mountain, THE mountain, Olympus.

A man at least 7 feet tall, and built like a pro-wrestler, is standing in front of me.

"God?" I ask nervously. Maybe I did die. *Crap! Crap! Crap!* "I died?"

"No, just 'a' god. I am Zeus," the man... errr god... ahh Zeus... says, in the deepest voice I've ever heard. "And no, you did not die. My brothers and I pulled you away to have a chat."

As Zeus stops talking, he sweeps his hand in front of him and two men, just as tall and built, walk from either side of me, making me jump.

Where Zeus has white, light hair, and the same color facial hair with dark gray eyes, one of his brother's has blonde wavy hair, no facial hair, and piercing blue eyes. The other brother is dark. Dark hair, dark facial hair, and dark, almost black eyes.

"Poseidon? Hades?" I ask. Now that my shock has worn off, my brain functions are starting to work again.

The blonde man bows his head and says, "Yes, I am Poseidon. It's nice to finally get to chat with you, Daughter."

Hades, the dark brother, steps forward and bows also, "I am Hades. As they have said, we have been wanting to have a word with you and thought now would be the best time to have it."

"Talk to me about what?" I ask. I'm getting a little nervous now. *Am I really standing here having a conversation with the Big Three?*

"To answer any questions you may have, that we feel we can answer," Zeus says, taking a seat on a boulder. The other two sit beside him.

"Questions?" I ask, sounding moronic.

"Yes, don't you have questions?" Hades asks, looking at me and then at his brothers like they might have gotten the wrong girl.

"Well, yes, I suppose I do. I'm just having a hard time thinking of them right now," I say honestly.

"Take some time, we have a little bit before we need to send you back," Poseidon states.

"Where are we?" I ask. It's the only thing I can think to ask of right now, even though I know the answer.

"Mt. Olympus," Zeus says.

"You guys live on top of Mt. Olympus?" I ask.

"No, this is just where we thought it might be more comfortable for you to talk with us," Poseidon says.

"And we're having this talk so that you can answer questions I might have?" I ask, yet another award-winning question.

"Yes," they say together but Zeus continues with, "within reason."

"Meaning, if I ask a question that you don't think I need to know the answer to, you won't answer?" I ask.

"Correct. There are things that you must find out for yourself," Hades states.

"Okay," I say, trying to sound more positive than I actually feel.

So, what are some questions I want to ask them? I know I had a bunch but now... now, I can't even remember my name. Poseidon had called me his daughter.

"You called me your daughter, what did you mean by that?" I ask, while looking at Poseidon.

"All Demi-gods are our children," Zeus says pointedly, but the way he is looking at Poseidon makes me feel like there is more to it.

"I don't know, I feel like you aren't telling me something. Is this something you can't tell me?" I ask.

Zeus bows his head and shakes it a little before

looking back up at me, "No, I suppose this is something you'll need to know so that other stuff makes more sense."

"Okay, so…." I urge.

"You must understand, we don't normally get involved in things down in the Inepti World, that's why we made Demi-gods. We can't personally do anything, it would cause the balance of the World to turn upside down and all would be destroyed. So, when we saw what our Demi-god, Vanessa, had in mind and that she started to act on her ideas, we decided we were going to need to step in and do something about it before she destroyed the World. We decided we'd make One. Our daughter. We chose your mother and father because they were as similar as one could be without being the same person. They held every value we wanted in the parents of the One we were willing to make," Zeus says.

"We could not have guessed at the level of evil Vanessa carried inside of her. If we had, we would have made it harder for her to find you and your parents. From the day she murdered your parents, we hoped she'd keep with her plan to see what Talents you'd have, which is why we held off on giving you your Talents until the very last second, on your birthday. There were many times we thought about just giving in and giving them to you. The amount of torture you were being put through, was torture to us as well, but just as we were about to give in, you would show strength and bravery beyond what we could have hoped for in you," Hades says, smiling encouraging at me.

"Each time you were knocked out or you passed out, we could see your strength grow ten times what it was before that round of torture began. It tore at us the amount of pain you were being put through, but we knew in the long run, the strength you'd receive from it, was more important. We are sorry about the pain and everything you went through. Again, we had no idea the amount of evil Vanessa had in her," Poseidon says a little sadly.

"My parents didn't get to raise me," I say.

"No, they did not, but you are everything that they were and more," Zeus says smiling at me.

"So, what did you do to make me 'your' daughter?" I ask. And now that I've asked it, I don't know if I really want the answer.

"We each gave a little of ourselves to you while you were in utero. If a doctor were to take a DNA sample from you, both of your parents' DNA would show up, as well as unknown DNA, which would be ours. In what we gave you, is every Talent that is known and unknown to the Demi-gods," Zeus says proudly.

"Is it safe for one person to have all these Talents?" I ask, slightly scared.

"It is for you but for anyone else, no," Hades states.

"Why is that?" I ask.

"Because of your makeup. You were made for this," Poseidon says.

"Literally," Hades says, winking at me.

People saying, 'literally', usually drives me crazy because they normally don't say it in the right context, but Hades said it correctly which makes me laugh.

"What's funny?" Zeus asks.

"I'm standing here talking with Zeus, Poseidon, and Hades... It's one of those surreal moments... that's not funny... but it's so not funny... that it makes you laugh," I say trying to stop myself from laughing.

The Big Three just look at each other, Hades shrugs his shoulders.

"She might be needing to get back down to her body, she's been out a little longer than we should have let her stay out," Poseidon says, looking at me with concern because I'm laughing so hard my eyes are watering.

"We'll leave you with this last thing, Daughter, and then you'll be returned back to your body," Zeus says.

"What you seek is what you'll find, when you go beyond the line," Hades states seriously. So serious, that my laughing cuts off instantly.

"Alone you'll go to bring all together those that are needed to do what needs to be done, but together as one you must be, to defeat what has begun," Poseidon adds. He disappears, as does Hades.

"Wait, what?" I ask, I'm trying my hardest to remember what they've both said. There's a ringing in my ears.

"Don't be scared, don't be brave, just be you, and all will be saved," Zeus says as he disappears.

"Zeus?" I say sleepily. "Poseidon? Hades? Come back. I can't... I can't remember... What did you say? Alone...? Together...? Scared...? Saved...? What does... this mean?"

I close my eyes and hear Zeus' booming voice in my head, *"Accept what is given. Absorb the energy. The time will come that you'll understand. Good luck, Daughter."*

Before I open my eyes, I can feel my body again. It feels heavy. I can hear everyone around me.

"It's stopped. She's not shining anymore," Libby's voice says from far away.

"It's like the time she Changed," Ty says. I can hear him walking towards me.

"Is she going to be okay?" Shae asks. It's so good to hear her voice. I had been afraid I would never hear it again.

"I'm okay," I say sleepily.

"Oh Emma!" They all exclaim. I hear them run

towards me and feel two people hugging me. By their scents, I know it's Libby and Shae.

"I'm okay, really. Just tired," I say again, but yawning this time.

"We'll let you sleep but we'll be back to check in on you soon," Libby says, I feel her and Shae get up off the bed.

"Ty?" I ask, searching with my hand. His hand instantly grabs mine.

"I'm not going anywhere," he says, bending down and kissing me on the cheek. I smile and then fall into a deep sleep.

When I had woken up three days later, I was weak. More so than I think I have ever been. I couldn't do anything by myself. Everyone was extremely worried about me. They thought that I used up all my energy, my Talent, to save Shae. They were still unsure how that had happened. I haven't gone into detail with them about anything yet.

I've been putting all my time and effort into getting my strength back and helping them locate Meredith, Doc, and Bill. They are still missing. The Trackers can't pick up a Signal of them. We are all afraid of what that means. They're either being

Cloaked or... I don't want to even think about the other option.

It took a month for me to regain the strength to get out of bed. Another month to walk any distance for a long period of time. Three months now and I'm just able to walk all the flights of stairs in the Estate without having to stop for a breath.

I found out the first day I fully woke up, that they had brought me home unconscious. Ty could tell I was alive, but my heartbeat was weak, so he wanted to get me back to the Estate as quickly as possible. He wanted me near Doc just as quickly. That's when they realized our Leaders were still not back.

They had been sending groups of five out looking for them. The parents who had made it back just before we moved to the Estate, were all back out actively looking for Meredith, Doc, and Bill as well.

The most recent group to be sent out was Charlie, Max, Clay, and two guys I had only met in passing, Jayce and Nick. They were to be back this evening. Ty had been staying behind to help me and taking turns with Libby to make sure I was Healing like I should have. I could tell he was torn between sending his Unit out without him and staying home with me.

When I voiced my concern, that he should go, that I would be fine, he told me that being away from me caused him more stress and he wouldn't be leaving me until he knew I was one hundred percent better.

So, I started to work harder to get back to normal but that only wore me out even more and actually made me worse. It also upset him and Libby, so I decided the only way to get us both back to our normal routines was to be patient and do what I was capable of and not push myself to the point of exhaustion, at least not every day.

I also learned the first day I was fully awake, that they took Elder Fadri to a European Demi-god headquarters. Someone had mentioned their family being stationed there and it being the safest place for our only surviving Elder. I had cried for all the Elder's we weren't able to save and my friends had to talk me down from my emotional spiral. They told me it wasn't my job to save everyone and there was no way I could have saved them all. I saved everyone that I could.

Speaking of saving someone, I haven't gotten to see Shae yet. I heard her voice the first time I sort of woke up back here at the Estate, but I haven't gotten to actually see her yet. I guess they only let her up to come see me because she was freaking out about it so much. They were afraid she was going to make herself sick unless they gave in and let her stay with me until I woke up. It was an argument after my first stirring or whatever you want to call it, that they made her go back to her room. When I had finally gotten the strength to walk out of my room, her room was my first stop. She wasn't there. Libby caught me in there and said that Shae was down in the pool.

Nobody has really told me how she's doing. They just say she was alive and doing exceptionally well. I decided to stop asking after the third denial and decided that I would find out for myself. But I found that extremely difficult as every time I went to go find her, she wasn't where I was looking. And as I've only now been able to walk the stairs by myself, I haven't been strong enough to go look for her. Today I was going to find her and get my answers.

As I make my way from the gym, where Ty was working out his frustrations, I see Libby up ahead of me.

"Hey Libs, hold up," I holler. My strength is back but my speed, not so much.

"Hey Em, what are you doing down here?" Libby asks, a little sternly.

"I came to see Ty, I was just heading up to get some lunch after I find Shae," I say as I catch up with her.

"You should go get lunch and get some rest afterwards. You've had a busy morning," Libby says, trying to not sound elusive but failing.

"How about you tell me where she is so that I can see her quicker? That way I can get some lunch faster and then a nap," I say with a little snark.

"I uh... I don't know where she is at the moment,

probably best for you to go get something to eat," Libby says.

"Okay, what's going on? Why does it feel like I'm not allowed to see Shae?"

"Does it feel that way?" Libby asks, actually sounding surprised.

"Yes, yes it does. I've been trying to see her... to check on her... since I woke up, but no one has had her come to me or take me to her, what's going on? Is she really okay?"

With a sigh, Libby says, "Yes, she's okay. She's better than okay, she's great. She's back to normal."

"Then what's the deal?"

"She doesn't know what to say to you and she feels like nothing is sufficient enough for what you did for her and she feels responsible for what happened to you."

"That's ridiculous. She doesn't need to say anything. And she is by no means responsible for what happened to me. Nobody is, they used the time I was passed out as a way for them to talk... to... me..." I trail off, forgetting that I hadn't told anyone about what happened with the Big Three.

Libby has stopped walking and is looking at me with her head tilted to the side and her eyebrows are raised, and asks, "Excuse me, what?"

I stop walking and look up at the ceiling, and then close my eyes.

Crap!

"Emma?" she asks, grabbing my arm gently.

"Okay, let's go get food and then go back to my room and I'll tell you all about it."

"Why can't you tell me now?"

"Because you're going to want to sit down for what I have to say and I need something to eat."

"It's that bad?"

"It's that weird."

"Weird?"

"Yeah."

She looks at me for a second, interlocks our arms, and starts leading us down the hall. She says, "Oookay, let's go."

We get to the dining hall and grab a couple of sandwiches, chips, soda-pop and a bag of chocolate chip cookies. Cooky has been adding sweet treats to the meals since we got back from the Elder's and because Meredith, Doc, and Bill are still missing. I think she's trying to keep our spirits up.

We walk back to my room in silence. We pass a few people as we're walking. They say hi and ask how I'm doing. I answer as nicely but as quickly as I can, I can tell Libby is about to her wits end.

We get to my room and she walks in first, and as I'm shutting the door, she says, "Okay, spill."

"Sit," I say as I point to the little table. She takes a seat, I sit in front of her. I take a bite of my sandwich, and she just stares at me. I look at her and then her food pointedly. She rolls her eyes and takes a bite of her sandwich too.

After she's taken a couple bites, she asks, "Can you please explain now?"

I think for a minute, trying to figure out the best way to tell her.

"Okay, so I passed out after putting Shae's spirit or whatever it was back in her body," I start to say but Libby interrupts.

"You did what?"

"Oh... I guess I haven't explained about that either," I say, grimacing.

"Umm no... no you haven't. We all thought you were able to Sense her very faint heartbeat where we couldn't Sense anything."

"No, I couldn't, she was gone," I say.

"Gone, gone?" Libby asks, choking up.

"Yeah."

"But you brought her back, how?"

"I saw a sliver of bright white light starting to rise from the middle of her. I'm guessing it was her soul or life essence or whatever, but I knew that I couldn't allow it to leave her completely. In the Vision I had of the battle at the Elder's, I saw the same thing leave Elder Selina and the Elder man, who ended up being Elder Fadri. When we got there, we were already too late for Elder Selina, but we were able to keep Vanessa

from touching Elder Fadri and saving his life. So...
when I saw the sliver of bright white light leaving
Shae, I knew I had to stop it or we'd lose her forever."

"Oh my gods," Libby breathes out in a whisper.

"Yeah."

"But how... how did you do it?"

"I honestly don't know, I just did this with my
hand," I show her how I fanned my fingers into the
palm of my left hand like I had done over Shae. "But
I needed both hands to push it... her... whatever you
wanna call it, back down. That's when I said I needed
both hands to save Shae."

"This isn't possible, I've never heard of anything
like this before," Libby says in disbelief.

"It gets stranger," I say.

"More?"

"Yes. So, I had my left hand on her light and I
started to use my mind to pull energy from around
me. From you guys, the mountain, from everything
that I could Feel close by that was releasing positive
energy. I sent the energy to my right hand, making
a ball of sorts, and as I was forcing Shae's light into
her, I pushed the ball of energy into her heart. I pulled
more energy in and sent another ball into her heart.
The third time I did this, pulling energy from further
out than just close by, using the trees from the forest,
the water from the river, and digging deeper into the
mountain, that's when the brightest of energy balls

was formed and I sent it into her. Shortly after, she took her first breath," I say, taking a deep breath of my own.

"We could see the balls of light in your hand but we didn't know what it was from. Ty and I were thinking it was Healing power," Libby says in awe.

"In a sense it was, but I was pulling it from all around us."

"And then what happened?"

I smile a little at the eagerness in Libby's voice.

"I tried to stand up, but everything felt numb. It felt like I went deaf too because I couldn't hear anything and then I thought I saw my light leave my body, that's when I passed out... or I did really die... or had an out of body experience, I'm not sure what happened."

"We rushed to you and checked your vitals, your pulse was extremely weak but you still had one. We all just assumed you had used way too much energy and caused yourself to pass out. But then I passed out myself, there was just so much going on."

"That makes sense."

"But you said 'they' used that as an opportunity to talk to you. Who's they?" Libby asks.

"Ookay, this is where it gets weird," I say a little shyly.

"Go on..." Libby urges.

"Okay so I was standing there looking around at

everyone and then a bright white light—" and so I tell Libby all about how I had met the Big Three.

CHAPTER 3 –
LEARNING ABOUT
THE BIG THREE

"Oh... my... gods..." is all Libby says when I have finished telling her about my meeting with the Big Three. Her mouth is hanging open slightly also.

"Yeah, I told you it got weirder."

"Yeah, weird," she says. She blinks a few times and shakes herself. "You think it really happened?"

"Can you explain... well me, any other way?"

Libby thinks for a couple of minutes, taking the last bite of her sandwich. She chews, swallows, and then takes a sip of her soda-pop.

"No, no I can't. Holy crap, Em! You are a true daughter of the gods?"

"We all are," I say, embarrassed.

"No, no we aren't. In the truest possible way, you are... you are..." her face goes blank for a split second and then her eyes go wide. "Oh Emma, this means you are a living god, er, goddess!"

"No! No, it doesn't!" I stammer out.

"You have god DNA, not just Demi-god DNA," she says, standing up and walking around the room.

"No, I have both, not just god DNA... which is what would make me a god or goddess," I say, trying to reason with her. She comes and sits back down.

"I don't think so," she says. "This would explain how you have all these Talents and how it all comes so easily to you, why you don't even have to think about doing it, it just comes naturally."

"I still think I'm more Demi-god than actual god... er goddess," I say in a pleading tone.

"I think you're something in between, something we've never heard of before, and probably never will again. Like Zeus said, they don't normally get involved directly. That's why we're here, why they made Demi's."

"Let's keep this between us, I really don't want it getting out that I have actual god DNA in me," I say, pleading again.

"Not just god DNA, Emma, the Big Three, that's freaking amazing," Libby says, in awe. She thinks for a minute and says, "But I can see where you wouldn't want this news to get out. I think if this got out to Vanessa, she'd rip the World's apart trying to find you. Although, I think you scared her enough that she might be taking a time-out for a little bit."

By World's, I know she means the other groups,

the Vampire's, Merfians, Fae Folk, and Werewolves. I shudder at the thought of her taking out her anger on them.

"I don't want to find out what her reaction would be if she were to find out about this."

"You have to tell Ty," Libby says, looking at me with concern.

"I will, I'll have to tell Shae as well. I feel like I owe her an explanation as to what happened to her and me, so that she doesn't feel responsible anymore and hopefully she'll talk to me again," I say and laugh a little. But then say sternly, "But other than those two, I don't want anyone else to know. No. One."

She holds her hand up and says, "I won't tell anyone. I'll let you tell Ty and Shae."

"Thank you," I say, reaching across the table and squeezing her hand. The thought of Vanessa has me thinking of something I had been wondering about while I was laid up in bed, healing and getting my strength back. "Libs, do you think it would be safe to go back to my house? The one Vanessa raised me in, in New York?"

"Why would you want to go back?"

"I don't know. Maybe to grab a couple of my actual things and look for any clues."

"I doubt she's been back there or even thinks you'll go back, so it might be okay, but we should talk to Ty and see what he thinks, since he's pretty much in charge right now."

"Still no word about Meredith, Doc, or Bill?"

"None," she says with sorrow.

"Maybe we can find something out at my old house. Maybe Vanessa left something there that I saw every day but never realized what it was, what it actually meant."

"That's not a bad idea..." Libby says and then looks at me with a look I had started to associate when she was in her Healing mode. "How are you feeling?"

"I actually feel really good. Didn't get tired at all walking up here and ate all of my lunch, look," I say as I point at my empty wrapper in front of me. I hadn't been able to eat a whole heck of a lot but today I finished my first meal.

"That's a good sign. Let's sit down with Ty and Shae, you can inform them about... well everything and then we'll talk to Ty about taking a group to New York, not only for a scout run but for you to get some of your things. I can only imagine how hard it's been for you. Your life has been turned upside down so many times in a short amount of time, I'm sure it would be nice to have some comfort things around you."

"It really would," I say, thinking about my favorite blanket and hoodies.

"I'll Run and get Ty and find Shae. Do you want them to come here?"

"Yeah, that'd be fine."

"Okay, I'll be back in a flash."

"Okay," I say as she stands up and goes to my door.

"Emma?" she says hesitantly at the door.

"Yeah.

"I'm really glad you didn't die-die."

"Me too, Libs, me too."

And then she Runs from the doorway, my door swinging shut behind her. I clear the table of our lunch wrappers and go into my bathroom and wash my face. I look in the mirror and my eyes look especially bright. Shaking my head, I go back into my room, sit on my bed, and wait. Thankfully I don't have to wait long. Soon there's a knock on my door.

"Who is it?"

"Ty."

"Oh, come on in," I say.

He walks in with a concerned look on his face at first but as soon as he sees me, his face relaxes, and he smiles his devastatingly handsome smile at me. He walks over and crawls onto the bed next to me.

"Hi," he says, kissing me on the cheek.

"Hi," I say back, butterflies erupting in my stomach.

"Libby said you needed to talk to me and Shae?"

"Yeah, they aren't here yet," I say, waving my hand around my room. "Obviously."

"So, you're saying we have a few minutes before

we're bombarded?"

"You could say that," I say giggling as he pulls me towards him.

He starts kissing me sweetly but just like all the other times, that doesn't last long. Soon, just like always, our kissing turns more passionate, more urgent. I put my hands in his hair and pull him closer to me. He reaches up and runs one of his hands down my arms, down my ribcage, down to my hip. His hand pauses there for a second, his thumb finding bare skin just above the top of my pants and the bottom of my tank. His thumb rubs back and forth for a couple of seconds before he continues down my leg, down behind my knee. He hikes my leg up and rolls so that I'm lying more on top of him than on the bed.

A soft moan escapes our mouths at the same time, which makes us smile. He runs his hands up my back and into my hair. I slide a hand down from the back of his head to his chest. I can feel his heart pounding underneath it.

Knock-Knock

We jump slightly at the sound of the knocking at the door.

Ty grumbles a little before he says, "Always getting interrupted."

I laugh and whisper, "We knew they'd be here

sooner or later."

"I was hoping for later... much, much later," he says as he kisses me one more time.

Knock-Knock

I slide off of him and we scoot up on the bed so we have our back against the headboard.

"Who is it?" I finally ask.

"Us," I hear Libby say from the other side.

"Come on in," I say, just as Ty says, "Go away."

The door opens and Libby walks in with Shae behind her. Shae looks almost scared. Libby is laughing and says, "Hey, at least I knocked."

"Thanks for that," I say, winking at her. I look at Shae and she looks close to tears. I get up and hurry over to her. I pull her into a hug and say, "Oh Shae!"

She starts to cry instantly. I turn her so I can see Ty and Libby. Ty's looking down at his hands and Libby has tears in her eyes now too.

"Shhhh... Shae, it's okay," I say, trying to sooth her.

"I'm... so... sorry... Em...ma..." Shae says in between sobs.

"You have nothing to be sorry about," I say, rubbing her back while holding her tightly.

"You... almost... died... because... of... meeeee..." she wails the last word.

"No, I didn't," I say.

She looks up at me with tears rolling down her face

"You... don't... have... to lie... to me," she says.

"No, Shae, listen, I didn't almost die. As soon as you are alright, I'll explain," I say.

"Here," Ty says, he's holding a cup of water and some tissue.

"Thanks," I say.

At the same time, Shae says, "Thaa...nks." It makes her smile and a small laugh escapes her.

After a few minutes of Shae calming herself down and we all get comfortable, I tell them about what had happened back at the battle.

I look at Shae first, her mouth is hanging open. She's stunned silent, no more tears. I look at Ty and he also looks stunned. If his eyebrows were any higher, they'd disappear under his hair. Shae's the first to talk.

"You actually saw my soul?" she asks.

"Soul. Life force. Life essence. It was something... It was you," I answer.

"And you had seen it coming out of the Elder's in your Vision?" Ty asks.

"Yes. That's how I knew I couldn't let it completely leave Shae. I knew if it got too far away from her, we would never get her back," I say, looking from him to Libby, to Shae. She has tears in her eyes again.

"So, I did really die?"

"I mean, yeah, but I think you were only really gone for a minute or two. It felt a lot longer than it actually was," I say, trying to reassure her.

"But I was gone, my heart had stopped beating?" she asks, looking at Libby.

Libby nods reluctantly.

"And you, you saved my life," Shae says, looking at me.

"I couldn't just watch you leave," I say.

"I... I will never be able to thank you enough... saying thank you doesn't even feel like enough... I haven't been around because I couldn't think of the right things to say. I knew you had saved me but I didn't know to this extent. I owe you my life," she says, starting to tear up again, she looks down at her hands.

"Shae, look at me," I don't continue until she's looking at me, tears running down her cheeks. "You don't have to say anything, ever. And you definitely don't owe me anything."

"I have to do something, I can't just let this go without... something," she says, looking around like she's looking for a gift of some kind.

"I'll tell you what I want," I say, thinking of something fast.

"What?!" she asks excitedly. "Anything."

"I want you to be happy. I want you to live your life like you did before. I want us to be friends. I want you to stop being scared around me, or whatever it is you've been. I want you to be the bad ass I met back at the Pit, the girl that became one of my first best friends. That's what I want."

"That's not enough," she says, sniffing.

"That's what I want, all I want," I say. "And I'll be pissed if you act any other way."

"Emma..." Shae trails off.

"Nope, I don't want you to feel obligated or whatever, I just want you to be you. Okay?" I say, looking at her with a smile.

She wipes a tear from her cheek and nods.

"Good," I say, smiling even bigger.

After a few minutes of quiet, Ty finally says, "Okay, now that that's covered, can we please talk about your meeting with the Big Three?"

"Uh, yes please," Shae says in agreement.

"Umm, yeah, of course," I say.

It's quiet again. I look at Libby, she shrugs. Shae looks stunned again. I look up at Ty and he's looking down at me with what I can only guess is awe in his eyes.

"What else can I say about it?" I ask, trying to prompt the conversation.

"How do you feel?" Shae asks.

"Same as before, I guess," I say with a shrug.

"No, I mean, knowing for sure why you are you," she says.

"Again, same as before. I still feel like me," I say.

Shae's eyes go big and she gasps, she yells, "You're a mother fucking goddess!"

"Shhhhh!" Libby and I say at the same time.

"No, I'm not," I say.

"That's what I said," Libby says to Shae, smiling smugly at me.

"And like I told you, I have Demi-god blood too," I say pointedly.

"I think you're something more than a Demi but not a full god," Ty suggests.

"I also said that," Libby says, again, smugly.

"It doesn't matter what I am because I am still me, the me I've always been," I say, a little more sternly than I had intended.

"But it explains how you can have all these Talents and from the sound of your... meeting," Shae says. "You have ALL the Talents and then some. Some we don't even know about. Like, putting souls back into dead people, Talents."

"You make it sound like I can raise the dead. That's not how it works. I have to be right there, just as a soul is leaving a body. Once it gets about here," I raise my hand above my head. "It disappears. At least that's what happened to Elder Selina's."

I see Libby and Shae shiver a little at the thought.

"What was it that the Big Three said at the end?" Ty asks, changing the subject from putting souls back in dead bodies to hopefully prevent more crying from Shae or because it was a little disturbing to think about. Either way, I'm grateful for the change of subject.

"Let me think," I say. I take a minute to try to remember. All of a sudden, as if I can hear them clear as day, I hear the Big Three's voices. "What you seek is what you'll find, when you go beyond the line. Alone you'll go to bring all together, those that are needed to do what needs to be done, but together as one you must be, to defeat what has begun. Don't be scared, don't be brave, just be you, and all will be saved."

"What happened after they told you this?" Ty asks.

"They each told me a part of it and then disappeared. I was starting to wake up or come back to my body, so I was a little confused. But Zeus then told me to accept what was being given to me, to absorb the energy. And with time I'd come to understand. Then I kind of woke up."

"The energy!" Libby exclaims.

"What?" I ask, sitting up.

"You were shining just like when you changed," Shae says.

"I kind of remember hearing someone say that," I say hesitantly as a faint memory of Libby's voice comes through my foggy memory of that moment. I point at Libby and say, "You said it."

"Yeah. You were shining and humming, or vibrating. That must be the energy Zeus was talking about," Libby says.

"What more could they have been giving me?" I ask.

"I don't think they were giving you anything you didn't already have. I think it was energy to get you back to your body and to Heal yourself. It took all we had to get you back to us, or at least we thought it was us doing it. Now I'm wondering if it was just you all along," Ty says, reaching for my hand and squeezing it gently.

"I am going to ask that you guys don't tell anyone about this," I say, looking at Shae and Ty. I glance at Libby and she just nods at me.

"Of course, we won't say anything to anyone," Ty says.

"Definitely not," Libby says.

"It'll just be between the four of us," Shae says in agreement.

"There really isn't any reason for anyone else to know about it. Nothing about you has changed. We all knew you were special and The One anyways," Libby says, smiling hugely at me.

"They don't need to know the details of how you saved Shae, either," Ty says.

"Everyone knows you saved me, but I agree, the details will just lead to more questions," Shae adds.

"We don't want this getting back to Vanessa," Ty says, looking concerned.

"Agreed," the girls and I say together.

I look at Libby and she nods, an encouraging gesture with her eyes brows wagging towards her brother.

"Speaking of Vanessa, I want to go back to my house in New York and do a couple things—" I start to say but I feel Ty tense beside me. So I hurry and add. "—hold on and let me tell you what I want to do before you go into protective mode about it. I want to get a couple of MY things from there and I want to see if there are any clues as to where Vanessa's and Chris' actual secret place is because they have to be somewhere. Somewhere, where Chris has lived the last 18 years. Where the Rifts call their home or homebase at the very least. I'm wondering if there's something at that house that I saw daily that didn't mean anything at the time but now could be the clue we need."

Ty had started to relax a little as I explained what I wanted but he hasn't fully relaxed.

"I told her I didn't think Vanessa would go back there but I also told her we'd run it by you first. What do you think?" Libby asks, looking at Ty.

"I don't like the thought of you going back to that house but I can understand why," he says. "Let me think about it. Maybe I can get a group together to go with us if Max, Charlie and Clay aren't back yet when we've decided to go."

"Thank you, Ty," I say, leaning into him and giving him a hug.

"I said I'd think about it," he says but he's hugging me back.

"But when it comes to Emma, you'd give her the world," Libby says smiling over at us.

"As long as the world is safe," he says, squeezing me tightly.

"I'm pretty sure she'd keep you safer than you her," Shae says, laughing.

We all laugh.

"You're probably not wrong there but for my sanity, let's pretend I'm the protector in this duo," he says, laughing harder. I nudge him with my shoulder. I don't think he understands how safe I feel with him near. I'll have to tell him soon, that I do feel like he's my protector.

CHAPTER 4 -
VISION PROBLEMS

T he last week has felt like things are getting back to normal, at least normal as far as my friendship with Shae. Meredith, Doc, and Bill are still missing, that isn't normal. Clay, Charlie, Max, Jayce, and Nick haven't gotten back yet and we haven't heard anything from them. I can tell Ty is starting to get concerned. Ty and I are sitting in the dining hall having breakfast with Libby. Shae isn't up yet.

Ty says, "I've been thinking about your request to go to your old house in New York and I think looking there for clues might be a good idea. Vanessa might be cocky enough to think we wouldn't dare go back there, even if she doesn't plan on going back, but maybe she's left somethings behind she feels are insignificant to her but huge for us to find."

"Really? We can go?" I ask, excited for the first time in months.

"Yeah, I talked to Travis, Ret, and Vinny and they're on board to go with us," Ty says as he takes a bite of his scramble.

"When can we go?" I ask, pushing my plate of food away, no longer hungry, excitement taking over.

"As soon as we've all eaten," Ty says, pushing my plate back towards me and looking at it and then at me pointedly. I pick up my fork and shovel some food in my mouth. He laughs and then says, "The sooner we get there and back, the better."

Phil, who is the tech guy here for the Guardian Room, comes up to Ty, holding out a black box, and says, "I was able to do what you asked, Sir. Here's the seven you asked for, for now."

"Thanks, Phil," Ty says, taking the box.

"What's that?" Libby asks, leaning over to try to see in the box but it's closed.

"I'll show you later, not here, top secret," Ty says, putting the box on his lap, under the table.

"Well, now I really want to know," Libby says.

"You'll find out, just stop drawing attention to it. It's something I've been working with Phil on since we moved to the Estate," Ty says, taking the last bite of his scramble and drinking the last of his juice.

I look at Libby and we start to eat faster. I see Alysa walk into the dining hall and she looks around until she sees us. She beelines it to us, walking fast.

"Have you guys seen Malysa?" she asks.

"Not yet," Libby says with concern. "Why?"

"I haven't seen her for a couple of days, I stopped by her room and she didn't answer. I thought maybe she was down here having breakfast already," Alysa says, her own concern thick in her voice.

"I saw her last night, she said she was really tired and going to bed early," Libby says, looking at me.

"Yeah, we were watching movies in the TV room and she kept falling asleep but it was late, it was nearly 10 o'clock," I say.

"I meant early, because we stayed in there for another movie," Libby clarifies. "We'll stop by her room when we head back upstairs."

"Tell her I'm looking for her, will ya?" Alysa asks.

"Sure thing," Libby replies.

Alysa has changed quite a bit since the battle at the Elder's. I think watching her sister die because of her selfishness really made her reevaluate her attitude and herself in general. The fact that Shae is okay doesn't seem to have made Alysa go back to her awful self.

"Let's go check on Shae, her not opening the door for Alysa isn't too surprising but with Shae feeling so tired last night, I just want to make sure she's okay," Libby says, as she gets up and takes her tray to the garbage cans and rack of dirty trays.

I stand, but Ty hands me the black box and grabs my tray and carries it over to the racks. The box doesn't feel too awfully heavy but it's not super light either. He takes the box into one hand and takes me hand in his other. Libby leads the way towards the stairs, we make our way up, and head towards Shae's room.

Once we're up in our hallway, Libby stops in front of Shae's room and knocks.

No answer.

She tries again but there is still no answer.

"Shae? It's Libby, Emma, and Ty," Libby says as she knocks again. "Can we come in?"

We hear a faint, "Yes," come from inside. Libby looks at me with wide eyes.

She opens the door and we hurry inside, Ty shuts the door behind us. It's dark, really dark. The curtains are pulled shut and it looks like Shae has put a blanket over the top of them to make it even darker.

"Shae? Honey, are you okay?" Libby asks, making her way towards the bed.

"Mmmm," is all we faintly hear.

"I'm going to turn the bathroom light on so we can see what's going on but not make it super bright in here, okay?" Ty says as he reaches into the bathroom.

Again, "Mmmm," is all we hear from the bed.

When we can see a little better, we see Shae lying on her bed, drenched in sweat.

"Shae!" Libby and I holler together.

Libby has her hand on her forehead and is checking her pulse in a blink of an eye. I jump on the bed and gently crawl to Shae's other side. Ty puts the black box on the little table and runs to the bathroom.

We can hear him turning on the water.

"Mmmmokay," Shae mumbles out.

"What's wrong?" Libby asks. She looks at me and says, "Her pulse is racing."

I put my hand on her wrist and check her pulse myself. Sure enough, it's beating so fast, there isn't a break between beats.

"Shae, can you open your eyes?" I ask.

"Head... hurts..." she pants out.

I put my hand on her forehead and I'm suddenly pulled into a scene that seems to be on a loop. Charlie, Clay, Max, Jayce, and Nick all being surprised by someone, they're caught off guard. Shae's Vision is stuck on repeat, playing their surprise over and over. The look of being startled and the beginning of terror to spread across at least Nick's face. I pull my mind out of the Vision and look down at Shae's face.

"She's stuck in a Vision... it's on repeat," I say in a strangled voice.

"What... what is it?" Libby says. Ty is placing a wet washcloth on Shae's neck.

I look into his eyes and I say, "The guys... It's Charlie, Clay, Max, Jayce, and Nick. They're caught off guard by something or someone. The Vision doesn't go any further than that scene. Just them, turning and surprise crossing their faces and at least Nick starting to look really scared, but it's just going over and over that scene."

"How do we get her out of it?" Libby asks, scared.

"I don't know," Ty says, concern in his voice. "I've never heard of this before with any Psychic."

"She's not actually hurt so we can't Heal her out of it," Libby says, running her hand across her own face, while keeping one of Shae's hands in her other.

"Emma, you try something," Ty suggests.

"Like what?" I ask, surprised.

"I don't know, just put your hands on her head and let your instincts take over," he says.

"Yeah, yeah... Place one of your thumbs over each of her eyebrows like this," Libby says, demonstrating by putting her thumbs, pads down, across Shae's forehead, just above her eyebrows. "Then wrap your hands around the back of her head. This is what we do when we get a Reading on someone or try to Heal a headwound."

"And then what?" I ask, as I place my hands where Libby suggested.

"Like Ty said, let your instincts take over," Libby says, going to stand by Ty.

I take a deep breath and close my eyes. I let my hands relax and then my arms, and then let the relaxation fill my body up. I can feel Shae's pulse through my thumbs. I can feel each time she's about to take a breath. I let my mind wander again and I'm pulled back into her Vision. This time, I'm not surprised. I look around and see Shae standing there with a hand over her mouth.

With my mind, I reach out to her.

"Shae?"

She looks up at me.

"Emma?" she asks in surprise, her voice in my head. *"How in the world? How are you here?"*

"I don't know but I'm here to help you. You're stuck in this Vision. We can't get you to wake up."

"I've been trying to get past this Scene, but I just can't."

"It's okay. You don't have to get past it, we just need you to wake up."

"I don't know how. I've been in here for too long I think."

"That's why I'm here."

She looks at me in surprise again.

"How?"

"I'm not sure," I say and then I try to walk over to her but find I'm cemented in place. *"I can't move, can you?"*

I watch as Shae takes a tentative step forward.

"Good, come over here to me."

"What about the guys?" Shae says but I see her staring at Charlie's face. They'd rekindled their Anima Gemella connection and it's stronger than ever.

"I don't know, but we need to get you out of here and then we can figure out what to do about the guys," I say, pleading with her. She takes another step towards me

and then another. I reach my hand out and she grabs hold. She's ice cold. All I can think about is getting her warm and getting her out of here.

I hear a gasp. I open my eyes and see Shae staring up at me, we're back in her room. I move over and sit beside her. Libby and Ty are back by our side in an instant. Libby checking Shae, Ty checking me.

"Are you okay?" he asks me, just as Libby is asking Shae the same thing.

"I think so," we both say at the same time. We all laugh a little.

I put my hand on Shae's hand and feel she's warm, not the ice cold she had been in her mind or her Vision, whatever it was we were just inside.

"Can you sit up?" Libby asks Shae.

Shae slides up to sit against her headboard. Ty hands her a small cup of water and she takes a small sip. She wipes her forehead with the back of her hand.

"How long was I in there for?" she asks with a shaky voice.

"We don't know. We found you like this. Do you remember telling us your head hurt?" Ty asks.

"I remember a faint voice asking me questions, but I don't remember talking to anyone until Emma showed up in my Vision. Which scared the hell out of me by the way," she says, laughing a little again.

"Sorry about that," I say, nudging her with my shoulder.

"Nope, I'm glad you showed up," she said, putting her head on my shoulder. "What made you come looking for me?"

"Alysa," we all say, causing us all to laugh a little, again.

"She's been keeping a close eye on you lately," Libby says.

"You mean acting like a sister?" Shae says.

"Better late than never," Ty murmurs.

"Emma told us about the Vision, is there anything else you remember?" Libby asks, getting us back on track.

"No, it was just the guys getting caught off guard, but I couldn't tell if it was serious or not," Shae says, rubbing her temples.

"Nick looked scared to me," I suggest.

"That's not too surprising," Ty says. "Nick isn't the bravest Guardian. He's usually sitting in front of a screen, but Billy and I were talking about how he needed to get out on a few missions and broaden his horizon. So, for him to be scared, it's not too concerning. Now if Charlie, Clay, or Max looked scared, that would be reason to send a search party out for them."

"They just looked surprised, not scared, just... caught off guard," Shae says, still rubbing her head.

"Headache?" Libby asks.

"Yeah, always after a Vision but this one is bad,

maybe because I was in for so long," Shae says, putting her head back against the headboard.

"Here, I'll take care of that," Libby says. She puts her hands on Shae's head like she had instructed me to do and she closes her eyes for a second. I see Shae tense and then relax, a small smile spreads across her face. Libby asks, "Better?"

"Much better, thank you," Shae says as she opens her eyes.

"When do you think your Vision started?" I ask.

"I'm not sure. I'd been thinking of Charlie all day yesterday, wishing we had a way to communicate. I thought I had a dream about him when I was still in the TV Room with you guys, and then I don't remember much after walking to my room," Shae says and then she looks around. "Did I put up that blanket?"

"You must have because it was up when we came in," Libby says.

"Huh... interesting, I must have been half in, half out when I got back to my room last night. I was in that Vision longer than I thought," she says, wiping her face with the washcloth one more time.

"How are you feeling now?" Libby asks.

"Worried," Shae answers.

"We'll figure out a way to get word to the guys to contact one of us or come home," Libby says, squeezing her best friends hand.

"Well, speaking of that," Ty says, walking over to the small table and picking the box up and walking back to the bed. He sits at the foot of it and turns so he's facing us. "I had Phil do some Trace Protecting on these."

He opens the box and pulls out two black, sleek looking things.

"What are those?" Libby says, leaning forward.

"Cellphones?" I ask in surprise.

"Yes, cellphones," Ty says, smiling at me and then his sister, and then at Shae.

"For real?" Shae says, leaning forward too.

"Yes, I figured it was time we figured out a way to have instant communication. Phil has been working on this since we got here. He's got quite a few programmed but I told him to put a rush on seven."

"Why seven?" Libby asks as he hands her a phone. Her eyes gleaming with excitement.

"So, when we go to New York, we can have communication with the Estate. We can communicate with them like a Walkie-Talkie or like a phone. We can also communicate with each other both ways. For Walkie-Talkie mode, this little switch on the side," Ty points to a tiny thing on the side of the phone, "has to show blue and the button below it is how you talk, by holding it in. It will also work with earpieces, but Phil hasn't finished with those yet. They'll be mostly used on missions. The phones are Untraceable and once you've touched your phone, only you can use it."

"These are so cool!" Shae exclaims.

"You're sure they're safe?" I ask.

"Yes. Phil has put them through every Demi and Inepti test we could think of, they're safe," Ty says, squeezing my hand.

I take the phone that he's offering me and as I use my thumb to swipe at the screen, I feel a zing.

"What was that?" I ask, looking at my finger, then the phone, and then at Ty.

"That's the technology doing a quick scan of you so that it knows that the phone belongs to you," Ty says, smiling.

"Cool," Libby says.

My phone screen lights up in a beautiful swirl of color and then my Mark appears on the screen. Eyes wide, I look at Shae and Libby and see their facial expressions mirroring mine.

"What the..." Shae trails off.

"Cool, huh?" Ty encourages.

"Uh, yeah!" we all exclaim.

"Like I said, they are unique to each owner and they are completely safe," Ty says.

"I've never had my own phone before," I say.

"Neither have we," Libby says.

"I wish Charlie had one," Shae says, sadly.

"He'll be okay," Ty says. "And everyone in the

Guard will have a phone for their next assignments."

"How can you be sure he'll be okay? My Vision…" Shay says, sniffling.

"Because he's Charlie. He's too stubborn to let anything happen to him and he's with the best group of guys we have in the Guard," Ty says reassuringly.

"You're right, he is stubborn," Shae says, laughing a teary laugh.

"Going to New York will keep us busy and maybe keep your mind off of things," I say.

"Ugh, I don't think I should go. I still feel kind of out of it and really tired. I'd also like to stay here in case the guys show up," Shae says.

"Are you sure? It might be good for you to get off the island," Libby says.

"No, I'm sure. I'll just take a nap and rest. Now that we have these," she holds up her phone. "We can keep in touch."

"We should probably get ready and go so we can get back by nightfall," Ty suggests.

"Do you want me to stay here with you?" Libby asks Shae.

"No, you go with them, I'll be alright," she says, sitting up and getting out of her bed.

I slide off her bed and head for the door.

"We'll have Alysa check on you throughout the day," Libby says as she opens the door.

"I'll be fine," Shae replies. "You guys just be safe

out there and check in with me so I don't go crazy with worry for you guys as well. I don't think I could handle getting stuck in a Vision again."

"We'll be alright," Ty says, ushering me and Libby out the door. He shuts the door behind us and we stop at Libby's door.

"Meet in Emma's room in half an hour?" Libby asks as she opens her door.

"Sounds good. I'll go let the guys know to meet us at the entrance," Ty says. He walks me the couple of feet over to my door. He grabs my hand and pulls it up to his mouth, kissing it gently before asking, "Are you sure you're up for this?"

"Yes, I feel fine and I'm feeling a little claustrophobic," I say, spreading my hand, the one he just kissed, out across his cheek.

"You have an entire island to use to stretch your legs, you don't have to stay inside the Estate," he says, leaning into my hand.

"I know but it's more of a feeling of needing to go and do something... to stop Vanessa, Chris, and the Rifts... not necessarily like I'm being smothered."

Ty bends down and kisses me sweetly on the cheek.

"We'll figure out a way to stop them, hopefully there will be a clue at your old house," he says, then he kisses me again, closer to my lips.

I turn my head a little towards him and our lips

touch. Instant need. Instant desire. I wrap my arms around his neck and pull him down to me as I stretch up on my tiptoes. Ty's hands wrap around my lower back and he pulls me into him. Fire is erupting inside my stomach. It's an ache I've only known when Ty kisses me, when he touches me. Our kiss deepens.

Ty runs his hands over my butt and lifts me up. I wrap my legs around his waist and he pushes me gently up against my bedroom door. When we're connected like this, it doesn't just feel like our bodies and our mouths are touching, it feels like our minds and our souls are connected. It's what I get lost in, that feeling of connection that goes deeper than just physical.

Cough-Cough

Giggle-Giggle

Ty pulls away in startlement and looks around. My head is spinning but I, too, look around. A couple of girls that I had only seen in passing were walking past. Two are covering their mouths trying not to giggle any louder and the third is looking at us with raised eyebrows.

"Sorry 'bout that," Ty says, letting me slide to the floor.

"Don't mind us, carry on," the girl with the raised

eyebrows says as they walk by, which causes the two other girls to really start to giggle. I can feel my face turning red.

"I'd say let's go in your room but if we're wanting to get to New York anytime soon today, we probably shouldn't, should we?" Ty asks, brushing a piece of stray hair back behind my ear.

I take a steadying breath and smile up at him. "We probably shouldn't, no."

He smiles, bends down and says, "I'll be back in—" he looks at his watch and his eyes get big in surprise "—in about 10 minutes."

"We were kissing for 20 minutes?" I ask in surprise.

"I guess so... but I'd call it making out because that wasn't just kissing," he says, winking at me.

My face going red, I shake my head and turn to my door, opening it. I turn to Ty and say, "See you in 10 minutes."

He gives me his smile that always makes my heartbeat quicken. But then he adds another wink and my heart feels like it's jumped into my throat. He turns and jogs down the hall.

That boy... he makes my heart do funny things and makes time stand still... I think to myself

Smiling like an idiot, I walk into my room and change. I put on my battle gear, not that I'm expecting anything to happen, but I'd rather be prepared than

be caught off guard. I grab my boots and pull them on.
When I look in the mirror, I see someone I'm starting
to recognize. A warrior. Someone who can hold
her own. Inner strength starting to shine through,
strength that I've had in me my entire life, but only
recently found.

Knock-Knock

I go to my door and open it. Libby walks in,
wearing similar clothes as me, only she looks like a
badass movie star about to play a role in some kick ass
action movie. Her Magikida is in a sleeve tied around
her thigh. I go to my dresser and pull my Magikida
out of the top drawer. I found out that my shirt has a
special pocket type sleeve in the back that a Magikida
fits perfectly in. I carefully slide it into place.

"Are you excited to go back to your house?" Libby
asks.

"I think I'm more nervous than excited. I don't
have any real fond memories from my time there. Like
I've said before, Vanessa wasn't the most nurturing
or loving mother figure. I went to school and came
home to basically spend time in my room. I read,
drew or painted pictures, and that's about the extent
of my time in that house. We had meals together but
looking back, I'm starting to realize how little of a
relationship Vanessa, and I actually had. I wonder

what all I was oblivious to as I spent most of my time in my room."

"Hopefully she left something behind that'll be a clue for us," Libby says, putting her arm around me in a one arm hug.

Knock-Knock

I open the door and see Ty standing there in his battle gear.

DAMN! I mentally shout in my head. His gear fits him way too well. Hugging in all the right places, his muscles rippling underneath as he steps to the side of my doorway.

"You guys look ready, the guys are down in the entrance, let's head down," he says. He motions for Libby to go first, I start to follow behind her. Ty pulls me back into my room and asks, "Have you seen yourself?"

He pulls us in front of my mirror, standing next to him, I look like I belong. I can see my muscles under my gear, not nearly as big as Ty's or Libby's for that matter but I can see muscles. I look at him, my eyes going from his face, down his body, and then back up to his eyes again.

"Have you seen yourself?" I counter ask.

"You look absolutely amazing in these," Ty says as he pulls a little on the side of my shirt, avoiding my question.

"Okay, love birds, let's go," Libby says half laughing, half exasperated from my doorway.

Ty nods his head towards my door and I laugh. I walk towards Libby, she rolls her eyes but then winks at me. Ty shuts my door and reaches for my hand before we start walking down the hall.

"Good luck," we hear from behind us. We turn and see Shae leaning out of her room. She's got a sandwich in her hand.

Good, she's eating something.

"Thanks, we'll let you know if we find anything," Libby says, smiling.

"Have Charlie call me on your phone if they make it back before us," Ty says.

"Will do," Shae says.

"Get some rest," I say.

"I'll try," she says, waving and then she disappears into her room.

"I tracked Alysa down and told her to check on her this afternoon," Libby says. "She assured me she would."

"Good," I say as we get to the stairs and start to make our way down.

CHAPTER 5

– GOING BACK

Travis, Ret, and Vinny are waiting for us just outside the entrance, sitting on the top steps. When they hear us open the front doors, they jump to their feet. They also look good in their battle gear but not nearly as good as Ty.

"Travis, Ret, Vinny, this is Emma," Ty says, pointing to me. "Emma, this is Travis, Ret, and Vinny."

Travis has a military haircut but short in the extreme. His hair is almost white it's so blonde. His light blue eyes shine bright with excitement but also kindness. He's tall like all the guys around here but not as tall as Ty.

Ret has red hair, a military haircut but not nearly as short as Travis'. He has green eyes, the same color as leaves, except the yellow green kind. He's shorter than Travis but not by much. He looks tense but also excited to be going on this outing with us. I'm not calling it a mission because I'm really hoping nothing happens at the house.

Vinny has dark brown hair and it's pulled back into a messy bun. He has brown eyes and he's the largest of the men standing on the steps and he's even bigger than Ty. He looks as if he never misses a chance to lift weights. The man is huge! He's probably the biggest guy I've seen so far, at least here at the Estate. However, he looks the most relaxed out of the three guys waiting for us.

"Nice to meet you," I say.

"We know who you are, Miss Emma, but it's nice to officially meet you," Travis says, shaking my hand. Ret just nods at me but Vinny comes up and shakes my hand as well.

"Nice to meet you," Vinny says. "We've heard all about you. You are a tiny little thing, aren't you?"

He doesn't say it in a demeaning way but the way he says it makes me laugh.

"Next to you, Vinny, we're all tiny," I say, looking up at him. His booming laugh makes me laugh harder.

"She's got a sense of humor too," Vinny says.

"So, are we flying there?" Ret asks, starting to lead us down the stairs.

"Umm, I was thinking maybe I'd Jump us," I say, looking up at Ty. "Would be a lot quicker."

"You sure you're up for that?" Libby asks, concern in her voice.

"Absolutely. I told you guys, I feel great," I say.

"I don't know. You just got your strength back,"

Libby says.

We look at Ty. I'm not asking for permission but as he's the person in charge, it's good to show him I respect his opinion, which I do.

Ty looks down, concern showing in his eyes for only a split second, but then he smiles and says, "I trust Emma and how she says she feels. If she says she's good and able, then she is."

I wink at him and look at Libby. She shrugs and turns to start walking down the steps.

"Ret, Vinny, Travis, these are for you," Ty says. Handing them their phones.

"Phones?" Ret asks, turning the phone over in his hand.

"Yes, so we can be in communication with each other and the Estate while we're out. That phone is to stay on you at all times," Ty says. He does a quick demonstration on how they work.

"Cool," Vinny says as he puts his phone in his pocket.

We walk down the stairs and stop. They all turn towards me.

Ty holds his hand out and says, "Ready?"

"Yup," I say confidently. I feel confident in my action but nervous about going back to that house. And hopeful that we find something useful. "I need everyone touching."

Libby grabs my free hand and then reaches for

Vinny's hand. Ret puts his hand on Vinny's shoulder. Travis puts his hand on Ty's shoulder.

"Ready?" I ask.

They all nod. I close my eyes and think of the house on the street I grew up on. I don't have to think long or hard about it. I grew up there. I know every inch of that house. Instead of having us just appear out of thin air, I make us Invisible. I take a step like I was going to walk up the sidewalk leading to the front door and when I open my eyes, we're there.

"Cool," Vinny says. I look at him and he looks over at me. "Whoa! We're see through!"

"I made us Invisible, just until we get inside. I thought it would be better than just appearing here, in case Vanessa has someone watching the house," I say.

"Good thinking," Ty says, squeezing my hand. He looks up and around. "Travis and Ret, you guys stay out here in front. Vinny, go around back, holler if you see or find anything. Girls, let's go in."

We reach the front door and I do a quick Scan of the house to see if anyone is inside. I don't Feel any Essences, so I lean down looking under the always empty flowerpot for the key that used to hide here. And it's here, Vanessa either forgot about it or never dreamt I'd come back. I slide the key into the lock and turn, it unlocks easily. Ty opens the door and swings the door into the house.

I stand in the doorway for a minute or two.

Looking into the entry way and up the stairs. I think of all the times I walked through this door, hollered a hello to my... to Vanessa and was greeted by nothing. She was either in her office or gone.

Thinking now about the relationship I thought was a healthy mother/daughter relationship when in reality, it wasn't anywhere near healthy. She never let me go do anything other than school and I was to come straight home after, but she was never here. She would come home in time for dinner. If she didn't bring something home, I was expected to have dinner ready by 7 o'clock.

I spent the weekends in the house or in the backyard, she had to work to give us this life we lived, or so she said. I never asked questions, I learned at a young age not to ask any. But I was blind. Maybe not blind, conditioned might be a better word. I was conditioned to think that my life was normal. It was far from it. I know now that she didn't work, she didn't have an Inepti job, so what was she doing when she was in her office or out of the house for 'work'?

Spurred by that thought, I step inside and walk past the stairs that lead up to our bedrooms. This house is huge. It easily could have housed a ten person family but the upstairs was made into two master suites, one for Vanessa, and one for me. I thought I was lucky, getting that much space to myself, when really it was so she didn't have to spend time with me. The downstairs, to the left is the dining room that leads straight into the kitchen. I always hoped we'd have gatherings big enough to use the dining room table, but we never did. We ate our meals at the island in the kitchen.

If you were to walk back out of the dining room and past the stairs, there's a hallway. A bathroom on the left, under the stairs. And to the right, a door leading into the large living room where I'd watch TV. The other door in the hallway was for her office, I wasn't allowed in there. And that thought has me walking straight to it. I hear the front door shut behind me and I don't have to turn to know that Libby and Ty are walking behind me. I let our Invisibility slip off.

"This is, was, Vanessa's office," I say, hesitating at the door. I was never allowed in here, like at all, even if Vanessa was home. I'd knock on the door and tell her food was ready. I realize now that I was scared of her because I never tried to snoop and go in. Vanessa made it very clear to never come in here. I turn the hand and push the door in, letting it swing open.

I don't know what I was expecting. Knowing who the real Vanessa is, maybe I was expecting dead bodies or something equally sinister but it looks like a normal office. Desk with a chair, computer, bookshelves, and file cabinets.

"Uh, that was anticlimactic," Libby says with a

little surprise in her tone.

"Right?" I say as a question.

"You guys were expecting something other than this too?" Ty asks.

"Yes," we say matter-of-factly.

"You tell us what you want us to do, Em. We'll follow your lead," Ty says, putting his hand on my lower back.

"Okay," I say, taking a minute to collect my thoughts. We came here for two reasons, and one is to see if we can find anything that tells us where Vanessa and Chris might be hiding with the Rifts. "Ty, check the file cabinets. Lib, look through her books. I honestly didn't know she had any of these."

"You didn't come in here?" Libby asks as she walks to the big bookshelf along the left wall.

"I wasn't allowed," I say. I walk to the desk and sit in the chair. Running my hand over the keyboard. I push the button to turn the computer on and wait. I watch Ty open the top drawer in the file cabinet and he starts thumbing through the papers. Libby is running her pointer finger across book after book on the bottom shelf.

After a few minutes, the computer turns on. Vanessa didn't set a password so getting in is simple. I open everything I possibly can. Web browsers. Files. Word documents. Picture folders.

"I'm not finding anything out of the ordinary,"

Libby says after what feels like hours have gone by in silence. I look up and see her flipping through a book.

"Me either," Ty says. "Was Vanessa a realtor?"

"No… at least, I don't think so. I don't think she actually worked. Why?" I ask.

"She's got a ton of folders on properties and information on them," Ty says. He walks over, holding out a folder for me. I grab it from him and open it. It's a small mom and pop store down the street.

"Why would she have this?" I ask.

"Maybe trying to figure out where we were hiding. Trying to find the Pit?" Ty suggests.

"That very well could be," I say, looking back at the computer. "I didn't find anything either. She either deleted everything on here or this was just a prop. There's nothing on here. Well except for our Greece trip. It looks as if she did a bunch of research on it and had the whole tip planned out. But how could she have done that if it was just a trick, to scare me?"

"Maybe she thought you did come in here and if you got on the computer, you'd find it and wouldn't think anything of it," Libby says, coming to stand behind me.

"Maybe…" I say.

"I'm going to go check the other rooms, what else is down here?" Ty asks.

"Kitchen and dining room back around on the other side of the house, living room is just over there,"

I say as I point to the wall, indicating the room next door. Ty nods and leaves.

"Want to go to your room?" Libby asks.

"Sure, it's looking like we might not be finding anything here after all," I say sullenly.

"You don't know that, we still have the rest of the house to go through," Libby says, wrapping her arm around my shoulders.

We walk back down the hall and start our way up the stairs. When we get to the top, to the landing, I turn to the right, and see my bedroom door. I had painted sunflowers on it last year. I turn the handle and push it open. It's just like I left it. You wouldn't guess I hadn't been back in almost four months.

I walk over and sit on my bed, grabbing my teddy bear, aka TedBear, I've had him since I was a small child. I can't remember not having this thing.

"I love your room, it's totally you," Libby says, looking around. I look around with her and see all the bright colors. I painted, colored, and drew in bright, happy colors. I did have a couple black and white, but only photographs I took.

"This was my sanctuary," I say. "I didn't know it was that at the time but looking at it through new eyes, eyes that have been opened to how my life was, I see that I made this my happy place."

Libby goes to my closet and finds a couple of duffel bags. She walks back over to me and puts them on my bed.

"What do you want to take?" she asks.

Right, we've got things to do and we need to get back to the Estate before dark.

"All my clothes should fit in one and then I'll grab some of my books and odds and ends to put in the other one," I say, standing and starting to go through my books.

I know I can't take everything in my room, so I just grab my favorite of everything. I take a couple of my paintings off the wall and put them in the bag I'm filling with just stuff. The paintings of mostly just flowers and the sky different times during the day or night.

I look over and see Libby is done packing my clothes. She's sitting on my bed, holding TedBear. I walk over and sit beside her.

"Have you noticed this before?" she asks, handing him over to me. She's pointing at the inside of his ear.

I look and notice, for the first time, a small stitching. It's a heart, the letter 'U', the letter 'E' and then 'M', '&', and 'D' underneath it.

"Do you think..." I start to ask but I have to take a breath to keep myself from crying. "Do you think this is from my parents? My real parents?"

"I think so," Libby says, wrapping her arms around me, squeezing gently.

"-Love you, Emma. Mom & Dad- Is that what it

means?" I ask, a tear falling down my cheek.

"I think so," Libby says again. I can hear she's crying too.

I hug the bear to me and let the tears fall. I think this is the first time I've cried for the parents I had. The parents I never really got to know, didn't get to know, and won't get to know. This bear is the only thing I have left of their love for me. Vanessa had to have known it was from them, why did she let me keep it all these years?

After a few minutes of letting myself cry for the life I should have had, I take a deep breath, and calm myself down. I open my eyes and look around the room. My feelings for this room no longer hold anything good for me. It's a reminder of what Vanessa took from me.

I look over at Libby and she's staring at the carpet. Her eyes red from crying with me but she looks pissed.

"Are you okay?" I ask.

Libby jumps, startled out of her thoughts. She smiles over at me but it doesn't reach her eyes. "Yes and no, torn really. I'm just thinking of everything Vanessa has taken from you. But also thankful in a way because it brought you to us."

"I know. Bittersweet," I say.

"Yeah," she says and then she stands up. "Ready? Should we go check the other rooms out?"

"Yeah, but only one other room is up here.

Another one I wasn't allowed in... Vanessa's bedroom."

"There's only two rooms up here?"

"Yeah, how lucky of me to have all this space... to myself?" I ask sarcastically.

Libby shakes her head but grabs the bag full of clothes and heads out the door. I grab the bag with random things and shut the door behind me as I step over to Libby. We put our bags down on the landing, right by the top stair. She gestures for me to go ahead and open the door. I don't hesitate, none of that anymore. I open the door and walk in. It's the complete opposite from my room. Gray walls, dark gray bedding, and nothing making it look like it belongs to someone. There doesn't look to be any personal items in here at all.

I walk over to the dresser and open the top drawer. Empty. Open the next drawer down, empty again.

Libby looks at me questioningly and then walks over to the closet and opens the French doors and we find it completely empty too. I look around the room and see a couple books on the small shelf by the bed. I walk over, kneel down, and grab a couple up and see their just random bird books. But there's a small sketch pad type book and I pick it up. The pages are blank but at the back are about ten pictures. I pull them out and flip through them.

"Libby, I might have found something, come look," I say.

Libby comes and sits beside me. I look at a picture and hand it to her. It looks like just a random picture of a forest with a beautiful hotel looking cabin. Then another of the ocean but there's a beach, and a village further down the beach, in the background. A waterfall. A beautiful, but creepy looking castle. A couple city pictures, one looks like downtown New York City. Another with the Golden Gate Bridge.

"What do you think?" Libby asks. "Other than the obvious, do they look familiar to you?"

"No, I've never been to any of these places except for the one of New York City, but this is just a picture of a popular spot downtown," I say and then a thought hits me. "Libby, what if these are pictures of places where some of the others live? Werewolves, Vampires, Merfians, Fae... those others..."

"Oh crap! You could be on to something. But, the city pictures? They don't live in places like that. If they're there, it's only for a visit. They don't like being around Inepties for long," Libby says. "Let's go show Ty."

I gather up the pictures and put them back in the sketch book I found them in and we head out of the room. I look around one more time. Nothing. Nothing in here shows that Vanessa ever lived here. I shut the door behind me and scoop up my bag before we start walking down the stairs. Once we get down to the bottom, I put my bag down by the front door, Libby following me.

"Ty?" I holler.

"Kitchen," we hear him shout from our right. We make our way through the dining room and I have no memory of ever using this room.

"Did you find anything?" Libby asks as we walk into the kitchen.

"No, I looked through everything in the living room but there wasn't much in there," Ty says, as he stands up from looking inside a cupboard by the stove. "Not much in here either."

"Emma might have found something, come look," Libby says. She gestures for me to show Ty the pictures. I spread the pictures out on the counter and Ty comes around to look at them with us.

"We think it might be pictures of where some Vampires, Werewolves..." I start to say.

"Fae and Merfians live?" Ty finishes for me.

"Yeah," Libby says.

"They are," Ty says. He picks up the waterfall picture and says, "This is a doorway into one of the Fae hollows. And this-" he holds up the picture with the forest and hotel that looks like a huge cabin "-this is Bane and Maisie's pack house in Montana."

"Was Vanessa doing surveillance for intel or planning something?" Libby asks.

"I'm not sure but either way, it's not good. I mean, the others don't keep their locations secret but if Vanessa is taking pictures and watching them, that's never good," Ty says. He turns to me and asks, "Do you need to go through anything else?"

"No, I'm done here," I say. He nods and helps me gather the pictures back up. I put them once again, back into the sketch book I found them in.

Just as we're getting to the dining room, the front door bangs open. Ty pushes me behind him, Libby jumps up to stand beside him. They're blocking me from whomever just came through the front door.

I love them for being so protective of me but, really?

I peak around and see Travis standing in the doorway. Ty and Libby relax. When I step around them, they both look at me sheepishly.

"We've got a problem," Travis says. He looks behind him, not in the least bit worried, but more annoyed than anything.

"What is it?" Ty asks, walking forward.

"Vinny caught someone in the backyard, kid says he knows Emma," Travis says, looking at me.

"Knows me?" I ask in surprise. Travis just nods. Ty and Libby look at me, I shrug at them. "I don't know who it could be."

As we walk to the front door, Ty picks up the two bags, and brings them outside. He puts them on the sidewalk and I put the scrapbook on top. I look to the right and see Vinny towering over someone curled in the fetal position on the grass. We run over to them.

"What's up?" Ty asks.

"This kid jumped the back fence and then tried to scamper away when he saw me standing by the back door. I ran and tackled him to the ground. He started yelling that he knew the Hart's and thought he heard something, so he was coming over to check it out because they hadn't been home in a while. Says his name is Zack," Vinny says, flexing his muscles a little when the kid, Zack, looks up at him.

Ty looks at me, but I just shrug. I don't know this person. Ty nods which is apparently a signal for Travis and Ret to pick the kid up. But as soon as he's standing, I realize kid is not the right description of him, he looks to be about my age, maybe a little older. He's tall but again, not as tall as Ty, but about the same height as Travis and Ret, just a smidge shorter than them. He's good looking in the 'popular kid' type of way.

"What's your business here?" Ty asks.

But instead of answering Ty, the kid... boy... man... looks at me and speaks directly to me.

"Emma, it's me Zack... Zack Wilder," he says.

Everyone looks at me. I feel embarrassed. I don't recognize this kid... Zack, I don't recognize him at all.

"I'm sorry, who are you?" I ask, trying to be polite.

I can see Travis and Ret tighten their hold on him. A threat to tell the truth.

"Emma, I'm your neighbor, you don't recognize me? I've lived next to you for the last ten years, we moved in when I was nine," Zack says, looking at me with raised eyebrows.

Ty looks at me, I shrug.

"I'm sorry, I still have no idea who you are. I wasn't allowed to socialize. Did we go to school together?" I ask, really embarrassed now. My cheeks are turning a little red.

"I was a grade above you, you really don't remember me? I used to walk home with... well not with you, but around you. Your mom scared me, so I didn't feel like I could really approach you," he says, looking down ashamed. "I really wanted to. You were always reading or doing some kind of art in the backyard. I actually did try once but your mom answered the door when I knocked and told me to leave and never to bother you or her again. So, I didn't."

"So, you watched her from afar?" Vinny asks, looking slightly disgusted.

"Well, yes... but not in a stalker type of way. Really, Emma, I was just kind of waiting for an opportunity to talk to you. I thought you at least knew about me," he says, looking sad. *He's only talking directly to me. Weird.* "When I hadn't seen you guys come back from your trip and then the strange men showed up, I figured you guys had moved. You'd graduated, so I thought maybe you'd left for college, and I had lost my chance to talk to you."

Ty is about to say something, and I bet I know what it is, but I put my hand on his arm. This guy, Zack, is willing to talk but it seems only to me. So, I nod at Ty, hoping he understands my gesture. He looks down and nods back.

I say, trying to reel in my urgency, "Okay, Zack. I have a couple questions. How did you know my... mom—" I trip over the word "—and I went on a trip?"

"Oh, she asked my mom some questions about Greece, my mom is a travel agent. I had overheard while I was getting my little sister out of the car from school," he says, eager to talk to me.

"Okay... and what about the guys at my house?" I ask, really wanting this answer.

"They were big, kind of scary looking. I was out in the yard playing with Molly, my little sister, and waved at one when he walked by. He didn't acknowledge he even saw me, so I thought it would be best if I took Molly inside. I told my mom what I saw, and she confirmed what I had thought, that you guys must have moved. I didn't think anything of it other than missing my chance to talk to you, until this afternoon when I looked out my bedroom window and saw—" he looks over at Vinny "—him, in the backyard."

"And you guys went to school together?" Ty asks, doubt thick in his tone.

"Yes," Zack answers shortly, not looking at Ty. I feel Ty stiffen beside me. I look up at him but he's staring at Zack, who's staring at me.

"I'm sorry, I don't remember you but—" I look at Ty "—that doesn't mean it's not the truth. Vanessa was strict, remember?"

Ty reluctantly looks away from Zack and looks at me, "Yeah, I suppose."

"Tell us more about the men," Travis says, he looks at me and I gesture for him and Ret to let him go.

Zack shakes his arms out and again, looks at me when he answers, "They were here for the last few months. I tried not to stare too much because they were like really scary looking. They haven't been back in, probably a week now, though."

I hear a weird vibrating sound and look over at Libby. She looks at me and then puts her hand in her pocket. She pulls her phone out and the look on her face about makes me bust out laughing.

"It's Shae!" she squeals. She steps away and answers.

Zack takes a tentative step towards me but Travis and Ret slightly block his path. He pulls his hands out of his pockets and holds them up in front of himself. He says, "I'm not going to hurt her."

"It's more for your protection," Vinny says, winking at me. He's relaxed quite a bit since we first came out here.

Zack eyes him questioningly and then playfully says, "So, where you been?"

I catch Ty's eyes narrowing slightly from beside me, but his stance is relaxed as well.

"Oh, I moved," I say, side stepping the question a little bit.

"That's too bad. For college? Will you be coming back for visits?" he asks, taking another tentative step towards me.

"Not for college, and no, I won't be coming back," I say. I feel Ty move a little closer to me.

"Why are you here? You said you were a grade above Emma? Are you still living at home?" Ret asks, speaking for the first time since we got here.

"I go to school at NYU, so I can live at home and help my parents with my sister when they're at work. Mom being a travel agent, has weird hours. Dad is a firefighter and also has weird hours," Zack again, doesn't look at Ret when he answers. "Plus, I've been on summer break."

"How old is your sister? Molly, isn't it?" I ask.

"She's six. I'd go get her but she's with our grandparents at the zoo while they're here for a visit," Zack says, smiling. He's got a great smile, but he's got nothing on Ty. The thought has me reaching over and putting my hand through Ty's arm, resting it on the inside of his elbow. Zack's eyes don't miss this gesture and I see his eyes tighten just a little. *Weird.*

"We have to leave," Libby says urgently. We all turn to her in surprise.

"Why?" Ty whispers.

"Shae said—" she glances at Zack "—the guys are back. And they need to talk to Emma."

Libby and Ty look at me. I nod.

"Okay, let's go," Ty says.

"Wait, Emma, how do I stay in contact with you?" Zack asks with panic in his tone.

"You don't," Travis says. Ty smirks at him. *Overprotective men.*

"Ummm…" I start to say.

"What if the men come back?" Zack asks quickly.

I look at Ty, his eyes are narrowed again, but nods.

I look at Zack and ask, "Do you have a cellphone?"

"Yeah," he pulls a black phone out of his pocket.

I pull mine out, "What's your number?"

"555-467-1122," he rambles quickly.

I enter the number and send a quick text.

Me- *It's Emma.* 4:48pm Thursday

Zack smiles and taps on his phone. My phone buzzes in my hand.

Zack- *Hi Emma ;)* 4:48pm *Thursady*

"Ready?" Libby asks, looking at me weird.

"Yup, bye Zack. Let me know if those men or if... my... mom—" no need to explain how she's not my mom "—comes back."

"I will. It was so good to finally get to talk to you and I guess officially meet," Zack smiles and winks. If he thinks he's got an effect on me, he's wrong. Maybe before Ty he would have, but he doesn't hold a candle to this man to my right.

Having had enough, Ty turns me and kisses me, deeply but also roughly. A lot rougher than he's ever kissed me, and in front of everyone. I still get the electrical zing that normally happens when we kiss. I pull away and look up at him, but he's looking over my shoulder. I glance back and see Zack glaring, fists clenched, for a quick second, but then he relaxes and just smiles sweetly.

Weird. That's weird. I'll have to remember to talk to Ty about this when we get back to the Estate.

"Let's go," Libby says, sounding annoyed.

Travis and Ret stop and grab my bags, putting the scrapbook inside the one it was sitting on, and then we start to walk down the street. I turn and see Zack starting to head back to his house. *It's so strange that I don't remember him.*

CHAPTER 6 -
NEWCOMERS

"L et's get around the block and we'll find a place for you to make us Invisible and then you can Jump us back to the Estate," Ty says, looking behind us, probably looking for Zack. I look back again but he's not there anymore.

"There's a park around the corner and a small tree grove surrounds it, that'll probably work," I suggest.

"Sounds good," Ty says. He reaches down and takes my hand.

"Did Shae say anything else about the guys and what they need?" I ask Libby.

"No, just that they needed to talk to you, but they're back at the Estate, so that's a good thing," Libby says, smiling. I'm sure she's thinking about being back in Max's arms.

We round the corner and as soon as the park comes into view, the guys pick up the pace. I don't mind, I'd like to get home too. There aren't too many kids playing, so slipping into the trees is easy. And making us Invisible, even easier. I check to make sure we're all touching, I think of the Estate, and take a step forward. I don't have to open my eyes to know we're home. It's so much quieter and smells of fresh air.

The front door opens and Max runs out.

"Libby!" he hollers. She drops my hand and runs to him. Their embrace has me smiling and gripping Ty's hand tightly. I know how they feel. Any time apart feels like an eternity. When they start making out, that's my cue to look away.

I look up at the door and see Charlie walking out, holding hands with Shae. Clay comes out behind them with Malory tucked under his arm. Alysa is the last to come out.

"Welcome home," I say to all the guys.

"It's good to be back," Charlie says, kissing Shae on the top of her head.

"So, how did it go?" Ty asks, shaking hands with Max and then Clay. He does the weird one-handed shake, hug thing, guys do, with Charlie. Holding my hand and Charlie holding Shae's, makes it even more awkward.

"On one hand, pretty disappointing. We didn't find any signs of Meredith, Doc, or Bill," Max says, shaking his head.

"And on the other hand?" Ty urges.

"You won't believe who we found!" Charlie says excitedly, looking at Ty and Libby.

"Who?" Ty and Libby ask at the same time.

"It's the reason we needed to talk to Emma," Charlie says, as he avoids answering Ty and Libby on purpose. Ty gives him the stop messing around look. Charlie just smiles. He's dragging out the suspense on purpose.

"Your cousins," Clay says, rolling his eyes at his brother.

"Tate and Tally?" Libby asks excitedly.

"Yeah," Charlie says, annoyed that Clay spilled the beans.

"Oooh, Emma please grant them permission to come to the Estate?" Libby asks, bouncing out of Max's arms and over to me.

"Who is it?" Alysa asks sounding annoyed, like her old self. "We don't want just anyone being allowed to the Estate."

"Relax, it's Tate and Tally," Charlie says.

"They're our cousins. Their dad is our dad's twin and their mom is our mom's twin. We look more like quadruplets than cousins," Libby says laughing.

"They're good," Ty says, squeezing me. "We can trust them."

"Even if it turns out we can't, there's not much they can do even if she grants them permission," Max says. "It's not like they can go and tell anyone how to get here. Only Emma can do that."

"That's true," Alysa says, flipping her hair behind her back.

"Okay, Charlie, since you know where they are, I'll give you their permission and then you can Jump them here," I say.

"Sounds good," Charlie says, kissing Shae quickly and then stepping over to me.

"I, Emma Hart, give Tate and Tally Conner permission to enter the Estate, Charlie O'Neal has permission to grant them entry by form of Jumping," I say, touching Charlie's elbow as I say it.

"I'll be back," he says and then he's gone.

"How long has it been since you've seen your cousins?" I ask Ty. He looks as excited as Libby.

"Oh, before we moved to The Pit. Mom and Dad have seen them when they've gone out Searching," Ty says, wrapping his arms around my waist, pulling me back into him.

"Why didn't they come to The Pit too?" I ask.

"They were traveling with their parents all over Europe. They were living over there when the battle at the school happened. Aunt Madison and Uncle David thought it would be safer for them to stay over there. They never got caught by the Rifts there, so maybe they were right, or they found their own way to hide out," Libby says. She's still bouncing on the balls of her feet.

"You seem really excited," I laugh.

"I am! Tally was like a sister when we were younger. Tate and Ty were pretty inseparable as well.

Everyone mistakes Tally and I for twins, and the boys for twin brothers. Just wait, you'll be blown away," Libby says shaking her head.

"Don't go falling in love with Tate," Ty says. I look up and he winks at me.

And then all of a sudden, Charlie is back, standing in front of us with two people that look like copies of Ty and Libby. Only, not really. Tate, his features look like Ty, it's uncanny but his coloring is the opposite. Ty's hair is dark brown with honey highlights and Tate's is the opposite. And Tate's eyes are like Libby's light green. Tally, has the same features, a carbon copy of Libby only her hair is the same as Tate's, honey colored with darker highlights. And Tally has the same color eyes as Ty, emerald green, only maybe a shade or two darker.

"Holy shit," Shae says. She's looking between the four of them.

"This is surreal," Max says.

"Libby!" Tally says excitedly. She runs forward and embraces Libby in a big, loving hug.

"Hey man," Tate says, coming forward to Ty. They also embrace. I drop Ty's hand so he can hug his cousin properly. Tate steps back and looks down at me. His eyes go wide. "This must be Emma?"

"Yes?" Ty says as a question, surprised that he was able to pick me out so quickly.

"I'm sorry, it's just your parents told our parents

about her," Tate says, looking at Ty. He looks at me, "Their description was pretty spot on but definitely didn't do you justice."

"She's taken," Charlie says, clapping him on the shoulder.

"I wasn't… I didn't…" Tate starts to stammer out.

"Ignore him," Shae says, patting Charlie on the chest. "He tried and failed with her."

We all go quiet, not sure how to handle that awkward statement.

"I didn't mean it in any way other than just letting him know. We all know the affect Emma has on people," Charlie says. Shae raises an eyebrow at him. "I just mean… I'm not saying she asks for it. I just… she's just… I'll shut up now."

Clay looks at Charlie and then at Shae with his eyebrows raised. Charlie looks slightly ashamed.

"Relax guys, I'm just kidding. Well, not really because it's true, but Charlie and I are good now. Charlie, I'm just flipping you shit. We do all know the affect she has on people," Shae says kissing Charlie on the cheek and winking at me. Charlie relaxes a little and pulls Shae into him.

"I'm sorry, the affect I have on people?" I ask, confused.

"Don't play…" Alysa starts to say but then looks at me with her head tilted to the side. She asks, "You really don't know the affect you have on people?"

"I honestly have no idea what you're talking about," I say honestly, I really don't.

"We won't dive into that right now," Libby says, smiling at me like she knows I'm telling the truth but wants to let me in on the secret that apparently everyone thinks they know about me. She pulls Tally and Tate by the hands and says, "Come in and see the new place."

"It's beautiful. And it's an entire island? That's awesome," Tally says. She sounds like she's trying really hard to help change the subject. She then adds, because I'm looking at her with a confused look, "Charlie told us a little about it."

Ty puts his arm back around me and we follow everyone inside. But he bends down and whispers into my ear, "Remind me, to remind you, how amazing you are whenever we're alone?"

I shake my head and keep walking.

We step into the foyer, and I see Tate and Tally staring up and around.

"Wow, this is truly amazing," Tally says. She turns to me and asks, "Your parents left this to you?"

"Yeah. Well actually, it's been in my mom's family for a long time and since I'm a Jamison, it's mine I guess," I say awkwardly.

We make our way through the Estate, giving a tour as we go. We find Tate and Tally rooms. We make our way back down to the Dining Hall.

"I'm starving," I say.

"Same," Libby says.

It's been such a long day. It feels like we were at my old house weeks ago, not just a short hour or so ago. Cookie has lasagna, garlic bread, and salad all set out. After introducing Tate and Tally to her, we load up some plates, and go find a table to sit at for our large group.

"So, you guys grew up together?" Malory asks Tally, after everyone has had time to eat a little of our dinner.

"Yeah, most of our childhood was spent together," Tally answers.

"Until your parents took their assignments in Europe, and then we only got to see you guys for, that one Christmas before everything changed?" Libby asks, looking sad.

Tally nods and continues to eat her food. She, too, looks sad.

"Wait, so none of you have met until today?" I ask.

"We were homeschooled as kids and spent most of our time over at Ty and Libby's. We did meet Charlie, Clay, and their parents a handful of times, I'm surprised you guys remember us," Tally answers, looking around at the table.

"Hard to forget someone who looks identical to your best friend," Charlie says, thumping Ty on the shoulder with his fist. "This is Shae, by the way, my girlfriend."

Shae waves in greeting. Tally and Tate wave back.

"I'm sorry, I guess we should introduce everyone to you guys," Libby says. "This is Max, my boyfriend, and his sister Malory. Her boyfriend Clay, who you already know. And Alysa, Shae's sister."

They all nod and say a quick hello as Libby says their name.

"How long do you guys get to stay for?" Clay asks, eating the last of his lasagna and taking some off of Malory's plate. She's turned talking to Alysa, not paying any more attention to our conversation.

"We aren't sure," Tate says. "We're in the States looking for someone, Arthur Blanc, from back home. We believe he was taken by Rifts in Paris and our intel shows he was moved to the States. We aren't sure why he was taken and moved. Some people in our region think he defected to the Rifts."

Ty sits up a little straighter and asks, "Did he have a position in your Guard?"

"He was one of our lead Guardians. Which is why I don't think he defected. He fought against the Rifts and had family taken from him just like everyone else. Not nearly as bad as here in the States, as the Rifts have only been in Europe and other countries for the last five to seven years. But still, Vanessa knows how to cause havoc," Tate says.

"Our Leaders are missing too. Meredith, who is

our Head Leader and her husband Jim— we call him Doc— and Bill, our Guard Commander. We aren't sure if Bill went missing first, and then Doc and Meredith went looking for him once they realized something was wrong, or if they all three went missing together. Maybe if we find them, we'll find Arthur too. We'll, also, need to get word out to the other Regions and see if any other Leaders are missing," Ty says. "I've got a bad feeling about this."

"So do we. Which is why we volunteered to come here," Tally says. "Mom and Dad weren't too keen on us leaving. But since we have connections here, Naomi, who is our Meredith, thought we'd have the best luck finding Arthur or at least getting more information."

"Why didn't your parents come?" Max asks.

"They've been out in the field for the last two months and Naomi didn't want to pull them off their Search to come here, when she had us she could send," Tate answers.

"And by your connections, you mean your family?" Alysa asks, paying more attention to our conversation than I thought she had been.

"Well, yes," Tally answers sheepishly, looking at Ty and Libby apologetically.

Libby laughs and says, "There's no reason to look like that, you know you can always call on us for help."

I yawn but try to hide it behind my hand.

"Tired?" Ty whispers, as he leans down to me.

"I'm fine," I say, lying. Because truthfully, I am pooped. The emotional rollercoaster from being at my old house, plus the physical exertion of Jumping us from one side of the country to the other, and then meeting Ty and Libby's cousins, has left me drained.

"You've had a busy day. And it's your first day back from being down for three months, it's okay to admit you're tired," Ty says, putting his arm around me.

I playfully glare at him before I say, "Okay, I'm tired."

"See that wasn't so hard, was it?" he kisses my forehead. I lean into him and breath in his scent coming from the center of his chest. "Want to go hangout in your room or mine, for a bit?"

"What about your cousins?" I ask. Looking at Tate and Tally. Tate is in a conversation with Charlie and Clay about the differences from here and back in their Region. Tally is talking to Libby and Max about something that has Libby blushing.

"They'll be fine and they'll be here in the morning," Ty says standing up. Everyone at the table looks at him. "Goodnight, everyone. Tate, Tally, we'll catch up more tomorrow."

Ty stacks our plates on top of each other and picks them up with one hand and offers his other hand out for me to take. I shake my head but smile as I take it.

"Goodnight," I say to everyone now looking at me. We walk over and put our plates on the pile by the garbage cans. He leads us to the stairs and takes his time walking up them beside me. I hadn't realized how sore I was until I stood up.

We finally make it to my floor and Ty asks, "Do you want to just go to sleep or would you like to hangout for a bit?"

"I'd like to hangout for a bit," I say, biting my bottom lip.

"Your room?" he asks, looking at the door.

"That works for me," I say, pulling him by the hand. I open the door and lead the way down the hall towards my door.

When we get to my room, I'm about to open my door, but Ty turns me towards him. He places his hands on my hips and pushes me gently against my door. I look up into his eyes and he has a look of need burning in them. I'm about to ask, 'what's the matter', but he's suddenly kissing me deeply.

Before we can get caught making out in the hall, yet again, I reach behind me and blindly find the doorknob on my door. I turn it and push it open. Without breaking our kiss, I grab Ty by the front of his shirt, and pull him into my room. He kicks the door shut with his foot, turns us, so I'm once again backed up against my bedroom door. He grips my hips tightly and lifts me up, I wrap my legs around his waist. I'm up higher so he doesn't have to bend down so far to kiss me.

"Bed?" I breathlessly ask as his lips leave mine and travel down my neck.

A moan deep down in Ty's throat escapes him as he nods. His lips are back on mine as he takes us to my bed. The softness of the bed is more comfortable than the door. I break our kiss for a second so I can scoot up on my bed and put my head on my pillow. Ty only has to crawl up a short distance. We're kissing again, Ty lying half on me, half on his side. I slide my left leg up and wrap it around his hips.

Ty grips my ankle for a second, then slides his hand up my calf, behind my knee, and pulls it up and over him more. He then continues to slide his hand up my thigh until it's resting on my lower back. He again, tries to pull me closer to him. I know what he wants. He wants to be closer. I want to be closer, but we are as close as we can get at the moment.

I'm not sure how long we lay like this making out but soon our kissing slows. Ty kisses my cheek, my nose, and then my forehead.

"I've been thinking about the conversation we were having back at The Pit, in the bathing pool," Ty starts to say. He looks down at me and smiles.

I turn red instantly, knowing exactly what conversation he's talking about. We were talking about our sexual history before we were interrupted by a couple of girls coming in for a swim.

"Mmmmmhmmm," I mumble out as a prompt for

him to continue.

"I was just wondering if you remember the question I asked you, that you never got a chance to answer?" he asks. He kisses my nose. Fire erupts in my stomach.

"I remember," I say nervously.

"And?" he encouragingly asks.

I take a deep breath and try to collect my thoughts so that I can tell him how I feel. What's the best way to tell someone you want them in every possible way but you are also, strangely, not ready for that step... yet. No matter how much your body craves them?

Honest, just be completely honest, no matter how embarrassing you might feel. I think to myself.

"In full disclosure, I might scare you away with how honest I'm about to be with you," I say, looking at Ty's nose because I can't bring myself to look him in the eye. Why is it when someone is being honest and truthful, it's so hard to look at the other person in the eye? But when someone is lying, they can stare at someone into the deepest parts of their eyes?

"Don't ever feel like you're going to scare me away with telling me the truth, I want you to always be honest with me," Ty says, pulling my chin up to where I end up having to look him in the eyes.

"Okay..." I say tentatively. I take a deep breath and continue, "I feel like you could be the person I take that step with, because even just kissing like we do and the bare minimum touching, it brings feelings to my stomach, my body, I've never experienced before. My body wants you. My mind and heart want you, but I don't think I'm actually ready for that step yet. I feel like I'll know when the time is right and there won't be any hesitation, I'll just know. I hope this doesn't scare you off or frustrates you, it's just how I feel, for now."

Ty sits up and for a fleeting second, my heart drops to my stomach, thinking he's going to stand up and walk out of my room. Except, he reaches for my hands, and pulls me up so that we're sitting with our backs against my headboard. He keeps ahold of one of my hands and kisses it sweetly.

"Emma, that's exactly how I feel. Although, I know I'm ready. I've been waiting for you. Not someone like you but you. If you were to tell me you were ready now, I'm all for it, but if you tell me we need to wait, I'm all for that too. Please don't ever feel like I'll pressure you to do something you aren't ready for and if I do make you feel pressured, call me out on it. I know we've only just met a few months ago, but I feel like my soul has known you for... well, forever... for eternity."

I lay my head on his shoulder and feel a tear fall down my cheek. I reach up and wipe it away. He didn't say it out right, but I feel like Ty's telling me I'm his Anima Gemella and I feel the same way. I also feel like that's something to admit or express, a little later in our relationship.

"Thank you for being so understanding. I'm sure it's confusing to hear someone pretty much tell you they want you but also not really," I laugh a shaky breath out. "I don't know how else to explain it, but I do know, you'll be the first to know when I'm ready."

Ty laughs and says, "Well, I'd appreciate that, and I do understand what you're saying. These feelings are new to me too, but I also have had a relationship where these feelings weren't there, so I know the difference. You've never been in a relationship, so you want to be completely certain these feelings are real."

"It's true, I've never been in a relationship but having been kissed before, I can say for certain, I have NEVER felt anything the way I feel when you kiss me," I say, turning my head and kissing his cheek. And to prove my point, even that small kiss leaves a zing on my lips. "And I don't think I'll feel this way with anyone but you."

Ty turns his head and kisses me. My heart rate picks up immediately. I place my hand on his neck to pull him closer and I can feel his heartbeat racing in his vein. If kissing like this can bring us these feelings, I can't imagine what it'll feel like when we take that next step.

After another unknown amount of time, our kissing slows once again. Ty slides his hand down my arm and I see out of the corner of my eye, his Mark peeking out from in side of his sleeve.

"Can I see your Mark?" I ask, realizing I've never seen it.

"I was wondering if you were ever going to ask," Ty laughs.

"Why not just show me?"

Ty shrugs as he turns his arm so I can see his Mark better. Ty's Mark looks like a Caduceus except for where there should be a staff, or in Shae's Mark, a Trident, Ty has a sword.

"This is the coolest one I've seen," I say, awestruck.

Ty just smiles and starts kissing me again.

CHAPTER 7 -
MADE IT OFFICIAL

Before my eyes can open, my mind registers I'm lying on top of another body. I take a deep breath and I'm rewarded with Ty's heavenly scent. I take another deep breath and relax into him. I nestle my cheek deeper into his chest and feel him take a deep breath in as well.

At some point last night, I fell asleep on Ty's shoulder. We'd stopped making out and talked a little more about our childhood. I brought up how he had kissed me in front of Zack and how it felt like he was marking his territory. He appologized and explained that Zack rubs him the wrong way.

The last thing I remember was sitting in comfortable silence, just listening to each other breathe. That sounds weird, but it was oddly soothing. Now, here I am, waking up having just slept with him. And slept as in sleeping, not the other meaning for slept. I wasn't kidding last night when I told him I wasn't ready for that step yet. Heck, we haven't even come out to people that we are in a relationship. And honestly, I didn't know we were officially in one until that's what he called it last night.

"Good morning," Ty says, squeezing my gently, pulling him closer to his chest.

"Good morning," I say, wrapping my arms around him. My stomach rumbles, which makes us laugh.

"Ready for breakfast?"

"Yeah, I'm starving. Yesterday took a lot out of me, I think I could eat two breakfast meals worth of food right now," I laugh.

"Let's go get you fed then. But first, I think I'll Run to my room. I need to shower and change," Ty says.

I reluctantly roll away from him and sit up. I say, as I discreetly smell myself, "I could use a shower as well."

"I'll be back in, half an hour?" he asks.

"Sounds good."

I walk him to the door and after a not so quick kiss, he steps out into the hall. I shut the door after watching him walk away, admiring his butt as he went. Smiling like a giddy little girl, I go into the bathroom, grab my toothbrush and toothpaste, and put it in the shower. I turn on the water and as I wait for the water to warm up, I strip my clothes off. Not wanting Ty to wait too long for me, I don't take as long of a shower as I would have liked.

I put undies and a bra on, socks, and then decide on jeans and a long sleeve t-shirt. Instead of braiding my hair today, I just put it in a loose bun on top of my head. I'm just getting my boots on when there's a soft knock on my door. As I walk over to open it, I grab my phone and see it's not quite 7:00 AM.

I open the door and find Ty wearing jeans and a nice fitting t-shirt. He smiles his heart stopping smile at me and kisses me quickly.

"Ready?" he asks.

"Yup," I answer, as I put my phone in my pocket and step out of my room.

He grabs my hand and we start walking down the hall.

"Emma, I've been meaning to ask you something and after our conversation last night, I feel like now would be a good time to ask," he starts to say as he holds the door open for me that leads down the stairs to the kitchen.

"Okay," I prompt.

"Will you, officially, be my girlfriend?" he asks and then winks at me.

I laugh and says, "Yes, as long as you'll be my boyfriend?"

"Absolutely, no doubt about it," he pulls me to him and kisses the top of my head.

"So, does this mean we go public?" I ask.

"Yeah, I think so. Although, I don't think anyone will be too surprised," Ty laughs.

"Not after Charlie's statement yesterday."

"He knew how I felt before I could admit it to myself."

"Why couldn't you?"

"I think it was mainly because it was hard to wrap my mind around such strong feelings for a girl I just met," he squeezes my hand. "But, that's how it goes sometimes, an instant connection with the right person."

"I felt... feel... the same way," I say giving his hand a squeeze back. Then a thought comes to me. "If Charlie knew how you felt, why did he try to get with me? Doesn't that upset you?"

"I was upset, but I reminded myself that you weren't mine, because I was too scared to come forward and tell you and see if you felt the same way. For me, my denial was to brood and try to ignore my feelings. In the end, it was the stupidest choice I've ever made. I think Charlie was in such denial about how he felt for Shae, he was doing everything to not feel it. Feeling like an absolute shit, for going for his best friend's girl– even though said best friend couldn't admit his feelings for the girl– it still felt better to him to feel like that, than to accept his feelings for Shae," Ty takes a breath and shakes his head. "Sometimes it's scary having such strong feelings. It's not right, but us guys, sometimes, handle those things by running from our feelings, which looks like we're running from the girl."

"In a way, I guess that makes sense," I say.

We've gotten down to the dining hall and everyone is sitting around the table we had sat at last night. In fact, it looks like they haven't even moved. The only indication they have, is that they're all wearing different clothes from last night. Ty and I go over to the food table and fill our plates with cinnamon rolls, eggs, and bacon. Ty grabs us a couple bottles of orange juice.

When we get back to the table we're greeted with a chorus of hello's and good mornings.

"You guys are all up early," Ty says as he takes a bite of his food.

"We decided to form a plan to propose to you and see if we can narrow down where the Rifts or Vanessa are hiding the Leaders," Max says.

"What are your ideas?" Ty asks.

"We don't really have any," Clay laughs embarrassingly.

"There are just so many places they could be hiding and not just here in the States," Tally says.

"So where do we start?" I ask.

"Maybe go to where you were being held and work our way out from there?" Libby suggests.

"That's not a bad idea," Charlie says.

"Haven't you guys done recon there after I was rescued and found nothing?" I ask.

"Yeah, but that was before the Leaders were taken.

There were still Rifts there but about a quarter of what was there when they had you. We never went back to check things out, but it would be a good place to start," Ty answers. "Charlie let's pull all the Units in and see what we have to work with, and we'll send a couple out on a scout. I don't want to send a whole Platoon if a smaller Unit will do."

"Roger that," Charlie says. He had finished eating just as Ty and I had gotten to the table, so he stands, kisses Shae, and then Runs from the Dining Room.

The other's break off into random conversations while Ty and I finish our breakfast. I'm just taking a drink of my orange juice when Charlie appears out of nowhere and sits next to Shae. I spit orange juice everywhere.

"Oh, sorry about that," Charlie says laughing. Ty goes to wipe the front of my shirt with a napkin but then decides against it and hands it to me. "So, are we going to talk about the elephant in the room yet or not?"

Everyone looks at him. Shae elbows him and shakes her head. Is he talking about the way he had been acting and has now seen the light or something else?

"Leave it alone," Libby hisses between her teeth. I look at her and she smiles at me sheepishly.

"What are you talking about?" I ask.

Shae glares at Charlie, trying to convey to keep his

mouth shut, even I can see the meaning in her look, but... Charlie is Charlie.

"I'm talking about you and Ty. Are you guys going to admit your feelings for each other and to us, or keep playing the clueless couple that isn't a couple, but sure acts like one?" Charlie asks. He smiles his smug smile, leans back, and pops a grape in his mouth that he took from Shae's plate.

Ty is about to say something, he doesn't look mad, he kind of looks relieved. He looks like Charlie just gave him a way to tell everyone that we are ready to admit how we feel. But, Charlie's attitude right now and the way he acted when he was denying his own feelings, has me pissed. I touch Ty's arm to stop him from saying anything just yet. I want to give Charlie a taste of his own medicine first. Ty looks at me with a questioning look, I wink at him, but for only him to see.

To everyone else and especially Charlie, I pull my most pissed off facial expression on and turn to Charlie, "Oh, I thought you were talking about maybe explaining to everyone why you had been acting the way you had been. Treating Shae like she was nothing and trying to get with anyone within arm's length, even her own sister. Now I get the whole twin fantasy thing some guys have but, those two are the most opposite twins you could ever meet."

Everyone stops talking immediately and looks

between Charlie and me. They glance around at Shae and Alysa as well. Shae looks shocked that I'm saying what I'm saying, but not pissed. For that, I'm thankful. Alysa looks ashamed.

"Shae and I have talked about all of this. I don't need to explain it to you," Charlie says, flustered.

"Oh, so your business is your business but me and Ty, that's something that needs to be discussed with everyone?" I ask. I hadn't thought I was going to be so serious but now that we're talking, I really do want to know what his thought process is on all of this.

"I... it's just..." Charlie starts to say. "We can all see how you guys feel about each other, we just want you to admit it too."

"Kind of like how we could all see the side stares you'd give Shae from across the room? How you always seemed to know where she was but pretended you didn't care? Kind of like how we could see you being a dick but you wouldn't admit it?" I say, crossing my arms across my chest. Ty puts his hand on my leg and gently squeezes.

"I was a dick! Okay! I can admit that," Charlie shouts. "I've told Shae that the three years leading up to her... death... were the worst years of my life! I wasted so much time denying how I truly felt. I wasn't with her because I was scared of how I felt! I thought being young meant testing the waters and getting experience when in reality, being with the person you're meant to be with is so much better. Having all the years you're meant to have with each other, that's so much better than things... than people... that don't matter. Being with the person that makes your heart skip a beat just by seeing them or just from catching their scent in the air as they walk by a room, that's what matters. Being with the person that scares you because of the strong feelings you have and not understanding how you can have such strong feelings for one person, that's what matters."

By the time Charlie is done talking, he's more or less whispering and has tears in his eyes. I've never seen him so quiet or look so sad.

Alysa clears her throat and says, "Since Charlie just spilled his truthful guts out, I'll go next. We never had sex, we fooled around but never took it to that level. Honest. I only acted like I did to piss Malysa off... sorry, Shae. I'm trying to change my ways and my attitude. Watching Shae die... was the worst experience of my life and I'll never forget it. I prayed to the gods to bring her back and if they did, I'd change. I'd do better, I'd be better. I'll admit that I was jealous of Shae. She had found her Anime Gemelle so young and I had hoped that Ty would be mine. But every day I tried to force it, it became clearer and clearer that we weren't meant to be together. That didn't stop me from trying. I thought if I could just show... prove to him that I was better than everyone, it would happen.

I thought since my conceited view was that Ty and I were the most beautiful of us all, things would change between us, but that's not how Anime Gemelle's work. We are destined for, who we are destined for, plain and simple. We can deny or try to force all we want but in the end, if it's meant to be, it will and if not, then it won't. Being with your Anime Gemelle is supposed to be as easy as breathing. They're supposed to bring you peace and feel like your safe place. I understand that now. I've also talked to Shae about all of this and as she's the only one that I needed to apologize to and ask for forgiveness, I guess since Charlie could open up, so could I–"

Libby interrupts her and asks, "You don't think you need to apologize to Ty and Emma as well?"

Alysa looks at Ty and me, ashamed. She says, "Yes, I do. And I will, but not right now. I just think Charlie is trying to get you guys to admit to yourselves how you feel so you don't waste any more time apart. And just so everyone is clear, Ty and I never had sex either. I didn't want to force him to do that, I wanted him to want to, and he never did."

Shae reaches across the table and squeezes her sister's hand. I can see their bond strengthening.

"Well, since everyone is being truthful," Ty says. Everyone holds their breath. He looks at me and I wink at him. "To be honest, Emma and I have sort of been together since we were at The Pit."

Everyone gasps.

"What?" Alysa asks in shock.

"I knew it!" Libby shouts and fist pumps the air.

"I told her I wanted to keep it quiet until we knew for sure what it was we were feeling and truthfully, I was scared. I was in denial. I, like most of us, have heard about how we'd feel when we'd meet our Anime Gemelle but to actually feel it is a whole other thing. Alysa, you say it should be as easy as breathing when in reality, Emma takes my breath away every time I see her. When we kiss–" I hear the girls gasp "–I forget to breathe. Being with her is easy. It's comfortable to just sit with her and not have to force conversation or anything," he takes my hand and holds it on top of the table. I know it's not the first time anyone has seen us hold hands. For him to be expressing himself the way he is and showing it with this gesture, has my heart skipping a beat, like it always does whenever Ty is involved. He kisses my hand and says, "We actually talked about this last night and made it official this morning."

"Nice man," Charlie says, raising his hand for a high five. Ty laughs and high fives him.

"Made it official how?" Shae asks, wiggling her eyebrows at us. She and Charlie make the perfect pair.

I laugh and say, "Not in the way you're thinking. We officially asked each other to be boyfriend/girlfriend."

"Oh... pssshh..." Shae says, looking legitimately disappointed.

"I'm so happy for you guys," Libby says as she gets up and walks over to me and hugs me.

"Doesn't it feel so much better to admit and accept these feelings?" Charlie asks. He looks like a weight has been lifted. Who knew refusing to let yourself feel how you truly feel, could make you seem so weighed down?

"Yeah, man, it does," Ty says, leaning in and kissing my head. I lean my head in and rest it on his shoulder.

The guys start talking about strategies on how they should do their recon on the place I was being held. I'll have to find a time to tell Ty I'd like to go. I want to see where I was being held and tortured, maybe that would give me better closure.

I feel vibrating on my leg. I put my hand to my poket and feel my phone buzzing. I look around and see no one else at the table has their phone out. I pull it out and see Zack is calling me.

"Ty, Zack's calling," I say in surprise.

Ty instantly turns to me and says, "Answer it. Guys, quiet."

I hit the answer button and say, "Hello? Zack?"

Zack replies in a whisper, *"Yeah, it's me... There are men back at your house... *there is a pause and I can hear a door opening*... I'm going to go to the back yard* *and get a better look."*

"No, Zack, stay in your house," I say. I stand up. I can't sit when I'm anxious. Ty stands with me. He motions to a corner of the dining hall where no one is sitting. He waves our table over but motions for them to be quiet.

"Put it on speaker," Ty suggests, so I do.

"No, it's okay, I can be quiet... I want to get a better look to give you a good description..." Zack says but he's so quiet I can barely hear him. I turn the volume up all the way. *"Oh shit... one of them saw me... shit... shit... shit..."*

I can hear wind blowing in the phone, like he's running. There's a sound of a door opening and shutting again. Loud footsteps running on wood floor.

"What's going on Zack?" I ask, panic in my tone.

"Molly, come with me! Mom, Dad, run! Hide!" I hear Zack yelling.

I look up at Ty, my eyes showing the anxiety and panic running through me. He looks around at Charlie and the guys. Libby and Shae are holding each other.

There's a sound of someone running on stairs and then a door shutting quietly.

"Zack, talk to me, what's going on?" I ask.

"They're in my house... Emma... they're in my house... I have my sister... I tried to get to my parents, but they were on the other side of the house... I told them to hide, I hope they listened... I hope... *faint screaming

and bangs*... *Oh fuck!...* *loud crashing sound*... *Emma! HELP!"*

The phone goes dead. I'm stunned and frozen. After I finally take a deep breath and realize I'm staring at a black, blank screen. I look up at Ty.

"We have to go, we have to go now!" I scream.

"Everyone, get your Magikida's and meet us in the foyer. We don't have time to change, go now!" Ty shouts.

Charlie grabs Shae and Clay, who's holding Malory's hand and Jumps them out of the room. I see Libby and Max Run from the room. Tate and Tally look at each other and then at Ty.

"We don't have a Magikida," Tate says.

"I'll get you guys some, just go wait in the foyer for us, that is if you want to come. This isn't your fight but we could use you," Ty says, hesitating for a moment.

"Of course we're going," Tally says in a manner that implies he's being silly.

Ty kisses me and says, "Go!"

I Jump to my room and grab my Magikida off my dresser. We definintely don't have time to change but I throw my battle gear top on. Having my Magikida secured on my back leaves my hands open which I feel like are a deadlier weapon than my Magikida. I Jump to the foyer and only find Tate and Tally.

"So, who is this Zack guy?" Tally asks.

"An old neighbor from where I used to live," I say, starting to pace.

"Where you lived with Vanessa?" Tate asks.

"Yeah... when we went back yesterday to see if she had left anything there and to get some of my stuff, he came over and told us that men showed up a couple months ago and moved a bunch of stuff out. I told him to call me if they showed up. I didn't think they'd show up so soon. I wonder if Vanessa had the place being watched," I say. I'm about to ask where everyone else is when Charlie appears with Clay.

"We talked the girls into staying," Clay says.

"Why can't they come?" I ask, defensively.

"Shae doesn't have a Talent that would keep her protected in a fight, other than being able to manipulate water. Malory could shift into an animal, but again, not very defensive," Charlie says, patting my shoulder.

"Alysa won't come, even though her Fire Talent is bad ass, but she's never taken any self-defense classes so when it comes to hand-to-hand, she'd lose," Clay says.

"What about Libby? She's an amazing Healer," I state.

"So is Ty but the difference is Ty has defensive skills. Emma, these girls are more than welcome to come but they don't know how to fight," Charlie says. "If they come and don't know how to fight, it puts us in a disadvantage because instead of fighting the Rifts, we'll be spending all of our time trying to keep the girls from being killed or taken. After the battle at the Elder's, they've realized they need more combat training."

"Don't worry, Emma, I've got your girl support," Tally says, smiling at me.

"What Talents do you have again?" Charlie asks.

"I play with Electricity. I'm also a Protector and Lie Detector. And don't worry, boys, I've had plenty of combat training," Tally says, punching Charlie in the arm. Hard enough that he grabs it.

"I can attest to that," Tate says, giving his sister knuckles.

Another second goes by and then Ty is standing in front of us, holding out two Magikida's to Tally and Tate. Max shows up a second after him.

"Ready?" Ty asks, looking at me. I nod, grabbing his hand.

"How are we getting there?" Tate asks, opening one of the front doors and walking out, Tally behind him.

When we get outside and down the steps, Ty looks at me and smiles.

"I'm going to Jump us," I say. I think Ty secretly enjoys watching people who don't know me, hear this news.

"What?" Tate says, looking at me. "No offense, but

you've had your Talents for how long?"

"Hmmmm about four months now," I say.

"No way can you Jump all of us... you're joking, right? Charlie's the one that can Jump people," he states, looking at Ty.

"She can," Charlie says. "I can't. I can do short distances with about four people, but my top number is three tag alongs for long distances."

Tate and Tally look at me skeptically.

"Just trust me," I say. I reach my hand out and Ty grabs it instantly. I offer my other hand to Tally. She takes it but looks at her brother and then shrugs. I look at Tate and say, "I need you to hold Tally's other hand."

Charlie, Clay, and Max know the drill, so they've already put their hands on each other's shoulders, Charlie's on Ty's.

Tate is still hesitant.

Ty says, "Tate, man, just do it. We need to hurry. The Rifts could be gone by now."

Shaking his head, Tate grabs hold of Tally's hand. The second I see they have a tight grip, I think of my old house, and take a step forward. At the same time, I make us Invisible. This is the first time I don't close my eyes. It's the strangest thing. One second I'm looking out on the grounds of the Estate and then I'm looking at my old house.

CHAPTER 8 -
BACK AGAIN ALREADY

"Incredible!" Tate says in astonishment.

"Whoa, and we're Invisible? What the hell? But not completely, I can see you guys," Tally states in shock.

"That's Emma too, you'll get used to it and her," Max says, patting my back as he walks by.

"It only looks like it's not complete because she's made us all Invisible to outside eyes, for us, we can see each other," Clay says, smiling at me.

Tate and Tally look at me in awe.

Trying to get their attention on something other than me, I turn to Ty, and ask, "What do we do? Go straight to Zack's house?"

"Charlie, Max, and Clay, you guys go check out Emma's house," Ty says, pointing to my old house. He then points to Zack's house and says, "The rest of us will go next door. Come over when you've cleared her house, but everyone turn your phones to Walkie-Talkie mode for easier communication."

"We don't have phones," Tally says.

"You'll be with us," Ty states.

Charlie, Clay, and Max start their way up towards my old house.

Ty leads the way towards Zack's house, or where I thought I saw Zack went yesterday. I'm behind Ty, Tally behind me, and Tate bringing up the rear.

"Can you tell if anyone is in there?" Ty asks, stopping at the front door.

I throw out my Senses, trying to find anyone in the house. I find only one presence.

"I can only Sense one," I say, panic thick in my tone.

"Let's go," Ty says. He tries to open the front door, but it's blocked by something.

"Back door?" Tate suggests.

"Yeah," Ty says. We follow him to the side of the house, to the gate in the fence. He opens it and we make our way to the back door but it's laying on it's hinges.

"Ty!?" I whisper shout.

"I know... come on, let's get in and see what we can find," he says, reaching behind himself and grabbing my hand. He squeezes to reassure me.

We walk into the kitchen and find, who I can only guess as Zack's parents, lying in a pool of blood. Their blank eyes a clear indication they're gone.

"Oh gods," I breath in slowly. "Where's Zack and Molly?"

"Are you sure you only Sensed one person?" Ty asks sadly.

"Yes," I say with a hitch, we're too late.

We clear the kitchen and make our way through the dining room. Once we get into the living room, we find the couch has been moved in front of the door, which is what had been keeping us from opening it.

"Emma's house is clear. We're on our way to you," Charlie's voice comes through mine and Ty's phones.

"We'll wait for them to get here, to help clear the house," Ty says as he walks slowly towards the stairs that lead up.

We don't have to wait long, the guys appear only a minute later.

"Emma, can you Sense where the person is in the house?" Ty asks.

I throw my Sense out and pinpoint the presence and find it upstairs.

"Upstairs," I whisper.

"And you're certain there is only one in the house, other than us?" Ty asks.

"Yes, just one other," I answer.

"Charlie, Max, Clay, finish clearing the downstairs and see if you can find anything about who broke in. Tate, Tally, Emma, follow me upstairs," Ty says as he takes the first step up.

"Wait," I say. And then I take the Invisibility off of us.

"Why did you do that?" Tate asks.

"Because if it's Zack or Molly hiding, do we want to explain why we're Invisible?" I counter ask.

"No, but what if it's a Rift?" he asks.

"I'll handle him," I say sternly. He looks at me with raised eyebrows and then at Ty, who shrugs and nods in agreement with me.

We make our way up the stairs and clear the first two rooms we come to. Both are bedrooms and both have been torn apart. The next room is a bathroom. The last room is a big bedroom, the master suite. We clear it and head back into the hall.

"What did we miss?" Tate asks, looking around.

"We've cleared everything up here," Tally states. She looks at me and asks, "Could you be wrong?"

"I could be, but I can Feel him, or her, now," I say. And it's true, I can Feel someone hiding and they're scared.

"What do you mean by that?" Tate asks, looking at me in astonishment.

"I can feel that they're scared," I answer.

I place my hand on the wall and start walking down the hall. When we get to the opposite of the bathroom, my hand warms and tingles.

"In here," I whispers.

"It's a wall," Tally whispers back.

Ty steps up next to me and runs his hands around the wall. It stops when it comes to what looks like a seam in the wallpaper. He pushes it and a small section of the wall pops out.

WHAM

The small section fly's open and slams into the solid portion of the wall. Luckily, our reflexes are on point, we all jump out of the way before it can hit us. Someone runs out holding a wooden stick and screams.

"BRING IT ON YOU BASTARDS!!"

I can see it's a boy but before I can say anything, Tate has swung out his leg and has knocked the kid back into the opened hidden space. Since he was up right, he slams his back and head into the solid part of the wall above the opening. Tate and Tally are on him, pinning him down.

"Wait, wait! STOP!" I shout. I throw out my hands and Freeze Tate before he can hit Zack again, now that I can see the kid, I see that it's him. "It's Zack."

Tally releases Zack's arms from behind his back and looks at Tate.

"Tate?" she asks uncertainly.

"I can't move, what the hell?" he says through clenched teeth.

"Oh, sorry," I say and unFreeze him. He looks at me with huge eyes.

I don't have time to explain to him the many

Talents I have, that'll have to wait until another time. I turn my attention to Zack.

"Are you okay?" I ask, kneeling next to him.

He rubs his head and rolls his shoulders, like he's trying to stretch them out. Tally must have really had a good lock on him. He stands with a little help from me.

"Yeah, I guess so," he says. Then a panic look comes across his face, he spins around in a circle, and yells, "My sister?! Where's Molly? She was with me. Where are my parents? Mom! Dad!"

He starts to turn towards the stairs, but Ty stops him. Ty looks at me with questioning eyes. Do we tell him or let him see for himself.

"Zack," I say in a low voice. I clear my throat and put my hand on his arm. He looks down at it and then back up at me. "Your parents... they're gone."

"What do you mean gone? Did those bastards take 'em? What about Molly? She was in there with me but I... we have to find her," he tries to push past Ty but he's no match for him. Zack turns and looks at me, I can see tears in his eyes.

"Zack, they didn't take your parents. They're... They're... I'm sorry but they're in the kitchen... they've been killed," I say with as much sympathy as I can, without starting to cry myself.

"No! NO!" Zack says, this time he pushes past Ty, only because he let him, and we follow him as he runs down the stairs, through the living room and dining room, and finally into the kitchen. He skids to a stop.

Thankfully, someone, has put a sheet over his parents. Zack walks over and kneels down at the head of them both. He flips the sheet off their face and he gasps.

"NOOO!" he screams.

I feel a tear run down my cheek. I wipe it away as quickly as I can.

"Zack?" I tentatively ask, walking over to him. I put my hand on his shoulder. He stiffens for a minute and then reaches up and puts his hand over mine. "I'm so sorry, but we need to ask some questions and we need to find your sister."

He jolts up and turns towards me, not letting go of my hand as he does it. I can feel Ty behind me, move closer. I squeeze Zack's hand in a gesture of support but then pull my hand out of his.

"You haven't found her?" Zack asks.

"She's not here," Tally says. Zack stares at her for a minute and then at Tate and then at Ty.

"But where is she? Did they take her?" he asks in frustration.

"We aren't sure," Clay says. "Tell us what happened."

"What do you mean you aren't sure? Where's my sister?" Zack snaps.

"Dude, we came to help you. We just got here.

Why don't you tell us what happened?" Charlie says, coming to stand next to Ty. The two of them could intimidate anyone.

I see Zack visibly gulp and takes a breath, trying to calm himself, I'm sure.

"Like I told Emma when I called her. I saw that the guys were back, only there were a couple more of them and this time a woman was with them, I didn't get a look at her face. I don't remember a lot about what they looked like, my head feels fuzzy. Anyways, when I saw that I had been caught looking, I ran. When I got to the kitchen, Molly was in there so I grabbed her and yelled for my parents to hide. I thought they were on the other side of the house, I didn't see them when I ran through the dining room and living room heading for the stairs. I knew the secret room was the only place we'd be safe. Once I got me and Molly in there, I heard bangs and screaming. My phone dropped and Molly started to cry. I tried to comfort her but then..."

"Then what?" Ty probes after a minute of waiting for Zack to continue on his own.

"I... I must have blacked out. I didn't come to until I heard the door opening, when you guys opened it," Zack answers sheepishly.

"Can you go get something of Molly's?" Ty asks.

"Why?" Zack asks snarkily. I look at him incredulously. If he didn't stop acting like this towards the guys that came to help him, they were going to knock him out again, and leave him here.

"I might be able to Track her," Ty says through tight lips. Yup, definitely on the verge of taking out some frustration on this kid.

"Do you have tracking dogs?" Zack asks.

"Something like that," Ty says with a smirk.

"She has a bunny she usually takes with her everywhere she goes," Zack says, stepping beside me.

"Clay, go with him," Ty says, nodding towards Zack as he walks back into the dining room.

"What's up?" Charlie asks, looking at Ty and then to where Clay and Zack have just disappeared.

"I don't trust him," Ty says.

"I don't either," Tally agrees. "I'm not getting a Reading that he's out right lying about something but there's something off about him."

"Maybe it's just from being traumatized? He just saw his dead parents and his little sister is missing, but given all of that, I too, am getting an off feeling about him," I admit reluctantly. I can't put my finger on what it is about him that's throwing me off but there's something. "I felt it when we first met."

"So, what do we do with him?" Charlie asks in a whisper.

I look at Ty and say quietly, "You aren't going to like this, but I think we need to take him back to the Estate with us until we figure this all out. If he is an innocent Inepti, we can't leave him here unprotected.

If he is something else, we can't just let him go."

Ty closes his eyes and shakes his head slowly. But then takes a deep breath, opens his eyes, and says, "Emma's right. We can't just leave him here. We'll take him back but one of us will be with him at all times."

"Maybe not you, man," Charlie laughs.

"What does that mean?" Ty asks, looking at him in shock.

"Dude, we can all tell you're about to take his head off with every look he gives Emma. The kid has a hard on for her," Charlie says laughing. And then looks at me and says, "Sorry, that was rude. I'm trying to be better."

"It's okay," I say, slightly embarrassed.

"He's not wrong," Max interjects. "I've been watching him and he can't take his eyes off of Emma. Even when someone else asks him a question, he answers but does it in a way that would suggest Emma asked the question, not a different person. I think Ty should always stay with Emma and we'll take on the task of taking turns being with Zack."

"Agreed," Tate and Tally say together.

"As long as he's at the Estate, he is to never be alone. And Emma, I know you don't like being told what to do, but I'd rather you not be alone with him. I know you can handle yourself and all that, but the guy has something about him that I don't like or trust, and not just that he can't keep his eyes off of you. So please, don't fight me on this and don't take it as a jealous boyfriend. I'm talking to you as the Commanding Officer at the moment," Ty says, tilting his head to the side, looking at me.

"I really don't think he'd hurt me but if that's the deal to allow him to come to the Estate, then I'll agree," I say. "And I don't think you're acting like a jealous boyfriend."

"Well, maybe a little jealous," Charlie says, laughing.

Ty glares at him but I say nothing. Ty has no reason to be jealous and I truly don't think he is being that way. Zack is just putting off weird vibes.

A second later, Zack enters the kitchen, looking worried, Clay coming in right behind him. Max motions Clay to go outside with him and they leave through the back door.

"Everything is gone," Zack says in a small voice.

"What do you mean?" Ty asks.

"All of Molly's stuff is gone. Her clothes. Her books. Her toys. All gone," he says, sitting down hard onto a barstool at the counter, putting his face in his hands.

Tally and Tate look at each other and then at Ty. Who then looks at me.

"What about her bedding? Anything she's touched multiple times, anything that'd have her essence on it?" I ask.

"Her essence?" Zack looks up from his hands, confusion in his eyes.

"It's hard to explain but is there nothing in her room that could help us Track her?" I ask again.

"No, nothing, it's all gone. Her bed was turned upside down. Her dresser knocked over. Hangers from the closet thrown around the room," he says sighing.

"They moved fast," Tally says in disbelief.

Tate is about to say something but Ty cuts him off.

"We'll talk more about this later," Ty says, cutting off whatever Tate was going to say. "We should go. We'll figure out a different way to find you sister."

Zack jumps up and grabs hold of my upper arms. Ty is instantly at my side, glaring daggers at Zack.

"You can't leave me! What if they come back? They'll kill me!" he screeches.

"Owe…" I say slowly as he's squeezing my arms really hard. I reach up and put my hands on his biceps. He's stronger than he looks. *Interesting.* "Zack, we aren't going to leave you. You're coming home with us."

Something flashes cross his eyes and had I not been staring into them, I wouldn't have seen it because as fast as it came, it was gone. He relaxes his hold on my arms but doesn't let me go. His touch becomes soft and a little too intimate for my liking.

Zack stares into my eyes and says, "I knew you'd

save me."

Tate steps up onto the other side of me and puts his hand on Zack's shoulder.

"Dude, you might let her go before her boyfriend rips your arms off your body," Tate says, nodding towards Ty. I look up at Ty and see he's not glaring at Zack anymore but he's not taking his eyes off of him either.

"Boyfriend?" Zack asks surprised but lets go of my arms reluctantly.

"Yes, boyfriend," Tally says, coming up and grabbing my hand before walking us away from the guys.

Tate takes my place and steps next to Ty, Charlie coming up behind them, and they cross their arms at the same time. I would have laughed if the tension in the room wasn't so thick.

"I say this as the Commanding Officer and not Emma's boyfriend," Ty says, stepping closer to Zack. "You. Will not. Touch. Her. Again. Understand?"

Zack scoffs and says, "Yeah right, not as her boyfriend? Dude, relax."

"I am not you're dude. If you agree to come with us, you will stay away from Emma and you will not touch her again," Ty says, more sternly and putting more authority in his voice.

"I'm not going to hurt her," Zack says. He then looks at me, "Honest, Emma. I won't hurt you. I didn't mean to hurt your arms just now. I'm just scared and worried about my sister. Seeing my parents.... I'm sorry, I really didn't mean to hurt you."

I say nothing and just nod. The sincerity I feel coming off of him can't be denied. However, I just can't put my finger on what it is about him that worries me.

"Zack," Ty says loudly, drawing Zack's attention back to him. "Whether you meant to or not, isn't in question. We know nothing about you, so from here on out, if you are to come home with us, you are to stay away from Emma and not touch her. Do you understand?"

Zack looks at me and then back at Ty, "Sure, man. Whatever."

I see Ty grit his teeth. It wasn't the verbal agreement he wanted but he wasn't going to push the issue. He'll give Zack a chance to step in line and if he doesn't, the poor guy won't know what hit him.

"Charlie, take Zack up to his room and help him pack a few things, we should get back," Ty says, glancing behind him to Charlie.

"Sure thing, Boss," Charlie says, stepping to the side and waving Zack to go back upstairs.

"Don't call me Boss," Ty says.

"But you are my boss," Charlie says, thumping Ty on the back. I can tell Charlie is trying to lighten the mood. One of the things I do like about him, he can't stand it when things get too serious.

Ty just shakes his head and steps to the side to let Zack by. Zack walks by, staring Ty in the eye as he does, even though he's a bit shorter, the gesture is taunting. I see Ty's hands ball into tight fists as he looks down at Zack.

"Ty?" I ask in a sweet and inviting way, trying to get his attention away from this stranger with a death wish. It works, Ty looks at me. "I need some fresh air, will you go outside with me?"

Ty looks back at Zack as he exits the kitchen with Charlie behind him. Charlie looks back at us and points to Zack and has a 'wow' look on his face.

"Yes," Ty says, letting out a deep breath. "Tate and Tally, wait for them to come back. Ask to borrow Charlie's phone and make an anonymous call to the authorities so they can come take care of his parents."

We walk outside. Clay and Max are on the far side of the yard, looking around.

"Hey," I say and pull Ty over to the other side of the house, where the side gate is, where we'll be leaving from. I put my hand on his chest when I have him leaning up against the house. "Breathe."

I feel his chest expand and relax as he takes a couple deep breaths in and out, while he stares into my eyes. I put other hand on his cheek and he leans into it, closing his eyes.

"Better?" I ask.

"Much better, thank you," he says, opening his

eyes. "I'm sorry."

"For what?" I ask.

"For letting that..." he takes a breath and relaxes again. "For letting Zack get under my skin. I don't know why but I just can't stand the way he looks and touches you."

"You know you have nothing to worry about, right?"

"I trust you with all that I am, I just don't trust him. I don't want you to ever be hurt, touched, or anything like what happened with Frank, ever again," Ty says, tensing up all over again.

I run my hand that's on his chest, up to the other side of his face so that I'm cupping it in my hands. I reach up on my tip toes and put my face close to his.

"You don't have to worry about that, I won't let anyone hurt me or touch me unless I want them to and you are the only one I want to touch me," I say, kissing him softly.

He wraps his hands around my back and pulls me closer to him.

"I know you can protect yourself but it's in my nature to want to protect you. I don't know if I'll ever be able to fully accept that you don't need my protection."

"I am naive in the ways of men. I need protection from my own self not really knowing or seeing the danger in the fakeness that comes with liars and cheaters, I trust too easily. I can see when someone is going to physically hurt me but the mind games, someone acting a certain way... lying... that's where I fall short. I'm learning how to use my Talents in that area but it's hard to shut down the part of my mind that instantly wants to trust someone. I'm trying to listen to the warning bells, even though the person isn't doing anything that really shows any danger. That's the protection I need."

"I can help you with that and I hope I never make you feel like I'm some overbearing, overprotective, buffoon of a boyfriend. But, I have a feeling there might be a few times when I come off that way because I will not allow anyone to hurt you in anyway, period."

"I understand that," I reach up and kiss him again. This kiss lasts a little longer. I pull away reluctantly. I smile up at him and ask, "Should I use a word to signal that you're inching towards the buffoon boyfriend, letting you know it's time to take a breath?"

"Just say my name the way you did in there, it snapped me out of my thoughts quickly," he kisses me again.

I giggle and pull away again, "Good to know."

"Emma, you truly don't understand the power you have over me."

"Power?"

"Not in the Talent sort of way but in the way

of a woman and a man. The way the sound of your voice makes my heartbeat speed up. The sight of you makes my heart stop and then pick up speed again. Everything about you... Just one word and you have my full attention," he turns us so I'm up against the house now. He bends down and kisses me passionately. I wrap my arms around his neck and pull him closer.

Cough-cough

We stop kissing and looking to the side. Everyone is standing there. They all have a look of surprise but happiness on their faces, except Zack. He looks pissed and he's glaring at Ty. When he sees me looking at him, his expression changes quickly and smiles sweetly at me.

I'm going to have to have a talk with him. Whatever feelings he might have had while I lived here, had better go away. The feelings aren't mutual and his jealousy will only get him hurt.

"We're ready Boss... Unless you and Emma would like a few minutes more alone," Charlie says, wiggling his eyebrows.

"Shut it," Ty says but he reluctantly steps away from me, reaching for one of my hands.

"To the park?" I ask.

"Yeah," Ty says. He gestures for everyone to start

walking. "Zack lead the way to the park."

"The park?" he asks, now staring at mine and Ty's interlocked fingers.

Ty looks at him and then me. Warning bells?

"I'm sure you know of the park down the street, you had to have taken your sister there to play?" I ask with concern.

"Oh, yeah... Sorry. I wasn't thinking," Zack says as he walks forward. In his snarky tone of voice, he looks at Ty and asks, "Am I allowed to talk to Emma with all of you around?"

"Go for it," Ty says. The more the guy talks, the more we'll learn from him.

"Wonderful," Zack says. When he turns to me, he's back to pleasant and the nice guy. *Does he have a multiple personality disorder?*

"What's up?" I ask.

"I've been wondering a few things," he starts to say. He gestures around at my friends, "Who are these guys? I've never seen them around your house before."

"Oh, ummm... New friends I've met since moving away," I say.

"And you're taking me to your new house?" he asks.

I look at Ty. What are we going to tell him about us? I see Ty shake his head quickly and shortly.

"Yeah, it's where we live," I say, gesturing to our group. We are getting close to the park. I speed up our pace a little.

"Is your car parked over here?" Zack asks, looking around.

"Ummm," I say. I look at Ty for help. How do we explain our traveling arrangement without telling him about us. Ty taps his forehead. It's a signal Libby told me to use and others, if they want me to speak to them Telepathically. I have to let my Shield down for it to work.

Ty, what do I tell him?

Don't worry. Tally will knock him out and then you'll grant him permission to the Estate. We'll just tell him he passed out from the shock of everything catching up to him. We'll keep him away from the classrooms and he'll only be allowed in certain areas of the Estate until we know more about him.

How is she going to knock him out?

A slight electrocution. A small smile crosses his face a little at that statement.

Electrocution? I let the panic soak into the word.

Don't worry, it won't hurt him. It'll be just enough to make him pass out.

"Emma?" Zack says, looking at me.

"Oh, what's that?" I ask him.

"I asked if your car was parked over here by the park?"

"Oh, well, we didn't drive?" I say it as a question. I've never been good at lying.

We walk through the park and into the tree grove. Zack looks at me skeptically.

"What are we…" he starts to ask but doesn't finish the question because Ty nods at Tally and she touches his arm and he lets out a little squeak before falling, Max catches him and puts him on the ground gently.

"That didn't really hurt him? Did it?" I ask Tally.

"No, I mean a little. It might have felt like how you get shocked by static electricity but maybe a little stronger. Not enough to hurt him severely but enough to make him pass out," she says, rubbing her hands together and I see blue flashes of electricity connecting her hands together.

"Interesting," I say. "You'll have to show me that when we get back to the Estate."

"You think you can handle it?" she asks, with a slightly wicked smile.

"Don't test her," Charlie says. He winks at me and says, "Our girl is all sorts of surprises and probably has that Talent, too."

"Really?" Tally asks.

I shrug and answer truthfully, "There isn't a Talent we've found I don't have."

"For real?" Tate asks, looking at Ty.

He just nods, smiling down at me.

"Doesn't mean I have them all," I say, hurriedly. I hate when they start making me feel like I'm weird for having all these Talents, even though I am, in fact, weird.

"We can talk later," Tally says, nudging me with her shoulder just like Libby does. The gesture makes me like her even more.

"Charlie, Jump Clay and Max back with you, and call a meeting for everyone to meet in the dining hall. We'll take Zack down to a Guardian room and lock him in there with Vinny or Ret, since they know of him. I'll explain to everyone what's going on," Ty instructs.

"You go it, Boss," Charlie says. Clay and Max grab hold of his shoulders and he's gone before Ty can reply.

"I wish he'd stop calling me that," Ty says, slightly embarrassed.

"But you are the Commanding Officer while Bill is missing," Tate says, grinning at him.

"Exactly, Bill is missing. I'm just acting Commander. I don't want Charlie to get in the habit of calling me Boss because when Bill is back, I don't want that title anymore," he says, reaching out for my hand. A signal to everyone, we are done talking about this subject.

Tate bends down, laughing a little, probably at Ty's discomfort, and starts to pick Zack up. Ty let's go of my hand to help him. They each throw one of Zack's arms around their shoulders. Tally takes my left hand and grabs her brother's free hand

Before Ty can grab my right hand, I reach up and

touch Zack's limp hand hanging over Ty's shoulder, and say, "I, Emma Hart, give Zack Wilder permission to enter the Estate.

I then grab Ty's hand, squeezing it gently, and Jump us back home.

CHAPTER 9 -
GUARDIAN LEVEL

W e're back at the Estate in an instant.

"That's truly amazing, Emma," Tally says, smiling down at me.

Sitting on the front steps, are Libby and Shae, waiting for us.

"Charlie filled us in quickly, he's got everyone waiting in the dining hall," Libby says as she stands up.

"Tate, will you help me take him down to the Guardian level?" Ty asks but before Tate can answer, Vinny and Ret are coming out of the front doors.

"We'll take him down. We've got a cot set up for him for now in Con-Room 4, until you decide what to do with him. We'll keep an eye on him," Vinny says. He winks at me and says, "Hello, Miss Emma."

"Hi, Vinny," I say smiling at him. "Please don't scare him too much if he wakes up before we get back down there. If he does wakeup, just tell him he blacked out again."

"Again?" Ret asked.

"Long story," Ty says. "We'll be down shortly."

"Rodger," Ret says as he and Vinny bend down and haul Zack up by the arms, in the same way Tate and Ty had been holding him. They hustle up the stairs like Zack weighs nothing.

"That guy, too?" Tate asks.

"What guy?" Libby asks first, echoing my thoughts.

"Vinny," Tate states.

"What about him?" Ty asks.

Tate looks at me and then at the now empty door way and back at me.

"Vinny has eyes for Emma too," he says matter-of-factly.

"Oh whatever, if anything, it's a brotherly thing," I say.

"If you say so," he says, shaking his head. "You've got some competition, Cuz."

Before Ty can respond, I say, "No, he doesn't."

I squeeze Ty's arm as I walk by and smile up at him.

"Like the girl said, no I don't," Ty says and I hear a thump. I glance back and see Tate rubbing his shoulder. Ty must have slugged him in the arm. I laugh silently to myself.

We walk into the dining hall and find it crammed packed with everyone. We walk to the stairs where Ty goes up a few steps so that he's above everyone, so he can see them all.

He clears his throat and speaks in a loud, commanding voice, "We've brought back a visitor. We are unsure of who he is, but we decided leaving him was not an option. As far as we know, he knows nothing of our World, our Talents. For the time being, he will not be allowed to wander around freely. He will be allowed in the dining hall, out on the grounds, and down in the Guardian level, but with an escort, always with an escort. Please keep all Talent practice confined in all designated areas. I know we practice outside but for the time being, until I say otherwise, no Talent practice out on the grounds. He is not a prisoner, but he isn't fully trusted, as we know nothing about him. Even with Emma's Protection on the Estate, we can't trust that what he sees might get into Vanessa or the Rift's hands. So, if you see him wandering alone, without a member of the Guard or one of my close people with him, assume he's ditched his escort. Please attach yourself to him until someone catches up to you. Alert me as soon as possible that he was wandering."

From somewhere in the middle of the sea of people, someone hollers, "How do we know who he is? There are a couple of new people here."

Ty looks down at me and touches his forehead.

What's up? I ask.

Can you send an image to all of them, of what Zack

looks like?

I can try.

I close my eyes and think of what Zack looks like, kind of like a picture. I open my mind up and send it out into all the minds in the Estate. I also send out, *Not to be wandering around alone.*

"Cool!" someone else in the crowd shouts.

"That's a helpful Talent," a girl near me says, smiling over at me. I smile back.

"Okay, that's all. Thank you for your help and cooperation. Back to your lessons or whatever it was you were doing before this meeting was called," Ty says.

He starts to step down but someone hollers out, "What about Meredith? Doc? Bill? Do we know what's happened to them?"

The room goes quiet. Ty takes a step back up and clears his throat again. Being in charge is hard for him but he handles it well.

"We haven't found anything about their disappearances, but we are working hard to find them. When we find out what's happened, we'll have another meeting. Until then, work hard. Do what they'd want you to do. Practice and build your Talents up. Dismissed," he says with finality.

Ty steps down and pulls me off to the side, waiting for everyone, except for our friends, to disperse. Charlie, Shae, Alysa, Malory, Libby, Max, Clay,

Tate, and Tally circle around us.

"Before we go down and talk to Zack, I need to warn you, Emma," Ty says, taking my hand. Libby puts her hand on my shoulder, a gesture of support.

"What's up?" I ask nervously.

"We're going down to the Guardian level. Not only is it where we have the Guardian Room set up to monitor the Estate but we also have the cells down there," Ty says.

"Okay," I say.

"We had to bring Frank here with us, he was on one of the jets you granted permission to come to the Estate," Libby says cautiously.

"Okay," I say again. I don't know why they're making a big deal about it. I figured they brought him. They wouldn't have just left him there.

"So, he's down in one of the cells," Charlie says in a way like he's talking to a slow child.

"I get that and I understand," I say. "Why are you guys acting like this?"

Ty straightens up and looks at Libby with raised eyebrows.

"Are you not afraid of him?" Libby asks.

"I mean, I don't want to sit down and have lunch with the guy but I'm not afraid of him," I answer honestly.

"After what he did to you and tried to do?" Shae asks, looking surprised.

"Yes, he hurt me, but he didn't win, because Ty showed up just in time. If I let myself be afraid of him, he will win. If I'm afraid of him, I'm giving him power over me, and I will not do that. He's a weak, nasty, coward, and if he does try something again, he'll realize the mistake he made coming after me," I, again, say honestly, no hate or anything in my tone, just matter-of-factly.

They're all staring at me in disbelief.

"What?" I ask, starting to feel embarrassed.

"It's just..." Libby starts to say.

"You are too good of a person," Shae says, shaking her head.

"It's not for Frank, that I feel this way, it's for my own peace of mind. I refuse to live my life scared. If I let myself, I wouldn't leave my room. Think of everything I've been through and everyone that's hurt me, I have plenty to be afraid of but I will not live that way."

More stares.

"Would you guys rather I hide in my room and never come out?" I ask, now getting a little irritated with them.

"We know what you've been through. We just have never heard you talk about how you feel about it," Libby says. "It takes a strong person to survive all that but it takes an incredible person to overcome it. I can't speak for everyone but I am in awe of you."

Everyone agrees with her.

"Again, there's two choices I have to choose from. I'm taking the choice that brings me the most peace. The one that gives me a better, happier, life," I say.

"Wow," Tate says, looking at me in a weird way.

"Okay, you all need to stop looking at me like that. Let's just go down and talk to Zack. If I happen to see Frank, I'll be fine. He's in a cell, right?" I ask.

Silence. I look around and finally stop on Ty and look at him expectantly.

"Uhh, yeah..." he sounds a little choked up but clears his throat. He continues with his normal voice. "Yeah, he's in a cell."

"Good, let's go," I start to walk out of the dining hall but realize I haven't been to the Guardian level yet. I turn and Ty almost runs into me, he jolts to a stop. I ask, "Which way?"

"There are a couple of ways to get there, the closest would be through the Hospital Wing," Ty says, pointing behind us.

"Lead the way," I say, waving them all on.

Libby, getting that I'm embarrassed by the way they were acting, grabs Max's hand and leads him to the front. She smiles at me apologetically. I smile back. I know they aren't meaning to embarrass me. I know that they truly don't understand where I'm coming from, but I don't like how they make me feel like I should be terrified of Frank.

They've all grown up being tall, beautiful people. Knowing who they are from birth. Knowing they'd have Talents and being trained to wield them. For the most part, or so far that I've heard, they've had two loving parents to help them grow. Being part of a community, no matter how secretive they had to be, bonded them together even closer. They can't understand where I'm coming from.

I grew up being picked on from the moment everyone became taller than me and realized I wasn't growing anymore. Not knowing that the 'loving mother' I thought I had, that I thought was only strict to keep me safe from the bullies at school, was actually the biggest bully of my life.

At a young age, I chose to look for the positive in my life. I couldn't go to friends' houses and they couldn't come over. Hell, I wasn't even allowed to have friends, so I found things that brought me joy.

Reading, drawing, and painting filled up my time so I didn't feel like I was missing out on anything. All the things I enjoyed, that helped fill the loneliness – the amount of loneliness that I am just now realizing I had– were choices I made to have a positive outlook. To bring me happiness. I could have moped around in my room or around the house, but looking back, that would have pissed Vanessa off. By choosing to find things that made me happy, probably kept her anger at bay. She treated me badly, more indifferently I guess than badly, but had I been a whiney child or a bitchy teenager, I can't imagine how Vanessa would have dealt with me. So, not only was choosing to not allow things to have the power to make me afraid or sad, I was actually saving my own life. Thinking of it that way, makes me not so embarrassed anymore, it makes me feel stronger.

As we walk, through the kitchen I feel my back straightening up a little more. It's time to feel proud of the way I am, for what I've made of myself from all the horrible situations I've been through, so far, in my life. As we get into the Hospital Wing, empty at the moment, I feel a tingle in my hands and look down and see them glowing a sunny, golden, yellow.

"Umm, what's happening?" I ask, holding my hands up, I stop walking.

"Uh oh," Libby and Ty say together.

"What?" I ask, marveling at my hands. It doesn't hurt, it's just warm.

"This is what you did when you Changed and then after you saved Shae," Libby states. "But it was you're entire body."

I ball my hands into fists and close my eyes. I pull my hands into my chest and take a deep breath. Opening my hands and placing them palm to palm, I interlock my fingers, making it look like I'm praying. Breathing slowly and evenly, I imagine I'm pulling the light from my hands, into my center, my heart, my soul. Now my whole body feel like the warmth I had in my hands.

I hear gasps from around me and hear a couple people stepping away from me. Ty has stayed close by. After the strange warmth has gone from my body, I slowly open my eyes.

I look down at my hands and see that the glowing light is gone. I look around and see everyone staring at me in awe. Tate and Tally looking on in disbelief.

"Are you okay?" Tally asks.

"Yup, I'm fine," I answer, unlocking my fingers and turning around. Everyone gasps, even Ty. All their mouths drop open. "What?"

"Look in the mirror," Shae says. Pointing at the mirror above one of the sinks.

I walk over and see that my eyes are glowing. The yellow, sun gold is shining through my eyes, making my blue eyes look as if the sun is behind them. It's a strange beauty. I close my eyes and feel that they are warm. I envision the light soaking into my brain and spreading out inside my body. When I open them again, they are my normal blue eyes.

"That was weird," I say.

"You controlled it," Libby says in astonishment, coming to stand in front of me, looking into my eyes.

"But what was it?" Tally says, walking up next to her.

"Her Power," Ty says with so much love, I look

over at him. "Isn't she the most beautiful creature you've ever seen?"

Shaking my head at him but winking to let him know I appreciate his statement, I ask, "Don't you mean Talent?"

"No, I mean Power. You've surpassed using the word Talent. That applies to a couple gifts one has been given. What you have, that's Power, from the looks of it, Power of the Sun," Ty says with unbiased admiration.

"She truly is The One, isn't she?" Tate asks.

"You had a doubt?" Shae asks.

"Yes and no. At first when your parents told us about her, I had doubts. But now, seeing with my own eyes, all that she-" Tate turns to me "-seeing all that you can do, I have no doubt anymore."

He bows his head and places his fist over his heart. Tally does the same.

"Oh stop, I'm still me, don't start with 'The One' crap again," I say. Waving them off. Yes, after having my conversation with The Big Three, I know now that I am The One, but I don't like when people treat me differently. And not everyone knows about the 'the conversation' and I'm keeping it that way. I still don't want people acting differently around me.

Tate glances at Ty, who is smiling his heart stopping smile at me and then looks at Tate and says, "You'll get used to her selflessness... Well, maybe, I'm still not one-hundred percent used to it."

"None of us are," Shae says, coming up and hugging me.

"You guys stop, we were on our way to go talk to Zack," and just as I finish saying his name, Vinny comes walking through a side door that I thought was a closet.

"He's awake and demanding to see Emma. I quote 'I don't give a damn what her macho boyfriend says, I want to see Emma, right now. Where the hell am I?' He settled back down when Ret got in his face. I assumed by boyfriend, he meant Ty," Vinny says, looking from me to Ty, with a slight sadness to his face.

"You're correct, Ty and Emma are official," Charlie says. He seems to have taken it upon himself to confirm any suggestions about Ty and I being together.

"Congrats," Vinny says, looking sheepishly at Ty.

"What did Ret do?" I ask, walking towards him, trying to get this conversation off my personal business.

"He just told the kid he better show respect to Ty. That the only reason he wasn't in a cell until we figured out who he is and what his deal is, was because Ty was allowing him to be out. He didn't like the mention of a cell," Vinny has a mischievous grin.

"This is the way to the Guardian Level, then?" I ask.

"Yeah, there's an elevator," he answers.

"An elevator?" I ask in surprise.

"Yeah, in case there's an emergency and we need to get multiple Guardians to the hospital room quickly. The garage is connected to the Guardian level and the elevator comes right down into the garage. So, if we come in from a battle, via air travel and then vehicle, we can get to Doc... err the Hospital Wing right away," Vinny says. Now he does look upset.

"How is Sara handling all this?" I ask as we load into the elevator, which is huge compared to the ones I've been in. It's at least four times the size as a normal hotel elevator.

"She's okay. We all understand that this is a way of life for us, that at any moment, a family member could go missing, be taken, or killed," Shae says.

"Understanding it and living it are two different things," I say.

"You're not wrong," Libby agrees. "But she really is okay. I think she's pouring herself into studying and working on her Healing Talent. She might have been second to Doc but she's just as good. She has said she wants to be ready for anything that comes to her."

When the elevator stops, I can feel the difference in temperature. We are definitely underground.

"Does the elevator just go between here and the Hospital Wing?" I ask.

"Yeah, it's the only real need for it," Vinny says as

he steps out.

"Whoever had the foresight that we'd need this place, did an amazing job," Clay says as he walks by, patting my shoulder.

I step out of the elevator and turn to my right and stop dead in my tracks. The garage is huge and it's modern. No dirt walls, they're all concrete, and hundreds of lights on the cement ceiling. I notice the ceiling is higher than the upper floors. There are at least twelve large SUV's parked in here, with room for more and larger vehicles if need be. There are bathrooms by the elevator.

"How big is the Guardian Level?" I ask.

"The same size as the first two floors," Ty says, grinning. "It's four times the size of what we had back at The Pit. Plus the garage part."

"That's amazing!" I exclaim. "It's bigger than the first floor?"

"Yeah, we'll show you," Ty says, taking my hand.

We are about to walk by a couple Guardian's that are servicing a couple rigs; changing the oil and checking the tires. They stand instantly when Ty gets closer and salute him the way we do, right hand fisted over their heart, and a bowed head. He salutes back. When they see me, they do the salute to me as well. I return the gesture.

"Why did they salute me?" I ask, not sure why they're saluting me, I'm not a Commanding Officer.

"They know who you are," Ty says, squeezing my hand.

"I'm not a Commanding Officer," I echo my thoughts out loud.

"You are higher up than a Commanding Officer," Libby says, coming to stand next to me.

"Yeah, you're up there with The Elder's, if not above them," Charlie says from behind us.

"No… No way I am," I say.

"Technically, you should be running the Guardian's while Bill's away," Ty says, looking down at me with a smile.

"To heck with that!" I screech, anxiety starting to course through my veins. "I'm just learning how to handle my Talents and how everything in this World works. There's no way I'd be able run the Guardian's or this place."

They all laugh.

"Which is why I never brought it up, although it was rude of me not to at least talk to you about it. I apologize," Ty says earnestly.

"No apology necessary. The Guardians are all yours and running this place for that matter," I say, my anxiety starting to subside.

I can tell Ty wants to say something more but we've gotten to two big sliding doors. They remind me of barn doors. Two Guardians standing by, pull them apart, wide enough for us to go through, four at a time. We walk into what looks like a staging area. Again, very modern, the concrete walls extend into here as well. Very nice lighting too but the ceilings aren't as tall as the garage. There are benches lining the walls and some folding chairs spread out through the room. The room is in a weird, sort of fat 'L' shape. To our right, is a door.

Ty pulls me to the left of the room and I see where there's a guard station.

"Hey Phil," Ty says as he walks up to the Guardian, Phil, behind the counter.

Phil jumps to attention and salutes Ty. After Ty has saluted back, Phil's about to lower his hand until he sees me. His eyes go wide and he salutes me. I salute back and he finally lowers his hand.

"What can I do for you, Sir?" Phil asks.

"Just showing Emma and a few of our new people around. Emma hasn't been down to check out the Guardian Level yet. Since we have a... visitor hanging out in Con-Room 4, I thought it would be a good chance for her to check it out," Ty says.

Phil nods and then sits down in his chair. Ty points to a door to the right of the counter and he leads us to it. Tate and Tally are the only ones that follow us. The others have either already been down here or aren't interested in what it all looks like. Behind the counter is a huge desk lined with monitors. I notice empty cells, all but one.

"That must be Frank?" I ask.

"Yeah, these monitor all the cells. Another thing whoever renovated this place, made sure we had state of the art surveillance for the grounds and for in here," Ty says. There are three other Guardian's sitting with Phil. As soon as they notice us, they jump to attention, and salute, first Ty, and then me. *I'm going to have to tell Ty to tell them all to stop saluting me, they really don't have to do that for me.*

We walk back behind them and I see another door. Ty walks to it and opens it, letting me, Tally, and Tate go through first. We walk in to what looks like storage and bathrooms immediately to our left. There are shelves with clean linens, pillows, and what looks like gray jumpsuits stacked up.

"This is just the storage closet for the cells. There are a couple first aid kits for minor issues, extra bedding, and stuff like that," Ty says.

We walk back out to the guard station and into the staging area where the rest of our group are waiting. To our left is a steel door with a little window at Ty's eye level.

"The cells are through there?" I ask.

"Yeah, and two interrogation rooms," Ty says. He knocks on the door twice and then a man's face appears behind the window.

"Who..." he starts to say but as soon as he sees Ty, he stops and opens the door. He salutes Ty and says,

"Hello, Sir."

Ty salutes back and moves to let me walk through the door first.

"Oh! Miss Emma!" the Guardian says in surprise and then salutes me hurriedly.

I salute back and say as we walk down the long, tight, hallway, "I really wish they'd stop saluting me."

"It's a sign of respect," Clay says. I look behind me and see that our entire group are back with us. "I don't think they'd stop even if asked to, well, unless they were ordered to do so."

Shaking my head, I turn and start walking again. It looks as if concrete was used to make all of the Guardian Level walls. The lighting isn't so bright in here but enough to see.

"How many cells are there?" I ask.

"40," Ty answers. I notice that the cells are numbered. Ty pulls out his key and unlocks number 11, on our left. We step inside and he explains, "We identify them as C-whatever number. So, this one is C-11. C-1 was the first cell on our right as we came in. Then C-2. Across the hall was C-3 and then C-4. Back across the hall for C-5 and C-6. It continues all the way down. Each one has a cot and toilet. If something crazy happens and all the cells are occupied, and we need more, three people can fit, with a little room, into one. They'd be cramped but then again, they're in trouble so it's not supposed to be comfortable."

"Which one is Frank in?" I ask as we step backout into the hall.

Ty looks down the hall and back at me.

"He's in C-28," he answers.

"He's pretty far from the guard station," I state.

"Benefits of being the only one here," Charlie snorts out. "He gets quiet seclusion to think about his actions. Lucky for me when I was in my timeout, thinking about my own actions, I wasn't near him. I was in C-9."

"Oh yeah, I forgot you were down here," I say, not in the least bit sympathetic.

"Me too," I hear Alysa say from behind us a little. "And I will do everything I can to not return."

"Which one were you in again?" Charlie asks.

"C-16," she answers gloomily.

Ty stops at C-23 and speaks in a lower voice, "We don't have to continue down. The interrogation rooms look like your typical room. Frank might try to cause a scene."

"I'd like to see all of the rooms, please. I like having visuals for everything. If Frank says anything, I can handle it. If not, I have all of you," I laugh out, waving at everyone in the small hall. I'm starting to wonder if this is why they all came down here for this part of the tour. Tally and Tate are the only ones that I'm sure haven't been down here. Libby said she'd come down with Shae to visit Charlie and Alysa when they were in their cells. And I know Ty's crew have all been down here as part of the Guard.

"Alright," Ty says with a sigh.

We continue walking and as we pass the small side walkway where Frank's cell is, it's quiet, no sound of any kind. It takes just another minute before we get to the end of the hall and there are two rooms on either side. Written in paint on the door on the left says, **INTERROGATION RM2**. The door on the right says, **INTERROGATION RM1**.

Ty pulls his key out again and unlocks **INTERROGATION RM1** and steps aside for me to enter. Sure enough, it's a run of the mill interrogation room. Table and two chairs. But unlike ones I've seen on TV, there is no mirror, but there are cameras on every corner of the ceiling. I look at the floor and see a drain.

"A drain?" I ask questioningly.

The guys all look at each other and grimace.

"Sometimes, there needs to be alternatives to just asking questions," Ty says, looking down at the drain.

"Oooh, you mean torture?" I ask in surprise.

"Sometimes, it gets these guys to talk when just talking doesn't work," Clay says.

"And sometimes, there's nothing that can be said that can be enough to stop the torture," I say as I start to walk back out of the room, having a flashback of my own torture interrogation for answers.

Ty gently grabs my elbow and pulls me back around.

"Emma, I truly am deeply sorry for what the Rifts did to you. They went straight to torture. We spend days... weeks... trying to 'talk out' the information we need. Hurting someone is always last resort and only if it's an emergency, do we ever go to torturing someone for answers. Please believe me when I say that we don't do it if we have any other options because nine times out of ten, we can get the person to talk using our Talents. The drains were here when we got here and we haven't used them once."

"No, I understand. I know that in this war, we have to use everything we can to get the answers we need but having been on the other side of the 'questioning' and not having the right answers, it just makes me cringe thinking about it," I say. And I truly do understand that sometimes they'll have to hurt someone to get what they need and I trust them to use that as the last resort. I turn and walk out of the room, our group parting to let me pass by them.

I get out into the hall and start walking back down, not thinking about waiting for Ty or anyone else to catch up. I can hear them murmuring in the interrogation room.

"Come for a conjugal visit?" a raspy voice says from my right. I stop dead in my tracks. The voice sends a shiver down my spine and not the good kind.

Taking a deep calming breath, I turn and look towards C-28 and see grimy hands holding onto the bars of the door.

"No, just checking out your home for the foreseeable future. It's... cozy," I say with a small laugh.

"Keep talking, you don't know what your voice does to me. Can you give me a whimper or maybe a scream like you used to? Just one?" Frank sneers.

I turn and walk down to stand in front of him and cross my arms in front of me.

I whisper out, "Do you really enjoy this?"

"Louder, I can't hear you," Frank begs.

"Tell me where Vanessa's hiding," I whisper again. I can hear the door of the interrogation room closing and the footsteps of my group making their way back down the hall.

"LOUDER! SCREAM!" Frank yells. He reaches through the bars, grabbing air, not coming anywhere close to me. His face is pressed as hard against the bars as he can get.

"EMMA!?" I hear Ty holler. A second later and he's standing next to me. "What are you doing?"

"Having a conversation with an old friend," I say, looking up at him. I look at Frank and smile sweetly.

"GAAHHH! I WILL HAVE YOU!" Frank screams again and starts throwing himself against the bars. "I WILL TELL YOU EVERYTHING YOU WANT TO KNOW!

JUST LET ME TOUCH YOU... LET ME HAVE YOU! YOU! ARE! MINE!"

Ty pushes me behind him, but I pat his arm, letting him know that I'm okay. He looks down at me, and I smile at him in reassurance. He gets a look of confusion on his face but moves aside. I see Charlie and Tate trying to get closer, but the little hall isn't that big and if any more people get in here, I'll be in reach of this lunatic. I wave them off. They stop and step back into the bigger sized hall. I see Shae and Libby poking their head around them.

"Frank, you will never touch me again. I doubt you'll see anything other than this cell and these Guardians, ever again," I whisper, not wanting to give him the satisfaction of hearing my voice any louder than that. He's a sick man. I turn to walk away, Ty puts his hand on my lower back and rubs his hand in gentle circles.

"SHE'S MINE! DON'T YOU DARE TOUCH HER!" Frank screams out at Ty. Ty stops and looks at Frank.

"She was never yours. Keep screaming Frank and we'll Muzzle you, permanently," Ty says through clinched teeth. I can feel his anger rising.

"Ty," I say in the way he told me to use when I can tell he's about to lose it. He looks down at me, his features softening. I reach up on my tiptoes and give him a small kiss on the lips, while cupping his face in my hands. "It's okay. I'm okay."

"NOOOO! THOSE ARE MY LIPS! YOU BITCH! I! WILL! HAVE! YOU!" Frank screams again. He throws himself at the bars again and then falls to the floor. "MINE! MINE! MINE!"

I grab Ty's hand and say, "Let's go."

We walk back out, everyone staring down at C-28 in shock, or horror, and then down at me. No one says anything until we're back out in the staging area. Ty walks over to talk to Phil. Phil and two other Guardians stand and leave the guard station and head down towards Frank's cell.

Ty is holding the door for them. He turns to me and says, "I'll be right back."

He walks through the door and heads back down the hall as well.

CHAPTER 10 -
A DIFFERENT FORM
OF TORTURE

"**I** guess there are other ways to torture someone, rather than with physical pain," Clay says, rubbing his neck with his hand, and looking sheepishly at me.

"I can guarantee he's in physical pain, just not in the way we're used to applying for torture interrogations," Tate says, laughing.

I turn bright red.

"I wasn't trying to torture him. I just wanted him to see he has no effect on me, that I'm not afraid of him," I say, embarrassed.

"He might not have an effect on you, but you sure have one on him," Shae says.

"That wasn't a normal reaction," Libby says, looking concerned. "I think his mind has been altered to feel like he needs you or something. Like he truly believes you are his and he needs you to live."

"Do you think Vanessa did something to him?" I

ask.

"Her or someone else she instructed to do it," Libby says, biting her lip.

"But why? Why Frank? How could she? Is there a Talent for that?" I ask.

"I think his lust for you was there and she saw it when he was so eager to torture you and how he reacted during and after. She probably took advantage of that feeling he had and amplified it. Silver Tongue's can get people to do anything if their target's mind is weak enough and the Silver Tongue has a good enough hold," Libby says, sitting down in a chair.

"Not to mention some Mentalists can alter memories and thoughts as well," Shae says, sitting down beside Libby.

"That's true too. And if she had both of those things done to Frank, that could explain his behavior. Just wanting you is one thing but being a raging, crazy person, that's a whole other thing," Libby says, looking up at me.

"So, what Frank has done to me, none of it could be his fault? Is there a way to make sure and cure him of whatever has happened to his mind?" I ask.

"Like I said, I think the feeling of being aroused while he tortured you was there before it was altered so severely. You said that he was stopped before he could assault you while you were being held by Vanessa. At that point, she might have seen what he was capable of and when you were saved, that's when she altered him. Sent him out as a double agent, if you want to call him that, to get info for her, to see if you had been rescued by Frank's own people. She used his want for you as a way for him to find you no matter what. I don't think Vanessa realized, or even knows, that to use a Silver Tongue and Mentalist on the same mind, can cause severe alterations. And who knows, maybe she does know and was hoping Frank would be killed in the process of whatever she had planned for him. Lucky for him, we don't usually kill first and ask question later," Libby says with a small smile.

"Is there a way to check if he's been altered? And then fix him, at least to his original mind and then maybe somehow be cured of those feelings so he doesn't hurt anyone else?" I ask again.

"Oh, we can definitely find out if his mind has been altered. Just like when Alysa tried to get Ty to be hers by force and we fixed him," Libby says. "But I don't know how deep the alteration goes. If it's too deep, it could kill Frank if we try to get it out. It all depends on how strong of a Silver Tongue and Mentalist were used. It would be helpful if Doc and Meredith were here for it all, so we'll have to wait for them to get home before we try."

We're all quiet, left thinking about Doc and Meredith, and Bill, coming home. They've been gone for too long without a word. If they were okay, they would have gotten word to us somehow.

Ty walks through the door a minute later and comes up to me. He looks pissed.

"What happened?" I ask.

"Frank kept running his mouth. He might not affect you the way he talks to you or about you but..." Ty takes a deep breath. "I can't stand it."

I ask again, "What happened?"

"We had to sedate him. He was slamming his body to the floor in a... disgusting show of... suggestion," Ty says, utterly disgusted. "Steve, one of the other Guardian's, Muzzled him. Meaning, Frank can't talk until Steve or someone else takes the Muzzle off."

"How do you Muzzle someone?" I ask. It's one I haven't heard of before now. I still have so much to learn.

"Kind of like how you Froze Tate, you took his ability to move away. So, with Muzzling, you just take their ability to talk away," he says, reaching for my hand.

"You should talk to your sister later, she has a theory about Frank and his behavior and I think she might be on to something," I say.

"Later," Ty says.

"Are we getting closer to where Zack is waiting for us?" I ask, changing the subject because I can tell Ty wants to stop talking and thinking about Frank and his grotesque obsession with me.

"One Emma stalker to the next," Charlie chuckles out.

"Takes one to know one," Clay says as he playfully punches his brother in the arm.

"I never stalked her. And we've been over this, can we drop it now?" Charlie asks, looking embarrassed.

"Never," Clay says simply. "You acted like a fool, I'll never let you hear the end of it."

"Clay..." Charlie warns.

"I'm just messing with you," Clay says, laughing. Malory playfully slaps his arm and pulls him away.

"Dick," Charlie says under his breath but not quiet enough.

"We all know how you feel and why you did what you did, he's just being a brother," Max says, leaning over and pushing Charlie in the shoulder.

"Emma, do you really believe me when I say I'm sorry?" Charlie asks, looking at me mournfully.

"I–" I'm getting ready to say I do but Libby interrupts me.

"Charlie," she starts to say and walks over to the guard station, asks for a piece of paper, and walks back over to Charlie. "Take this and crumple it up into a ball. Alysa, you should pay attention as well."

Charlie looks at her hesitantly but finally takes it and balls it up. He looks at it and then back at Libby.

"Now try to flatten it out and make it as smooth as

before but while you're doing it, say you're sorry to it," Libby instructs. Charlie looks at me, I think realization hits him but he does as she asks. He puts it on one of the benches and tries as hard as he can to smooth it out but it still has wrinkles. Alysa is looking between me and Charlie as well. She looks at Shae and I see tears well up in her eyes.

"I'm sorry... I'm so sorry...," he takes a breath and stands. He's holding the paper. "That's as good as it's going to get."

"Is it back to how it was before you crumpled it up?" Libby asks a little sternly.

"No," he says quietly.

"Did saying you were sorry, fix it?" Libby asks, sounding even more stern.

"No," Charlie says, looking at me with sad eyes.

"Doing damage and then thinking that just saying sorry will fix it, actually doesn't fix anything. Are you listening, Alysa?" Libby says, shooting a glance over to Alysa, who nods and wipes a tear away at the same time. "If you truly are sorry, which we all know you guys are, but if you are, action... not words... is the only way to show you are truly sorry for how you acted. I'm not saying you have to prove to Shae or Emma for the rest of your life how sorry you are for the way you both have behaved but stop apologizing and start showing it. And I know you are both trying, we've seen improvement. Don't fall back into old habits, work at being a better person."

I'm stunned. I look at Shae, she looks just as stunned.

"I will," Charlie says, looking at me and Shae. "I will be a better person."

Alysa walks over to Shae and sits beside her, "I'll be a better sister." She looks at me, "And a better friend."

There's silence for a good minute or two where we all look around at one another.

"Okay, so shall we continue on or do we have some more fun learning exercises to do down here?" Tally asks, trying to break the awkward silence. It works, we all start to laugh.

"No, let's go," I say.

Ty leads us through the door on the other side of the room. We walk into a breakroom, bathrooms to the left. All the Guardians in here stand at attention and salute us as we walk by. We walk into a huge hallway, it's at least three times the size as the one over by the cells.

Ty walks straight and there are two double doors on the right, and above them, it says, **ARMORY/ SUPPLIES**. At the end of the hall are more bathrooms. He unlocks the doors with his handy magic key. *I'm going to have to find out how I get one of those.* We walk in and there is floor to ceiling shelves everywhere, row upon row. Top to bottom, they are full of all sorts of weapons, Magikida's are the vast majority. On the right side, from the front of the room and for as far as I can see, are shelves of nothing but battle gear.

Ty leads us back out into the large hallway and turns the corner, and there is a long hallway stretched out in front of us. I can see maybe five or six doors along the hall.

The first door on the right is completely black. It doesn't have a sign or anything to indicate what's inside. Ty knocks once and then uses his key once again and opens the door. The room is nothing but monitors, whiteboards, and maps. There's a large round table in the middle of the room, it looks like the one from back in The Pit.

"This is the Surveillance room," Ty says. "We have eyes on every corner of the island. Not that we need it with your protection but we can never be too careful when it comes to Vanessa and the Rifts. And we have to stay on top of our Guardian abilities, we can't get lazy. We still run shifts and watch duties throughout the island. Always training and thinking of the best defensive moves if we were to be attacked here on the island. Again, just in case."

"It's good that you guys are staying on top of your game, better safe than sorry," I say.

Ty turns us and leads us back out the door, we continue to the right. Almost directly across from the Surveillance room, is a normal wooden door that has

CON-ROOM 1 painted on the door.

"This is conference room 1 or Con-Room 1, as the sign says. We have five conference rooms. Con-Room 1 is the largest and will be used for most meetings with all the Leaders, whenever that time will come," Ty opens the door and we step in. It looks like a typical conference room. Tables, chairs, and whiteboards. There seems to be a big screen TV on the back wall.

"Is the screen for streaming surveillance video from around the island while in a meeting?" I ask.

"Yes, and we can have conference meetings via video with other Regions on it as well. Say that Jenna can't make the next Leader's meeting but can join us via video, we just stream it over this," Ty says, waving a hand at the back wall.

"Wow, high tech!" I say.

"We are lucky to have this place," he says, squeezing my hand gently.

"So where is Zack?" I ask.

"Con-Room 4," Ty says, leading us out. Con-Room 3 is the room next, on the left, with Con-Room 2 across from it. Con-Room 5 down on the left, and here, Con-Room 4.

Ty knocks once, uses his key, and opens the door.

"It's locked?" I ask, as I step over to Ty, letting everyone else walk in to the room ahead of us.

"Couldn't chance him getting out," Ty says. "Even with Vinny and Ret with him. I don't trust him,

Emma."

"We'll figure out who he is," I say, patting his arm. "If he's not who he says he is."

I'm still having a hard time remembering him. I'm sure I would have seen him at least once or twice growing up. I could pick ninety-nine percent of the kids from my high-school out of a lineup if I had to, maybe he's part of the one percent I don't remember. Although, I honestly don't even remember his family either. When I saw his parents lying on the kitchen floor, there was no flash of memory, just sorrow for lost innocents. And I definitely don't remember there being a little girl next door. But being as I was secluded from most of the outside world until a couple months ago, I can't rely on my memory and what's true. He very well could be telling the truth, I just never saw him, or is family.

Ty leads us in after Malory and Clay walk in to the room. I look over and see Zack sitting at the table with a bottle of water in front of him. When he sees me his face lights up and he runs to me. Hugging me tightly.

"Oh Emma, you are here!" he says.

Ty clears his throat. I push Zack away, awkwardly. The guy acts like we're long lost best friends. He's making me feel really uncomfortable.

"Sorry, I was just excited to see a friendly face. These guys are making me feel like a prisoner. And then all these other people come in. The dudes, I remember from my house and that pretty girl. But the other hotties, I don't remember seeing them," he winks at Alysa. She glares at him.

"I'm sorry you've felt like a prisoner, you aren't one. But as we don't really know who you are, we have to be careful, you understand that right?" I ask.

"Careful with what? Where are we?" Zack asks.

"At our home," I answer simply.

"Which is where? They,"-he points to Vinny and Ret-"said I passed out. The last thing I remember is going into the trees by the park."

"Yeah, we think the adrenaline from the trauma that happened today, must have worn off and shock set in. One second you were talking and the next, my brother and cousin were catching you from falling on your face," Tally says, shrugging, pointing to Tate and Ty.

Zack's eyes tighten just a little as he looks at Tate and Ty.

"I thought you guys were brothers," he states.

"We get that a lot," Tate says. "But she's my sister, he's my cousin."

"And Ty's my brother," Libby says, coming up, waving hi. I can see she's trying to give him the benefit of the doubt. She smiles at me.

"You look more like her-" he points to Tally "-but also like the guys," Zack says. He's looking between the four of them so quick, it's making me dizzy.

"Twin siblings married twin siblings," Tally says and laughs. "We're the result."

"So, Zack," Ty starts to say, taking a seat at the table. He doesn't like it but he nods for me to sit next to Zack. I think Ty's starting to realize we'll get more out of Zack if he feels like he's getting closer to me. "Have you remembered anything more about the people you saw today?"

"Not yet, but I'm trying man, really I am," Zack says, rubbing his head.

"It's alright, it'll come to you. You still might be stressed or in shock from today," Libby says, smiling sweetly at him. His return smile is huge. Oh yeah, he definitely doesn't mind the way the girls look around here.

"What's the plan to find my sister?" Zack asks, looking at Ty.

"We'll get word out to some of our... friends and see if they can ask around and see what they find out," Ty says and by friends he means Werewolves, Vampires, Fae, and Merfians. I really hope the Merfian's don't know anything about a missing Inepti girl. They'd only know about her if she was dumped in their waters. I shudder, I don't want to think about that outcome.

"Who are you guys?" he asks, looking around the room. The girls have all taken seats, but the men are still standing. They are all wearing black colored clothing, nothing too menacing but still, they look tough.

"We're..." Ty starts to say.

"We're a type of special forces," I answer. That should explain why we're being secretive and using precaution with him without having to explain it all to him in detail.

"Like in the military?" Zack asks, surprised.

"Yeah, exactly, like the military," I say, smiling at him.

"Army? Navy? Marines? Air force?" Zack asks.

"None of those," I say. "We're part of a division people don't know about it. Top secret stuff."

"I didn't know you were interested in the military. You seemed more book smart than anything. Are you more tech support than soldier?" Zack says, laughing, thinking he's made a joke.

"She's our best... soldier," Shae says, using his term but adding a little more zing to her tone.

"That's cool. I thought about joining the Air Force," Zack says, puffing out his chest.

"Thought about, but didn't. Why not?" Alysa says, also sounding annoyed.

"Oh... Well, it's just... I get motion sickness pretty easily," he mumbles out.

"There's medicine for that," Alysa states.

"Umm... yeah..." Zack mumbles again.

"Zack, is there anything that could help us find

your sister? Anything that could identify the people that attacked your family?" I ask, trying to get the topic back on the situation at hand. We had three missing Leaders and now a supposed missing six-year-old.

"I'm sorry, I just can't remember," Zack says. "Every time I think about what they looked like... when I think about sneaking over to your backyard, my mind gets all blurry and I just remember being scared and running home and getting Molly and hiding."

"It's okay, like Libby said, it should come back to you after you get some good rest," I say, patting his hand. He turns his hand over quickly and grabs hold of my hand.

"Speaking of rest, do I have to stay in here? That cot isn't the most comfortable," Zack says, squeezing my hand gently.

I pull my hand free before Ty can say anything about it, I felt him tense when Zack grabbed it. I peak at him out of the corner of my eyes, he's staring at his hands on the table, a picture of calm, but I can feel the frustration emitting off of him.

"We'll see if we can find somewhere more comfortable for you," I say.

"Maybe something to eat too?" Zack asks.

"Oh, for sure!" Libby says as she jumps up. "It's about lunch time."

Since Libby stood, everyone else does too. Clay and Malory starting for the door, Max and Charlie behind them. Zack goes to stand too but looks around.

"I guess I have to stay here until further notice?" he asks.

"Sorry, Zack, just for a little while longer, okay?" I say, encouragingly with a smile.

"Alright," he says, smiling back at me.

"I'll send someone with some food," I add.

"You won't bring it yourself?" Zack asks anxiously.

"No, not this time. I've got some things to look into," I say apologetically.

"More important than making sure I'm okay?" he asks.

Ty is about to say something, but I put my hand in his and squeeze.

"Zack, I came down to check on you. If you want me to find your sister, I can't sit down here with you all day. My friends will keep you company and get you what you need," I say, as I turn to leave.

"Thank you," Zack says quietly. "I don't think I've said that since you showed up at my house. Thank you for getting me out of there and I know you'll find Molly."

I smile at him and nod. Then I really do leave and we walk back down the hall towards the garage.

"You okay?" Ty asks, grabbing my hand and

intertwining our fingers.

"Yeah," I answer tiredly. "The number of people we have to look for keep growing."

"Welcome to our World," Ty says. He doesn't say it with snark, just in a matter-of-fact way.

The tour is over so making it back to the garage and elevator takes little to no time. The short amount of time we've been down here and the numerous times I've been saluted, has me used to the gesture already. Just because they believe they need to show respect doesn't mean I have to give them a hard time about it.

We get into the elevator and ride it up to the Hospital Wing. Everyone is talking around me, but my mind is elsewhere. I'm trying my hardest to think about anytime I was outside of my house and maybe had gotten a glimpse of the cute boy next door but ignored him because I knew my mo... Vanessa, would never allow me to become friends with him, let alone date. Had I ever seen his little sister? Did I even know the couple that lived there? All answers are no and it all comes back to Vanessa keeping me locked away from everyone. Even though I was a neighbor, I am not a good source for knowing if Zack is telling the truth.

"Emma?" Ty says my name softly. I look around and see we're standing in line for food. I was really out of it if I zoned out from the Hospital Wing to the dining hall.

"Sorry, deep in thought," I say, grabbing the tray he's holding out for me.

"What are you thinking about?" he asks, grabbing a couple sandwiches, a couple bags of chips, two apples, a cup of pudding, and a couple bottles of water. I'm not too hungry so I just grab a sandwich and apple.

"I keep racking my brain to see if I can remember Zack but I can't. Although, I don't remember anyone that lived around me, if I'm honest. I remember kids in my class and some of the older and younger ones that went from elementary all the way through high-school with me, and that's only because they weren't very nice. Even the ones that were nice, stopped being nice after they invited me to parties but I wasn't allowed to go. I heard them saying they thought, I thought, I was too good to hang around with anyone. If they only knew the truth," I say, yawning.

"Nap time after lunch?" Ty asks.

"I'm okay," I say. "I really want to help figure out a way to find Doc, Meredith, and Bill. And Molly, now too."

"Emma, you're going to wear yourself out," Ty says, taking my tray for me and walking us over to the table our friends are sitting at, digging into their own lunches. "You are barely healed from the battle at the Elders. You need to rest, especially after Jumping multiple people clear across the country and back multiple times in a short amount of time."

"I know, but it feels like all I do is sleep," I say, yawning again. I smile, I can't help it.

"Sleep helps you heal, we've been over this," Ty says, setting our trays down.

"Alright, but only if you nap with me," I say.

"That is definitely something I can do," he leans over and kisses the top of my head.

Everyone is talking about Frank and what they think Vanessa did to him. Charlie insists that it's just Frank, he hasn't been altered. That Frank just wants me so bad that he's gone insane. I block out their conversation and focus on eating and thinking of where Vanessa could have taken our Leaders and possibly Molly.

The only place that I know of for sure is the place they had held me. Although, they might have moved after the guys rescued me. It's not a secret anymore. Unless they are keeping them there to trap us. I wonder if anyone knows where Chris lived in the years that him and Vanessa were apart, while she 'raised' me? Or were they apart?

"Hey," I say, loudly and startling everyone.

"I was just kidding," Charlie says.

Confused I say, "What?"

"He had said that we should use Frank's attraction to you as a way to get him to talk," Libby say, glaring at Charlie.

Thinking about it, I tilt my head sideways.

"That's not a bad idea," I say.

"What?!" Ty and Libby say at the same time, in shock.

"We need answers, and he was… is… a trained Guardian, he won't talk with your normal interrogation tactics, torture or not. I was just thinking, does anyone know where Chris lived while I was a child, while Vanessa was raising me?"

No one says anything, they just look around at each other.

"Exactly! Frank might know," I say. "He might know more than we think he does."

"I'm not going to let him touch you," Ty says, sounding pissed.

"Ty, he can't hurt me. He honestly has no effect on me," I say, grabbing his forearm and squeezing gently.

"He might say or do something that could hurt you," he says, placing his hand on mine.

"He's a gross, horny man. He's so lost in his lust, I don't think he can think straight," I say.

"So, we use that against him?" Libby asks, looking more intrigued than upset now.

"Can't be any worse than using physical torture, can it?" I ask.

"Honest Emma, I was just kidding. I don't like the idea of you going in there and getting him all riled up, who knows what he'll do," Charlie says sounding concerned.

"Okay, let's brainstorm and think of what he could possibly do to me," I say, looking around the table.

"He could..." Charlie starts to say and then stops, thinking harder. "He could break his bonds and attack you."

"What do you think I'll do? Lay down and take it?" I ask.

"No, you'd throw his ass across the room, probably through the wall and give him a dirt nap if it's through a wall that has dirt behind it," he says. I raise my eyebrows at him, signifying, 'see, there isn't anything to worry about then'.

"What are his Talents?" I ask Ty.

"Nothing extraordinary. Just the typical Guardian stuff; Super Strength, Super Speed, and a good fighter," he says.

"So, nothing that'll catch us by surprise?" I ask.

"Not unless Vanessa gave him something we don't know about," Ty says, looking around the table.

"If he had something we didn't know about, he would have used it to get to Emma when we were just down there," Max says. "The guy was throwing himself at the bars. I don't think he has anything hidden up his sleeve, so to speak."

"That's true," Libby says.

"So, we can interrogate him?" I ask.

Ty shakes his head and closes his eyes. I can tell he's warring with himself, between boyfriend and Commanding Officer. Letting out a huff of air, he opens his eyes.

"Yes, we can interrogate him, but," he says, holding up his finger. "I have stipulations."

"Of course you do," Libby laughs.

"Tally, Clay, and I will be in there with you," Ty starts to say and Charlie starts to splutter. "Charlie, Clay is a Mentalist, he can read Frank's mind and feed questions to Emma so that she doesn't have to get into his pervy mind. Tally is a Lie Detector, so she'll be able to tell if Frank is lying. And before you say you'll know if he's lying to you, Emma, I know you will, but I want you focused on getting answers from Frank. Let other people help you the way you help everyone."

He's really starting to get me because I was in fact about to object that I, if I concentrate hard enough, I can tell if Frank is lying. But, he's right, I need to let people help me and not over exert myself right now.

"Deal," I say.

"One more thing," he says.

"What's that?" I ask skeptically.

"You take a nap first," he says, smiling at me as he stands and takes our trays away.

I slump a little in my seat. He's laughing a little as he comes back to our table.

"I'm all amped up now, ready to go get some

answers. There's no way I can possibly sleep," I say.

Ty looks at me with eyebrows raised and taps his forehead.

What? I ask.

I can think of a way.

How?

Same way I put you to sleep last night.

My face turns red and I shake my head at him.

"That's not fair," I say. I start thinking about us kissing and lying in bed together.

"What did we miss?" Shae asks.

"They're having a private conversation," Libby says. Shae looks confused so Libby taps her head.

"Oh," Shae says.

"One hour, two tops. You need to rest," Ty urges.

"Emma, he's not wrong. If you're going to seduce torture Frank, you'll need to be rested," Libby says.

"Seduce? I don't know how to do that," I say, my voice raising up a little as I talk.

"You don't have to do anything different than what you did today. Just tease him a little and we'll dress you a little sluttier than what you're used to," Shae says, wagging her eyebrows.

"Uh, no you won't," I say.

"Not full-on slut, but showing more than what you're used to," Shae says laughing. "Come on Alysa, let's go through your outfits and pick your most modest one, it'll for sure be sluttier than what Emma

184   EMMA HART AND THE WEREWOLVES

has ever worn."

"I think that was supposed to be a dig, but I'll let it slide," Alysa says, standing up.

Shae kisses Charlie bye and she and her sister disappear up the stairs, my heart racing a little.

"You look scared," Ty says, his head tilted. "You don't have to do this, but you know Frank won't touch you."

"I'm not worried about Frank. I'm worried about what those two will put me in," I point upstairs, indicating Shae and Alysa.

"You aren't afraid that some sex crazed maniac that has a psychotic infatuation with you could possibly, highly unlikely but still could, get his hands on you, but you are afraid of clothes?" Tally asks.

"Yes," I say.

Tally tilts her head at me in confusion.

"Our Emma girl is modest and she's afraid of what horrors the girls are going to find for her to wear," Libby says, reaching across the table and patting my hand. "It wont be as bad as you think."

"You've seen what Alysa wears, how can you be so sure?" I ask.

She sits up straight and says, "Well, that's a good point. They'll find something decent, but I'm sure more provocative than what you're used to wearing."

"That's what I'm afraid of," I say.

"Girl, you have a tiny but rockin' body, show it

off," Tally says. She stands up and walks away.

"I'd like to agree on part of what Tally just said," Ty whispers into my hear. The little hair on my arm stands up from the goosebumps he's caused to pop up. He kisses my neck just below my ear.

"You don't play fair," I say, turning so I can kiss him quickly on the lips. He just winks at me. "Fine, one hour nap."

"We'll meet you guys in here in an hour," Ty says. I stand and as we walk for the stairs, Ty takes my hand.

"Are you really that eager for me to take a nap?" I ask, as we get into my hallway.

"I'm eager to get some alone time with you," Ty says, letting go of my hand and wrapping his arm around my back and pulling me close to him.

"That, I am eager for, too," I say, as we get to my door. Before we can start making out in the hall again, I open my door quickly and pull him inside. Before we've got the door shut, our mouths are on each other.

We make our way to my bed and lie down, kicking our shoes off as we go. Instead of breaking our kiss, Ty wraps his left arm around my back and lifts me up to him and scoots me back until my head lands on my pillow. His full weight is on me and it feels so good.

Our hands start to roam, mine finding the bottom of his shirt. I slide my hands beneath and feel the muscles on his back rippling under my touch. Ty stops kissing me for a second and as he stares into my eyes, reaches one hand behind his neck and starts to pull his shirt off. In one quick motion, it's off and flung towards the door. I look down at him hovering over me. I marvel at his upper body. At his muscles rippling with just the slightest action he makes.

His fingertip is under my chin, pulling my mouth back to his, kissing softly, but it doesn't take long before we're into a passionate, tongue tying, kiss. He slowly lowers himself back down but off to the side a little now. I run my hands up his back and down his arms. Most of my brain is lost in our kissing, but a small part is memorizing the way his muscles roll down his arms.

Before I know it, my head is lying on his chest, listening to his heart racing, but soft breathing. I can feel my heart is keeping pace with his. Ty starts to run his fingers through my hair and down my back. I feel his fingertips find bare skin from my shirt being lifted just a little down by my waist, he pulls it down, and smooths it out before he goes back to playing with my hair.

And soon, my eyes are drifting to sleep.

CHAPTER 11 -
THAT WENT WELL

"Emma?" I hear my name being called softly in my ear. Soft lips pressing against my forehead. "Emma?"

"Mmmmm," is the only thing I can say. I'm lost in blissful sleep.

"Em, we've been sleeping for two hours now, do you want to keep sleeping?" I hear Ty ask, as he runs his hand up and down my arm that I have slung over his bare stomach.

My brain is starting to wake up more, I roll onto my back and stretch. I was a lot more tired than I thought I was, I need to listen to Ty more, or at least listen to my body.

"No," I yawn, I laugh at my body's opposite reaction to my word. "We can continue this later, if that'll work for you?"

"I'd like that," Ty says, kissing me sweetly and then rolling off the bed.

"So, how is this going to work?" I ask. "Me interrogating Frank?"

"We'll think of questions and feed them to you Telepathically. Keep your mind open to us, but closed to Frank, can you do that?" Ty asks as he pulls his shirt over his head.

"Yeah, I think so," I say.

"If you accidently slip and see what Frank might be thinking, it could traumatize you," Ty says half joking.

"I know and I'll try hard not to slip up," I say. "There's no way I want to see into Frank's mind when it comes to me."

We put our shoes on and head out the door. Ty taking my hand instantly. I can't believe how a minor gesture can become a comforting thing in such a short amount of time.

"Promise me something?" I ask, as we walk our way down the stairs.

"Anything," he says without thinking.

"Apart from Frank attacking me, don't react to anything that he or I might say. I don't see myself saying anything that might cause you to have a bad reaction but I want to go with the flow and try to get as much information out of Frank as I can," I say.

He takes a deep breath and says, "Okay. Apart from him touching you or hurting you, I won't be your boyfriend in there, I'll be the Commanding Officer."

"Thank you," I say and pull him down to me so I

can kiss his cheek. "I really think he's our best bet at getting some answers."

"I hope so," Ty says. We walk down the last steps and find our group sitting at, what's apparently becoming, our table.

"Two hours on the dot," Clay says, smiling at us.

"We were gone for two hours?" I ask, looking at Ty then down at my watch, I see it's a little after 3:00pm.

"I might have told them it would be two hours instead of one," Ty says, smiling down at me.

"When?" I ask astonished.

"After you fell asleep," he says sheepishly. "You were really tired and you needed rest."

I give him a teasing glare but move on.

"Ready to see what Alysa and I picked out for you to wear?" Shae asks, standing up.

Instant dread.

"No," I croak out.

"I've never seen the color drain from someone's face so fast over clothes," Alysa says, laughing. She's holding a little bag in her hand. *Makeup? This is going to be my own sort of torture.*

"Oh, come on, you'll survive," Shae says, seeming to have read my mind.

"I don't want to see it," I stammer out. "If I see it before I put it on, it won't make it over my head. Let me see it for the first time when I look in the mirror."

"Are you sure?" Libby asks.

"Absolutely," I say.

"Well, let's go then," Shae says. Everyone stands to walk out.

Before Ty can say anything, which he's about to, Charlie raises his hand and stops him.

"We aren't going into the room with you guys, but Max, Tate, and I will be in the guard station watching the monitors. The girls are going to sit in the staging area and wait, in case Emma needs some girl support," Charlie rushes out before Ty can say anything.

Ty thinks for a minute and then nods. He turns and takes my hand and leads us through the kitchen and back to the elevator once again.

"While you're changing, I'll inform Phil what's going on and they can move Frank down to an interrogation room," Ty says, as we ride the elevator down the short ride. Soon the doors are opening once again into the huge garage.

We get into the staging area and everyone stops.

"You can use the bathrooms in the breakroom, they're more locker room style than the other ones down here. We'll be in here waiting," Ty says. He kisses me quickly and then walks towards the guard station.

The girls turn me and lead me to the bathrooms in the breakroom. Once inside, I go into a stall and take my clothes off. Someone, Shae probably, hands me my new outfit over the top of the stall door. At least it's black. I turn it until I find the tag in the back before I close my eyes and put it on. It's a dress. *Of course it is.* I can feel more cold air on my skin than I had before, because more skin is showing than before. I can also tell I'm going to have to go braless. *Wonderful.* I rip my bra off as quickly as I can and wrap it in my shirt, *my nice and comfy shirt,* I had been wearing. I open the stall door, step out, and toss my clothes over on to the bench against the wall.

Shae, Libby, Tally, and Alysa all gasp and put their hands to their mouths.

"That bad?" I ask.

"No," Shae says. "That good!"

Libby steers me over to the floor length mirror and I get a look at myself. The dress goes to about mid-thigh and is as tight as it can possibly get on me. The neckline plunges clear down to my sternum, showing off all my cleavage. The back scoops down to show most of my back. This dress definitely shows off all my curves.

"This fit you?" I ask Alysa skeptically.

"Well, I haven't worn it yet but I had gotten it for when I knew I wouldn't be wearing it for long," she answers, winking at me.

"Is this a nighty?" I ask in shock.

"No!" she exclaims. "Well, I was going to use it as one but it's for sure a dress."

I look back at myself in the mirror. My hair is still

pulled up in a messy bun and my cheeks have a faint pinkness to them, from my embarrassment.

"I don't think you need make up but let's do something with your hair," Alysa says. She comes forward and with more gentleness than I thought she had in her, she takes my hair out of my ponytail holder and lets it fall down my back. Having it in the bun all day leaves it curly and shiny. "Well, it doesn't look like we need to do anything with your hair either."

"Don't you think this is a little much?" I ask.

"Maybe but Frank won't be able to handle himself," Alysa says.

"Neither will Ty," Shae says, wiggling her eyebrows at me. I turn bright red and shake my head. "So does that blush mean you two have…"

"What?" I splutter out. "No, we have not."

"This dress won't help… or actually, it very well could help with that," Alysa says laughing at my expression.

"Let's go before you chicken out," Shae says.

Libby gives me an apologetic look and says, "If I didn't think this would work or if I didn't think you could handle it and Frank, I'd tell you to forget about it. But Emma, you look amazing and even more than that, you're a bad ass Demi-god, you got this!"

"Hell yes she does," Tally says, getting the door for me.

"Wait, shoes!" Alysa exclaims. She grabs some

little black flats and kneels in front of me. "This is what Shae and I disagreed on. She didn't think you'd wear heels."

"She's right," I say. The little flats fit perfectly. "Where did you get these?"

"Beth has The Closet finally set up and filled, in one of the outer buildings. It's a cute little cottage, in the wooded area next to the gym."

"Oh," is all I can say. I'm too nervous now.

"Ready?" Tally asks.

Taking a deep breath, I nod. She opens the door and we walk out into the breakroom. All conversation stops immediately. I look up and every pair of eyes are on me. Some of the guys that were in the middle of eating, have their food midair, and mouths wide open, frozen in place. The female Guardians are smiling encouragingly at me.

Does everyone know what I'm doing?

"Respect, gentlemen," Libby says.

Everyone in the room, jumps to attention, and salutes me. Shaking my head and feeling my face getting warmer than it ever has, I walk quickly to the door leading out to the staging area but stop before opening it.

Oh gods! Ty's out there. The guys are out there. I can't do this.

Once again, feeling as if she can read my mind, Libby says, "You have nothing to be afraid of, you look fantastic and you are a badass. You've got this!"

Without giving myself more time to think, and chicken out, I open the door and walk out. The guys are all standing around the guard station, talking to one another. But one by one, they all look our way. Mouths drop and eyes dang near pop out of their heads. Ty is behind the counter looking at the monitor when he looks up to see why Charlie has stopped talking to him, he was behind the counter with him too. Ty looks my way and I see shock and excitement cross his face. And then he gets the biggest smile I've ever seen, on his face. He slowly walks around the counter, out the door, and walks to me.

"Wow," is all he has to say. He looks me up and down and shakes his head a little. "I mean... just... Wow."

"Poor Frank," Charlie says morosely.

"Poor Frank indeed," Clay says.

"He doesn't stand a chance," Max says. He looks at Libby and gives her an apologetic smile and then looks down at the floor. I look at Tate and he's just staring at me, clenching, and unclenching his jaw muscles but he doesn't say anything.

"You look beautiful, Emma, so don't take this the wrong way but, Shae, Alysa, this was the most modest thing you could find?" Ty says, visually gulping.

"You okay there, brother?" Libby says, patting him on the arm. Ty shoots her a quick glare, but I see his cheeks turning a faint pink.

"It's the most modest thing I had, dress wise," Alysa answers him, trying not to laugh at his obvious staring. My cheeks get warmer.

"And all the dresses I own are for formal dances," Shae says. "This is what we thought would work best."

With a deep breath, Ty says, "You thought right, maybe a little too right."

"Sir, the…" one of the Guardians that were behind the counter earlier comes out from the door leading to the cells and interrogation rooms but stops dead when he sees me. "Holy mother of gods! Wow!"

"Mouth shut and eyes back in your head, Bran," Ty says.

"Uh, yes Sir, sorry Miss Emma," Bran says, saluting me and then turning to Ty again but he has to clear his throat before continuing, his eyes darting from Ty to me, "Sir, the prisoner is ready for you."

"Thank you," Ty says. Bran turns and I can hear his running footstep as he goes back down the hall. Ty turns to me, "Ready?"

"I guess so," I answer in a small voice.

"Good luck," Malory and Alysa say at the same time.

"You've got this," Libby says, hugging me.

"You're a badass, remember that," Shae says, giving me a side hug.

"Don't kill Frank, Ty," Charlie says, jokingly as he

looks at the monitors. I giggle at that a little. Charlie winks at me.

Tate holds the door open for me, Ty places his hand on my back and his hand touches my bare back. Warm tingles travel down to my toes. I hear a slight moan escape him. I look up at him and he just winks at me. Clay and Tally follow behind us, Tate starts to follow. Ty looks at him but Tate just shrugs. Ty nods, his indication it's okay for Tate to come too. The hall isn't big enough for more than two of their size of guys to walk down together.

When we get to the end of the hall, Bran and the other guy that was in the guard station earlier are standing on either side of Interrogation Room 1. They salute us but try not to look at me for too long. I can see the other guy trying really hard not to look but his eyes dart to me and away, quickly. Bran must have told him what I looked like and warned him about Ty's reaction to the staring.

Ty knocks on the door twice and then uses his key again and opens the door. We walk in and Phil is leaning up against the wall to the left of the room and Frank is sitting in the chair, facing us, at the table. Phil instantly pushes off the wall and salutes us. I watch as his eyes slowly slide from my face down to my chest, down to my toes, and back up again.

"You're dismissed, Phil," Ty says gruffly. I hide my smile by pretending my nose itches.

"Yes, Sir," Phil says. He looks quickly at the floor and walks even quicker out the door. I hear murmuring outside the door.

I hear scrapping and clanking of chains. I look over at Frank and he's straining with the shackles the guys put around his ankles and wrists, connecting him to the chair that I see now is bolted to the floor.

You guys go stand behind him. I want his eyes on me and not to be distracted by you guys making movements or anything like that.

Keep this open so we can communicate but block him out. Ty's voice says.

Yeah, you don't want to know what he's thinking. Clay's voice says, it's got a hint of disgust in it.

Tate and Tally just nod before they all walk behind Frank and lean against the wall. The good thing is, I can look at Ty and make Frank think I'm looking at him.

I look at Frank and I see him swallow hard.

"Like my new dress?" I ask, looking down at myself.

He just nods.

"Thanks, my friend loaned it to me," I say.

"You shouldn't give it back," Frank says huskily. "I can't imagine it looking better on anyone else."

"Well, that was nice of you to say," I say, forcing a sweet smile.

I see Clay grimace. Frank must be having a less

than desirable thought.

"I was hoping to ask you a few questions," I say as I slowly walk towards him.

Frank licks his lips and then bites down on his lip, before saying, "Ask me anything."

I reach for the chair and make sure I push my cleavage together for a better view. Frank actually lets out an audible groan.

You've almost got him, he'll be putty in your hands in a few more minutes. Clay's voice says.

I stay in this position and ask my first question.

"Frank, do you know where Chris lives?" I ask, adding a little sultriness to my tone.

"Why do you want to know where that bastard lives? I'm all the man you need, baby," Frank says, thrusting his hips up a little.

Barf.

Easy, Emma. Clay's voice says. *Don't let him think you're repulsed. I think he'll answer just about anything you ask him, if not, I'll at least see the answer in his head. We've got him. He's completely forgotten about us being in here. He thinks it's just you two.*

Ty nods at me in encouragement but I see him clinching his jaw muscles, his arms are crossed tightly over his chest.

I answer Frank, "Oh, I know but we've got some people missing and I was just hoping you could tell me where he lives so we could send some friends to pay him a visit and see if our missing people are there."

"You sure that's it?" Frank asks, licking his lips again.

I bend down a little more as I pull the chair out, a little more than I need to, but it has the affect I'm looking for, Frank's eyes open even wider.

"I'm sure," I say silkily.

"Same street as your house in New York. Brown house, white roof. I don't know the address," Frank says in a hurry. I look at Ty, he nods.

"Thank you for that," I say. I take a seat and with exaggerated movement, I scoot myself forward, making my boobs bounce as I do it.

"Daaaamn," Frank moans out. He pulls on his chains around his wrists. "Take these things off me baby, I want to show you something."

"In good time," I say. I put my hands on my knees, forcing my cleavage to bulge again. Apparently all it takes is a little boob to get guys to talk. "Do you know a Zack?"

"Why you asking me about all these guys?" Frank seethes.

"He's just a new friend, only a friend, but I don't know much about him. I was just wondering if you met a Zack while you were with Vanessa and the Rifts," I say, trying to sound like Zack was no big deal.

"I don't know no Zack," Frank says, not taking his eyes off my cleavage. I look up at Ty. I catch him looking there too and a small smile crosses my face. His cheeks turn pink again but nods for me to keep going.

"You don't remember a Zack living on the same street as me in New York?" I ask.

"Forget about the bastard Zack, let's talk about you and me and what I want to do to you," Frank says. I see Clay flinch.

"I just want to make sure Zack is a friend and not someone I need to be scared of," I say, urging him to answer me.

"The only person you need to worry about is me and what I'm going to do to you," Frank says and thrust his hips again. I see Tate reach for Ty, who had just taken a step forward.

"I know you don't want to hurt me, Frank," I say. I look at Ty and shake my head slightly at him. He takes a step back and runs a hand over his face.

"I don't?" Frank asks.

"I don't think so. I think you want to be a good man and answer my questions," I say, pulling down on my dress from my bellybutton, to show just a little more cleavage. Even though if there was any more showing, my boob would be hanging out.

"And if I'm a good man and answer you, what do I get?" Frank asks, licking his lips again.

Barf.

"I'll see what I can do," I say suggestively.

"I don't know about any Zack," Frank says, never taking his eyes off my chest. *What a buffoon.* "I only went to Chris' house a hand full of times before you and Vanessa left for Greece. I was there for a few minutes and then would return to my designated station, which is where you were taken, and we officially met. Do you remember that?"

My turn to grit my teeth.

Okay, we're done. Ty's voice says.

No, it's ok! I send out.

Tate pats him on the shoulder. Ty shakes his head and closes his eyes.

"I do," I say, trying to lighten my voice back up.

"Too bad Tim interrupted us that one time, do you remember that too? You were a little out of it, I might have taken some frustration out on you a little too much that day," Frank says with lust filled eyes.

I swallow back the bile rising in my throat. I see Tate and Tally are both holding Ty back.

Ty, it's okay. Clay, should I admit I remember or deny. I don't want this conversation to be in his hands. I mentally ask.

He wants you to admit you remember so that he can relive it with you, so deny. Clay's voice suggests.

"I must have been too out of it, I don't remember that at all," I say with fake sadness.

"I know you remember the night of your birthday, back at The Pit. If it weren't for that punk kid, I could have had you then. I was so close, you remember that, I know you do," Frank says, looking up from my chest for the first time.

"I do," I say.

"I would have been the best present you got all night... Hell for the rest of your life," Frank says, straining with his shackles around his ankles and pulling on his hands again. I can see him trying to reach for his crotch.

Double barf.

Focus, Emma. Clay's voice again.

I take a breath, making my chest rise and fall, drawing his attention back to my cleavage.

"Do you know where else Vanessa and the Rifts might be hiding?" I ask as I lean forward.

"I can't handle it anymore, just let me touch... let me feel you," Frank says, straining so hard on his wrists that veins in his neck pop out.

"Not just yet, I only have a few more questions for you," I say.

"And once the questions are done, you'll take these off me?" Frank asks, rattling the chains.

"I'll have someone take them off you, yes," I say. *And return you to your cell, you disgusting pig.*

Emma, easy. Your facial expression doesn't hide your disgust when you think like that. Tally's voice says.

"She has some places in different countries, I'm not sure where, I never went, but I heard some of her men saying when she was out of country and when she'd be home. I did hear about something in Europe," he finally answers.

Do you guys have any questions?

No, I think we're done. Ty's voice. I can Sense his frustration.

"Okay, Frank, one more question," I say. "How long was it until you decided to become a traitor?"

Without hesitation, he answers, "The moment I saw you."

"Which was when?" I ask, stunned.

"About a year before you guys left for Greece," Frank says, licking his lips. "You'd just gotten home from school. It was my first day undercover and I was surprised the Rifts were letting me in to their inner workings so quickly. We were at Chris' getting our instruction for the day and I watched you walk down the street. I had asked one of the other guys who you were, they said you were Vanessa's niece. You were our target the following year but when she wasn't home, we were to watch you. I knew in that moment, I'd do anything to have you. It wasn't too much longer after that, that Vanessa approached me. She'd somehow realized who I was and offered me a deal. I couldn't tell her where The Pit was, but I could give hints of its location and other info she didn't have before. And if I gave it to her, I'd get you in the end."

He strains against the chains again, thrusting

his hips. I see Clay and Ty looking at each other in astonishment.

"What info did you give her?" I ask.

"More questions? Come on Baby, I need you to help me take care of something," Frank says, suggestively thrusting at me.

"Just a couple more. Please Frank?" I ask in a forced pouty voice, when really, I just want to vomit.

"I told her when the next Leader conference would be and where I thought they'd be held. I told her where I thought the Elder's homebase was. I had overheard Bill having a conversation with Meredith one day about them, but they had caught me before they said the location again to confirm I had heard correctly," Frank says, breathing hard.

Okay, that's enough. We're good for now. Clay's voice says.

"Okay, thank you Frank," I say, I stand and turn away.

"Gods damn! Girl, that dress needs to come off now!" Frank hollers.

I turn around slowly. I push the chair in even slower, pushing my cleavage in and up even more. Once the chair hits the table, I stand straight. I smooth the dress down and stare at Frank.

"Come on now, take these off. I'm not going to make it much longer," Frank says, pulling up on his wrists again.

"Can I let you in on a little secret?" I ask seductively. The tone of my voice pulls Franks eyes up to my eyes.

He nods vigorously.

"You're never... going to touch me... again. And you'll never... see... what's under my dress," I say and turn and walk towards the door.

"YOU BITCH! YOU TEASE! YOU PROMISED!" Frank screams. He's really thrashing now.

I turn and see Tate and Clay surprising Frank, reminding him that they were in the room with us, they have their hands on his shoulders, holding him in place.

"I told you I had questions and I told you I'd have someone remove those," I point to his chains. "Once we were done. My friends here, will do just that. Have a good night, Frank."

"NOOOOO! I NEED TO HAVE YOU! YOU! ARE! MIIIINE!" Frank is screaming now.

The door opens and Phil, Bran, and the other guy walk in. Ty walks up beside me and leads me out the door. He's got a hold of my hand and he's pulling me down the hall. I start to shake. He looks down at me and once we're past about halfway, he pulls us off into one of the sides. I look at the cell door and see the number 15.

"Are you okay?" Ty asks.

"Yeah," I say. "I just hate acting like that with him.

I feel like I need a shower."

"You're shaking really bad," Ty says.

"Just my nerves finally unwinding," I say.

"Let's get you back to your room."

"Okay."

We step back out and make our way back down to the staging area. The girls jump up and run over to us.

"We heard everything!" Shae says, smiling.

"You did amazing," Libby says.

"Thanks," I say.

"Why are you shaking?" Alysa asks.

"Her nerves are shot," Ty answers for me.

"Should we wait to debrief until morning?" Max asks.

"Yes," Ty says. "I'm going to get her back to her room and hopefully that's where she'll stay for the rest of the night."

I don't have it in me to argue that a debriefing now would be best but I'm so tired.

"Get her there quickly," Libby says. "I don't think she's going to last much longer."

"I'm fine," I say, yawning with chattering teeth. "I just need to wash his sleaziness off of me."

Ty gets us to the garage door before I remember about my clothes.

"Libby?" I holler before we get through the door.

"Yeah?" she hurries over.

"Will you bring my clothes when you guys come

up? And check on Zack, did someone take him lunch? I completely forgot about that," I say, feeling awful.

"Yes, I sent lunch with Travis, he was relieving Vinny. I'll have one of the guys run down and check on him before we head up," Libby says. "And I'll get your clothes. Go take a shower and get some rest."

"Thanks," I say, smiling over at her.

I let Ty walk us into the garage. Maybe I should have changed before heading upstairs. All eyes are on me again.

"Show some respect," Ty bellows out. I can tell his nerves are on their last thread as well. I giggle. I'm not paying attention to everyone saluting us as we walk by and giving their halfhearted apologies. Ty looks down at me and asks, "What's funny?"

"You," I say, giggling again.

"Why me?" he says, smiling.

"Your boyfriendness is showing."

"Asking for them to show you respect, is me as their Commanding Officer."

"Yeah, but your glare and tone, are more boyfriend like than Commanding Officer."

"Well, I can't help it. You look too good in that dress."

I laugh again, "Oh stop."

We get to the elevator and I sway a little.

"Are you sure you're okay?" Ty asks with concern. He wraps his arm around me, holding me close to him.

"I'm just tired," I say.

As we step into the elevator, Ty scoops me up in his arms, he pushes the button to make us go up, with ease.

"So, is this boyfriend Ty or Commanding Officer Ty?" I ask, wrapping my arms around his neck.

"Boyfriend," he says before he presses his lips to mine.

I run my hands up onto the back of his head, into his hair, and pull him closer to me. I feel his left hand squeeze my knee and his right-hand slides around my back to my side and accidently grazes my side boob.

"Sorry," he mumbles and pulls his face away from mine and slides his hand back down.

"It's okay," I say, pulling at the back of his head, urging him to kiss me again. He eagerly obliges.

DING

The door to the elevator opens. Ty takes a small step out into the Hospital Wing and then stops. Letting the door shut behind us.

"What's wrong? I ask. I look around the room and everything looks normal.

"I need a minute," Ty says. I look up and his face his red.

"For?" I ask. He looks down at me and his eyes dart to my chest, and then he looks up at the ceiling.

"That's not helpful," he states and then chuckles.

At first I don't understand and then understanding hits like a pile of bricks. I let out a little giggle.

"I'm sorry," I say, giggling even harder.

"It's not funny," he says, through strained lips. He looks back down at me and grits his teeth. "Stop laughing. You're making... you're jiggling."

I laugh even louder.

"I'm sorry, really I am," I say, trying my best to stop laughing. "Hold on."

I think of my room and will myself to be there. In a blink of an eye, the bright light from the Hospital Wing is replaced by my dark room.

"Did you Jump us?" Ty asks.

"I thought it'd help both of our situations," I say, starting to giggle again.

"Thanks for that," he says. He sets me down gently and steps away.

"Are you better?" I ask, trying not to look down at... him.

"Embarrassingly, no," Ty says, turning away from me.

"You can't even look at me?" I ask through a giggle.

"You truly have no idea how amazing you look. Go take a shower and put on your baggiest clothes. I'll lay here and think about my life choices," Ty says, lying down on my bed slowly, looking as if he's in pain. I shake my head and laugh again.

I walk over to my dresser and grab my baggiest hoodie and a pair of sweats.

"I'll be out in a few minutes," I say.

He just mumbles something and throws an arm over his eyes. Giggling to myself as I go into my bathroom and turn on the shower. I look at myself in the mirror again, without nerves getting in the way. I don't look bad, but I don't think I'll be wearing this dress ever again. It's not my style and I'm not comfortable showing this much skin.

I peel it off and hang it on the hook on the back of the door. I take my undies off and step into the shower. The hot water instantly eases my tense shoulders. I shampoo my hair and then condition. I then wash my body and think about relaxing on my bed. My bed where Ty is currently lying down, trying to calm himself.

That thought has me tensing up again, and not in the bad way. I shake my head and go back to thinking relaxing thoughts. But my thoughts keep bringing up doing things with Ty because he's in the next room, on my bed. And I'm in here naked.

Gah, this shower is never going to end if I keep this up. Deciding I've had enough, I turn the water off and grab a towel and dry myself off. I step out and reach for my hoodie and sweats and put them on. Only now realizing, I didn't grab a fresh pair of undies or a bra.

CRAP! I silently scream in my head, thankful I'd ended the link between the guys and myself when we walked out of the interrogation room. *Oh well,* I think to myself. It'll be fine. I run a brush through my hair quickly and braid it into a loose side braid.

I open the door and see Ty is lying comfortably on my bed, arms behind his head. He looks over and smiles at me.

"Better?" he asks.

"Much," I say, walking over to him. "How are you doing?"

"Better too," he laughs. "Just barely though."

"Why's that?" I ask, trying not to laugh. It has to be difficult to be a man in that regard.

"Umm... well," he starts to say. "I started to calm down and then I thought about how you were in the next room... showering... and things escalated again. I had to hum to myself to block out the sound of the shower and force myself to think of unpleasant things."

"Like what?" I giggle.

"Charlie eating chicken," Ty laughs at my expression. "You'll understand the next time Cooky makes it. The guy goes to town without a care in the world, forgetting all manners, and it's gross."

He pats the bed beside him, so I crawl up and lay down. I put my head on his chest and drape my arm across his stomach. He rubs his fingers down my back, working out the knots in my muscle. His hand freezes for a second when he gets to the middle of my back. He flattens his hand out and rubs around, seeming to be looking for something. His hands stops and his whole body stiffens.

"What's the matter?" I yawn and look up at him. His massage was putting me to sleep.

"It's nothing," he says in a choked voice.

I move a little so I can see him better, which causes me to push my chest into the side of his torso. I see him close his eyes and take a deep breath.

"Ty? What's wrong?" I ask. He looks like he's in pain.

"It's too embarrassing," he says, running his hand, that isn't on my back, over his face.

"What?" I ask again.

"Ummm… you aren't wearing a bra, are you?" he breaths out. Now it's my turn to stiffen.

My head falls to his chest and I feel the heat of my face flare.

"No," I say in a small voice. "I forgot to grab one when I went in to shower and forgot about it again, when I saw you lying here when I came out. Here, I'll go grab one real quick."

I go to get up but Ty holds me tightly.

"Don't be silly, I'll be fine," I look at him and he winks. "I just need to think of Charlie and chicken a little more now."

My face reddens even more. I've never had a guy tell me in a roundabout way, that I was turning him on. I try to situate myself so that my chest isn't rubbing up against him so much.

"That's not helping," he groans and then laughs. "Just go back to how you were before I said anything. I shouldn't have said anything to begin with, I should have suffered in silence."

"Ty," I say, lightly smacking his stomach. "I don't want you to be uncomfortable."

"I don't mind this discomfort," he squeezes me to him. "I just have to not think about it."

"How's that going for you?" I laugh.

"Not too well," he laughs too. "My brain has a mind of it's own at the moment."

"Can I make a suggestion?" While I was in the shower, I had been thinking about mine and Ty's conversation about sex and how both of us were virgin's.

"Sure," he says, starting up his massage down my back again.

"It's more of a thought," I say, turning red. How do you tell a guy you'd like to explore more but not go all the way? Just say it?

"Okay," he says, sounding confused.

"I'm not sure how you'd feel about it," I start to say but my throat closes up. I cough to clear it. If my face heats up any more than it is now, we'll have to turn the AC up. A small laugh bubbles up and I speak my thought, "It might not help your current situation."

"What is it?" Ty asks, leaning away to try to look at me better. "Why are you so embarrassed?"

"You know how we talked about how we're both virgins and how I'm not ready for sex yet?" I ask in a rush.

"Yeah," Ty says in a questioning tone.

"I'm still not ready for that but, if you're willing, I'd be up for... a little more than just kissing and cuddling," I say tentatively.

"What do you have in mind?' Ty asks.

I slide my hand down his shirt, towards his waistline, he freezes. I lift his shirt and run my hand on his skin back up to his pecs. I trail a finger between his muscles, down to his abs. He finally unfreezes and relaxes.

"Maybe some touching and seeing, for now?" I suggest.

"Emma, we don't..." he takes a breath and puts his hand on mine that's tracing his ab muscles now. He coughs to clear his throat, "I can't concentrate with you doing that, it feels so good. We don't have to move our relationship to the next level. We have plenty of time."

"I know," I say. I sit up and move over the top of him, straddling his stomach. His hands go to my thighs, gripping hard, but gently. "I want to though, but if you don't, we don't have to."

I start to slide back off, to lie down beside him again. Face full of embarrassment again. *Maybe he wants to take it slow.* But his grip on my thighs tighten.

He says, "I want to, I just want to make sure you aren't feeling pressured."

"I don't, I want this too," I say as I lean down and kiss him. He runs his hands up my thighs, up my rib cage, and around to my back.

He pulls his head back into the pillow, indicting he wants me to stop kissing, so I do and lean away, "So when you say touching, what do you mean? I don't want to assume you mean something, and be totally wrong, and go too far. What are our perimeters?"

"I mean touching," I say. How do I explain this? "Like how you were rubbing my back, only on skin? And perimeters? Maybe keeping it North?"

He smiles at me, "Okay, that sounds good. And what about seeing?"

I thought that was obvious, but I guess he wants it explained so there aren't any misunderstandings. Which I get, it saves us both some embarrassing moments if we know what is to be expected.

"Everything can be off except underwear?" I say it as a question, heat rising up another notch on my face. Ty's eyes dart to my hoodie covered chest and back up to my face.

"Sounds good to me," he says as he pulls me down to him and kisses me deeply.

I reach down and pull his shirt up and over his head. I had thought about it during our first nap of the day today, about how it wasn't fair for me to get to enjoy him shirtless and me keep my shirt on. Why are girl boobs something to be covered at all times, unless in the confines of a bedroom or bathroom, but guys can walk around shirtless? Not that I want to run around shirtless but it's weird how one is more sexualized and made to be covered, when the other isn't even really thought of as anything other than a chest. If I want to see him shirtless, then I should be okay with him seeing me shirtless.

Getting my mind back into what we are doing, I pull myself away from kissing him, and run my hands over his muscles. In awe of his strength.

"You're amazing," I say, bending down and kissing him. How can this magnificent man be meant for me? Before I can spiral into self-doubt, I block those thoughts, and just enjoy our kissing.

After a few minutes of kissing, Ty's hands slide down my back and rest at the top of my hips but he pulls away just enough to ask, "Can I grab your ass?"

I nod. Technically it's below our perimeters but it's still out of the zone I truly was meaning was out of bounds. Ty's hands slide down my sweat covered rear and stops.

"Umm, no underwear either?" he asks, tensing, and pulling away from our kissing.

My forehead hits his barechest.

"No, I'm sorry. My nighttime clothes after a shower is a top and bottoms, nothing underneath. Autopilot was on when I was getting my things," I mumble into his warm skin.

Ty wraps his arms around me and roll us until he's on top, my legs wrapped around his waist.

"You're killing me, Em," he smiles down at me and then kisses me.

"Sorry," I mumble into his lips. I feel them spread into a smile.

I feel his hand slide up to my back and around to my stomach. His fingers skimming the little bit of skin showing from my hoodie riding up. He pulls it up a little more so that my stomach is in open air. He pulls away and looks at me with a raised eyebrow. I nod. Ty leans back and uses two hands to pull my hoodie up and over my head, I lie back down and watch the expressions cross his face. My face heating up, once again.

Ty's first expression is surprise. Then maybe a little awestruck. He smiles a big smile and then lust, or want, flashes in his eyes.

"You are beautiful," Ty says, leaning down so that our bare chests touch. He kisses me deeply, placing his hand on my side, fingers behind my back, and rubbing his thumb over my rib cage.

And we spend the next little while in our own little bubble of bliss.

CHAPTER 12 -
UNWANTED NEWS

When I open my eyes, I can tell its nighttime, there's no light coming in through my closed window shade. I roll over and find a shirtless Ty, sound asleep. Smiling, I curl into him, close my eyes, and instantly fall back to sleep.

. . . .

Daughter it's time to wake up. There is much to do. Now is the time to do what you must to pull together those that'll become one. Remember, you are the only one that can do what needs to be done.

. . . .

I jolt up, looking around. But I'm alone in my room. I look to where Ty had been sleeping, what feels like minutes ago, and find it empty. I look to the window and there's light shining through the crack in the shade. I reach for my light on my nightstand and turn it on, needing more light in my room.

I had heard Zeus' voice. It had been so clear, it sounded like he was here, in the room with me.

KNOCK-KNOCK

There's a soft knock at the door but before I can get off the bed to answer the door, it opens. Ty walks in holding a tray. A look of relief washes over his face. He takes the tray and puts it down on my dresser.

"You're finally awake," he says, definitely sounding relieved.

"Was I asleep for long?" I ask. "What time is it?"

"You've been sleeping awhile," he says coming and sitting next to me. I look down and see I have his t-shirt on from last night.

"Did you put this on me?" I ask.

"Yeah, I didn't want to leave you shirtless incase someone stopped in to check on you," he answers, shrugging.

"I'm so confused. How did you get this on me without me knowing or even remembering?" I ask.

"You've been pretty out of it," he says. "We were starting to get worried but your vitals have been fine. Sara came and checked on you and confirmed mine and Libby's thought that you were just tired."

"How long was I asleep for?" I ask.

Ty looks at his watch and says, "Coming up on about 22 hours. It's a little before 6:00pm, Saturday."

I laugh out a startled laugh and then yawn

"Why am I so tired?" I ask.

"You've been through a lot," he answers. "Even though you feel like what you did with Frank wasn't that big of a deal, subconsciously, it was a tremendous deal. Confronting a man who tortured you multiple times, and then attacked you... That takes a lot of mental strength. Stepping out of your comfort zone to interrogate him the way you did, takes a lot of mental strength. That's why you're so tired. Physically you're good, you're just mentally tired."

"Did anyone try to wake me up? We've got things we need to do. Or did you guys already have a meeting to decide what to do with what we found out about Frank?" I ask, sounding a little disappointed.

"We met but only discussed what he had said, we've been waiting for you to wake up to make any decisions. And yes, we did try to wake you up," Ty says, smiling at me. "You wouldn't budge."

"But I did wake up once, I remember it being dark in here and you were sleeping, too," I say, stretching and standing up.

"That must have been shortly after we fell asleep," he looks at me up and down. "After seeing you last night, I have a hard time not pulling that shirt off of you right now."

I turn red and he pulls me to him, kissing me.

"Last night was fun," I mumble into his lips. But

I can't get Zeus' words out of my head. "But we've got work to do and I've been sleeping for too long."

Ty chuckles and pulls away.

"I'll step out into the hall so you can change," he smiles down at me and then steps away. He walks by the dresser, to the door, and points at the food. "That's for you. Eat some of it, you haven't eaten in 24 hours."

He opens the door and walks out into the hall, shutting the door softly behind him. I wish we could spend all day in bed. Kissing and touching but we've got things to do. I shake my head and take Ty's shirt off, it smells like him. I put it on my bed, along with my sweats.

I go to my dresser, grab a piece of pizza off the plate, and take a big bite. I'm starving and I eat a whole slice before I realize it. I wipe my hands on a napkin Ty thoughtfully brought with my food. I reach into my drawer and grab a bra, underwear, and socks. I pull out some jeans and a long sleeve shirt, a light blue one today. I look over in the corner and see that my clothes that I forgot in the locker room yesterday, are folded nicely in a pile.

I scarf down another piece of pizza, crack open the pop that's on the tray, and take two big chugs before putting it down. Feeling much better, I walk into the bathroom and brush my teeth. I take my hair out of my, now messy, loose braid, and throw it up onto the top of my head in a messy bun.

I open my door and stick my head out.

"Ready," I say to Ty, he's leaning casually against the wall beside my door. I walk back into my room quickly and grab my tray, and holding my pop so it doesn't spill, and walk back out the door. Ty reaches around me and shuts the door but then takes the tray from my hand, freeing it for him to hold.

"Feel better?" he asks, as he looks at my now empty plate.

"So much better," I answer. I take another drink of my pop, finishing it with just a couple more pulls.

"I've sent a message to everyone, telling them to meet us down in one of the study rooms off of the foyer," Ty says. "We'll drop this tray off and head there. Ret is relieving Max from Zack duty."

"Oh Zack!" I exclaim. I'd completely forgotten about him. "How's he doing?"

"Annoying as ever," Ty says through gritted teeth. "He's been demanding to see you. He didn't believe any of us when we told him you weren't feeling well and were resting. It wasn't until Libby told him, that he finally relaxed. He told her he thought we were just trying to keep you from him."

"Why is he so attached to me?" I ask. "I barely know the guy."

"Sounds like he's had a thing for you for a long time and now that he's actually met you... I can't really blame the guy for feeling that way, as annoying as it is," Ty says.

"But that makes it feel even more awkward. He's been watching me for years and now, because we've met, talked a couple of times, he acts like a jealous boyfriend," I say.

"Are you uncomfortable around him?" Ty asks as we take the last stair down into the dining hall. He puts my tray on the pile by the garbage can and turns us around, walking us towards the foyer doors.

"No... Well, maybe a little. It just makes me uncomfortable how he acts," I say.

"You won't be alone with him and if he tries anything with you, let him have the full force of what you can do," Ty says, laughing a little at my shocked expression. "Okay, maybe not the full force."

We walk into the foyer, saying hello to some random people walking through. Ty holds the door open for me as we walk into the study, to the left of the foyer.

"There she is," Charlie says. "We've been worried about you."

"I'm okay. I was just a little tired," I say, smiling at him and everyone else in the room.

"The art of seduction for a newbie is hard work," Shae says, winking at me. My face turning red, which after yesterday and last night, should probably be a permanent shade of pink.

"I wasn't seducing him," I say, royally

embarrassed.

"The hell you weren't," Alysa says. "I don't mean to be offensive, but everyone watching you work Frank over, was getting seduced."

I crinkle up my nose in a grimace. I sit in the comfy chair, next to Libby, it's big enough for at least one more person. She wraps her arms around me and hugs gently. I put my face in my hands.

"I'm going to puke," I say. I probably shouldn't have eaten that pizza so fast.

"Don't be ridiculous," Alysa says. "You did what needed to be done to get answers. That's what a good Guardian does."

"I feel like a prostitute though," I say.

"You didn't sleep with him for answers," Shae says, reaching over from where she is sitting and pats my leg.

"And even if you would have, that's still not being a prostitute," Alysa says. I look at her and she shrugs. "Well, it's not. Prostitutes get paid with money. And if it were a man doing it to a woman, we wouldn't even be having this conversation, he'd be praised for doing what needed to be done."

"Okay, okay, we don't need to start the man vs woman moral compass debate right now," Shae says. "The point we're trying to make Emma, is that you don't need to be embarrassed. High-five yourself for a job well done and move on."

I look at Ty and he just grins at me, and winks. We'd talked about this last night before we'd fallen asleep.

"Okay, moving on then," I say. "Ty said you guys talked about what Frank had said?" A collective, 'yeah', is said around the room. "So, what do we do now? Send a group to the house he described as Chris'? Which I'm still shocked he lived on my street, and the group of Rifts that were at the place I had been taken to and tortured."

"That sounds like what we ought to do," Max says, standing over by the window.

"We'll do recon first. We don't need to go busting into someone's house if we aren't for sure it's Chris'. And I want to be extra careful when we go back to the Rift's hideout, that could be a trap," Ty says. I hear a small vibration sound and watch as Ty reaches into his pocket and pulls out his phone. He rolls his eyes and looks at me. "It's Ret. Zack is insisting that he talks to you, he says he remembers something, and he won't tell anyone but you."

"Could be just a way for him to see her," Tate says, crossing his arms over his chest.

"Could be," Ty agrees. "But, we'll have to find out."

"Luckily with Zack, you don't have to try anything to get answers from him, he'd willing do anything for you," Charlie says, winking. I feel like he's still teasing me.

"Charlie, time to stop teasing Emma," Shae says, standing up and patting her Anima Gemella on the chest.

"I'm not teasing her, it's fact. The guy has it hard for her," Charlie says, looking down into Shae's eyes. It's easy to see that he really only has feelings for her now. When he winks at me, it's more of a brother doing it to either tease, or make fun of his sister.

I roll my eyes at him, stand up, and say, "Let's go and find out what he remembers."

"Libby, why don't you go talk with Sara and figure out what can be sent out with the two recon groups. Charlie, go down and tell Lee, Karen, Shane, and Craig, they'll be going out on recon, to the house in New York. They won't leave until Monday. Most, if not all, of the Inepties will be at work that day. I want them in Con-Room 3, going over all we have on Chris and the pictures taken from when we were at Emma's house yesterday. Clay and Max, get all the original recon information we had from when we went to the Rift hideout the first time, when we found Emma, and meet me and Charlie in the Con-Room 1. I'll send Travis and Vinny there as well. After we talk with Zack, I'll find someone to switch out with Ret to stand guard over Zack, so that Ret can join the meeting as well," Ty says with authority.

"Got it, Boss," Charlie says. He kisses Shae and then leaves the room. She sways a little and by the look in her eyes, not from the kiss.

"Shae, are you okay?" I ask as I walk over to her.

"Vision…" she mumbles out.

"We've got her," Alysa says as she and Malory put Shae between them, holding her up with her arms around their shoulders. "We'll take her to her room. Go talk with Zack, she'll be okay."

I look at Libby pointedly. She nods. She'll go right to Shae's room when she's finished talking with Sara. I know Alysa is trying to change but I still don't fully trust her to tell us pertinent things.

"Ready?" I ask Ty.

He takes my hand and nods. I turn to take us the quickest way to the Hospital Wing, but Ty stops me.

"Where are you going?" he asks.

"To Zack?" I answer as a question.

"Oh, Libby found him a room. One of the very few that are left," he says, pulling me back around and towards the foyer. Again, as we walk through, we are greeted with hello's and salutes. We start our way up the stairs.

"Which floor is he on?" I ask.

"Same floor as me," Ty says

"Hmmm, I've never been to your room, which floor are you on?" I ask. I feel a little selfish for having never asked or been to his room.

"The fifth floor. I was one of the last to pick a room, you know, the whole 'Alysa messed with my mind' thing," Ty says, shrugging. He doesn't seem to hold a grudge against Alysa for doing what she did. Which doesn't surprise me, he's not the type to waste his time on grudges.

"Can I see your room sometime?" I ask.

"Would you like to?" he counter asks, seeming excited.

"Yes, absolutely," I say smiling up at him. We're just passing the fourth floor.

"After we talk to Zack, I'll show you," he says, pulling my hand up to his lips and kissing it sweetly.

We climb the rest of the stairs in silence, just enjoying each other's company. Ty opens the door to his floor and we walk down the hallway. I look at all the room doors, trying to figure out which one is his.

"Have you figured out which one is mine?" Ty asks.

"Is it in this hallway?" I counter ask.

"Yes," he answers with a smile.

"Have we passed it?"

"Yes," he smiles again.

"I'll guess when we are done with Zack. Which room is he in?"

"Last one on the right," he says, pointing. I look and see Ret standing outside.

"Miss Emma," he says, saluting me and then Ty.

"Hi Ret, nice to see you again," I say as I salute him back.

"He'll be happy to see you," Ret says thumbing behind him.

I knock on the door and Zack opens it.

"I said I will only talk to Em—" Zack starts to say angerly until he sees me. Then he excitedly exclaims, "Emma!"

He throws himself at me and pulls me into a big hug. I gently, but meaningfully, push him away.

"Hey, Zack," I say. "Can I come in?"

"Of course," he says jumping to the side and gestures me in by bending at the waist and waving his hand towards his room.

"Thank you," I say to be polite.

He goes to shut the door but Ty has his foot in the way. Zack opens the door back up and looks at Ty and then at me.

"Sorry, we're a package deal, kid," Ty says.

"Kid? You're what, a year older than me?" Zack asks scathingly.

Ty shrugs but walks into the room and sits in the chair in the corner. Zack glares at him. For a guy who is technically a guest, he's being awfully rude.

"How are you? They said you weren't feeling well?" Zack says, going to sit at the little two seat table. He waves for me to sit across from him, I oblige.

"I was just overly tired. It had been a long day and I've recently recovered from an... injury," I say. Steering the questions towards him, I ask, "I was told you remembered something but would only tell me? You know that all these people are on my side, your side, they're here to help you and help find your sister, right?"

"Why do I feel like a prisoner, then?" he counter asks, dodging my question.

"We've explained why you have a chaperone... an escort. You can't just go wandering around alone, not yet anyways," I say.

"Will I ever?" he asks.

"I don't know, that's not up to me," I say.

"Who's it up to then?" he smiles.

I nod towards Ty. Zack's smile disappears instantly and turns and looks at Ty, who just smiles and waves.

"You've got to be kidding me?" Zack says, putting his face in his hands.

"Nope, so start being nice," I say, like I'm scolding a misbehaving child. Then ask again, "What did you remember?"

"The people I saw, they were wearing black uniform type clothes, kind of like military. But not any military clothes I've ever seen. They said something about Montana and hoping to get back home soon," at the mention of Montana, Ty sits up straighter.

"Are you sure they said Montana?" he asks, trying to sound nonchalant.

I see Zack's eyes tighten slightly but he turns and answers with a nicer tone than I've heard him speak to Ty yet, "Yeah, I'm pretty sure. There isn't anywhere else that sounds like Montana, is there?"

Ty just shrugs and goes back to lounging in the chair.

"Is there anything else?" I ask.

"Nope, that's it so far," he says. "Oh well there was a woman with them."

"A woman?" Ty and I both ask at the same time.

"Yeah," Zack says. "I had mentioned her before but couldn't really remember her at the time."

"Do you now?" I say, waiting for him to describe Vanessa. But then I realize he knows what she looks like, he still thinks Vanessa is my mom.

"She had chin length blonde hair, pretty tall, and tan. She was beautiful," Zack says, smiling a sheepish smile at me. Not knowing who he just described and what it could possibly mean.

I control my voice and ask, "Are there any men that you can describe?"

Please don't, please don't!

"Well actually, yeah. Two of them I don't ever remember seeing. The other's, I remember being there before, when they were moving stuff out. These two new guys looked a little older than the others. Umm, one had dark brown hair, a little graying around here," he traces the outline of his face. "He was tan like the woman but tall, really tall, and huge. He would have made Ty look small, muscle wise."

My heart sinks.

"And the other guy?" Ty asks, he's sitting as still as a statue.

"He was just as tall but not as big, but still ripped. Like I said, a little older too. Light brown hair and dark brown, almost black skin," Zack says, looking between the two of us.

"And you couldn't have told us this because?" Ty asks, standing and walking over to us, he looks pissed.

"I wanted to see Emma," he smiles at me. If he didn't make things so awkward, I'd think he was a nice guy but there's just something off about him.

"I would have come up to see you anyways. From now on, if you remember anything, tell whoever is standing outside, please? It could be a matter of finding... Molly quickly or missing our chance," I say. I don't mention how he'd just described our missing Leaders. I pat his hand, which ends up being a mistake. He grabs my hand and holds it.

"For you, I will," he says.

I pull my hand away and stand up.

"You're leaving already? I thought we could hangout," he says, looking sad.

"To be honest Zack," I take a deep breath. This has to be done, "I'm not comfortable being alone with you. You act like we've known each other for years and years, when in reality we just met two days ago. You do things that are too familiar or intimate for people that just met."

"I'm sorry, I know. It's just I feel like I do know you," he says, his face looks embarrassed, but his eyes look... angry? He's throwing all sorts of warning signs.

"And she's telling you that by you saying that, it makes her uncomfortable," Ty says, coming to stand beside me.

"I'm sorry, I don't mean to make you feel that way," Zack says, looking down.

"I'm sure you don't but until we figure all this out, I'm going to keep my distance," I say and he looks up quickly with a scared look in his eyes. I continue with, "I don't mean I won't come up or talk with you again, I just mean, there will always be someone with us."

"Is this really what you want or what he wants?" Zack asks, nodding towards Ty.

"It's what I want," I say. "Ty just agrees with me. He trusts my instincts."

"And your instincts are telling you I.. what? Might hurt you?" Zack says, stepping back like I slapped him.

"No, I don't think so. Like I've said, we don't know you. We don't trust very easily, what we don't know," I say, trying to smile as kindly as I can at him. Trying to convey friendship but not so friendly he thinks there really is something here, or whatever it is he thinks.

My mind is a whirlwind of chaotic thoughts right now.

"Okay, I can understand that," he says, sounding crestfallen. "Can I at least have my phone back?"

"Yeah, I suppose that'd be okay," Ty says, reaching into his pocket and giving Zack his phone.

"We need to go," I say, I can feel Ty getting anxious the longer we stand here.

"You'll come back though?" he asks.

"I'll try," I say.

"Soon?" Zack pleads.

"When I can," I say walking towards the door.

"Okay," he sounds thoroughly defeated.

My mind is too crazy for me to think about comforting him, I nod at him, and walk out the door that Ty is holding open for me.

"Ret, I'll be sending someone to relieve you, I want you down in Con-Room 1 as soon as they get to you," Ty says urgently.

"Yes, Sir," Ret says with concern. He can tell whatever Zack told us, isn't what we had been expecting.

"Rain check on the bedroom tour?" Ty asks me as we walk towards the end of the hallway, to head downstairs.

"Absolutely," I say. "How long will it take you to find someone to relieve Ret?"

"Maybe 10, 15 minutes," he says. "Why?"

"I want to go check on Shae and fill them in on what Zack told us," I say.

"Okay, but make sure no one else is around. Malory and Alysa are fine, but no one else. We don't need word getting out that... I can't even say the words," Ty says, rubbing a hand down his face.

"I know, I'll be quick. Start telling the guys if I'm not there when you're ready to start," I say.

"You okay if I Run ahead? I feel like we need to get going on this information," Ty asks. I can feel how anxious he's starting to get.

"Yeah, go ahead," I say.

He kisses me on the cheek quickly and then he's gone. Instead of walking or Running to Shae's room, I Jump myself outside her door and knock. I hear a, "Come in," so I open the door and walk in. Alysa and Malory are sitting at the little table, chatting, or more like gossiping. Libby is reading a book, sitting on the bed with Shae, who is resting with a washcloth on over her eyes.

"Hey," I say as I come rushing in.

"What's wrong?" Libby says, jumping off the bed. Shae sits up gingerly and puts the washcloth on the nightstand. Alysa and Malory jump up and go stand next to the bed. I pace, from the window and back to the bed.

"Not good," I say.

"Emma, what's going on?" Alysa asks.

"Ty and I just talked to Zack. He remembered some things about who was at my house and who attacked his family," I say, still pacing. Libby comes and grabs my shoulders. She leads me to the little comfy chair and sits me down in it.

"Take a couple calming breaths and tell us what he told you," she says.

CHAPTER 13 -
MAKING A PLAN

"Holy shit!" Shae exclaims.

"For once I'm going to agree," Libby says. "Holy shit!"

"Is he sure that's what he saw?" Malory asks, starting to chew on her fingernails.

"Yes," I state.

"I mean, it could be anyone," Alysa says, sounding like she's not only trying to convince us, but herself too.

"It would be a pretty big coincidence that three people matching the same description of our missing Leaders were to show up at my old house," I say.

"But if it was them, what were they doing there? And who were they with?" Shae asks.

"Do we know any Demi groups from Montana?" I ask.

"No, but..." Libby starts to say. She looks around the room at the other girls and then stops on me. "Bane and Maisie have their homebase there."

"Okay, so maybe it's not as bad as we think,"

Malory says, hopeful.

"If it's not so bad, why did they attack Emma's neighbor and his family for him just snooping around? Why did they kill his parents and take the little girl?" Shae asks.

We all look at each other and shrug.

"No, this isn't good," Libby says.

"Is this what you were having a Vision about?" I ask Shae.

"Oh that, no, it was nothing," Shae says, glancing at me. Malory and Alysa start talking about being scared of what it could mean if our Leaders have abandoned us, Libby goes to them and tries to comfort them. Shae juts her chin out at the three of them and then nods her head towards the door. Like she wants them to leave.

I can't think of a way to get them to leave and I know Libby won't leave us, so I tap my forehead at Shae. She nods.

What's up? I ask.

My Vision was about you. Her tone has a hint of accusation.

What about me?

You leave us and go somewhere alone.

I have no plans to do that.

Don't you? What about what The Big Three told you?

I hadn't made any plans on what to do about that or where to go.

I think Zack just gave you your first direction.

You won't tell anyone?

Emma... There's pleading in her tone now.

Ty won't let me go alone and you know The Big Three said I'd have to go alone. If you tell Libby, she'll feel like she has to tell Ty. If any of the guys find out, they won't let me go and they'll all definitely tell Ty.

Alright, but I'll be Looking for you and if I get a Vision that you're in trouble, I'm sending the whole damn Guard to you.

That sounds good to me.

"What's going on?" Alysa asks, finally looking at Shae and I.

"Nothing," we say at the same time.

"Were you guys having a 'private' conversation?" she asks.

"It's about her personal life, Alysa, butt out," Shae says.

"Ooooh?" Alysa is intrigued now.

I make a show of rolling my eyes and then lie, well sort of, by saying, "I'm just weirded out about Zack's... affection."

"Oh, well haven't you figured out that everyone wants you?" Alysa asks. She doesn't say it in a vindictive or snarky way, just matter-of-factly.

"They do not," I say.

"Okay," she says, flipping her hair and walking towards the door.

"Clay and Max don't. And neither does Charlie, not now anyways," I say quickly.

"Just because they don't act like it, doesn't mean they don't," she says as she gets to the door. "And we know how Charlie feels."

"Alysa," I say. Ignoring the Charlie statement. I truly believe that him witnessing Shae die and then be brought back, has changed him and cured him of his lust for me. "You can't possibly think that all the men here want me?"

"All their reactions to you in that dress yesterday says they do," she replies.

"Just because they thought she looked nice," Libby starts to say and then sees Alysa's look of disbelief at Libby's use of the word nice, has Libby switching up her adjective. "Fine, just because they thought she looked good... looked smokin'... in that dress, doesn't mean they want her. You can admire the way someone looks but have no actual feeling of attraction for them."

"Give one example," Alysa says.

"Every man in this place," I say. "All you women in this place. If you were to wear that dress and walk around, you would have been getting stares as well."

"But no takers," Alysa says. "I guarantee you that if you weren't officially with Ty, you would have had all the single guys tripping over each other, asking to escort you back to your room."

"Alysa, you'd have 'takers' if you were nicer. Emma has so many admirers because she is the nicest, sweetest, most selfless person to ever walk the Earth," Shae says.

"I'm trying to change," Alysa says as she opens the door and walks out.

Malory walks to the door too, but before she leaves, she says, "She really is trying."

"We know," Shae says, sounding like she means it.

Malory gives a small smile and then shuts the door behind her.

"So, what were you two really talking about?" Libby asks. "I know you're concerned about Zack, but I also know you could have said that out loud. What's up?"

Deciding to go another route with Libby I say, "Well, I was asking her about tips on guys. What they like and ideas on what to do to have fun without going all the way."

Shae had just taken a drink of water and must have inhaled at the same time she took a drink because she starts coughing. Libby looks at her and then at me.

"Is that really what you were talking about?" she asks Shae.

"Yyyup," she splutters out.

"You didn't think you could ask that out loud?" Libby asks me.

Thinking fast I ask, "What do you think Alysa would have had to say about that?"

"Think about it. Alysa already thinks Emma is naive and playing dumb with how the guys feel about her. Emma would never hear the end of it. Also, how Alysa wanted Ty, I just don't think it would have went well," Shae says.

"Okay, that's true," Libby says.

"And plus, I had just dumped a massive information bomb on you guys. Me switching topics was more for me to calm myself mentally, so I didn't start to spiral out of control," I say. Which technically wasn't a lie, I had been starting to spiral.

"So you and Ty are..." Libby says, I can tell she wants to be a good friend but doesn't really want to hear about her brother's sex, or lack thereof, life.

"No... Well, not really," I say, turning red. "We're moving the relationship along. Even though we just made it official the other day, I think we've both been pretty certain about how we felt about each other. So, taking the next step feels right. Not sex, I'm not ready for that. I haven't told him this yet, but I had always told myself I wanted to wait until at least after high school and possibly marriage, before I'd take that step with someone. After never getting to date anyone in high school, the prospect of losing my virginity IN high school went out the window and making my mind up to wait until my wedding night, became something I really thought I wanted."

"And now?" Libby asks.

"I can see myself wanting to take that step with Ty, but not right now. We've only known each other for three… four-ish months now. And I truly feel that when you know the person is right, you'll just know, and I feel that way about Ty too but," I take a breath. I'd never had anyone to talk to about this kind of stuff before, now that I'm spilling my guts about it, I can't seem to stop. "But, I feel like giving yourself to someone like that, in that way, should mean something. Doing that with someone shouldn't just be because you're both attracted to each other, or just horny, or whatever. It's the way babies are made. How we continue on and I feel like an act that important is something to cherish. It's a way for two souls to communicate, to connect. Sure, or at least I assume, it can be fun and not just about making babies. I know that, but I don't think it should just be done to say you've done it or because someone thinks they have to do it to keep a relationship or get a relationship."

Libby and Shae are sitting silent, just staring.

"I've never heard someone explain sex like that before," Libby says. "But I totally agree."

"It's how I felt too," Shae says. "Which is why I told Charlie we aren't having sex again until we've been bonded as Anima Gemella."

"Really?" Libby asks in shock.

"Yes," Shae answers.

"How did he take that news?" I ask.

"He said whatever I wanted to do he was onboard," Shae says. She laughs and says, "I told him sex was off the table, but we can do other stuff."

"Which is what you were telling Emma about?" Libby asks.

"Mmmmmhmmm," Shae says, looking at me, nodding, like she's trying to convince us all that's what we were talking about.

"Well, I don't need to know what you told her she should do with my brother, that's too much information for me," Libby says, acting like she's plugging her ears.

"We decided on touching north of the boarder and keeping the southern area covered," I say and then laugh at Libby's crinkled nose.

"Even that is too much information," she laughs.

"How did Ty take the other news?" Shae asks.

Her bringing it up makes me realize I've been in here a lot longer than I had originally planned. I look at my watch and see that sure enough, I've been in here for at least 45 minutes.

"Shoot, I have to go," I jump up. "Ty was going to tell the guys what Zack told us and start making a plan on what we should do."

I get a pointed look at Shae, ignoring her so I don't draw attention to her, I walk to the door.

"Tell him we'll help any way we can," Libby says as she lies back down on the bed and picks up her book. Shae lies back down and puts the washcloth back over her eyes.

"Will do, see ya," I say as I leave.

Once I'm out in the hall, I Jump myself down to the hall outside Con-Room 1. I can hear talking inside. I knock a couple times and go in. All eyes turn towards me. I wave at everyone and mouth, 'sorry,' to Ty. He waves me in and points to a chair next to Tate. I walk over and sit.

Ty continues on, he must have just started telling the guys because he's telling them that Zack had described Doc, Meredith, and Bill to us. I look around the room and watch their expressions. They all go a little paler and shock and anger cross most of their faces.

When I get to Tate, I stare for a moment and then quickly look away. Even though he could be Ty's carbon copy, with only a few tweaks, the feeling I get when I look at Ty, doesn't come when I look at Tate. It must really be a deeper connection that we have, not just based on looks. Which I knew but it's nice to have definitive proof right in front of me.

"So, what do we do?" Max asks.

"We..." Ty starts to say. He rubs a hand over his face. He looks at me and I smile an encouraging smile at him. "We continue with our original plan. The other Unit will go do recon on the house that could be Chris' and we'll go back to the Rift's hideout and see if we can find out anything there. This information that I just told you, does not leave this room, is that understood?"

"Yes, Sir," they all say at the same time.

"What do we do if they come back?" Clay asks.

"If they come back while we're still here, we'll quarantine them and interrogate them. I'll inform the Units that are staying here to protect the Island and Estate, to quarantine them and notify me immediately if they return while we are away. We shouldn't be gone for more than a couple of days. We'll spend a day or two doing surveillance and then a day executing a sweep. We'll return the day after that or even that evening, depends on what we find," Ty answers, sounding more confident as he speaks. Leading really is his strong suit.

"Will Emma be coming with us?" Charlie asks.

"If she would like to come, she's more than welcome to," Ty says, nodding in my direction. I smile a timid smile back.

If what Shae saw is true, the best time for me to 'sneak' away would be while these guys are gone. Ty will be pissed when he gets back but I'll already be gone. What do I tell him is the reason I need to stay? Do I come up with a legitimate reason or do I make up a lie? I'm not very good at lying.

"When are we leaving?" Vinny asks.

"Monday. Both Units will leave Monday and return no later than Friday evening," Ty states. "Use this time to go over the intel we have on the Rift hideout. Look for places they could set traps for us and find all entrances into the place. It very well could be our exit that saves us if we get into trouble. There are enough folders for everyone."

I can't help but think that maybe I should put off my excursion until after the guys get home. I instantly get a calming feeling, no the guys will be fine. I need to go. But how?

"Emma, can I have a word?" Ty asks, walking over to me. He's in Commanding Officer mode.

"Mmmmmhmmm, sure," I nod, standing and walking over to a corner of the room so we can have a private conversation.

"Please don't take this the wrong way, but I don't think you should come with us, not this time at least," Ty says, getting straight to the point. "And before you disagree and argue your point, I only think this because you still have some healing to do. I'd hate for you to come along and overexert yourself and ruin the progress you've made since the battle at the Elder's. You really pushed your boundaries there and I think you need to sit this one out."

I pretend to glare at him and pretend to think. I don't want to show him that he's given me my out that

I needed.

"It's my choice though?" I ask.

"It's always your choice," Ty says. "But this is coming from a Healer and Commanding Officer, not from your boyfriend who wants to keep you safe and far away from the people that hurt you."

"Can I have the day to think about it?" I ask, still pretending.

"Absolutely, take tomorrow too, if you'd like," Ty says, happy to hear I'm willing to consider staying home.

If you only knew my real plans, you'd insist on me coming with you. To keep me from doing the other crazier, more dangerous thing. I think to myself.

I put my hand to his face and nod.

"Do I get a folder?" I ask, turning towards the table. I see all the guys are doing as Ty had said, pouring over the papers, looking for anything they might have missed the first time.

"Yes, there's one for you too. If you do end up going, you'll need to know your way around the place, since the last time you were there, you were..." Ty says, wincing and trailing off. Probably remember the state in which he found me.

"Out of it?" I say, giving a nicer way to put that I was unconscious most of the time. Hurt. Tortured. Close to death. Those all seem too harsh, although true, very very true, but still.

"Ugh, yeah," Ty says.

He walks us over to the table and picks a folder up for me. I know I could have it memorized in less than a minute, but I need to get back to my room to start my own plan. I'll go over the folder too, to see if I can help them in anyway but I need to figure out my first move.

"Is it okay if I take this to my room?" I ask.

"Sure, you feeling okay?" he asks.

I force myself to yawn and says, "Just a little tired."

Ty nods, like he knew he'd been right to suggest I stay home. I feel bad for feigning my tiredness and tricking Ty into thinking I really should stay home but for the sake of everyone, this is the best thing. I can feel how right it is for me to do this.

I stand on my tiptoes and kiss his cheek.

"Come up later when you're done down here?" I ask.

"You know I will," he says and winks. I smile and leave the room.

I Jump myself to the dining hall to see if there's any more pizza. The room is empty and all the food is gone.

I wonder if Cooky has anything in the kitchen. I think to myself.

I walk into the kitchen and find Cooky sitting at her little desk in the corner. She looks up and smiles at me.

"Hello dear Emma," she says, smiling warmly at

me.

"Hi Cooky," I say, smiling back, and walking over to her.

"What can I do for you?"

"I was wondering if there is anything to eat?"

"Oh, absolutely," she says jumping up. "What are you in the mood for?"

"Just a sandwich and an apple would be great," I say and as I see her head for the fridge, I hurriedly say, "I can make it, you can go back to what you were doing."

"I don't mind Sweets, it's what I'm here for," she says, smiling widely at me. I reluctantly let her make me a sandwich. She winks at me as she puts a brownie on the side, by the apple. "It's all about balance."

"Thank you," I say, giving her a hug and take the paper plate she's offering me. I wave goodbye as I walk out into the dining hall. I Jump myself to my room, not even thinking if the food would make the Jump but I look down and see it's still nicely laid out on my plate.

Sitting at my little table, I start eating, and making my plan.

I have to go to Montana first. I'll go to Bane and Maisie's and see what I can find out from them. If werewolves were with our Leaders, we have a bigger problem than we thought. I'll have to make my next move after I find out what I can from there.

My plan is flimsy, more of a 'see how it goes' type

of thing. Ty wouldn't like it and honestly, I don't like it much either but what else can I do?

I finish eating while I look through the folder. When I'm done eating, I throw my plate away. I get a drink of water out of my sink before brushing my teeth and take a quick shower. I put on a tank-top and sweats and go lie down on my bed. I'll rest while I wait for Ty.

CHAPTER 14 -
NOT MUCH OF A PLAN

B *right beautiful colors are swirling around me.*
I feel like I'm standing in a kaleidoscope. Every
once in a while a flame will zip around me, being chased
by a blue ball of water. They'll combine and a fountain
of color erupts from it and joins the swirling colors. The
next second, the water is being chased by the fire, and
then another burst of color when they join. I stand here,
staring and watching. Mesmerized by the colors. Then all
of a sudden, a ball of water and fire collide right in front
of my face, causing me to flinch away, squeezing my eyes
shut tight.

When I open my eyes, I'm staring at the ceiling
in my room. That was a bizarre dream. I roll over and
I'm surprised to see Ty sleeping next to me. I don't
remember him coming in last night. I think back to
the last thing I was thinking about and realize that as
soon as my head hit my pillow, I was asleep.

I look at my watch and see it's just after 5:00am.
I've been sleeping for more than 14 hours? I turn my back
to Ty and scoot myself into him. He instantly wraps

his arms around me, even in sleep he wants me close. I can feel he's wearing sweats, but no shirt. His warmth is comforting. I pull his arm up to my chest and hug it to me.

"Mmmmmm," he moans happily, starting to wake up. I grin. He squeezes me closer to him and kisses the back of my head. "Good morning, Em."

"Good morning," I say, turning towards him. I place my hand on the middle of his chest and kiss his lips softly.

"Is it okay that I let myself in last night?" he asks, looking down at me with concern. "I came in and saw you were sleeping. I tried to wake you, but you were sound asleep."

"Absolutely, it's totally fine that you crawled into bed with me," I say, patting his chest. "I quite like waking up to you."

"I really like it too," he says, kissing my forehead.

I'm about to make a move, to maybe get our morning started on an even happier note, but then my stomach growls.

"Breakfast?" he asks.

I'm torn between feeding my stomach and feeding my need to be closer to Ty. My stomach growls even louder. Well, that'll ruin the mood if it continues to do that, so I decide it'll be better to feed my stomach at the moment.

"Yeah, I suppose so," I say.

"I'll Run to my room and change, I'll be back in 5 minutes," he says as he bends down and kisses me. He's about to pull away but my desire has me clutching him to me.

I run my fingers into his hair at the back of his head and pull him back down to me so that he's lying on top of me. Our kiss becomes intense, full of passion.

GUUUUURRRLLLLLLGGGGG

My stomach basically screams at me. How embarrassing.

Ty laughs and slowly pulls away. I see my desire mirrored in his eyes.

"Continue this later?" he asks.

"Bet your butt we will," I say, reluctantly letting him up.

"Bet my butt?" he asks, laughing as he stands and takes a step away from me, reaching for his shirt that he had folded and put on my dresser.

"Yeah, I don't know, it just came out," I say, turning pink. "It basically means, count on it."

"I like it," he says, holding out a hand to help me out of bed.

I stand up and stretch. Ty inhales sharply and then I hear him gulp loudly. I look at him. He's staring at my chest. I look down and see that it's apparently cold in here, or I'm more aroused than I thought. I cover my boobs and turn pink.

"Sorry," I say.

"I'm not," he says with a wide grin. He goes to step closer to me, desire burning bright in his eyes, and trying really hard to keep from looking back down at my chest.

GUUUUURRRLLLLLLGGGGG

I put my hands over my stomach, willing it to shut up.

"I'm starting to feel like you have a guard dog in there," Ty says laughing.

"It's ruining all my fun," I say.

"We've got plenty of time," Ty says, leaning in and kissing me quickly. "I'll be back."

He disappears out the door before I can say anything. I go into the bathroom and brush my teeth. I brush my hair out and braid it into my signature side braid.

GUUUUURRRLLLLLLGGGGG

"You hush," I say to my stomach. I go out into my room and pull jeans and a black t-shirt out of my drawers, along with socks, a bra, and undies. I get dressed and as I'm tying my shoes, there's a soft knock on my door.

"Coming," I say, I stand and go to the door. As I expected, it's Ty. He has changed and is wearing almost the same thing as me. I smile at him and then notice his hair is wet. "Quick shower?"

"It was necessary," he says, cheeks turning a light pink. I tilt my head at him, wondering why taking a necessary shower would make him embarrassed. Seeing my confusion he says, "It was a cold one."

It takes me a second too long to understand his meaning, but then I do, and I'm trying not to laugh hysterically.

"I'm sorry, you poor guy," I say, patting his arm as I walk out of my door and shutting it behind me. I snort really loud because I'm trying so hard not to laugh.

He grabs me around the waist and pulls me to him. He bends his head down and growls in my ear, "I can see how... remorseful you are."

He kisses my ear and then starts to laugh.

"I really am. I can't imagine how uncomfortable that must be for you, painful even. Us girls have it easy in that respect," I say, taking a step forward as he had started to walk, me still in his arms.

"I don't think you girls get as... excited as we do," Ty says, stepping to the side of me so we can walk easier, and takes my hand.

"I think you'd be surprised. Just because we don't

have anything that's a big 'tell' that we're excited, doesn't mean we don't get just as excited as you men."

"Really?" he asks, looking at me with a big grin.

"Well, yeah," I say. "I mean, I think our real excitement is more singular, has more of an emotional attachment, than you guys', but it can be a pretty powerful feeling."

"What do you mean by 'singular'?"

"I think guys get excited when they see a pretty girl, whether they're wearing provocative clothes or not wearing clothes, no matter who they are or what they are to them," I start to say. We've reached the stairs and start walking down. "A friend, girlfriend, or just a random girl can excite a guy if they're attracted to them. Women, we can look at a nice-looking man and think they look nice, but we don't get really excited, not like men. Usually, it takes more of a connection for a girl to get to the same level as a guy, not always, but usually."

"That just proves my point, women don't get as excited as men," Ty says, hip bumping me.

"I'm not explaining it right," I say, laughing. "We get just as excited, but it's saved for special guys, not free for everyone."

"I think I understand," Ty says. "You're saying women can look at a good-looking guy and appreciate how he looks but not have sexual feelings for him. But men, if they find a woman attractive, they instantly are aroused?"

"Yeah, that's pretty much it," I say. "And just because a man finds a woman attractive or is aroused, doesn't mean he wants to have sex with her. His body is just reacting and showing his attraction to her."

"Give me an example because I feel like you're making us men seem like horny dogs," he smiles down at me, letting me know he's not offended.

"No, I don't mean that at all. It's just the way our bodies were made. I'm not explaining it right," I say. I do however have an example I can give him.

"Give me an example then," he urges.

"You and Alysa," I say, looking at him. His face falls. I got him.

"Oh..." he thinks for a minute and then he shakes his head. "I guess you're right. I can't deny she's not attractive, but I can say for certain I never wanted to have sex with her."

"It's not a bad thing," I say, nudging him as we walk into the dining hall. "One of our genders had to be easily ready to go or our species would never have survived."

"It's biology and primal," he laughs.

"Exactly," I say, laughing with him. "What a weird conversation to have. I didn't mean to make it so serious."

"I don't mind," Ty says, reaching for trays for the both of us. "Having weird conversations is the best way to get to know each other better."

"Agreed," I say, smiling as I pile some gravy on to my biscuits. I scoop some scrambled eggs and put them next to them. Cooky has a yummy looking berry mixture so I scoop some of that onto my plate as well.

Ty steers us to our table and we sit. I look around, the dining hall is still pretty empty, it's not even 6:00am yet. We eat in silence for a few minutes and watch as more people come in. I love that Ty and I can have weird, serious, conversations but can also sit in amiable silence.

I glance up and see Libby and Max walking in. She waves at us. Max says something to her, and she nods. She leaves him at the food table and walks over to us.

"Hi guys," she says, smiling widely at us.

"Hey, Sis," Ty says, nodding at her.

"Hi," I say, smiling back.

Libby looks at Ty and then at me, and then back to Ty. She raises her eyebrows at him.

"What?" Ty asks in confusion.

"I've gone to your room the last couple of nights to talk to you, but you haven't been there. It had been pretty late when I went and waited longer each night," Libby says pointedly. She looks at me and winks, she's going to give her brother a hard time. "Have you been sleeping over at one of my best friend's place?"

Ty had just taken a drink of juice and it sprays everywhere. I hand him a napkin and he wipes his face and then the table. He glares at Libby.

"What if I have?" he says. "We're both adults, Mom."

Libby rolls her eyes at the mom comment.

"So should I just come to Emma's room from now on if I need to talk to you," she asks.

"Mine or hers," Ty says matter-of-factly. "What did you need to talk to me about?"

"Do you know when Mom and Dad are going to be coming back?" she asks.

"No, why?" Ty says.

"Just wondering," Libby says, looking away and towards Max. He looks like he's about to dump one of the trays. "Oh, I better go help him."

Charlie and Shae come in soon after, waving good morning before heading to get food. Clay and Malory, followed by Alysa walk in next.

"Morning," Shae says as she gets to the table, sitting next to Libby, who had sat down next to me. Max sits across the table from us.

"Morning," Ty and I say at the same time.

"Hey, Boss-man," Charlie says, sitting next to Max. "Mrs. Boss-man."

Ty shakes his head but doesn't say anything.

Malory and Alysa sit at the end of the table, still a part of our group but still their own little click. Clay sits next to Charlie. Small conversations breakout among everyone. I lean my head on Ty's shoulder and just enjoy everyone's presence. I know soon, I won't be surrounded by my friends and the comfort they bring me.

I'm not sure how much time goes by but after multiple conversation changes, Tate walks in, looking exhausted.

"What's with Tate?" I ask, pointing towards him.

Ty looks at his watch and says, "He was on Zack duty last night. His shift just ended, it's a little after 7 o'clock. Ret just took over."

When Tate gets to the table he yawns and says, "Are we still meeting at 8?"

"Yeah, I just want to go over everything and see if anyone has found anything new," Ty says. "It shouldn't take more than an hour, and then you can go get some rest. How did it go last night?"

"Uneventful," Tate says. "Do you still think he's a danger to us?"

When he says 'us', he looks at me.

Ty clears his throat, seeing I'd caught on to Tate's meaning. "No, I don't think so. I'll go have a talk with him and if he agrees, I'll allow him out of his room with an escort."

"I'll do it," Tally says, walking up to the table.

"You'd rather stay here and babysit an Inepti than go out on an assignment?" Tate asks in surprise.

"As much as I love you boys, I'd like to have some time with the girls. Plus, someone must be assigned to Zack, might as well be me," Tally says, biting into a huge strawberry.

"I'll assign Chaton and Brock too. You guys can choose which eight hour shift you want," Ty says.

"I'll take the second shift, 4pm-midnight," Tally says eagerly.

"Sounds good. I'll see if Chaton can take the first shift. I need Ret in on the meeting this morning. I'll go up and have a talk with Zack and explain the rules, and what's expected of him. Hurry down when you've finished eating," Ty says to the guys.

"I'm going to go out on the grounds and look over the folder again, I think I might have seen something when I went through it last night," I say.

He nods, stands, and kisses me on the top of the head and leaves, taking our empty trays with him. I smile after him like a lovesick puppy dog.

"You two make a good couple," Tally says. "You've brought a side out of him I've never seen before."

"Really? How so?" I ask. But before she can answer, Shae falls out of her chair.

"Shae?!" we all exclaim. Charlie is kneeling beside her in a second.

Libby squeezes between Alysa and Malory.

"Shae?" Libby says tentatively. "Can you hear me?"

"Vision," Shae says through gritted teeth.

"I'll take her to her room," Charlie says. He lifts her up easily in his massive arms and Runs from the room.

"Two in a short amount of time," Alysa says, looking worried. "I don't think that's ever happened."

"There's a lot about to happen, I can feel it," Libby says. She looks at me. "I'll go be with Shae. You go do your studying. She won't be able to tell us anything for a little while and if she does, I'll call you."

"Are you sure?" concern soaked in my question.

"Yes, definitely," Libby pats my arm and then Runs from the room too.

I stand, waving goodbye to everyone, and walk to the stairs. I walk myself up to my room and grab the folder. I make my way back downstairs and through the foyer. When I open the door, I'm greeted by sunlight, and fresh air. I walk out and to the right, there's a big tree in the middle of inviting green grass. I go over to it and put my back against it and open the folder.

My mind doesn't see the words on the page. I'm thinking about reason's Doc and Meredith would be involved with what happened at my house and Zack's. Bill, he could have gone in undercover. I just don't know what to think. I can't believe they'd be willing participants in murdering innocent people. My brain rejects the thought that they did it. Zack described them perfectly but what if there are people that look similar.

I look around the grounds and watch as people practice hand to hand combat. They all look similar but have their own unique attributes. It's possible that the three people Zack saw weren't our Leader's at all, but our minds instantly put their faces to the people.

"Hey!" I hear someone yell. "Where's your escort?"

I look up and see one of the guys that was teaching combat moves to a couple girls, jogging after... Zack?

He's smiling and jogging towards me.

"Zack?" I ask, stunned. "What are you doing out here?"

"I came to find you," he says, smiling. I'm too stunned to stand. He reaches me and plops down beside me, lying on his side. Smiling like he doesn't have a care in the world.

"Oh Miss Emma, I didn't see you out here," the combat instructor says, coming to stop in front of me. He salutes, and as he does so, Zack looks from him to me. I reciprocate the gesture. "Shall I return him to his room?"

"No, it's okay. I'm sure his escort will be out shortly," I say, smiling up at the big man.

"Yes, ma'am," he says. He looks at Zack and then back at me and adds, "I'll just be over here continuing with the lesson. Holler if you need me, my name is Finn."

"Thanks, Finn," I say, smiling to reassure him I'll be fine.

"So, what chya doin'?" Zack asks nonchalantly.

"Studying," I say curtly. "What are you doing away from your room and escort?"

"Oh, Ty said I could venture out," Zack says.

"Mmm, I don't think he meant for you to do it alone."

"It's not my fault that big oaf of a man fell asleep," Zack says, shrugging. "I wanted to get out of my room and see you. You weren't answering my texts or calls."

"Chaton fell asleep?" I ask skeptically. "And I don't use my phone while I'm home."

"Is that his name?" he asks, picking at a blade of grass. "I've had so many guards, I've lost track of their names."

"Zack, this isn't showing Ty you can be trusted," I say as I shut my folder. "The first chance you get, you sneak away."

"What should I have done?" he asks. I can tell he's playing dumb.

"You should have waited until Chaton woke up."

"You're right, I should have but, I'm here now," he smiles cockily at me. "So, what are you doing out here by yourself?"

"Like I said, studying."

"What're you studying for?"

"A mission."

"You can't go on a mission!" he exclaims, anger crossing his face.

"Excuse me?" I say indignantly, my eyebrows

shooting up.

"I'm sorry, it's just..." he takes a breath. "I feel protective over you."

"Well, don't. I can take care of myself," I say, annoyed at his reaction.

"I'm sure you can," he says, his tone lightening. "Can I help you?"

"No," I say.

"Does it have to do with my sister?"

"It could."

"Then I want to help."

"No, you're an..." I'm about to call him an Inepti but he wouldn't know what that is and I don't want to... well, can't... explain it to him. So, I change it to what he will understand, "You're a civilian."

"I can fight. I've been starting to fight MMA," he says, flexing.

"That's all well and good but the answer is still no."

"Come on, Emma," he says, reaching over but before he can touch me, I stand.

"I think it's time you go back to your room," I say. I wave Finn over, he stopped his instruction again, as soon as he saw me stand up. He runs over quickly.

"Can I help you, Miss Emma?" Finn asks, looking at me and down at Zack, who is getting up off the grass slowly.

"Please take Zack back to his room," I instruct.

"No need for that, my escort is lumbering out here," Zack says, pointing towards the front steps. Sure enough, Chaton is walking out in a pissed off manner.

"There you are you fucking weasel," Chaton says as he gets to us. "Excuse my language Miss Emma, but he pretended he needed to go to the bathroom when I was showing him the main floor. He must have snuck out a window. I searched the entire floor and went back to his room, hoping he'd gone back up. But when I started asking people I passed, they said they saw him heading outside."

"You didn't fall asleep?" I ask him.

"What? Absolutely not," he says, looking at Zack like he would like to knock his head off.

"You lied to me?" I ask Zack pointedly.

"It was a white lie. No harm, no foul," he says shrugging and trying to smile what I think is a smile he uses when he's trying to get out of trouble.

"Zack, to me, a lie is a lie, no matter how big or small it is," I say, shaking my head.

"I'm sorry," he says like a little kid.

Rolling my eyes and turning to Chaton, I say, "Take him to his room, his adventuring privileges have been revoked."

"What?" Zack asks in shocked horror. "You can't do that."

"She just did," Finn says.

"Please, Emma, I won't lie again. Honest, I knew that if I told you I snuck away, you'd make me go right back inside. Can't you understand how much I wanted to be out?" Zack pleads, his tone changing once again.

"Yes, Zack, I do understand that. And you had that freedom, but with an escort. Chaton was showing you what we have, or had, to offer you but you chose to take it upon yourself to do what you wanted. That doesn't show me you can be trusted, to follow the rules. Chaton, please take him back to his room. Finn, would you mind accompanying them?"

"Two now?" Zack says, throwing his hands up in the air.

"Actions speak louder than words," I say, sitting back down by the tree. "Show me and the others that you can be trusted, and you'll get a little more leeway back."

Shaking his head, Zack lets Finn and Chaton escort him back to his room. He looks back a couple times before they disappear through the front doors. I put my head back and close my eyes.

"Emma?" I hear someone calling my name. I open my eyes and see Ty standing in front of me. "Nice nap?"

"I guess so. I hadn't realized I'd fallen asleep," I say. I look at my watch and my eyes go wide. "Two hours ago."

"So, maybe it would be a good idea for you to stay

home?" Ty suggests, sitting down beside me.

I fake being reluctant to respond, he has no idea I have other plans.

"Yeah, I guess it'd be better if I didn't go with you guys," I say. It's not a lie, it's actually very true. Feeling slightly hypocritical after scolding Zack about lying but I tell myself I'm not lying. *But isn't holding out the truth, still a type of lie?*

Before I can mentally get into it with myself, Ty interrupts my internal argument.

"Did you find anything in there?" Ty asks, pointing at the folder that had slid to the grass while I slept. I pick it up and open it to a page I remember seeing something.

"Actually, I think so," I show him the page. "Does this look like a strange place to have a storm cellar?"

In the middle of their building, which is the shape of a square with a lawn in the middle, there is what looks like a door that leads down into the ground, like a storm cellar.

"I don't remember seeing this picture the first time we went," he says, pulling the paper closer to himself. "We'll have to check that out when we go. Anything else?"

"No, that's all that I could see that looked out of the ordinary in a place that doesn't have storms strong enough to warrant underground safety or whatever it might be."

"Good find, thanks Emma," he says.

I smile over at him and rest my head on his shoulder.

"What time do you guys leave tomorrow?" I ask.

"Early. We want to get into position before daylight hits the Rifts hideout," Ty says, putting his right arm across my legs, tucking his hand under my right calf. "So, we'll leave well before the sun is up."

"Have you thought about Montana and going to visit with Bane and Maisie?" I ask as nonchalantly as I can.

"I have and we need to talk to Tate and Tally about that," he says, yawning.

"Why them?"

"They've been up there before, so they'll know where to go."

"Is there anywhere they haven't been?" I ask with quiet laughter.

"Down to visit the Merfians I'd guess," Ty laughs too.

I laugh out loud and say, "Yeah, I guess that place would be hard to go for an extended amount of time."

"They've gone out to talk with them, but the Merking and Merqueen came up to the surface for the visit."

"Tate and Tally have travelled a lot, haven't they?"

"Yeah, one of the benefits of being based in Europe, I guess."

"Do you wish you could have travelled more?" I ask, leaning away to get a good look up at him.

"Sometimes but we've been so busy here, I don't feel like I've had a free moment to feel like I've missed out," Ty says honestly. "Being in one place and being able to train, has gotten me to where I am today. There aren't a lot of Guardians that could be where my men and I are physically and being trained for combat, at our younger age. I'm Bill's second because I'm more advanced and skilled than all of the senior Guardians. My Unit and the second Unit train in a way that would make some of the senior Guardians and their Units, faint. I'm not trying to sound egotistical or anything, we just train to be at the top, to be here when the call comes in for action. That call came when Bill, Doc, and Meredith went missing, or presumably went missing. I still can't believe they'd willingly do what Zack said they did."

"I can't believe it either. Hopefully we'll have some answers by the end of next week. And speaking of Zack," I start to say. Ty leans away to look down at me. "Have you talked to Finn or Chaton?"

"No, why?" he asks curiously.

"Zack snuck away from Chaton on their Estate tour and came looking for me. Zack found me out here and lied about sneaking away. When Chaton finally caught up to him and told me what really happened, I was pissed. I don't like being lied to," my voice faulters a little at the word lie. I hate being lied to but here I am about to lie to Ty and my friends. *Again, hypocrite much? Ugh, hopefully I can sneak out of here without having to lie.* "I revoked his privileges to wander. He wasn't happy."

"What an idiot," Ty says. He exhales and adds, "I'll tell Tally and Brock to be extra vigilant, to do what they need to, to stay awake."

"His impatience and lying has put him back where he was at when he first got here," I sigh. "If he'd just stayed with Chaton, he would still have a little more freedom."

"You are a hard one to stay away from," Ty says, bending down and kissing me sweetly on the lips.

"Ty?" we turn at Ty's name being called from the front steps of the Estate. It's Charlie.

"What's up?" Ty asks.

"We're ready for you," Charlie says. He nods in my direction, a quick hello. He must be in battle ready mode. Ty nods back at him. Charlie turns and Runs back inside.

"You coming back inside?" Ty asks. "You can join the meeting, even if you aren't going with us."

"No, thank you. I think I'll sit out here a little longer. It's so nice to be outside," I say, leaning my head back against the tree.

"Okay, I'll find you once our meeting is over," Ty says.

"Sounds good," I say.

Ty leans in and kisses me before he stands up and Runs away.

I lean my head back and close my eyes. And rethink my plan. I need it to be better planned out rather than the 'fly by the seat of my pants' idea I have right now.

So, what is the first thing I need to do? After just talking to Ty, maybe talking to Tally can give me some information I don't have. Like where Bane and Maisie's homebase is in Montana. That's a good starting point. I'll go to the Werewolves first and talk to them. If they don't have any idea what I'm talking about or haven't seen our Leader's, then I'll decide on who to go to next. Maybe they'll be able to point me in the right direction.

There isn't a whole lot I can plan after that, not knowing what Bane and Maisie might know, or not know. That's as planned out as I can get, I suppose. I stand up and wipe my backside off. Another thing I can do, is get a backpack for supplies. I don't know what all to expect from the other Regions, so I probably need to pack some water and at least snacks, to get me by if I need them.

I open my eyes, stand up, and start to walk around the Estate, looking for The Closet and Beth. It doesn't take me long once I get by the gym. Just like Alysa said.

I walk up and it has an actual door this time. The

cottage is super cute on the outside. I try the handle and it turns, opening the door slightly. I push it open and walk inside.

"Hello?" I call.

"Back here, hun," Beth's voice says from the back of the room.

"Hi Beth, it's me Emma," I say. "I was wondering if you---"

Before I can finish, she interrupts and says, "A backpack?"

I laugh. She always knows what you need before you can tell her.

"Yes, ma'am," I say.

"I have this one right here," she says, walking out from behind the counter. She walks towards one single black backpack sitting on top of a shelf.

"How do you know things like this?" I ask, concerned now. I hope she can't See what I need it for, I'm sure she'd tell Ty if she did.

"It's just a Talent I have," and as if she can Read my mind, she adds, "I don't know the why or when something is needed. I just get a glimpse of it and I know I need to get it as soon as possible. This backpack has been with me for about six months."

"What?" I exclaim. "That's well before I even came to be with you guys."

"Like I said, I don't know the why or when. I just looked for a backpack when the image came to me."

"That's interesting," I say.

"It's something," Beth says, laughing, as she walks back behind the counter, holding the backpack.

"Well, I'll take it," I say.

Beth types something into her computer and then hands me the backpack.

"You're all set," she says.

"Thank you," I say. "Oh, how's my balance?"

"You are pretty well set for some time," she says, looking at the screen.

"Really?" I ask. "I feel like all I do is sleep."

"You've done more than that," Beth says. "Don't you worry."

I'm about to say something else but I hear the front door open and a bunch of girl voices reach us.

"Thanks again, Beth," I say, nodding at her as she walks around the counter.

She puts her hand on my back and walks with me for a few steps before she says, "You are most welcome, Miss Emma."

She turns and walks towards the girls, looking at the wall of swimsuits.

Once I get outside, I Jump myself to my room. I put my folder on my table and put my backpack in my closet, towards the back right corner. Now to get supplies.

I walk down to the dining hall and into the kitchen. Cooky is sitting at her desk again. She turns when she hears me come in.

"Hi Sweets," she says, beaming.

"Hi, Cooky," I say, returning an equally large smile.

"What can I do for you?" she asks.

"I was wondering if I could take some bottled water and snack type stuff up to my room. With all the sleeping I've been doing, I shouldn't be as hungry as I am, but I have been starving. I'd hate to bother you every time I need something or make a mess trying to find something in the wee hours of the morning."

"Oh my dear, it wouldn't be a bother at all but I can get you set up. What are you thinking?" she asks, standing up and going to one of her pantries.

"Maybe some granola bars, packaged crackers... Umm, some muffins I can wrap up or put in baggies. Some apples. Umm...Do we have any jerky or pepperoni sticks?"

"We've got it all, Sweets," she says. I follow her into the pantry, and she starts handing me multiples of things. My pile starts to get too much for my arms, so Cooky grabs an empty box lying on the floor. "Here, throw all that in here and then we'll add the rest to it."

When we've finished, the box is full of everything I had asked about. Cooky had even used plastic wrap to wrap some muffins for me.

"Thank you so much, Cooky, this is great," I say.

"If you need more, don't you worry about coming

in and help yourself, just don't tell anyone I'm letting you have free rein, I'd hate for people to think it's a free for all in here," she winks at me.

"I really do appreciate you doing this for me," I say, sincerely.

"Emma, darling, you have done so much for us, it's the least I can do," Cooky says, cupping my face in her hand. "Now, what else did you need?"

"Water?" I ask.

"Right," Cooky says. She grabs a plastic bag and starts putting water bottle after water bottle in it. When it looks like it's as full as it can get without ripping, she hands the bag to me. "You got it?"

After juggling the box and looping the bag's handles onto my arm, I finally feel like it's all secure.

"Got it," I say, smiling warmly at her.

"Okay, well if you need anything else, you just come and get it," she says. "Even if I'm not here."

"Thank you," I say once more. I sure hope she doesn't feel like I tricked or betrayed her when she finds out when I've left, that these snacks weren't necessarily meant for my midnight snacking.

I step out into the dining hall and see there aren't very many people in here. The few that are, aren't paying any attention to me, so I Jump myself to my room. I'm just putting my goods into the closet when there's a knock at my door.

CHAPTER 15 -
THREE LITTLE WORDS

I open my door and Ty is standing there, looking godlike as usual. But this time, he's in just shorts. Swim trunks, actually. I tilt my head to the side and look at him questioningly.

"I was wondering if you'd like to go for a swim?" Ty asks.

"Oh," I say in surprise. "Yeah, sure!"

"Get changed, I'll wait out here," he says with a smile.

I hurry and change into my swimsuit but put some shorts and a tank top over the top of it. I grab my phone and put it in my back pocket. As I slip my sandals on, I open my door, and see he's leaning against the wall across from my room. When he looks up, he pushes off the wall with his upper back, and I see his abs ripple as he does it. Catching myself staring, I pull my eyes up to his face, and smile sheepishly.

"I'm ready," I say.

He smiles back and takes my hand. We walk in

silence for a few minutes. I'm about to break the silence and ask how the meeting went but Ty beats me to it with his own silence breaker.

"Your comment about being outside made me realize, we haven't really done anything fun since we got here," he states. "So, I thought, if you were up for it, we should go for a swim."

"I'm definitely up for it," I say. I love swimming. Thinking about our last encounter at the beach, has me asking, "Pool or ocean?"

"Pool for now. I don't think I could handle watching you swim with sharks again," he says. "Even though it's what started to break the Love Spell Alysa put on me, I'm still traumatized by the thought of you and a shark being that close to each other."

"She was fine," I say.

"Only because you were able to talk to her," he says, laughing.

"Maybe," I say, not wanting to think about what might have happened had she caught a different Demi out there.

We walk in silence as we walk through the halls. Every girl we pass, eyes Ty's upper body, and then they look away quickly when they see me noticing their ogling.

"These poor girls," I say, after we've passed another group of looky-loo's.

"What about them?" he asks, glancing behind us.

"You haven't noticed them staring at you?"

"Have they?"

"We've passed at least 15 girls and you haven't noticed any of them?"

"No," he says honestly.

"Oh, then I really feel bad for them."

"Why?"

"Because you're a god amongst Demi-gods."

"All the guys look like me," he says casually.

"No, they don't," I state.

"What? Yes, they do. Just like all the girls look the same," he says.

"You guys are similar, just like the girls are similar, but there are slight differences," I say, looking up at him. "You really can't see the differences?"

"No," he says uncertainly. "There's differences?"

"Yes," I laugh out. "You are slightly more defined than any of you friends. Not only taller but more muscular. Your skin is a little bit smoother looking as well. And the girls? Some have a little bit bigger... assets than others. Not enough to cause a huge uproar but enough that I can tell a difference."

"You're kidding," Ty says. "No way."

"Maybe I notice it because I'm new," I say. "Or maybe I notice it because I grew up noticing the differences in everyone around me."

Ty looks down at me and says, "You know why I don't notice the differences?"

"Why?"

"Because no one, no other woman here, holds a candle to you. You are the most captivatingly beautiful creature I've ever met," he says. He stops suddenly, and pulls me to him, wrapping his left arm around my back, pulling me to him. He puts his right hand behind my head and bringing his face down to mine. Our kiss is instantly passionate.

We part after a good long minute of kissing, both of us breathless.

"I just feel bad for the girls that won't ever get to call you theirs," I say, taking a deep breath, to calm myself down.

"I will always be yours, Emma, just yours," he says, kissing me softly on the nose. Before I can respond, he takes my hand, and we start walking again. My heart swells with so much love for this man that the thought of what I'm going to do, feeling like I'm deceiving him, makes me feel like crying.

I'm about to spill my guts out of shame and guilt, when I feel my phone buzz from my back pocket. I reach behind me and see a new text from Shae.

Shae: *Don't. You are doing the right thing. 11:36pm Sunday*

I close the phone and make a mental note to ask her if she saw me telling him and what the outcome was when I did.

"Everything okay?" Ty asks. He must have felt me tense.

"Just thinking," I say. *Not a lie.*

"About?" he asks.

"Everything," I sigh. *Still not a lie.*

"You know everything will work out in the end, right?"

"I hope so," *If you only knew what I had planned, but apparently I'm not supposed to tell you.*

We get to the gym and Ty holds the door open for me. We walk through and head to the pool. There are a few people doing laps when we walk in. We grab a couple towels from the shelf by the door and walk over to the other side of the room and put our stuff on some empty chairs.

Before I can say something that'll give away what I have planned for when he leaves, I dive in, and go down to the bottom of the pool. I stay there for a minute, trying to get my mind right. I look up and see Ty's wobbly reflection above the water. I see him dive in a second later. I push off the bottom and swim to him, he looks at me with concern. I kiss him on the lips and then swim to the surface.

When my head is above the water, I see that we're the only ones in the pool. I hadn't noticed the other people getting out. Ty is beside me in another second.

"You okay?" he asks.

"Yeah, why?" I counter ask.

"You stayed down there for quite a while. When you didn't come up right away, I gave you some space for a minute. But then it felt weird, just staring at you through the water. Is something bothering you?"

"No, well yes, but no. I'm just thinking about everything," I say. I go with something that isn't a lie. "I can't wrap my head around Meredith, Doc, and Bill leaving us to join the Rifts. I can't imagine them being a part of attacking innocent people. I can't think of any reason they would do that except for that they weren't in their right minds and if they weren't, then we have a big problem. If the Rifts can catch them, they can catch any of us."

"Okay," Ty says. "Come over here."

We swim down to the shallow part of the pool, at least where Ty can touch, and off to the side, and he pulls me towards him.

"Take a breath and try to calm down," Ty says. "We will figure this out. I agree with you. If, and I do mean if, our Leaders had anything to do with what happened at your old house and attacking Zack's family, there is a good explanation. As far as the Rifts, they can only catch you if your guard is down. You have so many Talents, Emma, you are so powerful, they'll have a hard time catching you again. We all believe in you. It's time you start believing in yourself as well."

Ty's right. Everyone in the World could believe in me but it doesn't matter unless I believe in myself. In the same sense, if I believe in myself and everyone else doubts me, it doesn't matter because my opinion about myself is all that matters. My inner strength is what makes me strong, not what everyone else believes to be true.

"You're right, I do. I just don't know how to do it without doubt creeping in or the thought of feeling like I'm being self-centered taking hold."

"Well for one, Vanessa raised you to feel self-conscious and to not believe you're deserving of anything good. She couldn't have you going out and making friends and not relying on her for everything. So, you need to retrain your brain and block out her voice, that has become your inner voice when it comes to believing in yourself."

"You are so right," I say.

"Although, the plus side, if there is one, to the way she raised you, is that you are the most selfless, kind, caring, and sweet person, we, and I do mean all of us, have ever met. You wouldn't be if she hadn't treated you the way she had. So, on that note, she made you her biggest threat."

"If I think of my up bringing like that, I can feel a different way about it. Do you think I would have been any different had my actual parents raised me?"

"I think you'd be a closer version of the you that you are now but it's hard to say. We are all made from nature, meaning how we resemble our parents and family. But, we also have a lot of nurture in our make-up, as in, how we were raised. Not knowing your parents and their family, except your aunt and uncle, which, they could be the complete opposites. Look at Shae and Alysa, for that comparison. My point, we can't know how you would have turned out had your parents raised you. It will drive you crazy trying to figure it out, all 'what if's'. So, just accept how incredible you are and trust your instincts, your inner voice, not Vanessa's."

"Thank you, Ty," I say, smiling. And then add, smile fading, "But, I'm more worried about you. About our friends and everyone else, too."

"Of course you are," Ty says, kissing my forehead. "That's what I love most about you. Your selflessness. But you have to remember we train for this, whatever happened to Bill, Doc, and Meredith, believe that it happened in either a complete and utter surprise or they put up one hell of a fight."

I'm still stunned by Ty's use of the word 'love'. He still didn't come right out and tell me he loves me but it was pretty dang close. But I pull my thoughts away from that and look at him seriously.

"Ty, I know what the Rifts are capable of doing.

I wouldn't wish it on anyone. Just thinking of them getting their hands on you," I take a deep breath. "I'd tear this world a part to find you and then tear them limb from limb for even thinking of hurting you."

"Easy, Em," Ty says, but he's smiling.

"I'm serious," I say, stubbornly.

"I know you are, and I love that about you," he says.

"There's that word again," I say. And then I slap a hand over my mouth. I didn't mean to say it out loud.

"What word?" Ty asks. I just shake my head, hand still over my mouth. Ty repeats his question, "What word?"

"Nothing. Never mind," I say, my face growing hot. I don't know why I'm embarrassed. He's the one who has been saying it, well not IT but using the word.

Ty thinks for a minute and says, "Love?"

I feel my eyes go big and feel my head nodding without me making a conscience decision to do so.

"Have I not told you I love you?" Ty asks.

My eyes go even wider. I shake my head, and squeak out, "No."

"I could have sworn I said it out loud. Hmmm, I must have always been thinking it," he says, nonchalantly. He looks me in the eyes and says, very sweetly but seriously, "Emma, I love you. With everything that I am, I love you."

My heart literally stops and I realize I've stopped

breathing as well. As I take a slow breath in, and my heart starts beating again, I say, "I love you too, Ty. More than I ever thought possible."

Ty pulls me to him and we're kissing. This kiss feels different though. It's not urgent. It feels meaningful and deeper than any kiss we've shared. I wrap my legs around Ty's waist, and he presses me up against the pool wall.

Our kiss might have started off feeling different, but it turns to an all too familiar fiercely passionate kiss. I ran my hands down from the back of Ty's head and down to his neck, down to his shoulders, and finally to his biceps. I wrap my hands around the back of his arm and then slide my hands on to his back and then back up to his neck, where I try to pull him closer.

Ty's hands have been on my lower back, and he slowly moves one hand to my side, and up my rib cage, up to my neck, trying to pull me closer too. He moves his other hand out and does the same movement until his hand is behind my upper back, pressing me into his chest. He uses his hips to hold me to the pool wall.

I suddenly feel something... pressing against my rear. I gasp and pull away. I look at Ty and see he's blushing. He pulls his hips away just a little and the feeling goes away, but I slid down the wall a little. His hands instantly go to my ass to keep me from completely falling into the pool. I gasp again.

"Sorry," he says. He lifts me up and puts me on

the edge of the pool. He steps beside me and puts his forehead on my knee. I can feel his skin is warm.

"It's okay. Don't apologize," I say, running my fingers through his wet hair. I'm trying not to laugh. I really do feel bad for him. "Don't be embarrassed."

He just shakes his head. "I can't even go for an innocent swim with my girlfriend without... something popping up and ruining it."

I can't help it anymore, I start laughing hysterically. Ty looks up and shoots me a mock glare.

"You think that was an innocent swim?" I ask. "I'm pretty sure our making out was making the temperature of the pool go up a couple degrees."

Ty shakes his head but then he starts to laugh as well.

"And the... pop up, didn't bother me, it just surprised me is all," I say. "And then you went and put your hands on my ass. Again, it didn't bother me, just caught me by surprise."

"Really?" he asks, surprised.

"Mmmmhmmm," I say, as I keep running my hands through his hair.

"Do you want to get back in? I think I have it under control again," he says.

I slide off the edge and press up against him. He's so much taller than me that I can't even touch the bottom of the pool without my head going under water, so I grab hold of his arms and let myself float.

He dips his upper body down into the water so that we're level, eye to eye, with each other.

"Hi," I say with a smile.

"Hi," Ty says, laughing. But his smile, that stops my heart, spreads across his face and he kisses me sweetly on the nose.

I wrap my arms around his neck and pull myself to him. I kiss him on the cheek, and then down his jawline, onto his neck. I kiss my way up and down, noticing the vein in his neck, so I make a trail down to his collarbone, and then up to his ear. Ty lets out a soft moan.

"You have no idea how good that feels," he groans.

I smile and give his earlobe a quick kiss and kiss my way back to his cheek. He doesn't let me kiss his cheek though, he turns his face and catches my lips with his. And we start our make out session again.

I'm not sure how long we've been like this but I hear the pool room doors open and hear a gasp and then giggles. We break apart and look over and see a bunch of girls standing just inside the pool.

"Sorry, we'll come back later," one of them says.

"No, that's okay," Ty says, he looks down at me. And looks up at the ceiling and nods.

"Yeah, we were just leaving," I say.

"Looked like it," one says, quieter, but still loud enough for us to hear.

Ty helps me out and when I turn as I'm putting

my towel on, and grabbing my clothes and phone, the girls gasp.

"Oh, Miss Emma, we didn't know it was you and..." the girl that spoke first says. She salutes me and then gulps when she sees Ty standing beside me with a towel around his waist. She hurriedly salutes him and says, "Sir."

The other girls do the same. I think the one standing in the back, with the red face, is the girl that had made the 'looked like it' comment.

"No worries," I say, as we walk by. They all avert their eyes to the floor, trying with everything they have not to stare at Ty. I giggle a little.

We step out of the pool doors and Ty pulls me to him.

"Jump us to your room," he says into my ear. He doesn't have to ask me twice. And it's getting to where I don't have to really concentrate on my room anymore. This time, I put us right beside my bed.

Ty tosses his phone onto my nightstand and then rips his towel off, mine as well. I drop my things in my arms into a pile on the floor as he wraps his arms around my waist and flings us to my bed. I'm on top of him for just a second before he rolls us and now I'm under him, with his comforting weight pressing me into my mattress. I can't help but giggle. He's kissing me and then, maybe to get me back for the neck kissing in the pool, he's kissing down my neck, but he doesn't stop at my shoulder. He kisses over my collarbone, across to my other collarbone and up the other side of my neck.

I let out a gasp and he stops at my earlobe. As he kisses it gently, another gasp escapes my lips. He runs his left hand from my shoulder, down my arm, and onto my hip where he squeezes gently.

Time always seems to disappear when Ty and I are like this because it feels like only minutes have passed, when his phone starts to ring. Ty rolls to the side and grabs his phone off the nightstand.

"It's 2 o'clock already?" Ty asks in surprise. He sits up and answers his phone. "Yeah..."-he looks done at me and then sighs- "I'll be right there."

I get up off my bed and go to my dresser and pull out a bra, undies, jeans, and t-shirt.

"I can't believe it's 2 already," I say.

"Me either. I told the guys to meet me at 2 for another meeting. I didn't think I'd lose track of time like that, but I should have known better. Time spent with you seems to go too fast."

I laugh, "I was thinking the same. Go, I'll meet you for lunch, well, I guess dinner."

"Cooky might still have lunch out," Ty says.

"I'll check after I shower."

"Okay. I'll Run to my room and shower real fast. I'll see you later?"

"Yup," I say, kissing him on the cheek.

"I love you," he whispers into my ear.

"I love you, too," I say, kissing him again.

Ty leaves and I head to my bathroom, smiling like crazy and giddy as all get out. I don't think I've ever been this happy in my life.

After I've taken a long shower and calmed myself down, I get dressed, and Run down to the dining hall. Luckily, Cooky does have lunch stuff out still. It smells like tacos. I go and make a couple and sit at the table that has become our groups table.

I've eaten one and starting to eat another when Shae walks in through the doors from the foyer.

"Finally," she says, walking over to me.

"I'm sorry?" I mumble out around the bite I had just taken.

"I've been waiting for you and Ty to come up for air for the last hour and a half."

"Ummm how did you...?" I trail off.

"I don't pick and choose what I See, I just knew what I was seeing was today and that I had to talk to you."

"Well, that's embarrassing," I say, turning bright red.

"I didn't See it all, just you guys kissing and then me down here waiting to talk to you," she says, seriously. I wait a minute to see if she's going to be her usual self and ask about what I'd be embarrassed about, but she doesn't.

"Oh," I say, relieved. "What's up?"

"You got my text?"

"Yes, thank you for that, but what was it about? I mean, obviously not to tell Ty my plan but…"

"If you tell Ty your plan," Shae says, lowering her voice, even though we're the only ones in the dining hall. "He'll attach someone to you so you can't leave."

"He wouldn't?" I ask in disbelief and then think about how protective he is and how me going out on my own, for who knows how long, is his definition of not safe. "Okay, yes he would."

"I can tell what you have to do is important and has to do with what the Big Three told you, so I won't say anything to anyone. Unless, like I said earlier, I See you become in a dangerous situation, or I See the Rifts closing in on you."

"How is it you See so much of me?"

"I've recently realized I'm your Seer."

"My what?" I ask.

"Seer," she states. "Some Elders have them. A Demi with a Psychic Talent, becomes super aware of that Elder and their Visions focus on that one Elder. Not all the Visions, just most of them. I've been keeping track of my Visions, not in detail, just who and what they're about. For the last two months, nine out of ten pertain to you. So as your Seer, I'm obligated to never speak about your Visions other than with you or if I need to send someone to help you. Our Link might have already been started or we connected in a different way when you saved me. All I know is I'm your Seer."

My taco I had been eating is frozen halfway to my mouth, which is hanging open in shock. My senses come back to me, and I put my taco down, and wipe my hands and mouth with a napkin.

"I'm sorry but I'm not..." I start to say but Shae interrupts me.

"Don't say you're not important enough to deserve a Seer because out of everyone in the history of ever, you are the only one who actually does need one. You are about to go out and single handedly save the World."

"No, no I'm not. I'm only bringing everyone together to save us from Vanessa and her followers," I state.

"Same thing"

"No, it's not."

"Emma, what will happen if you don't do what the Big Three told you to do?"

"Vanessa wins"

"It's the end of the World. You doing it saves us all."

"No pressure," I say as I push my plate away, not hungry anymore. "So you won't tell anyone unless I'm in danger?"

"Yup, only if I see you're going to be in danger or

in immediate need of help."

"They won't get mad at you for holding out on them?"

"They understand the Demi and Seer relationship."

"What if they ask you if you know where I went?"

"I'll tell them that you went somewhere that the Big Three instructed. I honestly don't know where you're going first, so I won't be lying. I'll tell them about me being your Seer and I'm keeping an 'eye' on you. They'll have to respect that, even if they don't like it."

I feel better about not putting Shae in the middle of all this, even though neither of us asked for it. Knowing about Seers is fascinating but also a relief that Demi-gods have to respect the relationship the Seer and Demi have with each other.

I sigh, "Okay..."

"I'm going to go, but I wanted to give you this just in case you need some cash along the way," Shae says, as she gives me a huge bundle of cash.

"What in the–" I start to say but Shae cuts me off.

"If you need food or a place to stay, use it. Put it away though, so no one sees it," Shae says. She doesn't continue until I've stuffed it into the pocket of my shorts. "Don't worry about saying goodbye to me or any of the other girls. If you do, they'll think something is off. Just act normal tonight. You can text them once you've gotten to your first destination. Also, the best time to talk to Tally will be while she's on Zack duty tonight."

"How..." I start to ask. I had been thinking about how to say goodbye to the girls without causing suspicion and when to talk to Tally. "Seer stuff?"

Shae taps her temple and winks.

"Oh, and we can try out an idea I've been thinking about recently. While you're out, try to connect with me Mentally. Try when you're relaxed and trying to sleep. I want to see if we can connect that way. I've been thinking about that since you pulled me out of the vision about the guys running into Tate and Tally."

"You think that'll work long distance?"

"Only one way to find out."

"Okay," I say. "I'll try."

"See you Em, be safe," Shae says. She salutes me and then Runs from the dining hall.

"Bye, Shae," I say to the empty space in front of me.

CHAPTER 16 -
WELL IT'S A START

Not hungry anymore, I take my uneaten taco and wrap it up in a napkin. I glance down at my watch and see it's a little after 3 o'clock. Not knowing where Tally is right now. I contemplate on what to do.

I decide to go into the kitchen, but I don't find Cooky. I go into pantry and grab a couple more granola bars and find some dried fruit that will come in handy. I also grab some more water. I leave a note for Cooky, telling her I grabbed a couple more things.

I Jump myself to my room and add the new supplies to my earlier haul. I put the money that Shae gave me into the bottom of the backpack. I'm still not sure what to do before Tally's on duty, so I lay down. But instead of sleep finding me, I get restless. I sit up and look around my room. I walk to my sliding glass door and look outside. It looks like a nice day out, so I decide to go outside to walk around.

I make my way down the hall and the stairs leading to the foyer. I wave and say hi to people who stop and salute me. Once I'm outside, I find Finn finishing up with a group of Demi's.

"Hi, Finn," I say, waving as I get closer.

"Miss Emma," Finn says, saluting me.

"Are you done for the day, or do you have a minute?" I ask.

"I am done for the day, what can I do for you?"

"I'd like to practice a few defensive moves with you if you don't mind. I had just started when we left the Pit."

"Wouldn't you prefer to work with Ty?" Finn asks hesitantly.

"I feel like he holds back with me. I don't need 100% strength right away, but I need more than what I think he allows to spar with me."

"I can understand that, you are a tiny thing," Finn says, then he turns red. "My apologies for the offense."

"I'm not offended. It's the truth. I am smaller than the normal Demi which is why I think people will underestimate me. I'd like to have some self-defense and combat moves down."

"I'm more than happy to help but, excuse me again, don't you have infinite Talents?"

"I don't know about infinite, but I'd like to be prepared for anything. I don't know if my Talents will last forever or for a short time. I'd like to be able to have some hand-to-hand combat training added to my strengths."

Finn thinks for a minute and looks me up and down, "You're right, it would benefit you greatly."

"Thank you," I say.

"With your size, I would guess most Rifts, or anyone wanting to harm or capture you, would see your size as your weakness and try to just over power you. So, I think we should practice a straight on attack from me. I'll adjust as you defend, you adjust as well, and I'll stop if I have any pointers or concerns about a move you should or shouldn't do. Sound good?"

"Perfect," I say smiling. I add, "I have one condition."

"Yes, Ma'am."

"Try to really get me. I don't want a false sense of protection when in reality, you were actually taking it super easy on me."

"No ma'am. I am a combat instructor. I won't let you leave with a false sense of anything. I will start off slow, to see what you can do, and from there, I'll increase my speed and strength."

"Thank you, Finn."

He salutes and then starts walking around me, like a lion starts stalking its prey. I don't let him out of my sight, never turning my back. He lunges at me and I dip, dive, and spin away from him.

"Very good," he says.

We spend the next little while doing this and at one point he lunged and anticipated my move and caught me around my waist. He slammed me to the ground, pinning me. He explained I had started to show signs of what my move was going to be so I needed to work on waiting until the last minute to do it.

After another bit of time, I'm pinning Finn down, after punching him in the stomach. My knee is on his chest and my hands on his biceps. Knowing there's not much I can really do after this, I fling myself up and over his head, in a summersault, front flip type move, and put about ten feet between us.

He's breathing hard and is slow to roll over.

"Very good, Miss Emma," he says, panting.

Our watches chime, I look down and see it's saying it's 5 o'clock already, it's dinner time.

"Wow, more time went by than I thought," I say.

"Let's stop for this evening. And honestly, I think you've got pretty much everything down. Whether Ty, or your other instructor, were taking it easy on you, you handled everything I could think of to throw at you very well. We can keep practicing but I don't think you need instruction, just practice so it comes more naturally."

"Thank you, Finn. I needed to hear that," I don't commit to another time because I don't know when I'll be back. "I'm going to go get cleaned up and head to dinner. See you."

"You are most welcome, Miss Emma," he salutes

me and I return the gesture.

I jog through the grounds and up the front steps. Once I'm in the foyer, I Jump myself to my room.

I take a quick shower and change into another pair of shorts and tank top. I let my hair fall down my back. I make my way down to the dining hall. I find the girls are sitting around our table. The guys must still be in their meeting.

Cooky made spaghetti, garlic bread, and a nice green salad. After my training with Finn, I'm famished. I load up on everything and grab two bottles of water. Walking to the table, I realize this could be my last meal with my friends for who knows how long.

"Hi," I say, a little more choked up than I mean to sound."

"Hey," they say.

Libby looks at me with concern. She tilts her head and says, "You okay?"

I clear my throat and say, "Yeah, something was just in my throat."

Shae looks at me like I need to pull it together.

"You guys been here long?" I ask, looking at their empty plates. I check my watch, it's 5:45PM.

"We got here about 20 minutes ago," Alysa says. "Malory and I were just about to leave."

"Oh okay, have a good night," I say, nodding in their direction.

"Night, Emma," Malory smiles over at me. Alysa waves bye as they get up and take their trays away.

"Tally on Zack duty?" I ask.

"Yeah," Libby says. "Poor thing. I don't know why she volunteered."

"It makes her feel like she's working, even if it's boring," Shae says, shrugging.

"What have you guys been up to today?" I ask, as I take a bite of my food.

"I've been in the Hospital Wing making sure everything's ready in case the guys come home and have an emergency," Libby says as she spins her empty water bottle around in her hands. "Sara has been holding it down pretty good since Doc... went missing. I've been trying to help keep her company as much as I can."

"I've been resting," Shae says. "I've been super tired today."

"Do you think you're going to have another Vision?" Libby asks, leaning in to look into Shae's eyes better.

"Maybe, or it's just from all the ones I've had," she says, glancing at me quickly and then back at Libby. If Libby noticed, she doesn't say anything.

"You should get some rest," Libby says. "Head up to your room and I'll send Charlie up if I see him. I'll come check on you myself in a couple of hours."

"That's not a bad idea," Shae says. I look over at

her and see she's got tears in her eyes.

What's wrong? I ask through our Seer's link.

I'm going to miss you. Shae says and even her voice in her mind sounds sad.

Miss me because I'm going to be gone or because something happens? I ask.

I would tell or show you if I saw something like that. I'm going to miss you because you're going to be gone and I can't tell when you'll be home or when I'll see you again.

I'm going to miss you too. I say, trying to put all the emotion I feel into my mental tone of voice.

Shae stands and says, "Good night, Libby... Emma. See you later, Emma."

"Bye," I say. I want to get up and give her a hug, but I know that would just make Libby suspicious.

I take another bite of my food and push my plate away.

"Not hungry?" Libby asks.

"I had lunch not too long ago," I answer honestly.

"After your training outside I'm surprised you didn't build up a bigger appetite."

I choke on the drink of water I just took and cough out a, "What?"

"I was making my way back from The Closet and saw you outside with Finn."

"Oh," I stammer out.

"What was that about?"

"Oh well, I wanted to get back into doing some

combat training but you know how all the guys are, they take it easy on me. I had remembered seeing Finn outside with a group of Demi's and thought he might be able to instruct me a little and I was right. He didn't take it easy at all. In fact, I might have a couple bruises," I laugh. Then add quickly, "Don't tell Ty. I asked Finn not to take it easy on me. I wanted to see what I could handle."

"That's a good idea," Libby sighs. "It's probably time for Shae and I to get some training under our belts too. It's actually really ridiculous of us to not have had any training yet."

"You should get Alysa and Malory to join you guys. I definitely recommend Finn," I say.

"Thanks, that's good to know. Maybe you can help him with our lessons?"

I take the last bite of my spaghetti, which is a big one, and make a noncommittal sound as I eat.

"What are you doing after you are finished eating?" Libby asks when I've taken a drink of water.

"I think I'm going to go visit Tally. I feel like I haven't had any time to get to know her," I say.

"Oh, that's a great idea. I know you guys will hit it off," Libby says, clapping her hands together excitedly.

"What about you?"

"I'm going to go back into the Hospital Wing for a little bit longer. Everything is set up, but I want to make sure we are absolutely ready for anything Ty and the guys might bring back."

"I hope they find something," I say, sighing.

"Me too," Libby says sadly. "I just can't imagine Meredith, Doc, and Bill deserting us and going to Vanessa's side. Something just doesn't feel right about it."

"I know, I feel the same. I haven't known them as long as you guys have but I never once got a feeling they were anything other than what they said. They had plenty of opportunities to let Vanessa know where you guys were. I can't imagine waiting until they were on a super isolated, secure island, to decide now was the perfect time leave," I say, getting up with my tray. "No, something definitely isn't right about any of this."

"Where are you going?" Libby asks, standing with her tray.

"I'm going to go talk to Tally."

"Have fun," she says.

"Thanks, Lib," I say. I add in my head, *For being my first best friend and showing me what true friendship is all about.*

"See you later," Libby says. She dumps her tray and then waves as she walks in the opposite direction as me.

I dump my plate off and walk up the stairs, taking my time, trying to think of what to say to Tally. *How do I get information without her getting suspicious?*

I make my way up to Ty's floor. I see Tally sitting on the floor, her back to the wall, just to the right of Zack's door.

"Hey," I say, when I get closer to her.

She springs up to her feet and salutes me.

"Emma," she says, startled that I caught her off guard. "Hey, sorry I was just..."

"It's okay," I say, not sure why she's apologizing. "No need to be sorry, I'd be sitting too. In fact, why don't we?"

"Why don't we what?" she asks.

"Sit," I say, pointing down to where she had just been sitting. I put my back to the wall, on the other side of Zack's door, and slide down. It takes Tally a second of thinking and her eyebrows pulling together before she slides back down to sit. "So, how's it going so far?"

"He's been pretty quiet," she says, looking at me confused. "He poked his head out once and saw I was out here. He flirted for a minute, trying to see if I'd take him for a walk, but I told him he'd lost that privilege when he tricked Chanton. He pouted and tried to flirt some more but when he realized he wasn't getting anywhere with me, he shrugged and went back into his room."

I shake my head, "He's something else."

"Can I ask what you're doing here?" Tally asks. "Not to be rude."

"Oh," I say, my turn to be caught off guard. "I just wanted to come and talk with you. I feel like we haven't had a chance to visit since you guys got here. You, Libby, Ty, and Tate are so close, I thought it was time to come have a chat."

"Oh gosh," she looks relieved. "I thought I had done something wrong and was in trouble."

"Why would I be here if you were in trouble?"

"Well, you're Emma... The One," she says.

"That doesn't mean anything, I have no power or authority here," I say.

Tally leans forward, bringing one of her legs up and, and, tilts her head at me. "You have a lot more authority here than you think you do."

"I don't know about that," I say, deflecting because I don't want to get into that right now. "But no, I just wanted to come talk to you. Get to know you better."

"Well, what do you want to know?" Tally asks, looking more relaxed.

"Ty said you and Tate got to travel a lot, how was that?" I ask.

"It was alright," she answers. "Don't get me wrong, I've seen some amazing places, some of the most beautiful places in the World, but traveling so much made it hard to have a real home. We have a house in the U.K., just outside of London, but it's not a home. We aren't home for more than a week before we have new orders and are sent out again."

"How do you not have an accent?"

"Our parents were born and raised in the U.S. and we were born here. I don't think we stayed in a place long enough to pick up any accents. When we were younger, we'd travel with our parents and would be left at the headquarters if they needed to go out to do recon. We learned how to speak all the languages at a young age which is why I think the Elders wanted us out there, traveling and not have a real homebase."

"That's impressive, how many languages can you speak?" I ask.

"All 23 of the main ones," she answers.

"Is that another Talent that you guys have?" I ask, shocked.

"No, just a product of our upbringing."

"Wow, I'm impressed. No wonder Naomi likes to send you guys out so much. Where's your favorite place to visit?"

"The U.S. It's more home than anywhere else and I really do miss Libby and Ty. We don't always get to come visit when we are sent here but we always contact Ty and Libby to let them know we're 'here'," she says while putting air quotes around the word here.

"Ty did mention that you went up to Montana and got to visit Bane and Maisie. How was that?" I ask, finally seeing an opening to get some information without giving too much away and making Tally suspicious.

"It was pretty cool. Bane and Maisie are probably my favorite Leaders out of them all. Their homebase in Montana is beautiful. If an Inepti were to stumble across it, it would look like a lodge resort. It's right up next to a mountain, deep in the forest, so an Inepti actually coming across it, is highly unlikely."

"Oh, that sounds wonderful. Do you mind...?" I start to ask. I don't feel right invading her mind and taking the picture of the place she's talking about. I think asking is going to make her super suspicious though.

"Do I mind what?" she asks.

Thinking fast of an excuse that isn't a lie, I say, "This is going to sound crazy, but having been raised by Vanessa, I never got to go anywhere other than school, home, and the pool on occasion. I was wondering if you'd mind letting me see their place through your mind?"

Tally looks at me for a second and then smiles, "Sure. How do I do that?"

"Just think of their place, and I'll use my Telepathy to look inside your mind to see it."

"So, all I have to do is think about their place?"

"Yup," I say.

"You won't see anything else?" she asks, looking at me shyly.

"Not unless you're thinking of it as well as

thinking of their homebase," I say, now thinking she's hiding something too.

"Okay," she says. "You could have just looked while I was talking about it?"

"I feel like that would have been invading your privacy and I never want to use my Talents to the point of hurting someone."

Tally looks at me and her eyes soften just a little, "You might have been raised by Vanessa but you are definitely nothing like her."

"Thank the gods for that," I laugh.

"Okay, so I'm just going to close my eyes and think of their place," I watch as she closes her eyes. A second later, she says, "Okay, got it."

I close my eyes too and think about stepping into Tally's mind. When I do, I see a huge mountain in front of me. Trees as far as my eyes can see. I turn around and see a huge cabin in front me. Tally was right, it looks more like a lodge resort than a cozy little cabin in the forest. I turn around again and try to see as much detail as I can.

I notice there are quite a few smaller cabin's spread out around the large one. A paved road leads away from the lodge. I take a couple steps to the left and see a four-car garage. I walk the other way and see where the trees have been cleared away and see a landing pad for a helicopter. Tally must not be thinking of anyone being there because I don't see anyone walking around.

It's a start, I think to myself. *I know for sure where I'll be starting my journey.* Just as I'm about to step out of her mind, the scene changes and all I see is Ret's face.

"Shit," I hear Tally say from far away.

I open my eyes and see Tally staring at me in horror. I curl my lips around my teeth and hold it in a tight line, trying not to smile.

"Did you see?" she asks.

"Bane and Maisie's place?" I ask, playing dumb. "Yup."

"That's all?"

"Well…" I say, smiling at her. She puts her face in her hands and I can see it turning red, all the way up to her ears. "I can pretend that I didn't see that last part."

"Oh gods," Tally says now. She pulls her knees up to her and puts her face to them, wrapping her arms around her legs.

"It's okay, Tally," I say, reaching over and patting her arm. "Do you like Ret?"

She shakes her head for a second, stops, and then nods.

"Yes," she muffles out.

I laugh. I reach over and try to pull her arms away. "Don't be embarrassed. He's a good-looking man."

"It's not just that he's good-looking," she finally lifts her head. "He's funny, kind, and an amazing fighter. I was watching him train when we first got here and I was blown away."

"So, you've talked to him?"

"Yes..."

"And..."

"I think he's my Anima Gemella," she groans out.

I clap my hands together, "Really?"

"Yes," she sighs and then looks at me with huge eyes. "You can't say anything to anyone. He and I just started talking. In fact, he's supposed to come up at 7 to hangout."

We look at our watches and I see that it's 6:45pm.

"I'll go then," I say standing up. But before I can walk away, Zack's door opens.

"I thought I heard people talking out here," he says, beaming at me. "I would have came out sooner had I known it was you, Emma."

"Hey, Zack," I say curtly. "I just came to talk to Tally. I'm about to leave."

Panic crosses his eyes, and he reaches out and grabs my arm and pulls me towards him, "Don't leave, please."

He catches me by surprise so I fall into him when he pulls me to him. He wraps his arms around me and pulls me into his room, shutting the door before Tally or I know what's happening.

I hear the click of the lock and then Tally is banging on the door.

"Zack! Open this door right now before I break it down!" she yells.

He still has his arms around me when my head catches up to what is happening. I push away from him and surprisingly he lets me go. I step away from him, into his room.

"What the hell, Zack?" I say.

"I'm sorry, I just…" he starts to say, taking a step towards me. "I just want to talk."

"This-" I say, pointing at him and then making a circling gesture to him and me, "-is not the way to get me to want to stay and talk. This is creepy as hell."

"I'm sorry," he says, but he walks towards me, and he has a smirk on his face that doesn't match his apology. "I feel like we haven't had a minute alone to talk since I got here."

"Why would I want to be alone with you?" I say, my heart beating fast. I know I could get out of here easily, but I don't want to give away that I have Talents.

"To talk," he says, coming closer. I take a couple steps further back.

Tally has stopped banging and screaming at the door.

"What do we have to talk about?"

"I don't know but I'm sure we can think of something," he smiles.

"Do you not see how creepy you are being?"

"Damn it, Emma! I just want to talk," he yells, making me jump. This is the first time he's ever talked like this, with anger, to me. "Why don't you want to talk to me?"

"Because you make me feel uncomfortable," I say, honestly.

"I don't mean to," he says, taking another step. I take another step away but find my back up against the furthest wall from the door.

"Please, stop," I say, putting up my hand. "Just don't come any closer and we can talk."

Zack stops walking and puts his hands up in front of himself.

"Okay," he says.

We stand staring at each other quietly for a minute.

"You want to talk, so talk," I say.

"Are you really with Ty?" he asks. I can see him trying to control his anger.

"Yes, I am," I answer and I see his jaw muscles clench.

He thinks for a minute and then says, "Have you guys found anything more about my sister?"

"They're hoping to find something out tomorrow when they leave on their mission."

"Are you going?"

"No," I answer honestly again.

His eyes light up and he takes a step towards me

again.

"Zack, I said to stop coming closer to me and I meant it," I say. I can feel my fingers starting to get warm. I look down and see that they're a little red. I clench them into fists and wiggle them. *Stay calm, Emma. He can't hurt you, but you can hurt him really bad. Stay calm.* I take a deep breath and let it out slowly.

"Sorry," he says, taking a step back. "I just feel drawn to you."

I look at him with my eyebrows raised. "We hardly know each other, Zack. I think you're just scared from losing your family and you're latching on to me because you feel like you know me. But you don't. We never spoke until just the other day."

"That's not true, I know you."

"Just because you saw me around, doesn't mean you know me."

"Well, I want to get to know you better."

"Locking me in your room with you, isn't the way to do that, and I know you know this is wrong."

Zack thinks for a minute and then I see something change in his eyes. Then they fill with tears and he sits on his bed.

"I'm sorry, you're right," he says into his hands. "It's just... I am scared. My parents are gone and my sister... UGH! She has to be so scared. That is if she's not... if she's not..."

He doesn't finish what he's trying to say and starts to bawl into his hands. I walk over to him and put my arm around his shoulders.

"It's okay, Zack, we'll find her. She'll be okay," I say, hoping to the gods that I'm not lying to him.

"Promise me something?" he mumbles through his hands.

"I can't promise anything but go ahead," I say.

He takes a deep breath and looks down into my eyes, his eyes wet from his tears, "Let me go with you when you go to look for her?"

I shake my head, "Zack, I can't do that, it's too dangerous."

"But you'll be going, won't you?"

"When we get a lead of where she's at, yes I'll be going."

He puts his face in his hands again and cries. I pat his shoulder and he leans into me, putting his head on the top of my head. It's a little awkward since I'm so much shorter than him but I can't just let him cry. He wraps an arm around my waist, holding me to him. I go stiff instantly. Feeling like this is starting to get to intimate. And when he puts his hand on my thigh, I stand up.

Luckily, he just stays on the bed.

"Sorry," he huffs out and then he wipes his eyes.

I take the opportunity to walk towards the door just as there's a loud bang on it.

"EMMA!" I hear Ty's voice say from the other side.

"Hang on," I yell. I run to the door and unlock it.

Ty, Charlie, Max, Clay, Tate, Tally, and Ret are all outside my door, breathing heavy and looking ready for a fight.

"Easy," I say, putting my hand on Ty's chest. "I'm fine."

"What the hell?" Charlie says. "Tally said he pulled you in here and locked the door."

"He did," I say. "He just wanted to talk."

"I'm not so sure that's all he wanted," Clay says, glaring at Zack.

"I wouldn't hurt her," he says, standing up, and walking over to the door.

I step closer to Ty. One, to keep some distance between Zack and me. And two, to make sure Ty doesn't charge him. I feel Ty tense as Zack gets closer.

"We just talked," I tell Ty, reaching up and pulling his face down to look at me. "He didn't touch me. Well, he did hug me when we were talking about his family."

Ty doesn't relax.

"I think that's enough talking for one day," Ty says. "Someone will bring you some dinner."

"Gee, thanks," Zack says through clinched teeth.

"Try anything like that again, to any of the girls," Ty warns. "And you'll find yourself in one of the cells. I'm being lenient with you because you've lost your family and you're some place foreign to you but keep pissing me off and I won't be so nice. Grabbing Emma, let alone anyone, and forcing them to talk to you, is a sure way to really piss me off."

I see Zack take a deep breath and when he exhales, I see his facial expression change, "I'm sorry. You're right. I won't do that again."

"Don't apologize to me," Ty says. "Apologize to Emma."

"I'm sorry, Emma. I won't do that again," he repeats himself.

"Thank you," I say. "Good night, Zack."

"Good night," he says.

Charlie reaches in and shuts the door. I look around everyone looking at me, except for Tally. She's staring at the door.

"What's wrong?" I ask her.

"I don't know," she says. "I can't say for sure, but I think you need to stay away from him. He lied when he said he wouldn't do it again. I couldn't tell what he meant by that other than he lied. I'll see if I can pick anything else up on my shift."

"I'll hang back and see if I can help her," Ret says.

I turn to hide my smile, but I look up at Ty. He's looking at Tally and then looks down at me.

"She's never wrong with her Lie Detection," he says.

"Okay, I won't be around him," I say, clearing my face of the smile I had for Ret and Tally. "Even though I wasn't here to talk to him anyways. I was just visiting with Tally."

Charlie and Max lead us down the hall. Ty looks down at me as he takes my hand and starts to walk. Clay and Tate bringing up the rear.

"So, you were there to talk to Tally? About what?" Ty asks.

"Nothing in particular. I just haven't had a chance to talk to her to get to know her so I thought I'd spend a little time with her," I say, nonchalantly. "She told me about some of the places she's visited. It was really interesting."

"They definitely have some good stories," Ty says.

We stop after walking a minute. I look around and see we've stopped in front of someone's room.

"What are we–" I start to say and Ty interrupts me.

"I have a little bit of time before I need to get back down to the Con-Room, I thought I'd finally show you my room since we're here," he says, pointing with his thumb over his shoulder

I smile and clap my hands, "Eeek, yay! Yes please!"

Clay and Tate walk past us, Tate looks back behind him when he walks and give Ty a head nod, and then laughs. I shake my head and look back at Ty's door.

"Ready?" he asks.

"Yes," I say eagerly.

Ty opens his bedroom door and lets me walk in

first. His room is exactly how I thought it would be. Just like all the other rooms, the layout is the same, but he has bookshelves lining every wall space.

"Oh my gosh, Ty... This is amazing," I say quietly. "Where did all these books come from?"

I walk in and start looking at the first bookshelf and see so many classics.

"I've had them for years. My grandparents helped build my personal library and then when we had to move into The Pit, I had to put them in a storage area, my room wasn't big enough. So, I just kept a couple of my favorites."

"This truly is amazing," I say in awe.

"You're welcome to come in here any time you like. I know the Estate has multiple libraries but consider this your own personal one as well," he says, walking up behind me and putting his hands on my shoulders.

I turn in his arms and wrap my arms around his neck. Getting up on my tiptoes, I reach up and kiss him softly. His hands slide from my back down to my hips and he pulls me to him.

Ty takes a couple steps back until he's sitting on his bed. He spreads his legs and I step between them. Our kiss becomes more passionate. I wrap my arms completely around Ty's neck, pulling him closer. Following my lead, he wraps his arms around my waist. He leans back, lying down, and pulls me with him so that I'm lying on top of him.

Time once again means nothing as we lay here and make out. We get lost in our kissing and touching. Being with Ty is like nothing I've ever experienced. Kissing him makes my heart race and stop, simultaneously. I'm sure if we did this for too long, I'd probably have heart failure.

I'm now on my side, with one of my legs hitched over Ty's thigh. We've stopped kissing, our noses are still touching though, and he's running his hand from my calf up to my rib cage. The sensation of the soft touch has me relaxing into a puddle on his bed. I open my eyes and see that his eyes are closed as well.

"I could lay here and listen to our silence for days," I say. "This is the most peaceful, relaxing moment I think I've had since everything changed."

"Mmmm," Ty says. "I couldn't agree more."

But all too soon, Ty's pocket starts to vibrate. He pulls his phone out and looks to see that Charlie is calling.

"Hello," Ty says. There's a pause when Charlie's talking. Ty chuckles and says, "Yeah, I'll be there in a couple of minutes."

"It's time already?" I ask.

"Seems like it," Ty says. He doesn't move though.

"What time are you guys leaving tomorrow?" I ask.

"We're going to leave well before the sun comes

up so we can get into position before anyone can see us. We've decided not to wait, we're going in at daybreak. I'm not sure if there are any Rifts still left where they had you but just to be on the safe side, I want to be set up and ready to go well before the sun rises."

"Oh, okay."

"Are you sure you're okay with not going?"

"No, I'm not. I don't like that you guys are going without me, but I think it's for the best," I say honestly. I truly don't like that I'm not going with them but with my ulterior motives and still withholding my true meaning behind it, I still feel like a big old hypocritical liar. But I smile and add, "This time."

"We'll be back before you know it," he says, leaning in and kissing my nose.

And I won't be here when you do get back, I think to myself as I close my eyes. I can feel tears starting to form in my eyes, but I force them back down. *I will not cry.*

Ty's phone buzzes again but he doesn't take it out of his pocket this time.

"Okay, okay," he grumbles. "I'm coming."

I roll away from him and get up. He does the same but comes to me and pulls me into a hug and he puts his hands on my face. He bends and kisses me gently.

"I love you, Emma," he says into my lips.

"I love you too, Ty," I whisper back. I kiss him one more time and then his phone starts to buzz again.

"I'll beat them all," he says.

I laugh and step back but take his hand.

We leave his room and as we walk down his hall, I yawn unexpectedly.

"Tired?" Ty asks.

"I guess," I say. "Maybe a little."

"Have you had dinner?"

"I did, before I went and talked with Tally."

"You should go lie down," he says, stopping and turning me as we get to the staircase. "I'll come to you when we're done with our final meeting."

"Promise?" I ask.

"Promise," he says, as he leans in and kisses me.

"Okay," I say with a sigh.

Ty walks me to my room and we kiss again until his phone starts buzzing in his pocket. He pulls it out and looks at who's calling and what time it is now.

"Crap, I'm really late," he says, running his hand through his hair. "I'll see you in a few."

He leans down and kisses me softly again.

"Bye, see you soon," I say, reaching behind me and opening my door.

He kisses my hand before he lets go and walks down the hall. His phone ringing again. This time he answers it.

"Yeah, yeah, I'm coming," he growls. There's a

pause, and he laughs, and then says, "No, you idiot. I'm heading that way now."

His voice drifts away and when he goes through the door at the end of the hall, I walk into my room. I close my door and lean my back against it, waiting for my heart to stop trying to escape my chest.

CHAPTER 17 -
THE JOURNEY BEGINS

After a minute of calming down, I push off the door and go to my closet where I have my backpack and duffel bags stored away. I grab my backpack, one duffel bag, and put it on my bed. I go back to the closet and grab the food and water I've been accumulating.

I grab my Magikida and put it at the bottom of my duffel bag that, lucky enough, has a hidden pocket, the same width and length of the bag. The bottom is hard so that whatever you put in the pocket doesn't rip out the bottom and the top is also hard, so it doesn't leave a lump where my Magikida sits. I grab a couple pairs of pants, shorts, t-shirts, long sleeve shirts, a hoodie, a pair of sweats, socks, underwear, a couple sports bras, and a pair of running shoes and pack them in the duffel bag.

In my backpack, I load all the food and put some bottles of water in there. The rest of the water goes into my duffel bag. I look around my room, not sure what else to pack. I'll pack my bathroom stuff in the morning, just before I leave, along with my phone charger. I'm not sure if I'll be somewhere where I can charge it but I'm bringing it just in case.

It's better to have it and not need it, than to need it and not have it. I think to myself.

I pick my duffel bag up, pleased to find it's not too heavy, and I place it back in my closet. I put my backpack on top of it and as I'm stepping over to my bed, I look around my room to make sure nothing looks out of place or out of the ordinary. When I sit down on my bed, a feeling of heaviness settles over me.

"Am I wrong not to talk to Ty and everyone else about this?" I ask myself out loud. It takes me two seconds of thinking about Ty arguing about how dangerous and crazy it would be for me to leave on my own. Libby would agree with him, as well as the other guys. The only one who would be on my side would be Shae and it's because she can See that I have to do this alone. I lay down, putting my hands to my stomach, and answer myself in my head. *No, talking this out would only make it harder for me to leave because Ty would put a Guardian on me quicker than he put one on Zack. It would also make it a true lie, me leaving without saying goodbye. Right now, it's just me omitting the truth by not telling him my plans. I know this is what I'm supposed to do.*

I roll over and close my eyes. I try to clear my head

and not think about what I'm about to do. And how upset everyone will be with me when they find out.

As I start to wake up, I vaguely remember Ty coming in and telling me it was just after 10 o'clock. He kissed me on the forehead, and I fell right back to sleep. Now, as I'm becoming more aware, I feel an arm draped over my waist and a warm body to my back. I hear his soft breathing in my ear. I snuggle closer to him and hug his arm to my chest.

"Mmmmm," he whispers into my ear. "Good morning."

"I'm sorry, I didn't mean to wake you," I say. I look at my watch and see it's just a little after 1am.

"It's okay, my alarm was going to make sure I was awake by 1:30 anyways. This just gives us a little more time before I have to get up and leave."

"You said you wanted to be there before the sun comes up, what time is that exactly?" I ask as I turn towards him. He turns to his back and I put my head on his chest. As I wrap my arm around his stomach, he wraps his around me, pulling me in tight.

"The sun will rise at 7:07 there, 4:07 here, so we're leaving at 2. Charlie is going to Jump us a block away from the motel we rented. The same room we brought you back to when we found you."

"Oh the memories," I say, sarcastically.

"If I could," he says through clenched teeth. "I'd burn the Rifts place down to the ground. But not knowing if it's theirs or if they took it from someone, I can't do that."

"I don't like what they did to me but being there... led me to you. Don't get me wrong, I have no desire to go back there on vacation but because it brought me you, I can't hate it completely."

"You are something else," he says, kissing my forehead.

We've been making out for a little bit when I hear a buzzing sound. I roll to my nightstand and grab my phone.

"That's your phone," I say, as I see my screen is still a blank.

"I swear..." Ty says as he rolls over and reaches into his pants on the floor.

Pants?! I scream in my head. I sit up and put my back against my headboard. *He was sleeping in his underwear?*

"Hello?" he growls out as he answers his phone. He sits up as the caller is talking. "No, I'll be right there."

"Is everything okay?"

"Something about surveillance video of activity at the Rift's hideout," Ty says, getting out of bed and bending down, grabbing his pants. He's always worn sweats or shorts, which is why I'm surprised to see he's wearing black boxers. He clears his throat and says, "Everything okay?"

I look up at him quickly, embarrassed he caught me gawking, "Ah, yeah... sorry. You're just, ah... Umm, you're in your underwear."

He chuckles as he pulls his pants up. He smiles and says, "Are they any different from shorts?"

"Other than having an extra layer of fabric between me and your..." my face now flames even hotter. "Never mind."

I jump out of bed and walk towards the bathroom. Ready to lock myself in there until the end of time. Before I get to the door though, Ty's hand gently grabs my arm. He pulls my back to his chest and hugs me tight.

"I'm sorry, I should have thought about how it would make you feel. I was just in a hurry to get back to you, I didn't think about grabbing sweats or shorts. I see that you're not comfortable with this so from now on, I'll make sure I change before I come to your room, or you come to mine. I'm sorry," he says, kissing the back of my head.

"It's just... I'm not em—" I take a deep breath. "—Okay, yes, I'm embarrassed. Not because you're wearing just your boxers, there really isn't any difference between them and shorts. It's because..."

I'm so embarrassed that my face could probably cook a marshmallow right now.

"Because why?" Ty asks.

"I don't want to say," I admit, putting my face down onto his arm.

"Why?" he asks. "It can't be that bad."

"It made me think... to say..." I'm so mortified by my embarrassment, that I can't find the right words. We stand in silence for a few minutes, Ty letting me find the words to explain. When I finally find them, they tumble out and then it's a word explosion, "It made me think of... to picture... to think about how close... you were to me. Even though a pair of shorts or sweats isn't much fabric added on, it's an extra layer between what I want to do. And just thinking of you laying next me, closer than we have been, even by one layer of clothing, it made me think and I'm embarrassed by that thought."

I feel Ty go still. I can hear him swallow loudly and then he whispers slowly, "What you want to do?"

"Oh gods," I say, stepping out of his arms, as I turn to face him, I put my face into my hands. "I didn't mean... I don't... I mean, I do, just not right now. I... make me stop talking!"

I hear Ty step to me quickly. He pulls my hands from my face and his lips are on mine in an instant. His hands move up from my hands, up my arms and grab my face, pulling me to him. I put my hands on his biceps and when he puts his hands behind my back, I slide mine up behind his neck.

"So that thought you had," Ty starts to say as he pulls his lips from mine so we can breathe for a second, he kisses me softly on the neck.

"Nope, we're going to forget I brought up anything about... that," I say. "And definitely going to forget about me talking about your man bit."

"Man bit?" Ty says, laughing in my ear.

"We aren't talking about it," I say, laughing also.

"But if we wanted to talk about it," he says. "I'd be okay with it."

"Oh, I'm sure you would be," I say. His phone buzzes in his pocket, saving me from saying anything else that'll leave me red faced and embarrassed.

"Crap, I forgot," Ty says. He grabs his phone and pulls it out, "Yeah, I'll be right down."

The realization that I don't know when I'll see Ty again, has my throat closing off and tears coming to my eyes.

"Ty," I choke out.

"Hey, why the tears?" he says, bending down to look me in the eyes. "I was only teasing. I promise. I would never do anything that would make you feel uncomfortable or anything you aren't ready for, even talking about it."

"It's not that," I say, sniffling and he wipes a tear off my face. "I just realized you're leaving and I don't know when I'll see you again."

Because I'm leaving too. I add in my head.

"I'll be back in a couple of days. Sooner if we don't find anything," Ty says, kissing my forehead as he pulls me to him.

"I know, it's just—" I take a breath "—I'm going to miss you."

"I'm going to miss you too, Em," he pulls me into a hug and squeezes gently. His phone starts vibrating again. "Ugh!!"

"It's okay, you go. You guys need to get going anyways. The sun will be up before you know it."

He leans down and kisses me one more time.

"I love you, Emma," he whispers against my lips.

"I love you too, Ty," I say and kiss him quickly. He hugs me and then he lets go and walks towards the door. I have a horrible feeling that something is going to happen. "Be careful, please. Come back the way you're leaving."

"I will, get some rest," he says from my door. He nods at me and then leaves my room.

I sit on my bed and try to control my breathing.

Zeus, Poseidon, Hades... if you guys can hear me, please keep a watch over Ty and the guys as they go out on their mission. I have a bad feeling, but I don't know if it's from me feeling guilty for leaving without anyone knowing except for Shae, or if something bad is going to happen to the guys. I know I need to do this on my own, but I don't want to regret leaving and not going with them. Just please, keep them safe.

I lie back down but end up just staring at the ceiling for an hour or so. I decide to get up and I go into my bathroom and take a quick shower. I'm not sure when I'll get another chance to take a real shower. When I get out, I braid my hair. I wrap a couple of extra ponytail holders around my hairbrush to make sure I have some in case the one in my hair breaks.

I get dressed in my battle gear but add a hoodie over the top. I add my toothbrush, toothpaste, hairbrush, and grab my little bathroom bag that holds my feminine products in it and put it all into my duffel bag.

As I grab my phone off my bedside table, I feel it buzz. I unplug it from the charger and look at the message.

Ty- *I love you, Em. I'll see you soon.* 3:42am Monday
Me- *I love you too, Ty. Be safe. :-** 3:42am Monday

After I hit send, I unplug my charger and into my duffel bag.

I make my bed, trying not to picture Ty lying there. I pick up the pillow he's been sleeping on for the last little while and breathe it in. It smells like him. A couple of tears leak from my eyes.

I won't do this now. I take a deep breath and push the emotions down, at least for now.

I turn off my phone and put it in the side pocket on my backpack. After I sling the crossbody strap on my duffel bag over my head and across my chest, I put my backpack onto my back.

Taking one more look around my room, I check for anything else I might need. Nothing stands out to me, so I take another deep breath, and send out a thought to Shae.

This is it, Shae. I'm heading out. I'll keep in touch through our Link, but my phone will be off until I get somewhere permanent. I know everyone will be upset with me and probably with you once they find out you knew I was leaving, and you'll get the brunt of their wrath, so thank you for that, I owe you. Please keep me posted on Ty and the guys. Let me know as soon as they get home and what they find.

I'm about to Jump when a sleepy voice from Shae comes into my mind.

Be careful. Keep your guard up. Don't trust anyone. Use your Talents every step of the way. Don't feel bad and like you're being intrusive if you look into someone's mind because that could be the difference between staying safe or getting taken again or worse, killed. You were given these Talents to use them, not to feel self-conscious about them. You are the strongest and bravest person I know. Don't worry about anyone here, I'll take care of them.

I'll keep you posted on the guys. You just worry about yourself and your mission.

I wipe another tear from my face. *Bye, Shae.*

Bye, Em.

I put a Non-Trackable glamour on myself and my things. Then, I make myself Invisible and close my eyes. I think about the lodge looking place that Tally shared with me not even 12 hours ago. In my mind's eye, I think about the road that I saw leading to Bane's house. If I Jump down the road a mile or two and walk in, that would be better received than having some random stranger just appear out of nowhere in their front yard.

Let's hope thinking of the road is good enough. Since I didn't get to see where I want to Jump, I'm not sure how this will work. I make up my mind, and take, yet another, deep breath, and take my step into the scary, unknown.

Let the journey begin.

CHAPTER 18

– WEREWOLVES IN MONTANA

I can hear the birds chirping their predawn song but then they go silent. They've probably felt the shift in the air as I appear out of nowhere, Invisible. Before I open my eyes, I feel the soft, crisp breeze twirl around me. As I open my eyes, the birds start chirping again.

I look up and down the road but see nothing but pitch black as the sun hasn't risen yet. I'm not sure if I have a Talent for night vision, but I try anyways. I relax my mind and eyes and think about being able to see. It doesn't take more than a second of trying to be able to see, before it feels like the moon has started shining a million times brighter to light up the road. I look up at the crescent moon and I can tell it's still shining just the same as it always has. I realize, I do in fact, have Night Vision.

So cool!

I'm not sure which way is the way to Bane's house.

I open my Senses and let myself feel which way to go. I feel a tugging on my Senses to go to the left. Adjusting my bags, I start walking up the road.

As I'm walking, I look around and see nothing but beautiful trees. The only clearing is the road. If I were to step off the road and walk through the forest, I wouldn't be able to be seen. That thought has me trying to look closer through the trees, to see if anyone is out there. They may have their own guards set up, to alert the house if anyone is coming.

Using my Senses, I feel if I can Sense anyone out there. I don't feel anything that would be big enough to be a Werewolf. Only small things, which could be anything from rabbits, squirrels, chipmunks, birds, or any other small forest animal.

Keeping my Senses open, I continue walking down the road. I'm not sure how far away from the house I am but soon I can feel larger presences up ahead. Knowing I can't walk in there Invisible, and just appear out of nowhere- which was the whole reason I Jumped down the road- I let my Invisibility slip off me.

I see a bend in the road coming up and I remember seeing something similar when Tally showed me this place. I prepare myself for what I might be faced with and pick up my pace. When I walk around the bend, I'm blown away by what I see.

Bane and his family have cleared away a huge area

of the trees. It looks as if they used them to build their cabins. There are quite a few more little cabins that have been added from what Tally had shown me. And by little cabins, I don't mean little. They are as big as the two-story houses in New York, but next to the lodge, they look small.

Seeing the big one, the lodge looking one, in person has me speechless. It sits facing the road and is nestled up against the side of the mountain, with trees all around it. It has a wraparound porch, and on the corners of the porch that I can see, there are a couple of swings. There are chairs spread out with little tables here and there as well. It's three stories tall but wider than it is tall.

I try to count the little cabins and stop counting when I get to 14. They've made their own little town in here, tucked away in the forest. I can see how they'd need to do that but seeing it in person is just amazing.

As I get closer, I see men coming out of the lodge, and a couple coming out of the smaller cabins. They all look similar to Bane in that they have dark hair, some with short hair, some with longer. They all have dark facial hair and brown eyes. They do, however, have varying shades of skin tone. But there is one, in particular, that looks as if he could be Bane's twin, only taller. He walks in front of all the other men and stops about 20 yards from me. He stands with his feet apart and crosses his arms over his massive chest.

When I stop after taking a few more steps towards him, he asks in a deep voice with a hint of an Irish accent, "Can we help you?"

I search his thoughts quickly and see that he thinks I'm a lost hiker.

"Yeah, I think you can," I say. "I'm Emma Hart and I'm—"

The man interrupts me and quickly says, "Emma Hart?"

"Yes, sir," I answer. "I met Bane and Maisie a couple of months ago. I was hoping I could talk with them. Are they home?"

He looks at me with a slight glare, the other men around him fidget and look uneasy.

"What do you want to talk to them about?" he growls.

I check his thoughts again and he doesn't believe I am who I say I am.

"Can I ask who you are?" I counter ask.

"My name is Bronson Woods, son of Lexie. First grandson to Bane and Maisie," he states matter-of-factly and proudly.

"It's nice to meet you Bronson. Did your grandparents tell you they met me?"

"They debriefed us when they got back, yes," he states. "But how do I know you are who you say you are, you could be anyone."

"That's a good question," I say honestly. I smile

kindly at him and add, "You'll just have to trust me."

"We have a hard time trusting those we don't know," he says.

"I can understand that, because I too, feel the same way. But I'm going to have to trust you as much as you trust me. I have no way to prove to you who I am other than, you trusting that I'm not lying, and I will not lie to you."

Bronson tilts his head to the side and looks at me.

"You look just as Grandmother described you to look," he says. He walks to me and slowly makes his way around me. Looking me up and down, sizing me up. "She did mention you were a tiny thing. Most Demi's and therefore, Rifts, are quite larger than you."

"This is all true," I say, agreeing.

He stops right in front of me. I tilt my head all the way back to look at him. He's taller than Ty. I don't show any signs of backing away. I don't feel threatened by Bronson. I don't feel any warning bells going off in my head, telling me I'm in danger. I can feel he can be dangerous but he's only projecting protectiveness right now.

"Grandfather heard through the ranks that you have a unique Mark. May I see it?" he asks, putting his left hand out to me, palm up.

I don't hesitate, I pull my sleeve up from my wrist and place my hand in his, with the back of my hand on his palm. He stares into my eyes for a second longer and then looks down at my Mark. I watch his eyes and see his expression go from uncertainty to disbelief to wonder. He takes his right hand and runs his pointer finger over my Mark.

"It's real," he says over his shoulder to the other Weremen. I see them relax immediately. "You are Emma Hart."

"I am," I say, nodding.

"Welcome," he says as he releases my hand. As he steps back and away from me, he turns to the side and opens his arms away from him, in a gesture as if he's opening the area up to me.

"Thank you," I say. I take a step towards the other Weremen and they all start to salute me. "Oh, you don't need to do that."

"We know the significance that you bring, we show the respect that is due to you," one of the men says. He has a Spanish accent. He adds, "I am Felix, son of Aleck, second grandson to Bane and Maisie."

I turn to Bronson who is saluting me as well. I salute back to all the men and then Bronson comes to stand beside me.

"Is Bane here?" I ask, as Bronson gestures for me to walk towards the lodge.

"He is not," Bronson says. "He and Grandmother had business to attend to at my Uncle Ondrei's. Uncle Xander went as well."

Feeling disappointed I ask, "Do you know when

they'll be home?"

"I do not," he says. He looks at me again, deciding on something, and then adds, "A demon was spotted outside of Uncle Ondrei's region. Grandfather's help was requested."

I stop walking at the word demon and look up in shock at Bronson. I stammer out, "Ah... a real demon?"

"Yes," he states, looking at me with his eyebrows pinched together. He thinks for a minute and then he smiles, "I have forgotten that you are a young one. Very new to not only our World but life itself."

"How old are you?" I ask. I know Bane and Maisie have been married for close to two hundred years and if Bronson is their grandson, he must be up there as well.

"I was born in 1845," he states.

I laugh out a startled laugh. I wasn't expecting him to be this old.

"Well then, to you I am very young," I laugh.

"That you are, Miss Emma," he says as he chuckles. I can feel him starting to relax a little more as we continue walking.

I look around the closer we get to the lodge and I see Werewomen and children starting to come out of the other cabins. Bronson waves and nods at them. They smile and come closer. As we walk up the steps to the lodge, the massive front doors open and three women stand there, looking as fierce as the men had

EMMA HART AND THE WEREWOLVES

when they met me.

"Maude, Akeila, Zahina… this is Miss Emma Hart," Bronson says, gesturing towards me. I smile at them at the same time I take a peek at their minds. Just like Bronson, they are unsure of who I am.

They nod at me and look at Bronson.

"Maude is the first daughter of Helia, 19th grandchild of Bane and Maisie," Bronson says. The olive skinned Werewoman nods. He points to the darker skinned of the Werewomen and says, "Zahina is the second daughter of Lysander, and 20th grandchild. And Akeila is the first daughter of Sophia, 18th grandchild. We call them the Triplets, as they were born within days of each other. They also don't go anywhere without each other."

"Wow, it's really nice to meet you," I say, nodding at them.

"Is she really the Emma Hart?" Akeila asks in a Russian accent.

"She is, she showed me the Mark that Grandfather told us about," Bronson says, nodding in my direction.

The women relax immediately. Zahina walks down the steps and stretches out her arms and leans in for a hug. I tentatively hug her back.

"It's nice to meet you Miss Emma, welcome," she says in her own African accent, as she steps away. All three of them salute me.

"Thank you," I say. "I was just telling Bronson I

came to talk with Bane and Maisie, but it sounds like I've missed them."

"Yes, trouble at Uncle Ondrei's," Maude says, and she too has her own slight accent, New Zealand this time. She hugs me when I get closer. "Please come in. I apologize for our uncertainty, but one can never be too careful."

"I understand," I say, walking into the lodge. I stop in my tracks and my mouth hangs open. I don't know what I was expecting, maybe a hotel set up, but what I see is nothing like a hotel.

The entire floor is open, with support beams scattered throughout. There's a huge kitchen to the right, a lounge area to the left, and a massive dining room table straight ahead. The whole back wall is made of windows. I turn around in a circle and take in the huge room.

"Wow," I say in awe. As I take in the house, I soak in the Sense of these Werewolves. After spending time with my friends, I can tell that Demi-gods and Werewolves have different Essences. I'm hoping I can now differentiate between the two.

"Our grandparents wanted an open, spacious living space," Akeila says, laughing. "The upper levels are all rooms."

"It's beautiful," I say, walking more into the room.

"Are you hungry?" Zahina asks. "We were making breakfast when you arrived."

"I'm okay for now, thank you though," I say. I look out the window and see that the sun is just starting to shine through the trees. I think about Ty and the guys starting their move on the Rift's hideout.

Bronson gestures to one of the sitting areas. I go and sit down, taking my bags off and putting them by my feet.

"So, tell me about the demon," I say. "I've only been a part of this World for a few months and have yet to hear of or see one."

"Over the last hundred years, they have gotten smarter and more difficult to catch and dispose of quickly. The Demi-gods have worked hard to try to keep them under control but with Vanessa and the Rifts causing problems the last 10 years, we and the Vampires, have upped our part in fighting against them. Demons threaten our way of life just as much as they do Demi-gods and Inepties. Grandfather has instilled in us the desire to protect Inepties just as he did before he was changed," Bronson says.

"And each of you have a Region you protect?" I ask. "I didn't really get to go into too much detail with your grandparents when I met them. It was kind of a whirlwind of a meeting."

"Our parents have a Region and they are the Pack Leaders. And each Pack Leader has sub-packs. We are our sub-pack leaders but as the first grandchildren to Bane and Maisie, we work as liaisons between all the

Regions, so that our parents can stay and make sure everything is running smoothly," Maude says, sitting down in an over sized chair. "We were here for a meeting with Grandfather when he was called away. He instructed us to stay until he returned."

"Excuse me for a second," Zahina says. As she stands, she says, "I need to go check on breakfast."

"We'll come help," Maude says, grabbing Akeila's hand.

"See, nowhere without the others," Bronson says, laughing.

"I'm sorry, but I can't ignore the fact that you each have your own slight accent. Where are you guys from?" I ask.

"I was born in Ireland," Bronson says. "My mother is the Pack Leader for Europe but her homebase is in Ireland in the Crone Woods. Maude was born in New Zealand. Her mother is the Pack Leader there and her homebase is in the Victoria Forest Park. Akeila's mother is the Pack Leader of Asia. Her homebase is in the Karakan Pine Forest in Russia and that's where Akeila was born. Zahina's father is the Pack Leader in Africa, and his homebase is in the Conga Rainforest, and that's where Zahina was born."

Felix walks around the couch with a plate piled high with breakfast foods. Bronson raises an eyebrow at him, but Felix ignores him. He smiles at me and says, "My father is the Pack Leader of South America.

His homebase is in Rio de Janeiro in the Tijuca National Park."

"Wow, this is all so amazing," I say. "You all must have some pretty unique last names."

"No, our surname is all the same," Bronson says. "Woods, after Grandfather."

"Even your aunts?" I ask.

"Yes," he says. "People marry into our family and become part of our family. Whether they are man or woman. You marry one of our relatives, your last name becomes Woods."

"That's pretty cool," I say. "None of the men argued about keeping their names?"

"No," he chuckles. "My father, Liam, I guess told Grandfather that if he was willing to take the chance and change into a Werewolf, changing his name wasn't that big of a deal. I think any of the men that have maybe hesitated about it, Father talks to them and they see exactly what he means. Changing one's name is not a big deal in the scheme of all the things changing."

I laugh, "Yeah, I guess you're right. It's a pretty small thing considering everything. Where are all your spouses and children?"

"Our spouses are here with us. They're out in our cabins. Our children are all very much grown as they are all about one hundred and twenty years old," Bronson says, smiling.

I put my palm to my forehead and say, "You look so young that I keep forgetting you're..."

"Old?" Felix laughs around a mouthful of food.

"Well, yeah," I say. "So you have grandchildren of your own?"

"A few million," Bronson states matter-of-factly.

"I'm sorry?" I ask, stunned

"Six of the seven children of Bane and Maisie's, each had six kids each, all starting as soon as they got married at eighteen. In thirteen years, our grandparents had thirty-six grandchildren. That's me, Felix, and the Triplets' generation. We each had six children, again starting as soon as we got married at eighteen. I think the last time we counted there were over 362 million of us grandchildren, give or take. Vanessa and the Rifts have killed quite a few of the 8th and 9th generation during their uprising and they don't hesitate to take one of us out if we're caught alone. The only one of us that has never gotten married and had kids, is Uncle Xander. Grandmother says it's because he hasn't found the one who calls to his heart. She doesn't allow him to travel alone," Bronson explains.

"I'm sorry, there's over three-hundred million of you?" I ask, dumbfounded.

"Yes," Felix says again.

"Where?" I'm completely shocked at this news.

"We're all over," Bronson laughs. "Our sub-packs

have sub-packs, that have sub-packs, and so on. We prefer to be in the woods but it's not possible for us all, so we set up territories inside of the Regions for sub-packs to manage. Any city you go to, we have a sub-pack there. Small town? We have a sub-pack, it's a small one, but we're there. Somewhere that seems deserted? We're there," Bronson says.

"That's incredible. How do you keep track of who's great grandchild times three and who's great grandchild times four? And all your nephews and nieces?" my mind is about to blow from trying to think about it.

"We don't keep track of how many 'greats' go in front of our names. Grandmother and Grandfather are the only ones with the title, Grandmother and Grandfather. Everyone else is Grandpa or Grandma or a variation of it. My grandkids call me Pops, all of them. And then you've got your Auntie, Uncle, and then cousins, and then of course our siblings. My nephews and nieces who were born in the late 1800's, call me Uncle Bronson, just like my nephews and nieces that were born in the early 2000's," Bronson says, leaning back into the couch.

"I can see how that would keep things simple," I say. "I just can't wrap my head around a family that big. I can't imagine that you've all been together at the same time."

"No, that is one of the downsides. We have never

had a family reunion where everyone was in the same place at the same time. But we all get out and visit. Like I said, we're everywhere," Bronson laughs.

I'm thinking about how crazy this all sounds when Maude walks back over to us.

"Miss Emma, are you sure we can't make you a plate of food?" Maude asks.

"It's really good," Felix says around a big bite in his mouth.

"Excuse our cousin, his manner's are lacking when Grandmother isn't home," Maude says.

My stomach growls and gives away how hungry I actually am.

"Sure, Maude, just some eggs and toast will be fine, please," I say, politely.

She claps her hands together and runs back to the kitchen. I see the other two Werewomen clap when she gets back to them and they hurriedly put some food onto a plate.

Akeila and Zahina bring over their plates, while Maude carries her own and mine in her hands. She hands me a plate full of eggs, toast, berries, and bacon.

"I thought you could use a little more than just eggs and toast," Maude says, shrugging.

"Thank you, this is very kind of you guys," I say. I take a bite of the eggs and it tastes so good. I look at my watch and see I've been here for an hour already.

"So, Miss Emma," Bronson says. "What is it you

needed to talk to our grandparents about? Maybe we can help you."

"I'm looking for some information about an attack at an Inepti home. And looking for clues as to where our Leaders, Meredith, Doc, and Bill, may have gone to," I say, I put my fork down. Thinking of what Zack told us has me not really hungry anymore. I add, "We haven't seen them since before the battle at the Elder's."

"We haven't seen them," Felix says, putting his plate on the table beside the couch he's sitting on. "What made you think of coming to talk to Grandfather?"

"The Inepti said he thought the people that killed his parents and took his little sister, said they were heading to Montana," I say.

Akeila and Zahina share a look of concern.

"Sounds like Rifts," Maude says. "They are the only people I know that take children."

"That's what we thought too," I say. "Have you guys or your grandparents heard of any Rift activity going on in Montana? More than normal I guess?"

"There were a couple pockets of them in Helena and Billings but our sub-packs took care of them to the point they packed up and left. I haven't heard of anything since before your battle at the Elder's," Bronson says. His eyebrows pinch together. "It's too bad Uncle Xander went with Grandfather and

Grandmother, he would have been one to ask too."

"Does he have a sub-pack here?" I ask.

"Uncle Xander is the Roamer. He travels between each Region when he feels like it or when he's needed," Zahina says.

"I wonder," I start to say, then look around at the Werewolves sitting around on couches with me.

"What's that?" Akeila asks.

"Well, I wonder if I could go to your Uncle Ondrei's and maybe find Bane there," I say. "The sooner I find answers, the sooner I can go home."

"How did you get here?" Zahina asks.

"I Jumped," I say, matter-of-factly.

"That's impressive," Akeila states. "For a young one, you are very powerful."

"You heard what Grandfather said," Maude says, smiling at me. "She's the One."

"Do you think you can Jump yourself to Australia?" Felix asks, sitting up.

"Is that where Ondrei's Region is?" I ask.

"Yes," Felix answers.

"There's only one way to find out," I say. "I do need to intrude into one of your minds."

"What do you mean?" Bronson asks.

"Since I've never been there, I need one of you to show me, in your mind, as much detail about Ondrei's place as possible," I try to explain.

"How will you see that?" Akeila asks.

"I use Telepathy and look at what you show me. You just relax and focus on Ondrei's place and that's all I'll see because I don't dig around when I'm in someone's mind," I state.

"Does it hurt?" Zahina asks.

"Not at all," I say, smiling at her. Hopefully putting them all at ease.

"I'll do it," Bronson says. "I've been there recently, so I know what it looks like."

"Thank you," I say. Bronson comes over and sits by me on the couch. I turn to him and take steadying breaths. "Just relax and close your eyes. Think about Ondrei's place. Add as much detail as you can. What roads lead to it? What's in the surrounding area? How many houses are around?"

I close my eyes and let myself relax as well. I let my Senses roam and I find Bronson's mind. He's thinking about a map and looking at Australia. It's like his mind zooms in and he's focusing on Brisbane. His mental vision changes to in person view. He's standing in a square, surrounded by people and small shopping stands. He turns and walks to a dock where there are boats tied up. He gets in one and takes it out to an island. There's a sign that says, 'Welcome to North Stradbroke Island'. He walks around and disappears into a dense forest. His mental vision changes again and this time he's higher up from the ground. I realize he's changed into his Wolf form. He runs so fast it's as if he's Running. He's running through the trees, but I can see a dirt lane that stays parallel with him. His mental vision changes once again and we are in a clearing similar to Bane's. Only there is a huge mansion sitting amongst the trees. Instead of everything looking like a cabin, like Bane's, Ondrei's looks more modern. But just like Bane's, this seems to be a little village. There are smaller houses sprinkled around the mansion.

Bronson's vision turns slowly, looking at everything in the area. He stops and stares at the mansion. Nothing changes for a couple of minutes, so I pull myself back and open my eyes.

"Thank you, Bronson, that was perfect," I say.

"How do you feel, Cousin?" Maude asks, coming and standing in front of him.

"Perfectly fine," he smiles at her and then me. "I couldn't even tell you were in there."

"That's the point," I say. "At least it should be. I'm sure Vanessa and the Rifts have a different opinion about that but that's why we are different from each other."

"When will you leave?" Akeila asks.

"Now, I suppose," I say, standing. I pick my bags back up and sling them on like I did before leaving my room.

"Well," Zahina says, standing with me. "It was very nice meeting you."

"It was nice meeting you all, as well," I say, hugging the Werewomen one more time.

"We will spread the word about your journey and make sure that our families welcome you with open arms," Maude says. "If you find yourself in trouble, just search out one of our sub-packs and they will get you in touch with a Pack Leader."

"Thank you," I say, feeling a lot better about this journey now that I have allies around the World.

"Excuse us, we need to go call in the troops to eat," Akeila says.

Zahina, Akeila, and Maude salute me one more time and then walk back to the kitchen.

Felix and Bronson walk me back outside and to the road.

"Please don't hesitate to reach out if you need anything," Bronson says.

"Thank you," I say.

"Happy travels," Felix says. A Werewoman hollers his name. He salutes me quickly and then turns and his face beams when he sees her. He runs to her and scoops her up in his arms and kisses her. It must be his wife.

"Be safe," Bronson says.

"I will. Bye Bronson, thanks for everything.

"Goodbye, Miss Emma," he says as he salutes me

I start walking back down the road. When I look back behind me, he's walking back towards the lodge.

I make myself Invisible and stop in the middle of the road. I close my eyes and think about what Bronson had showed me. I decide to Jump to Brisbane and then make my way to the Island from there

I just hope I can Jump that far. I think to myself

Have faith in yourself, Daughter. I hear Zeus' booming voice in my head. I jump a little as it startled me. I wait for him to say something else, but he doesn't

I close my eyes again and think of Brisbane. I remember the square and how there were little side streets, like alleys. I decide to try my best at Jumping to one of those, hoping nothing has changed since the last time Bronson was there.

"Here goes nothing," I whisper out loud.

CHAPTER 19

- AUSTRALIAN WEREWOLVES

I land on solid ground and hear nothing but silence beyond the alley I Jumped in to. I open my eyes and see nothing but pitch black. I check my watch to see it says it's almost 3am. *What the heck? I forgot about the time zones.* I use my Night Vision once again. I look around me and thankfully see that no carts or boxes or anything like that had been put in this alleyway. I had seen it a couple of times in Bronson's mental vision of the square. He had been thinking about how he'd spent a good five minutes once just turning around slowly, taking in everything. He'd passed this alleyway three times before deciding to head to the dock.

I look around and see no one in the square so I let my Invisibility slip off. I step out into the square. There are booths and carts set up everywhere. Everyone trying to sell the next best thing. They must trust no one to steal if they leave it out overnight.

I'll have to remember this place if I need to come back for more supplies. Now that I know I can Jump here. I think as I walk past a stand with dried fruits and nuts.

I stop at a stand that's selling maps and I buy one of the area, leaving the money under a rock next to the rest of the maps on the table. I see a few more stands with things that might come in handy. Blankets that look like they can be folded up into a small roll but also look warm. Leather work that have gnarly looking knifes or daggers in them. There're also stands with plain t-shirts and jeans, socks, and underwear. Tennis shoes, boots, sandals, and even fancy shoes.

Yeah, I'm really going to need to remember this place.

I keep walking and make my way to the dock, just like Bronson had when he was showing me this place. I get to the end of the sidewalk and I'm about to start walking down the dock, when I feel like I'm being watched

Pretending to look at the map, I turn around like I'm trying to figure out where to go next. I see a man standing at the edge of the square, staring at me. *It's so dark, how can he see me?* I look back down at my map, but not really looking at it at all, I send my mind out and see if I can pick up anything from him.

Who is this? She looks lost. It's late, maybe I can help her find her way. She looks like... but no—

I stop listening and look around, trying to see if I can find somewhere to literally disappear. I see a row of paddle boards set up just down the sidewalk from me. I start walking towards them. Once I get behind the first row, I turn quickly to make sure no one can see me and I hurriedly slip my Invisibility on. Within 20 seconds, the man is walking down the paddle boards. I scrunch down, being careful I don't knock my bags into anything and put myself between the ends of two boards.

"Where the hell did she go?" the man grunts out. He picks up his pace and walks the rest of the way down and then turns.

I don't know who that guy was, he didn't give anything away as to who he might be. So, from now on, I'm Invisible. Or I need to figure out a way to detect if I'm being followed or watched.

I stand and hurry to the dock. Not waiting any longer to get to North Stradbroke Island, I close my eyes and think about Ondrei's place and the road that leads to it. This time, I plan on staying Invisible until I see the place. I'll then walk back down the road and take my Invisibility off.

I Jump myself to the road and use my Senses to guide me in the correct direction. I feel the tug to head straight. Walking, I notice the scenery is similar to Bane's road, in the sense that it's surrounded by trees, not as dense as in Montana but it would still be easy to disappear into these trees. These trees, however, are not the Pine trees in Montana at Bane's homebase. The only ones I recognize are the Eucalyptus trees.

I only have to walk about 5 minutes and go around one bend in the road, before I come to a huge wrought iron gate.

Hmmm, I don't remember Seeing this in Bronson's memory. I think to myself.

I take a step closer until I can reach out and touch the gate. I can see the opening into Ondrei's place. I look around the best I can and try to Read the area. From what I can see, it looks exactly like Bronson's memory. Nothing screams out there is danger nearby, so, I walk back down the road and slip my Invisibility off. I do, however, put up all my Defenses in case I'm attacked for some reason.

I turn back and walk to the gate. As I'm approaching, I see four Weremen running towards me. They don't look happy.

"What do you want?" one of them growls out.

"I'm Emma Hart, I'm here to see Bane and Maisie Woods," I say calmly.

"Wait here," the one who addressed me first says roughly.

The three Weremen who stay, stand in front of me, on the other side of gate. They stand with their feet shoulder width apart and arms crossed over their massive chests.

It doesn't take long for the Wereman to come back but he has an even angrier Wereman with him, he looks more like Bane than the other Weremen.

"What do you want?" the new Wereman demands.

"I'd like to see Bane and Maisie, please," I say, again staying calm. The unease rolling off this Wereman has me becoming very uncomfortable.

"At this time of night?" he growls. "Who said they were here?"

"Bronson," I state. I look at my watch and see it's a little after 3am Tuesday. *Tuesday?*

The new Wereman glares at me.

"He would have informed us if you were coming," he growls.

"I just left there," I say. Australia must be hours and hours ahead of us and even Montana. Montana is already three hours ahead of us at home.

He glares at me again and I scan his thoughts quickly. He doesn't believe anything I'm saying but he opens the gate with a nod.

Is the gate magic? Or are there cameras and the guard watching, opened it? I ask myself. *Probably the latter.*

I step in and immediately two of the other Weremen grab one of my upper arms.

"I'm not here to fight anyone," I say as calmly as I can.

"We'll see about that," the new one says. "Take her to the chambers. I'll be there to speak with her shortly."

He turns and runs back to the main house.

"Why am I being imprisoned?" I ask frantically. I know I could get out of here if I wanted to, but I have to show these Werewolves I don't mean any harm.

My four guardsmen don't answer me. The one that ran and got the other Wereman, the one who seems to be in charge, steps in front and when he starts to walk away, the two holding me usher me along. The last one follows right behind me.

I get a chance to see the main house in person before we turn and head across the way. The main house is impressive. It looks more castle than mansion now that I see it. There are a couple towers towards the back, by the mountain side.

I wonder if that's where the guard station is, it's where I'd put them if this were my place.

I'm led to a small house, smaller than any of the houses around the main house, it looks to be maybe big enough for two rooms inside. It has four smaller outer buildings around it, two on each side, all maybe big enough for one or two people to reside.

The first Wereman points towards the first tiny building to the left of the small house, as he climbs the two steps leading to the front door of the small house. The Two Weremen holding me, walk me to the tiny building and then stop, letting the one behind us, step around and he opens the door. When he steps to the side, the other two let go of my arms and nod in the direction of the open door. I see that there is an oversized mail slot in the middle of the door.

Not wanting to cause trouble I walk into the tiny building. It's just one room with a bed. I walk to the middle of the room and turn towards the Weremen.

"Can I please talk to Bane or even Ondrei?" I ask. "I've met Bane before, he can clear all of this up immediately."

One of the Weremen walks in and demands, "Give me your bags."

"I have nothing to hide," I say. I hand over my bags and realize I have my Magikida. *I hope that pocket keeps it hidden, I doubt they'll think to kindly about some stranger showing up with a hidden sword.*

The Wereman takes my bags and steps back through the doors. The one holding the door handle, without saying a word, shuts the door. I hear a key enter the keyhole and the sound of a heavy lock is slid into place.

I go and sit on the bed. I relax my mind and try to Link up with Shae.

Shae, are you there? I send out.

After waiting for 10 minutes for her to answer, I give up. I walk over to the one window in the room that, luckily, faces the main house, and look out. I stand and stare out for, I don't know how long, before I see the Wereman that I think is in charge, walk out of the front door.

"Finally," I say, as I watch him walk to the small house. I go and sit on the bed and wait for him to come to me. I only have to wait a couple more minutes before I hear a key in the keyhole.

I sit up straight when he walks in and he closes the door behind him. I hear the lock slide into place again.

"Who are you?" he demands.

"I'm Emma Hart," I answer.

"I don't believe you."

"Ask Bane to come verify, he's met me before," I stammer out. "Or get ahold of Bronson, I literally just left him at Bane's. I promise, I'm Emma Hart."

He glares at me and says, "I can't just take your word for it."

"What's your name?" I ask kindly, smiling at him. I try to force myself to stay calm and show him kindness, getting irritated at him won't help me.

He glares again but thankfully answers me, "My name is Xander."

"Oh, your Bane and Maisie's son," I say excitedly. "They must have told you they met me when they came to The Pit a couple months ago."

"They debriefed us, yes. But that doesn't mean you are the Emma Hart."

"How can I prove it?" I ask. "Do you want to see my Mark? Bronson was convinced once he saw it."

I start to pull my sleeve up but Xander stops me

and says, "No, Marks can be faked. I'll try to get in touch with Father or Bronson and have them verify who you are before we move forward with anything."

"Wait, your dad isn't here?" I ask hurriedly.

Xander stills for a minute, maybe kicking himself for letting that information slip.

Thankfully again he tells the truth, "Father and Mother left, there was trouble back in Montana. Weirdly enough, you say you just came from there."

"I did, about—," I look at my watch and do the math from when I got here and what time it showed "—45 minutes ago. Everything was fine. There was no danger there."

What in the World has happened!?

"Interesting that you were there and then Father was pulled away to go back there because there's been a threat of an attack," Xander growls out angrily, walking towards me. He gets right in front of me, so close I can see the vein in his neck pulsing fast with his heartbeat.

I don't back away or show how scared I'm becoming.

"I am no threat to anyone, I'm on your side," I say, trying to sound strong, but my voice cracks at the end.

"We'll see about that," he says and then turns and walks out of the room with two large strides. He knocks on the door and someone on the other side unlocks it and opens it for him. Xander doesn't look back when he walks through the door and shuts it behind him, and it's locked again.

Shae, please! Answer me! I shout out in my head. I don't have my phone to call her, it's in my bag. I have no way to get in touch with anyone. *Maybe this wasn't such a good idea.*

I go and lie down on the bed. I wait for Shae to answer me and wait for Xander to come back. He must have gotten ahold of Bane or Bronson by now. But no one comes for quite some time. My stomach starts to gurgle from hunger. I look at my watch and see that it's just after noon.

I've been here for about 10 hours already?

A little while later, I hear something at the door, not a key going into the keyhole, but something else scraping against the door. I sit up and wait. After a couple seconds, the oversized mail slot opens and a little face appears.

"Hello," I say to the little face. I walk over to the door and kneel down. It's a little girl.

"Hi," she says shyly. "I heard Uncle Xander say you're Emma Hart. But he doesn't believe you."

"I wish he would," I say. "What's your name?"

"Gurley," she says. I don't know what it is about little kids and accents but it's one of the cutest things in the World.

"Hi Gurley, I'm Emma. It's nice to meet you," I say smiling. "So, what are you doing here?"

"Well, I just had lunch and I thought you might be hungry. Even if you aren't the Emma all the old ones are talking about, I still think you should get something to eat. None of the old ones had even thought to bring you something to eat. I was only able to sneak a roll and a bottle of water," she says as she pushes a roll through the large mail slot, that I'm now understanding could be for this reason right here. She's now passing the water bottle through.

"You are very kind and thoughtful, Gurley, thank you," I say. "As much as I appreciate you doing this, I don't want you to do anything you'll get in trouble for, just for me, okay?"

"I won't get in trouble," she says with a beaming smile.

"How old are you, Gurley?" I ask.

"Six!" she says excitedly. "I just had my birthday."

"Well, happy birthday," I say smiling at her. "You are a truly kind little girl."

"I wish I could stay longer and talk to you, you're nice. But, I have to get back to finish my lesson for today. I'm learning how to count by tens."

"You are so smart."

"I'll try to come back after dinner."

"Please don't get into trouble."

"I already said I won't, silly," she laughs. "Bye, maybe Emma."

I laugh, "Bye Gurley and thank you again."

She sticks her hand up to the slot and waves and I wave back. She lets the slot door swing shut and then I'm alone again. I don't have another visitor until Gurley comes back in the evening. She doesn't stay long but brings me two rolls and another bottle of water.

Shae! Are you there? I reach out again. I've lost count of how many times I've tried to contact her, but it hasn't worked yet. I guess our Link isn't strong enough yet for this great of a distance.

The last time I looked at my watch it was 3:37am. I'm waking up now to the sound of a light tapping on the door. I roll over so I can see it and see the slot door open and little Gurley's face shining through.

"Good morning," I say, happy to see her.

"Good morning," she says brightly.

"How are you today?"

"I'm good. Did you sleep okay?"

"I did, thank you."

"I'm so excited. I was able to sneak an apple and a muffin today!" she says excitedly. "Aaand an orange juice and bottle of water."

"Oh, Gurley, you are my angel," I say as I walk over to the door. I look at my watch, it's 6:58am, Wednesday.

She starts to push things through one by one.

"I can't stay, my class is starting soon," she says looking sad.

"Does nobody notice you taking these and coming here?"

"No, they aren't really watching you because you haven't caused problems. At least that's what Uncle Macalla said. I heard him talking to my Aunty and my momma last night."

"I don't mean any of you harm. I just came to talk to your Grandfather and Grandmother."

"I wish they were still here," Gurley says sadly.

"Me too," I say.

"I'm sorry I have to go but I'll be back at lunch."

"Please be careful."

"I will."

She waves and leaves.

I go back to my bed and lie down. With nothing to really do, I try to sleep. It helps pass the time. Besides escaping, which I know I can, I'm going to have to wait and be patient for them to decide I'm not trouble or until they get ahold of Bronson or Bane. Surely they would have gotten ahold of them by now. Unless there really is trouble going on back in Montana.

Lunch comes and goes with Gurley bringing me half of her sandwich and another bottle of water. She doesn't stay long and I watch through the window as she skips away. And sure enough, no one notices her. In fact, I don't see any Werewolves outside.

Being here is starting to remind me a little of my time back with the Rifts. One of biggest differences is

I'm not getting beaten and the even bigger difference is, I can get out of here anytime I want. But waiting and being patient will allow me to bond with these guys better than just breaking out. I might be able to show them I am who I say I am, but that might also scare them away. I have to keep telling myself this because if it weren't for Gurley, I might have already lost my mind and gotten out of here.

When the sun goes down, I look at my watch and see it's a little after 8 o'clock, still Wednesday. I stand and look out my window, waiting to see if Gurley comes, even though she's about 2 hours later than she was last night. But instead of Gurley's little self, I see two large Weremen walking my way.

I hurriedly go to my bed and sit down. I hear the key in the lock and then the door opens. Xander and another Wereman that looks identical to him, walk in. Someone on the outside shuts the door and locks it.

Do they really think I'm going to try to escape with these huge Weremen in here with me? I think, annoyed, to myself.

"Hello," the new one says. "I'm Ondrei Woods. Fourth son of Bane. My twin here says you say you are Emma Hart?"

"It's nice to meet you," I say standing. "Yes, I am Emma Hart."

"You look exactly as Mother and Father stated you did," Ondrei says. "Xander, why didn't you say she matched their description?"

"Didn't cross my mind," he grunts.

"Yes, I'm sure it didn't," Ondrei says, smiling at his brother. "May I see your Mark?"

"Yes," I say. I look at him and then at Xander. "I tried to show Xander but he said Mark's can be faked."

Ondrei gives Xander a look but then looks back at me with a smile. I push my sleeve up and hold out my arm and Ondrei takes it. He looks at it and then shows it to Xander.

"I don't think this one could have been faked," Ondrei says. "Everything Father and Mother have said about her has been true. Even after talking to Bronson and the Triplets, I believe she is the Emma Hart. What other proof do you need?"

Xander just stands here and glares at me. After a minute he answers his brother, "I guess nothing."

"I'm sorry for the precautions. We were finally able to get ahold of Father and they'll be returning in the morning. It took a bit longer than normal to get a hold of them. They were tracking down the sub-pack that had taken off to hunt the demon," Ondrei says.

"So, they weren't in Montana?" I ask, looking at him and then pointedly at Xander.

"No," Ondrei answers, looking at Xander also. "Is that what he told you?"

"Yes," I answer. "He basically said it was quite the coincidence that I had just been in Montana and now there was trouble there."

"Xander," Ondrei says, sighing and putting his hand to his twins shoulder. "Why must you lie to our friend?"

"I was trying to get a reaction from her," Xander admits.

I shake my head and put a hand on my hip.

"Did you even call Bronson yesterday?" I ask.

"Yesterday?" Ondrei asks. "Didn't you just get here this afternoon?"

"What?" I say, dumbfounded. "No, I got here yesterday morning, sometime after 3am."

"Xander, are you kidding me?" Ondrei says angrily.

"I was testing her," he answers, nonchalantly.

"My apologies, Miss Emma. My brother tends to believe the worst in people," Ondrei says, he salutes me and then elbows his brother. Xander reluctantly salutes me also.

Before anyone can say another word, we hear screaming.

CHAPTER 20 -
ON TO IRELAND

We run to the window and look outside. There are flames coming from the main house. One of the towers is on fire down at the bottom, the flames making its way upwards. And the other side of the main house is smoking like a fire has just started but hasn't fully caught on yet. Looking around to what I can see, I see other houses are on fire also.

"Ondrei, let me out, I can help," I plead, as the two Weremen head for the door.

"Absolutely not," Xander says. "You will stay here until I feel certain you are who you say you are."

"Xander, don't you think—" Ondrei starts to argue my case but Xander cuts him off.

"We don't have time for this, your home is on fire," he yells as he runs through the door. He shouts at someone to the side of the door, "Lock this behind us and then get the water hoses strung out!"

"I'll be back," Ondrei says. The door swings shut

behind him and the lock is clicked into place.

"Enough is enough," I say out loud. I look out the window and see that Xander and Ondrei have stopped a few feet away from my tiny room, pointing at Werewolves as they come to help with the fire. I Jump myself to them.

"What the—" Xander says, startled.

"I was only staying in there to be polite, a courtesy to Bane but I've had enough of your crap. I am Emma Hart and I can help with this," I say, waving my hand around.

I Run to the main house. As I get closer, I can see Gurley in an upstairs window of the tower that's on fire. She's banging on it and looks like she's screaming for help. All the other Werewolves are running around scared and trying to figure out how to get the fire out.

I take a calming breath and let my instincts take over. I start to roll my hands around and blue mist type stuff starts to form. When it's the size of a basketball, I throw it at the main house. As it hits the fire, it's instantly extinguished. I move my hands side to side, like I'm wiping steam off a mirror or window. I cover all the houses that are on fire. All fires are out within minutes.

I Jump myself to Gurley.

"Sweet girl," I say. "Are you okay?"

"I'm so scared. I want my mommy and daddy."

"I'll take you down now. Is anyone else up there?"

I ask, pointing up.

"No, I was the only one in this part of the house," she says. "I was just going to do a little extra schoolwork before bed since Mommy says I wasn't allowed to go outside. Something about scary people lurking around."

Not wanting to ask her anything more about the 'scary people' I reach down, with my arms spread out and she wraps her arms around my neck. I pick her up in a hugging embrace and she wraps her legs around me.

"Close your eyes, I don't want to make you sick," I say. "I'm going to Jump us back outside to where your Uncle Ondrei and Xander are standing."

"He's not my Uncle Ondrei, he's my Grandpappy," she giggles in my ear.

"Okay, let's get you down to your Grandpappy."

I look down at her to make sure her eyes are closed and then I Jump us back down.

"What the—" Ondrei says.

"She was trapped in the tower," I say, handing her over to him. "I saw her and wanted to get her out."

"But how did you do that?" Xander asks, awestruck. "You were there and then you weren't. And now you're here..."

"It's what we call Jumping. It's the ability to Teleport," I say.

"What did you do to put out the fire?" Ondrei asks.

"You had blue gel looking stuff coming out of your hands."

"I think it was a Water Talent," I answer honestly.

"You think?" Ondrei asks.

"I've never used a Water Talent like that before or even knew I had one, so yes, I think it was a Water Talent," I answer again, honestly.

"Amazing," Ondrei says. He looks at Xander, who looks just as impressed.

"If it weren't for Gurley," I say her name and the two Weremen look at me shocked. "I would have been dehydrated and might not have been able to do that. She has been bringing me water and a little something to eat since I got here."

"Did you?" Ondrei asks her, holding her out from himself so he can see her a little better.

"Yes, Grandpappy. She's very nice, I believe she's Emma," Gurley states. She then puts her head on his shoulder.

"I do too, my sweet girl," he says, rubbing her back. "That was a very nice thing you did for her."

Before anyone says anything, we hear a Werewoman yelling.

"Gurley! Where are you? Gurley!"

"She's over here, Aroha," Ondrei says. The Werewoman comes running to us.

"Oh, my sweet baby," she says as she takes Gurley from Ondrei. "I was so worried about you."

"I'm okay Momma, Emma Hart saved me," Gurley says, smiling at me.

"Emma—" Aroha looks at me "—Hart. Yes, yes you are! You are her! Thank you so much for saving my little girl."

"She's an absolute angel," I say. "You've got a special one there."

"That I do," she says. She salutes me and then walks away, kissing Gurley as she goes.

I stand with Ondrei and Xander and watch as they help families find their family members that had gotten confused and lost during the fire. It doesn't take long before all the families are back together and heading back to their houses, if they aren't the ones that had caught on fire. They're scared but all safe.

I ask Ondrei, "I didn't think much could kill a Werewolf, but fire can?"

"Fire can't kill us adults, but we can get hurt badly from it. The young ones are the only ones that can die because they haven't made the change yet. Which is why Aroha was so worried about Gurley."

I shudder, "I can understand her worry."

"Sir," a Wereman comes up to Ondrei. When he sees me, he salutes me, and hands me my bags. "I brought these for you, Miss Emma."

Word gets around fast around here. I think to myself as I put my backpack on and then sling my duffle bag strap across my body.

"Thank you," I say to him.

"Everything's in it," Xander says from beside me. I look at him and nod.

"Yes, Par, what did you guys find?" Ondrei asks.

"There was a hole cut... well, melted through the fence just to the side of the main house. It looks as if someone broke in, set fire to the tower, then as they were making it to the other side of the house, either ran out of fuel or couldn't quite finish getting everything to light. Miss Emma was able to put the fire out quickly, but significant damage has been done to you home, Sir," the new Wereman, Par, says. "Six homes are complete loses and seven may be salvageable but it's bad. The seven remaining have smoke damage."

"Thank you, Par," Ondrei says, looking worried. "I want 24-hour patrol, pairs, four on each wall. Check in with each other at every crossing and corner. I want hourly reports to Wassily. He will be in contact with me."

"Are you leaving, Sir?" Par asks.

Ondrei looks at me and then at Xander, "I think we'll be taking the women and children to Lexie's. Hourly reports, understand? Anything, and I mean anything, that looks out of the ordinary gets reported immediately and then checked by groups of fours. Spread the word for all the women and children to meet here in 20 minutes. No need to pack anything,

Lexie will have everything we need."

"Yes, Sir," Par says. He nods to Ondrei and Xander and then salutes me.

"We're going where?" I ask.

"My sister Lexie's in Ireland. My wife, Shalien is there visiting her. But it's also a good place to take the women and children. We'll send word for Father to meet us there," Ondrei states. "Xander, do you agree?"

"Yes," he says immediately. "The Rifts won't expect us to go there, it's further away than some other places but big enough for the women and children to feel at home and safe."

"Lexie's place is in the Crone Woods, right?" I ask.

"Yes,the Crone Woods," Ondrei says.

"How do you guys typically get from place to place?" I ask.

"We usually swim or Run," Xander answers.

"I can Jump all of us, but I need to be told about the Woods. I'd have to see it in one of your minds. It would literally take a second for us to get there. These kids have been through enough for one night, let me make this trip quick and easy for them," I plead.

I see Xander about to protest. He and Ondrei share a look. Ondrei looks excited. I can already tell that Ondrei is the free-spirit and the one that's up for adventure, out of these twins.

Ondrei just laughs and says excitedly, "That would be wonderful! What an experience this will be!"

"Fine but you must Jump me first, to make sure you take us where we want to go," Xander states.

"Where else would I take you?" I ask.

"Well, if you're a Rift, nowhere good," he growls.

"I... am... not... a Rift," I hiss through my teeth, pissed off. "How dare you!"

"That's enough Xander, you saw what she did to put the fires out and she saved little Gurley. You know she's who she says she is, it's time to stop this ridiculousness. Apologize to Emma, now," Ondrei orders.

"I'm—" Xander swallows and clears his throat "—sorry."

I glare at him for a second and then say, in an irritated tone of voice, "Fine, I accept. And yes, I will Jump you first. You'll have to show me her place."

"How do I do that?" Xander asks.

"Close your eyes and just think about it. As much detail as possible, the better," I say. I take a couple breaths, trying to calm myself down. "Then I'll look into your mind and I'll see it too."

"What?" Xander asks.

"It won't hurt and I won't see anything except for what you are thinking about," I say to reassure him.

He looks at me for a second and for the first time since I got here, he takes a step in the direction of trusting me as he shuts his eyes.

"Fine, but let's make this quick," he says snarkily.

"Just tell me when you're ready," I say back just as snarkily.

It takes a second but then Xander says, "Okay, ready."

I close my eyes and Look into Xander's mind. The view is beautiful but in an other worldly way. There are a lot of leafless trees, except for the very top, but from his mental view I can't tell if it's leaves or moss. There is also moss growing on everything down on the forest floor. It makes the area look very green.

Xander's mental view doesn't change, we just stay right here in this one spot.

"Are we not going to move from here?" I ask.

"No, you will Jump me to that spot, and then once you've Jumped us back, you will Jump us all to that spot and then we will walk to Lexie's," Xander states. "There is no reason to show you more when you have us to lead you to her."

"That's fine," I say. I look at Ondrei as he shakes his head at his twin.

Just before we leave, I see Werewomen and children making their way over to where we're standing. I check my watch, it's 9:07pm.

"We'll be back in a blink of an eye," I tell Ondrei. He smiles and nods at me. "Ready, Xander?"

"I guess so," he grunts.

"Take my hand and close your eyes," I say, holding my hand out for him.

When Xander's hand touches me, I feel a zap. He pulls his hand back. I shake my hand, ignoring the zap, but I offer it to him again, nodding at him encouragingly. He takes it again, this time ignoring the strange zap, and he closes his eyes. I Jump us to the spot in the Crone Woods he had shown me. It's daylight, early even. I look at my watch and it's changed from 9:07pm to 10:07am. It's still Wednesday at least.

"Open your eyes," I say. Even with my eyes shut, I could have felt the difference. The air is a lot cooler and the smell is, well, greener. Which is hard to explain but it just smells green. Fresh, but in a mossy way, I guess. North Stradbroke Island smelt like what you'd think a hot island would smell like, which is sea and dirt.

I watch as Xander opens his eyes. His expression changes from his sourpuss look he had on, to amazement, to awe, and then relaxed.

"Okay, I believe you now," he states.

"Really?" I laugh. "It took me Jumping us all the way to Ireland for you to believe me?"

He just shrugs and smiles. His smile softens his face to the point I can see how handsome he is and the differences he does have from Ondrei. I shake myself inwardly. *Stop checking him out.*

"Okay, ready to go back and get everyone else?" I ask.

Xander just nods and closes his eyes. Jumping is so easy now that I just have to think about where I want to go and allow myself to be there, and I'm there.

"Absolutely astonishing," Ondrei exclaims. "How was it brother?"

"Truly amazing," Xander says, surprising me. He let's go of my hand and steps to his brother's side. "Miss Emma definitely has her Talents."

"He finally believes," I say, rolling my eyes and then I laugh out loud.

"He's a hard one to convince sometimes," Ondrei laughs.

"Let's get going," Xander says, annoyed.

Ondrei and I have one more laugh before I pull myself together.

"What do you need from us?" Xander asks.

"I just need everyone standing and holding hands or touching a shoulder or something. We just need to be connected by a touch," I say.

"Can I hold your hand, Emma?" I hear Gurley say from behind me. I turn and see her standing there with her mother and a couple other children that look older than her.

"Let's not bother Miss Emma," Aroha says.

"She's no bother at all," I say. "As long as you don't mind."

"Not at all," Aroha smiles.

I hold my hand out to Gurley and she walks up to

me and takes my hand.

"Everyone, please hold hands," Ondrei says loudly for everyone to hear. There's about 50 of us standing around.

One by one, everyone takes a hand. Xander takes my hand and that zap gets me again. I look up at Xander's face and see him looking at me questioningly. I look at Ondrei and he reaches forward and grabs Xander's shoulder, while he holds another child's hand beside him.

"Everyone holding on?" I ask. A resounding yes goes around the group. "Okay, close your eyes just so you don't get sick or startled."

I count to ten and then Jump us to Crone Woods.

"Excellent," Ondrei says. I look at him and see him looking around. "Absolutely amazing!"

"You can all open your eyes now," I hear Xander say. He let's go of my hand but before he can take a step away, I sway. The ground tilts just for a second. Xander's hands are on me but on my arms now, steadying me. The zap goes from my arms down to my toes. I put my hand to my forehead and ignore the tingling feeling.

"Are you okay?" Ondrei asks, concerned.

"Yes, I'm fine. Just got a little dizzy for a minute," I answer.

"Is that normal?" Xander asks.

"Jumping 50ish people? I think so," I laugh

timidly. "I'll be fine, I promise."

I pat his hands, hoping he believes me so he'll take his massive hands off my arms. He must see it in my eyes because he nods and steps away. He starts walking around the Werewomen and children. I can hear him asking if everyone was okay and if everyone was here. Everyone made the trip just fine.

"That was pretty neat," Gurley says from beside me.

"Better than Jumping from the tower down to your Grandpappy?"

"So much better," she laughs. A couple of kids run up to her and she takes off with them. They're running up the road without a care in the World.

"Walk with me?" Ondrei asks. I see Xander walk ahead of us with some Werewomen, talking to them, and laughing at some of the kids.

"Sure," I say.

"I don't think I'll be able to thank you for what you've done for my family," he states. "First putting out the fire that probably would have taken us a couple hours to get out. Even with our speed, getting the hoses set up and going, we can't speed up the flow of the water. Not to mention saving Gurley, losing her would have been a tremendous loss to us all. And then making our trip to a safer location for the women and children, so much quicker and easier. So many things to show gratitude for in a short amount of time."

"No thanks necessary," I say honestly. "I help when I see help needed."

"Well, you have won another place to call home, shall you ever need it. If not a permanent home, at least a safe haven. Consider my home always open to you, Miss Emma," Ondrei says as he salutes me.

"That's very kind, thank you," I say, saluting him back. I look in front of us and see Xander giving a little boy a shoulder ride.

"Give him some time," Ondrei says. I look at him and see him smiling ahead of us at his brother. "I can already see him starting to warm up to you."

"Oh, no need for that," I say. "I understand his need to be vigilant when it comes to his family. When it comes to Vanessa and the Rifts, you can't be too careful."

"This is all true, but I haven't seen the light in Xander's eyes in awhile, and it's there, now," Ondrei states.

"It's probably from all the excitement," I say, feeling uncomfortable at the implications of Ondrei's words. "Xander doesn't seem like the type of Werewolf that likes to stay put for too long."

"That he doesn't," Ondrei says. "I do think that once he finds the one that calls to his heart, he'll be able to stay in one place."

"It really is something when you meet your person, isn't it," I say.

"Have you met yours?" Ondrei asks.

"I have," I say beaming. "His name is Ty Conner. He's a Demi-god back home."

"Was it love at first sight?"

"Kind of more at first touch," I laugh. "He literally took my pain away. His touch was the only thing that stopped the pain until I let Doc heal me."

"Doc is your medic?"

"Yes, he's one of the reasons I'm out here," I say. "Doc, Meredith, who is our Leader, and Bill, our Guardian Commander, are all missing. There's also a little girl that's gone missing. I was hoping to talk to your father about if he's heard or seen anything."

"You'll get some answers tomorrow when they get to Lexie's."

"I hope so, I'd love to get home before Ty does."

"Why's that?"

"I didn't exactly tell him I was leaving."

"Brave woman! Shalien would be one angry Werewolf if I ever left without telling her."

"I only did it because he wouldn't have let me leave. He would have done everything he could to keep me there. Even stay home from his own mission and I couldn't do that to the Unit. They need their leader."

"Does Ty not trust in you and your abilities?"

"After the battle at the Elder's, he's very protective over me because he feels like I overdo it sometimes if it means helping someone. He's not wrong there, I do tend to do that more often than not," I laugh. "I think since I'm still so new to this World, he wants me to move slowly instead of jumping in feet first and see how I handle it all."

"Like Jumping 50 of us well over sixteen and a half thousand kilometers?" Ondrei asks.

"Something like that," I laugh.

"Are you really okay? You look a little pale."

"I'll be okay, I might need to eat my weight in food, but I'll be okay."

"I truly am sorry for the way you were treated. I will be having a talk with the men in my family to remind them who is in charge at my home. No matter what Xander says, those men should have reported to me directly."

"Xander was just being protective, I get it," I say.

"But he didn't even show you the decency of bringing you something to eat. It took a six-year-old to keep you from becoming dehydrated and starved."

"He had his reasons." *Why am I standing up for him? He was a total ass to me.*

"He and I will be having a conversation, and you best believe, Father and Mother will be hearing about this as well."

"Ondrei, please, don't cause trouble. I swore, I didn't want to cause problems and I meant that, no matter what. Maybe just remind him that even if he believes someone to be a Rift, they still deserve food," I force a laugh, to try to convince Ondrei to drop it.

I look up and I finally see Lexie's place coming into view. It looks more modern than the last two places I have visited but it's still rustic looking. It's huge and is a beautiful mountain home. It resembles Bane's place more than Ondrei's. It's smaller than Bane's but still looks like an expensive mountain resort, but also homier in a way.

"Did you let your wife and sister know we were coming?" I ask. Realizing now how strange it would be for Lexie and Shalien to see us all walking in. Some of the Werewomen and kids have ash from the fire smeared on their faces.

"I did. I sent a quick word when you had taken Xander on his experiment Jump. I also sent a message to Father," he answers.

"I remember Bane saying something about Telecommunicating," I say.

"That's only when we're in Wolf form," Ondrei says. "We use cellphones if we're in human form."

"Oh, okay," I stammer out, slightly embarrassed that I assumed they didn't have cellphones.

As we get closer, a beautiful dark skinned Werewoman comes out of the main house and meets us. Ondrei walks to her and embraces her in an intimate hug and kisses her passionately. He steps to the side and beams widely at me.

"Miss Emma Hart, let me introduce you to my

magnificent wife, Shalien Woods. My Love, this is the Miss Emma Hart," Ondrei says lovingly.

"It's nice to meet you," I say, sticking my hand out to shake Shalien outstretched hand.

"The honor is all mine," she says. After shaking my hand, she salutes me. And then she steps forward and hugs me tightly. "Thank you for what you did for my family and delivering them so quickly to us here."

"I did what anyone would have done," I state.

"She's a modest one," Ondrei laughs out, as he pulls his wife back to him into his arms.

We turn and walk towards the house.

"I'd ask how the trip was but as we just got your message not even 2 minutes ago, My Love, I'd say it was pretty uneventful," Shalien laughs.

"Uneventful but also very eventful," Ondrei says laughing boisterously. "You must ask Miss Emma if she can Jump you somewhere. It's so instantaneous, it doesn't seem real. It's the most wonderfully bizarre thing to happen to me since I went through the Change."

"Maybe someday you can do that for me," Shalien says to me.

"I'm sure I can make that happen," I laugh along with everyone.

As we get closer to the house, a Werewoman that resembles Maisie almost to a T, meets us at the bottom of the steps.

"Sister," Ondrei exclaims as he walks to her and gives her a big hug.

"Baby brother," she says fondly in a beautiful Irish accent. Ondrei steps away, laughing even harder.

"All these years and generations later and she still refers to me as her baby brother," he laughs.

"Well, it's not a lie. You were Mother and Father's last-born child," the Werewoman says, smiling. She turns to me and instead of shaking my hand, she pulls me into a hug, and says, "And you must be Miss Emma Hart. It is so very nice to finally meet you, I am Lexie first born to Bane and Maisie."

"It's nice to meet you as well, Lexie, thank you for opening your home to me," I say warmly.

"Oh, it's my pleasure," she says, turning and walking with me up the stairs. The others follow us. When we get inside, I see Xander sitting at a huge dining room table. I look around the room and it looks similar to Bane and Maisie's home. It has the same open floor plan but it's flipped. Lexie's kitchen and dining room are on the left, her lounging areas are on the right.

As Lexie is leading me to the table, I feel like my vision is getting blurry. I close my eyes for a second and shake my head slightly. When I open my eyes, I see Xander staring at me.

"Are you okay?" he asks.

"I'm—" I slur out "—I'm fine."

"I think she's going to pass out," I hear Xander say. I hear a scraping of wood on... maybe the floor? I'm not sure. The sound seems to come from far away.

My vision has gone extremely blurry. The last thing I remember hearing is a curse word in an Australian accent. The last thing I feel is a zap of electricity zooming through my body before I'm sucked into the blackness.

CHAPTER 21 -
CAT'S OUT OF THE BAG

I start to come to when something cold is put on my forehead.

"Ughhh," I moan out loud because my head is throbbing. I put my hand to my head and feel a cold washcloth sitting on my forehead.

"Emma?" I hear my name from beside me. "Emma dear?"

I open my eyes and see Ondrei standing behind Shalien and Lexie standing behind Xander, who's kneeling beside me. I look around and see I'm lying on a couch. I look back at the Werewolves and see concern in their eyes, even Xander's.

He doesn't seem to be the type to worry about a stranger, I must have really scared them.

"What happened?" I ask.

"You fainted," Xander answers.

"Ugh…" I groan. "Not again."

"Does this happen often?" Lexie asks, as she sits by my feet. I sit up to give her some space and realize my bags aren't on me. I look down at the floor and see them leaning against the corner of the couch.

"Well, when I overexert myself, I sometime faint afterwards. My head hurts but I'll be fine," I say.

"Jumping us here overexerted you?" Xander asks.

"Yes, it looks like it did," I say.

"Did you know it would be too much for you?" he asks a little angerly.

"No," I answer honestly. "I have Jumped more than 50 people at one time before today."

"And what happened then?" Shalien asks.

"I passed out for a couple of hours," I say. "How long was I out for this time?"

"Just 10 minutes," Ondrei says.

"Well, that has to be a good sign," I laugh. Xander glares at me. "I'll be fine. I just need to get something to eat and maybe take it easy for an hour or so."

"Why would you risk yourself to help us? We could have gotten here Running and swimming, it would have taken us a couple of days, but we would have made it just fine," Xander says.

"Like I said before, if I can help in anyway, I'm going to help," I say. "And I don't think those little ones can Run and they definitely wouldn't have been able to swim nearly as fast and as far. There weren't enough grown Werewolves to hold them to Run with them. This was the quickest and easiest way to get them here quickly and safely."

"At your expense," Xander states. I see Ondrei and

Shalien share a look and they look at Lexie before they look back at Xander.

"Being a little tired and hungry is worth it," I say.

"I don't understand," Xander growls as he gets up and stalks away.

"What doesn't he get?" I ask. "I Jumped us because I knew I could, even if it meant I got a little tired. It's really not a big deal."

"Oh, but it is dear," Lexie says. "You see, we've always gotten along with Demi-gods and the other Beings, but none have gone out of their way to help us, let alone put themselves in danger. Especially since Vanessa started her invasions."

"I was there when she ambushed Mother and Father in Paris so that she could talk to them. She offered them all sorts of things if they, meaning we, defected and came to her side. Father having been a Demi-god and having the Demi code in his blood, he refused. None of us ever thought twice about it. Vanessa is all that is wrong with the world. Greedy, ruthless, selfish, entitled, and just plain mean," Ondrei says.

"Okay, I'm still not following," I say, maybe I'm more tired than I thought. "What does that have to do with me helping?"

"You knew there was a chance you'd be affected, possibly hurt by Jumping our family here, immediately after putting the fire out, which probably took some energy as well," Lexie says. "Xander, actually all of us, are just surprised that you would do all of that, for us. For Werewolves."

"I would do it for anyone," I say. "Isn't part of being a Demi-god helping when help is needed?"

"It is," Lexie says. "But it's been a little different since Vanessa."

"How so?" I ask.

"For the last few years, Beings of all the Realms have taken up the philosophy to help their kind first. If they can help other Beings after, later, without losing some of their own people or getting hurt, then they help," Ondrei states. "Vanessa has done a great job instilling distrust and fear into everyone."

"But you guys are dang near indestructible," I say, which makes them chuckle. "No, I'm serious. How could she cause you to fear anyone?"

"It is true that we, adult Werewolves are hard to dispose of but our young, the future of our kind, are as vulnerable as Inepties, just as your youth are, because the change doesn't happen until later. Our fear doesn't come from who will hurt us, it's what could happen to our young," Lexie states.

"Not only that, but putting our trust into someone, just to have it blow up in our face, so to speak, and have it come back to hurt us in the end, is painful. Trusting someone wholeheartedly and finding out they aren't who they say they are, that can hurt worse than a physical wound. Finding out someone lied can be a deep wound to the heart and soul, that may never heal. Once someone has been lied to, and I don't mean little lies, but a big lie, like who someone is and what their intentions are, that can scar someone deeply and change their lives and view of the world, forever," Shalien says.

"Did that happen to Xander?" I ask, suddenly realizing why he has such a distrust in strangers. Shalien looks at Ondrei who looks at Lexie.

"It did," Ondrei says sadly. "But it's not our story to tell. However, I can tell you, you are the first Being out of our family, that I've seen Xander warm up to so quickly. He must sense you are trustworthy."

"So please, don't break that trust," Lexie says with an edge of protectiveness in her voice.

"I have no desire to break my trust with any of you," I say. "I say what I mean and mean what I say. I'm only here trying to find answers about our lost Leaders and a little girl. I don't mean any harm to any of you, and I will help you all anyway I can."

"We believe you," Ondrei smiles at me.

"Now, how about something to eat?" Lexie says, patting my foot.

"Yes please, that would be wonderful," I say as my stomach starts to gurgle.

"We had breakfast a couple of hours ago, are you okay with something reheated?" Lexie asks.

"Oh, yes, that's absolutely fine," I say, I turn to stand but get dizzy and sit back down.

"You stay and rest, we'll bring you the food," Shalien says, patting my shoulder.

"No, it's okay. The sooner I get up and start walking around, the better I'll be," I say as I try to stand again, this time going slower. When I don't get dizzy, I laugh and say, "I think slow is key."

I start to grab my bags, but Ondrei grabs them out of my hands.

"It's the least I can do," he says, smiling.

"Thank you," I smile back.

I follow Lexie to the kitchen, Ondrei and Shalien following behind me.

"Have a seat at the island, I'll get somethings on a plate and get it warming up for you," Lexie says. "Ondrei, how much would you like?"

"I ate before we came," he states without thinking as he kisses his wife on the temple.

"Why is Miss Emma so hungry then? Or did putting out the fire and Jumping everyone here take that much energy from you?" Lexie asks as she goes to the refrigerator.

"That should be a question for Xander but since he's not here," Ondrei says, looking slightly ashamed. "I don't think Miss Emma has had much to eat since she arrived at my home. I was unaware she arrived yesterday morning until just shortly before the fire and chaos began."

"I'm sorry, what?" Lexie says, turning around and crossing her arms across her chest.

"Xander took it upon himself to test Miss Emma to see if she was telling the truth or not," Ondrei explains. "I think he was seeing how long she would stay in the Chambers before trying to escape."

"The Prison Chambers?" Shalien asks surprised.

"Yes, My Love," he says, nodding. "She never complained about being in there. Our sweet Gurley was sneaking what food she could grab and water, out to her. Although, I think had Gurley not done that, Emma wouldn't have complained anyways. Miss Emma never tried to escape, as far as I'm aware, until the fire. I wanted to let her out, but Xander was still skeptical of her. We locked her in there but within seconds, she was standing beside us and then suddenly, she was putting the fire out. It was truly amazing to watch."

"We need to have a word with our dear brother about how he treats people," Lexie says angerly.

"He was protecting his family," I say hurriedly. "Am I thrilled I was locked up and not given any food? No, but I can understand his reasoning."

"Be that as it may, he needs to show at least the bare minimum and feed someone he's holding until he's sure they mean no harm. And to do it in someone else's Region without informing the Leader?" Lexie fumes. "No, that's not acceptable."

Realizing I should keep my mouth shut, that these Beings have ways of doing and not doing things, is none of my business. Whether I'm the one that was imprisoned or not. My opinion in the matter doesn't mean anything, as it shouldn't. Their rules have worked for hundreds of years, I'm not going to cross any lines here trying to smooth it over.

The microwave dings and Lexie walks to it and pulls out my plate with a towel.

"The plate is hot but that just means the food is too," Lexie says kindly to me. "Please accept my apologies for how my brother treated you while you were at Ondrei's. You will not receive that treatment here."

Okay, I was going to keep my mouth shut but they're acting like Xander did it just to be mean or spiteful.

"Can I ask you something?" I ask.

"Of course," Lexie says.

"If Bronson would have told me that your parents were here, at your place, would you have been so openminded if I just showed up unannounced, out of the blue?" I ask.

Lexie is quiet for a minute as she thinks about my question.

"I suppose not but I would have been on the phone immediately to my son to confirm what you were saying to be true," Lexie finally answers. "Which brings me to my next question, why didn't Bronson call you, Ondrei, to let you know she was coming?"

"That, I don't know," he says. "According to Xander, Miss Emma said she'd only just left Bronson's when she arrived at my gate. He didn't believe her, but he should have called Bronson to confirm."

"I will be contacting my son shortly and ask him his reasoning behind not calling right away," Lexie says shortly. "Miss Emma, please enjoy your breakfast. I'll have someone come and show you to your room so you can get some decent rest. Please excuse me."

"Thank you, Lexie," I say.

She nods, salutes me, and walks from the kitchen, towards a staircase.

"So, Miss Emma, tell us about yourself," Shalien says. She gets up and grabs three cups from a cupboard and places them in front of Ondrei and me. She grabs a pitcher of water from the refrigerator and fills up our cups.

"What would you like to know?" I ask, after swallowing the bite of breakfast casserole I had in my mouth. I also add, "What did Bane and Maisie tell you about me in their debriefing?"

"They told us what you looked like and how strong they could tell you already were. They told us about what Vanessa did to you and your parents," Ondrei says sadly. He then adds more cheerfully, "They thought you were brave for how you handled meeting all the Leader's of the Realms."

"Is that what you guys call it? The Realms?" I ask. "I like that, it sounds... right."

"Yes, and that's pretty much all they told us," Ondrei says with a smile.

"Well, I guess there's not much to say," I state. "I was raised isolated from everyone and everything so that I would only rely on Vanessa. I'm starting to think I was only allowed to go to school so that she could do her evil bidding without me becoming suspicious. Come to think of it, I don't really know what she did during the day. My one spot of happiness was supposed to be our trip to Greece, but that just turned out to be her ploy to try to get me to Change earlier than my birthday."

"You deserved to have been raised so much differently," Shalien says, patting my hand.

"While I was growing up, I didn't think anything of it. I thought what Vanessa was showing me was love but it wasn't. Now that I've been with the Demigods, I know what it truly feels like to be shown kindness and what it feels like when people care," I smile at them. I take another bite of my breakfast, realizing it's all gone. *I was a lot hungrier than I thought I was, apparently.*

"Except for Xander," Ondrei says, shaking his head.

"Except for Xander, what?" Xander's voice comes

404 EMMA HART AND THE WEREWOLVES

from behind me.

I'm turning just as he's walking into the kitchen and comes to stand beside me.

"Miss Emma was just talking about how she's only known what kindness feels like and what it feels like to be cared for from her short time with the Demi-gods," Shalien says.

Ondrei adds, "And I said except for Xander. You know we're going to have a talk about the way you treated her at my place, right?"

"Yes, I know. But just so you know, Lexie beat you to the punch. She really laid into me a couple of minutes ago. I'm to be Emma's... sorry, Miss Emma's personal tour guide while we're here and if we leave from here, I'm to accompany her until we find Father and Mother or until you get the answers you're looking for," Xander says, looking at me.

"I don't need a babysitter," I say, annoyed.

"It wasn't my idea," Xander says, putting his hands up by his shoulders, palms out. "Lexie thinks it would be a good idea for me to get to know you better and to make sure you get everything you need."

"Well, I appreciate the gesture, but no thank you," I say. "I have to do this alone."

"Who says?" Xander asks.

Not wanting to tell them anything to do with the Big Three, I just say, "I just have to."

"She won't take that as an answer," he laughs.

"She doesn't have to," I say getting a little irritated. "This is my journey. I say what I need and don't need."

"Okay," Xander smirks.

I get up before I say anything out of irritation and take my plate to the sink, and rinse it off. I put it in one of the three dishwashers. When I turn around, I yawn.

"Tired?" Shalien asks.

"Yeah, a little," I answer honestly, while trying to simmer my tone of voice back down.

"Lexie asked me to show you to your room," Xander states.

"Of course she did," I say under my breath. But with their Super Hearing, they all hear me.

"Shall we?" Xander asks as he scoops up my bags.

"Lead the way," I say, sweeping my hand in front of me. But before we leave, I turn to Ondrei and Shalien, "Thank you and please tell Lexie thank you for breakfast."

"We'll pass it on to her," Ondrei says with a smile.

"Have a good morning, Miss Emma, get some sleep," Shalien says.

"Thank you," I say.

Xander walks towards the staircase Lexie headed up earlier. I follow behind him up until we get to the third floor. He waits and then walks beside me. We walk in silence until he stops in front of a beautiful mahogany door with a wrought iron handle.

"This is you," he says as he opens the door.

I step through the door and enter a decent size living room. There's a couch and two comfy looking chairs that surround a coffee table. To the left is a small kitchenette, with a sink, small counter, and a minifridge. It's just big enough a person wouldn't have to go down to the main kitchen for a drink or snack but not big enough to make a meal. There's no stove or oven. Xander steps ahead of me and walks to the door ahead of us. He opens the door and I see the bedroom. A fluffy looking queen size, four poster bed, with a canopy is straight in front of us. A lounge chair to my right, sits in the corner. A full vanity is behind the door, in the left corner. There's a bathroom door to my left and a dresser in the corner to the left of the bed. Two large nightstands are on both sides of the bed, with a lamp on each one. I walk to the huge window, it's bigger than I am, possibly twice as big. Looking out I see the clearing getting brighter as the sun moves higher in the sky.

I turn and see Xander putting my bags down on the lounge chair.

"Thank you," I say.

He walks over to me before he says anything.

"Miss Emma, I need to apologize—" he starts to say but I interrupt him.

"Your siblings think you need to, I don't think you do," I say, putting a hand up to stop him. "You were being cautious and protective of your family. I probably would have done the same, maybe not exactly the same, but I would have been just as protective."

"No, this isn't coming from my brother or sister coming down hard on me for the way I treated you. This is coming from me. I don't think I was wrong in holding you until we could verify you were telling the truth about yourself but I was wrong for not telling Ondrei right away and definitely wrong for not calling Bronson as soon as you arrived. I'm also in the wrong for keeping food from you. The bare essentials should always be given. For all of this that I have done wrong, I'm sorry," Xander says, sticking out his hand.

I reach out and shake it. I immediately feel the zap of electricity and a pull towards him. I pull my hand back quickly and put them behind my back.

"You felt that too?" Xander asks.

"Yes," I answer hesitantly but honestly. And keeping with being truthful, I add, "I don't know what that is or what it means but Xander, I have someone back home. My Anima Gemella. Do you know what I mean when I say that?"

"It's what you Demi-gods call the person that you've found that calls to your heart, your Mate," he states. "I don't know what this feeling is that happens every time we come into contact, but my intuition is that I'm supposed to stay with you. My intuitions are never wrong."

"Never?" I ask skeptically.

"Not ever," he says bluntly. "I don't think this is the feeling of our hearts calling out to each other. I think it's like the feeling of two puzzle pieces falling into place with each other."

"You know what puzzles are?" I laugh.

"Why wouldn't I?" he asks questioningly.

"I'm sorry, it's just a bizarre thought of a Werewolf sitting down putting a puzzle together," I laugh again. "I'm sorry, I think I'm just tired, and I'm finding things a little funnier than I normally would. I do agree with you though. This feeling doesn't feel like the feelings I get when I'm with Ty, my Anima Gemella. There is a pull though. I guess I'll have to accept your offer, or Lexie's offer, of you accompanying me until we figure out what this could mean."

"I'm glad we've had this talk to clarify this feeling, it was throwing me off," Xander says. He salutes and then adds, "I'll leave you to get some rest. Lexie made sure the bathroom was stocked with anything you might need. Have a good rest, Miss Emma."

"Thank you, Xander," I say back. He nods and then leaves my room, quietly shutting the door behind him.

I yawn and decide to take a shower first before going to bed. *I've been in these clothes for two days, I think. Time has been weird with all the Jumping I've been doing.* I walk to my duffle bag and find my phone sitting on top. *Oooh, no... I'm going to have to turn this on and see what messages I have waiting for me.* I'm happy to see they have an outlet like we have back home. So, I grab my phone and phone charger, and take it to the nightstand closest to the bathroom. I plug my charger into the wall and then plug it into my phone. I go back to my bag and pull out a pair of underwear, my pair of sweats, and a long sleeve shirt, the room is a little chilly. I grab my bathroom bag, hairbrush, and walk to the bathroom.

The shower is a stand-alone shower, no tub. Two big fluffy dark gray towels hang on the handles on the shower door. A mirror takes up the whole wall behind the bathroom door. The toilet is in a separate little room, with its own door. I go to turn on the shower and find it has one of those showerheads that dumps about a gallon of water a second. It looks absolutely delightful!

I strip out of my clothes, take my hair out of my braid, and step into the shower. *Best. Shower. Ever!* I don't keep track of time, but I wash my hair and body twice. I also just let the water pour over me, letting some of the stress I have been feeling slip down the drain with the water.

I get out and wrap one of the towels on top of my head and then wrap the other around my body. I walk over to the mirror and wipe the little bit of condensation off of it. I take out my toothbrush and tooth paste and brush my teeth. I pull the towel off my head and pat my hair dry. I brush my hair and re-braid it around and down to the side.

I change into my undies, sweats, and shirt. I hang my towels back up on the shower door. I shut the light off in the bathroom and walk back into my room. I turn the lamp on that is on the nightstand that my phone is charging on and then go turn the light switch off for the overhead light. I shut the curtains and the room darkens as if it's in the middle of the night.

I go back to the bed and pull the blankets down and crawl into it. It feels like I'm being hugged by a soft, fluffy, cloud. *I could close my eyes and go right to sleep.* I think to myself. *But I need to check my phone and check in with Shae.*

I roll over and grab my phone and turn it on, closing my eyes to rest them while I wait. It takes a couple of seconds to turn on. I know when it's on before I even look at it, I hear a ding after ding, after another one. I don't even try to keep track at the number of notifications I have when I finally look at my screen. My screen shows 12:11pm, Wednesday. I see that I have 54 text message notifications and 14 missed calls. *54 text?! Oh. My. Goodness.* I shake my head and open my phone.

I check my missed calls first. I have four from Shae, three from Libby, five from Ty, and two from

Zack. *I won't be returning any of these phone calls. I'll handle my angry friends via the coward's way, text message.*

I open my text message app and see that 15 are from Ty, 12 are from Shae, 8 are from Libby, and 19 are from Zack. Shaking my head, I open Ty's message thread as he's the last one who messaged me.

Ty- *Hey, just checking in, I miss you! How's it going?* 5:47am Monday

Ty- *You must be sleeping. We're heading out. I'll talk to you later. Love you :-** 6:02am Monday

Ty- *We're back at the motel. Rift's place was a bust. Nothing was there. I'll tell you more when I see you. We're going to check it again, a quick sweep, tomorrow, and if there's still nothing, we'll come home.* 9:52pm Monday

Ty- *Ok, you must be in bed. Sleep well, love you Em.* 10:12pm Monday

Ty- *Good morning, Beautiful* 5:02am Tuesday

Ty- *Emma, is everything ok?* 5:26am Tuesday

Ty- *Well, we're heading out. I'll try calling later. Love you.* 5:58am Tuesday

Ty- *We're coming home. Libby and Shae have both said they haven't heard from you. Are you ok?* 3:56pm Tuesday

Ty- *Emma, where are you? What's going on?* 4:23pm Tuesday

Ty- *I'm freaking out, where are you? I've searched the*

Estate and island. 5:31pm Tuesday

Ty- *Emma, please call me.* 6:00pm Tuesday

Ty- *At least tell me you're ok.* 6:52pm Tuesday

Ty- *Shae finally told me a little of what's going on.* 7:45pm Tuesday

Ty- *I'm a little upset about the way you went about this.* 7:49pm Tuesday

Ty- *After talking to Libby, I can understand why you did it this way. Please call or text to let me know you're ok. Please. I love you, Emma.* 8:15pm Tuesday

I close my eyes and sigh. I knew he'd be upset but seeing his texts and watching them progressively get filled more and more with worry breaks my heart. But he's right, this was the only way. *Well, the cat's out of the bag now.*

Me- *Ty, I am sorry. I am safe and doing fine. I'm so sorry. I didn't tell you because I knew you wouldn't let me go and would have definitely stopped me from going alone.* 12:19pm Wednesday

I close out his message thread and open the next one, Shae's.

Shae- *Let me know when you get to your first location.* 7:01am Monday

Shae- *Libby is asking where you are.* 9:07am Monday

Shae- *Libby is getting frantic.* 1:21pm Monday

Shae- *Libby said she tried calling and texting you. I told her you were fine. Now she's suspicious.* 3:36pm Monday

Shae- *I had to tell Libby you had to go on a journey. She was about to call Ty.* 7:00pm Monday

Shae- *Guys aren't back yet. No word. Not a bad sign.* 8:44am Monday

Shae- *Where are you?* 10:01am Monday

Shae- *I tried calling a couple of times. I kept having a feeling I needed to call you. Is everything ok? Please call or reply ASAP.* 6:05am Tuesday

Shae- *I'm starting to worry.* 9:13am Tuesday

Shae- *EMMA! Please reply!* 12:43pm Tuesday

Shae- *The guys are home. Ty is frantic.* 4:04am Tuesday

Shae- *Ty was about to freak out. I told him a snippet of what you're doing. He wanted to know everything. I didn't tell him. He's pissed. It's ok, I can handle him. Please call!* 7:45pm Tuesday

I send Shae a quick message.

Me- *I'm fine and where I need to be. I won't tell you where, so that way you don't lie to everyone if or when, they ask you. Just know, I went to Montana, and got sent somewhere else, just to be sent somewhere else again. I need to talk to you about our Link, but in private.* *12:20pm Wednesday*

I close out of Shae's messages and click on Libby, who's next.

Libby- *Hey, are you feeling ok?* *9:15am Monday*

Libby- *I stopped by your room but you weren't there.* *12:52pm Monday*

Libby- *Where are you, Em?* *2:31m Monday*

Libby- *If you don't reply, I'm going to have to call Ty.* *3:29pm Monday*

Libby- *Shae told me you're on a journey? What the heck does that mean?* *6:50pm Monday*

Libby- *I'm so worried, please reply or text soon.* *8:30pm Monday*

Libby- *Emma, where are you?* *4:47am Tuesday*

Libby- *Shae says I need to be patient and leave you be because you're busy. Busy with what? I won't text or call you again for a while, but please know I'm so worried.* *9:07am Tuesday*

Oh, Libby. I think to myself. I send her a quick text.

Me- *Lib, I'm sorry. I know you're probably confused why Shae knows where and what I'm doing. It's because she's my Seer. I hope you understand I didn't tell you because I know how much you care about me and how protective you are of me, and for those reasons, I couldn't tell you.* 12:21pm Wednesday

I close Libby's text thread and open the last thread. I don't know why I'm dreading Zack's so much more than the others. No, dread isn't the right word. I'm more annoyed that he texted me 16 times. I open his thread and start reading.

Zack- *Hey!* 2:23am Sunday

Zack- *Can you come see me?* 7:16am Sunday

Zack- *Emma, please, I'm bored.* 7:58am Sunday

Zack- *Hey, can you come talk?* 8:27am Monday

Zack- *Are you still mad at me?* 8:34am Monday

Zack- *My babysitter won't go get you for me.* 8:46am Monday

Zack- *Emma, please. I apologized. Talk to me.* 8:57am Monday

Zack- *Seriously? You won't even text me back?* 9:10am Monday

Zack- *I'm sorry, please. I'm so bored.* 9:18am Monday

Zack- *Emma??* 9:25am Monday

Zack- *Emma?* 9:28am Monday

Zack- *E* 9:32am Monday

Zack- *M* 9:32am Monday

Zack- *M* 9:32am Monday

Zack- *A 9:32am Monday*

Zack- *I'm gonna go crazy if you don't talk to me.* 9:47am Monday

Zack- *Ok fine. I won't text you until you text me back* 9:53am Monday

Zack- *I know I said I'd wait but I can't. Why won't you talk to me? I said I was sorry.* 10:58am Monday

Zack- *Ok fiiiine. I'll wait. For real this time.* 11:22am Monday

And I thought I was annoyed before reading those text? I think to myself, more annoyed than ever. 16 texts of the 19 in 3 hours seems excessive. Not that he deserves a reply or that I owe him a response, I send Zack a message of his own, only because I'll feel bad if I don't.

Me- *Zack, you can't text me like that. I'm not at your beck and call.* 12:22pm Wednesday

I close out of Zack's thread and close out of my text message app. I put my phone on the nightstand and lay on my side and close my eyes for a minute. I wait for the onslaught of messages to come.

CHAPTER 22 - COMMUNICATION

My eyes aren't closed for long when I hear it start to ring. I open my eyes and look and see it's Ty calling.

Taking a deep breath, I answer.

"Hello?"

"Emma?"

"Hi, Ty," I say happily. It's so good to hear his voice.

Silence for a minute.

"Do you know how worried I've been?" his voice breaks.

"I'm sorry, really I am," I say, pleadingly. I hate hearing his voice like this.

"Emma, you don't need to apologize. I do."

"What?" I ask, stunned.

"What kind of Anima Gemella am I, if my love doesn't feel like she can talk to me because she's afraid I'll keep her from doing something. Force her to stay?"

"Ty, you are the most amazing man I know. I know everything you do or would do is for my protection. I know that sometimes I don't think of my own safety when it comes to doing something for someone else, so you sometimes have to think about it for me. And I know that I'm new to this World and I kind of jumped in feet first, not really giving myself time to adjust, but... I don't have a choice. It's all or nothing and I just have to learn along the way."

"*I know, Em. I just feel awful that you felt you couldn't talk to me about this because you thought I'd control you and make the decision for you. I don't want you to feel like that, ever. I know I need to dial back my protectiveness because I do want to keep you safe with everything that I am. Just the thought of losing you again, even though we didn't lose you, it was damn close and felt like we did, I don't want to feel that way again. It's a pain that goes so much deeper than just my heart. However, you are the strongest, bravest, and most badass Demi-god in history, and you are the one that protects us all, so I have to rein in my instinct to immediately reject anything that'll put you in harm's way. I'll work on that.*"

"Thank you, Ty. I appreciate that, but I know I could have handled this maybe a different way. I just didn't want to lie outright to your face if I had talked to you and then you put a guard on me. I would have lied to get away. I wouldn't have really had to do much lying, I would have just Jumped. But from that point on, I would have had to lie about every step along the way. I wouldn't have been able to tell you where I was or where I was going next, for fear you'd come get me."

"*I definitely would have put a guard on you and you're right, that wouldn't have done anything but piss you off. I think you did the right thing. This way, I had time to sit and think about it. Libby and I talked, and she said basically what you said. It gave me time to think about how I've been projecting my fears of losing you on to you and not trusting in you and your Power. I'm going to work on that too, I promise.*"

"I love you, Ty."

"*I love you too, Em,*" he's quiet for a minute. He then asks, "*So can you tell me what you're up to? Shae refused to tell me anything other than that you weren't on the Island and you were on your own mission.*"

"Did she tell you she's my Seer?"

"*What? No! When did that happen?*"

"She said that for the last few months she's been having Visions and they've mostly been about me. She thinks when I went into her Vision and pulled her out was when she really began to feel my presence in her mind. She also thinks that when I saved her, it connected us in a different way."

"*It makes sense that you'd have a Seer. And if I'm honest, it's not a surprise that it's Shae. You two do have a connection,*" I hear a faint holler from his end of the phone call. "*Just a second, they're here.*"

"Who? Who are where?" I ask.

"*I sent a group text to everyone that you replied to*

my texts and that I was calling you. They're meeting me outside of Zack's room. I'm on duty tonight."

"Why? Where's Brock?"

"He's been complaining of a migraine since before his shift ended this morning. Chaton took over a little early for him so he could go lie down. Around noon, he was in the Hospital Wing. Sara is keeping an eye on him."

"I didn't think Demi's got sick?"

"We don't, which is why he's there. Having a headache can happen if we get dehydrated but it's usually fixed quickly if we drink enough water. What Brock has, it's not that. We aren't sure what's going on. Libby has been helping Sara and they can't figure out what's going on."

"That's strange."

"I'm going to put you on speaker. Libby, Shae, Charlie, Max, Clay, Tate, and Tally are here. Alysa and Malory asked to be filled in later. They're at their combat lesson."

"I'm sorry, their what?" I half chuckle out.

"You've inspired all of us to get training," Libby says. *"I'm mad at you by the way."*

"I'm sorry," I say sincerely. "To all of you. I really am but you have to realize I did this the only way I thought I could without being stopped. Having done this, this way, let you all have time to think about it before reacting rashly. I know this is what I'm supposed to be doing right now."

"This has to do with what the Big Three said, right?" Libby asks.

"The Big Three what?" Charlie asks.

"Crap, sorry," Libby says.

"Don't worry about the Big Three," I hear Shae say.

"I want to know though," Charlie says.

"It's okay," I say. "I should probably tell the guys now anyways. I'm not going into all the details but here it is in a shorter version. When I was... out of it... right after the battle at the Elders, the Big Three came and visited me, subconsciously or maybe I went and visited them. I'm not really sure. Anyways, they told me I needed to join all the Worlds together, which the Werewolves call Realms, and I really like that so that's what I'll be calling our different Beings and their Worlds from now on. Okay, anyways, I needed to get us all joined together, closer than we are, to help fight against Vanessa. They said it was up to me and me alone. So, I had been trying to think of what to do and then made a plan to execute where I needed to go first."

"You're with the Werewolves?" Ty asks, shocked and a little angerly.

"What? You're with the Werewolves?" Charlie asks even more shocked.

"Did you not pick up when she said 'the Werewolves'?" Clay asks him.

"Yes, I did but she reads so much I thought it was

from something she picked up from reading. I didn't immediately assume she was with them," Charlie states defensively.

"Are you with the Werewolves?" Libby asks.

"Yes," I say. "After Zack had said he heard the people at his house say something about going back to Montana, that's when I decided I'd visit Bane first."

"Did you find anything out?" Max asks.

"Bane and Maisie weren't... here," I say. "They'd left just before I got here to go to their son, Ondrei's region in Australia. There was a demon in his Region causing problems. I visited with Bane's grandsons, Bronson and Felix, and his granddaughters, Zahina, Maude, and Akeila, before coming to Australia. Having done so, I have bonded with them pretty well."

"Did they say anything about Doc, Meredith, and Bill?" Clay asks,

At the same time, Max asks, *"A demon?"*

Ty is being awfully quiet.

I answer Clay first, "No, they haven't seen Doc, Meredith, and Bill or even heard about them being in Montana. Yes, a demon, Max. Apparently, they're still causing problems. The other Realms, at least the Werewolves and Vampires, have been trying to keep them under control but they've apparently become harder to send back to where they come from."

"Are you safe?" Ty finally asks and I hear a couple people say something but can't hear them over Ty.

"Guys, we'll talk about demons later."

"Yes, I am," I answer him reassuringly.

"When will you be home?" Libby asks.

"Not until after I talk to Bane and Maisie," I state. "I'll keep in touch better, now that you guys know what I'm up to and I'll keep my phone turned on. I had turned it off so that I wouldn't be tempted to reply right away, I'm sorry about that as well. I also didn't want you guys to try to track my phone, even though I put a Non-Trackable glamour around myself and my things, I didn't know if there was a different way to Track me."

"I doubt there's anything or anyone in the World or any of the Realms, that would be able to Track you if you put a Non-Trackable glamour on yourself," Shae laughs. *"You're Talents are unsurpassable."*

"She's not wrong," Libby agrees and laughs.

I yawn and try to laugh with them but I just end up yawning again.

"We'll let you go," Ty says. *"You sound tired. What time is it there?"*

I pull my phone away from my ear and check the time. I put my phone back to my ear and say, "It's almost 1pm."

"That doesn't seem right if you're in—," Tate starts to say but Shae interrupts him

"You get some rest, we'll be in touch," she says and then the phone call is cut off.

Of course, Tate would know what time it is in Australia. I'm sure Tally knows as well. With all the traveling they've done and get to do, they must know the time differences. I don't know how they do it. I still feel a little jet lagged from all the time zones I've Jumped through.

I put my phone back down on the table and close my eyes. I'm just about to fall asleep when I hear my notification of a new text message.

I pull my phone to me and look. It's from Ty.

Ty- *I love you. 12:59pm Wednesday*

Me- *I love you too. 12:59pm Wednesday*

Ty- *I don't like this. I don't like not having you here. 12:59pm Wednesday*

Me- *I know, I'm sorry. 12:59pm Wednesday*

Ty- *How's Australia? Do you like it? 12:59pm Wednesday*

Me- *You guys haven't heard? 1:00pm Wednesday*

Ty- *No, heard what? 1:00pm Wednesday*

Me- *Ondrei's place was attacked. Burned a good chunk of his home. 1:00pm Wednesday*

Ty- *Shit! Rifts? How? Why? 1:00pm Wednesday*

Ty- *This is something you should have told us while on the phone. 1:00pm Wednesday*

Me- *I didn't really get a chance to say anything and I thought you guys would have already known. 1:00pm Wednesday*

Ty- *I haven't been in contact with Bane since our Leaders went missing.* 1:00pm Wednesday

Me- *I'll hopefully be able to talk to him tomorrow. And yes, I think it was Rifts that started the fires. I don't know how it happened. The Werewolves didn't hear or Sense anyone in the area out of the ordinary. They found a section of the fence melted beside Ondrei's house. The only thing I can think of is the Rift's knew I'd be there. They can't fight Werewolves easily, so they probably thought burning down where they thought I might be would be quicker, easier. But I was 'locked' away on the perimeter of the grounds, in their Chambers.* 1:01pm Wednesday

Ty- *Wait, what?* 1:01pm Wednesday

Me- *Ty, it's fine. I'm fine. It was a precaution Xander was making. I easily Jumped out to help with the fire. It's a long story. Just know I'm safe and okay.* 1:01pm Wednesday

Ty- *Xander? Where are you? I'll come to you and help you.* 1:01pm Wednesday

I don't reply right away. I know I can trust him but there's just something stopping me from telling him exactly where I'm at right now.

Ty- *Em? You still there?* 1:03pm Wednesday

Me- *I don't think I should tell you. I think someone there told the Rifts. I KNOW it wasn't you but if I say in a text where I'm at and someone steals your phone or reads your mind....* 1:03pm Wednesday

Ty- *You think someone here is a spy?* 1:03pm Wednesday

Me- *I find it highly unlikely it to be a coincidence that the first time the Rifts attack a Werewolves' homebase is when I'm there. No, someone told. How else would they have known where I was going?* 1:04pm Wednesday

Ty- *Who all did you talk to about where you were going?* 1:04pm Wednesday

Me- *Shae was the only one who knew I was leaving but she didn't even know where I was going for sure. I asked Tally a little bit about Bane and Maisie's place but she had no idea I was planning on going there either.* 1:04pm Wednesday

Me- *There is not one person there I would even begin to think would betray our trust. But I'm sure at some point in Vanessa's life, people thought the same about her too.* 1:04pm Wednesday

Ty- *I don't know. I'll do some checking.* 1:05pm Wednesday

Me- *Be careful.* 1:05pm Wednesday

Ty- *YOU be careful.* 1:05pm Wednesday

Me- *I'm with a bunch of Werewolves, I'm as safe as can be.* 1:05pm Wednesday

Ty- *Only you would say that. hahaha* 1:05pm Wednesday

I laugh and close my eyes for a second.

DING-ALINGDING-ALING**DING-ALING*

I open my eyes and see another text. I must have fallen asleep because it comes in at 10 minutes after Ty's last text.

Ty- *You still there?* 1:15pm Wednesday

Me- *Yeah but fading fast. My sleep schedule is all sorts of out of whack. In Australia it was 21 hours ahead of home and here, it's only 10 hours ahead.* 1:15pm Wednesday

Ty- *Get some rest. But please keep in touch. I've never been so anxious in all my life and I've been on countless missions. Having you out there by yourself, scares me more than anything I've ever faced.* 1:15pm Wednesday

Me- *I will. But I'm keeping my ringer off, so I won't be replying right away if I'm in the middle of something. So don't panic if I don't reply immediately.* 1:15pm Wednesday

Ty- *I'll try. :-D* 1:15pm Wednesday

Me- *I love you and miss you. :-** 1:15pm Wednesday

Ty- *I love you and miss you too! :-** 1:15pm Wednesday

I turn my ringer off before I put my phone back down on the table. I roll over and fall instantly to sleep.

◆ ◆ ◆

Bodies everywhere. Blood on every surface.

I turn in a circle but all I see are my dead friends, countless Werewolves lay motionless as well. Libby and Shae are sprawled out to my right with a handful of Demi's I don't recognize. Alysa, Malory, and Charlie lie to the left and in front of me. Clay and Max are a little to their left. And lying right in front of me is Ty.

"NO!" I scream as I fall to my knees.

"No…" I whimper.

"You've done this," a deep voice says. It sounds like it's coming from every direction.

"Done what?" I cry out.

"What you see in front of you," the voice booms.

"How? How have I done this?"

"By fighting against me!" it bellows.

"Who are you?" I ask with a shaky voice, looking around me frantically.

"I am the one true king, the king of gods, the one who those who want greatness seek out."

"Zeus?" I ask, but I already know it's not him. This voice is deeper and more evil sounding.

"NO!" the voice booms, making me cover my ears. "He is nothing compared to me. He only exists BECAUSE of me!"

"I don't understand. I don't know who you are. So how can I be fighting against you?"

"Your dearest aunt and uncle, puny Demi-gods, figured out how to communicate with me and have vowed their allegiance to me and in return I have shown them things your pathetic gods could only dream of. So by fighting against Vanessa and Chris, you fight against me," as the voice is speaking, his volume increases, and the tone becomes very seductive. I have to close my eyes and cover my ears because of how loud he's getting. "Join me and all will be forgiven. Join me and become my queen. We will conquer all Worlds, not just your own."

In my mind, I see a very tall man, muscular to the extreme, dark brown hair, and eyes so dark, they look black. And he's as naked as a person can be. And his business is hanging out. Even though this is all in my head, I can still feel my face turning red as my mental vision travels up and down this mountain of a man's body.

"This could all be yours, My Queen," the man says with the voice I've been hearing. He gestures with his hand from his chest to his lower half, "All you have to do is vow yourself to me. Vow yourself and become the strongest Demi-god, the strongest woman to walk the Worlds."

He stretches his hand out to me. I know if I accept his hand, take hold, I'll be vowing to him that I am his.

In a flash, I see Ty's smiling face. It makes this man's face dull in comparison. Ty's kindness and true love shines through, breaking whatever hold this strange, scary man, is trying to put on me.

My eyes fly open. I stand and straighten my shoulders and stand taller. My hands ball into fists at my side.

"No," I say strongly. "I don't know who you are and I don't like the way you're talking. I don't want to be your queen or anyone's queen for that matter."

"You say that now, but you'll change your mind. You! Will! Be! Mine!" he shouts.

"NO! I WON'T!" I shout back louder.

With a burst of light coming from me, and a gasp of air, I sit up in bed. My eyes blinking fast from the light still lingering in the room. I take deep breaths to calm myself. I hear faint running steps from outside my door.

Confused and not knowing what's going on, I jump out of bed and run to the corner of my room, using the dresser as a block between me and whoever is outside.

"Emma!" I hear a muffled shout from out front, passed the living room.

Living room? Oh yeah, I'm in Lexie's home.

There's a loud bang followed by another shout, "Emma!"

Even though I know where I'm at, I'm still

confused, so I stay put beside the dresser. I hear running footsteps again. My bedroom door flies open.

I throw out my hands and Freeze whoever is bursting through my door. Using my Telekinesis, I turn on the lights.

I see Xander, Ondrei, and three teenage looking boys, maybe my age, standing in front of me.

"Oh, sorry," I stammer out and un-Freeze them.

They stumble into each other.

"Are you okay?" Xander asks, rushing over to me.

"We heard shouting and the air went unnaturally cold. We couldn't move, we were frozen just as you had frozen us a moment ago," Ondrei says.

"There was more shouting," one of the teenage boys says. His voice is a little deeper than I was expecting. He looks at me, his eyes travel down for a second, and then his eyes fly to the ceiling, his cheeks turning pink. I look down and see that I'm revealing how cold I must feel. I cover my arms over my chest, feeling my own face turn a little red.

"We could tell it was coming from your room," the smaller of the three boys says, his eyes are also averting mine.

Xander scrunches down so he's at eye level with me and asks again, "Are you okay?"

Letting out the breath I was holding, I whisper out, "Yes, I think so."

Xander relaxes and stands up. He steps over to the

foot of the bed and grabs the throw blanket and wraps it around my shoulders.

Great, he must have noticed too. How embarrassing.

"What happened? Who were you arguing with?" Ondrei asks, thankfully pulling me out of my embarrassing thoughts.

I walk over to the bed and sit down, shaking a little.

"Blaze, go get Miss Emma some water," Xander demands. He looks at me and then adds, "Please."

The smaller of the three boys nods and leaves the room. The other two boys just look at each other with confused looks.

"I'm not sure," I answer, honestly.

"About which question?" Ondrei asks.

"Both. I don't know what happened and I don't know who you heard or who I was arguing with, if you could hear him too," I say.

"We could hear muffled shouts but couldn't understand any of it," Ondrei says.

Blaze walks back in and hands me a glass of water.

"Thank you," I say, before taking a drink. He just nods and then goes to stand next to the other two boys.

"Why don't you tell us what happened?" Xander suggests.

"I must have been sleeping, having a dream, but I hadn't realized I was still asleep, it felt so real," I take a breath, reminding myself what I saw wasn't actually real. "I was suddenly surrounded by everyone, but you were all dead. Demi's and Werewolves. Then there was a voice."

I tell them about what the guy had told me and how when I closed my eyes, I could see him, a stranger. And I tell them all that happened while my eyes were closed and then, when I told him no, that's when I woke up.

"What was that bright light from?" asks the teen that is more muscular out of the three.

"That was me," I say a little sheepishly.

"You?" they all ask at once.

"Yeah, it's one of my Talents," I say.

"One of?" Ondrei asks.

I nod.

"Well, it felt like sunlight. It was warm and I could feel the goodness in it," Blaze states.

They all nod.

"We'll try to get ahold of Father and ask him if he knows anything about who that guy could have been. And you're sure you've never seen him before?" Ondrei asks.

"I've never seen him before that dream," I answer

"Derk, tell the Force to stand down, but bring Units A and B back," Ondrei says. The tallest one, with the deep voice, nods, salutes me, and leaves the room. "Blaze, go tell your mother what happened and then you can go back to your service work. I'll go out and do a perimeter sweep, Slade you can come with me."

Blaze nods, salutes me, and leaves. Xander nods to Ondrei and salutes me too as he leaves. Slade, the strongest of the three teenagers, salutes me as well, and then follows Ondrei out the door.

"Force?" I ask Xander.

"That's what we call our elite guard at each homebase. When we pull all the best of the Forces together, we are called the Elite Force. When there is a big battle or threat, that's when the Elite Force comes together."

"We? You're part of the Elite Force?'

"Yes, I'm the 'Bill' of the Elite Force."

"Meaning you're the... well for lack of a better description, the Commanding Officer?"

Xander laughs and says, "Yes, that's the best way to explain it. Except Bill is the Commanding Officer for your Guardians in the States, I'm the Commanding Officer for all the Elite, from all over the World."

"Wow, that's intense. Did you volunteer or get elected for that position?"

"A little of both, I guess. Since I don't have a homebase of my own, with my own pack and Force to run, like Lexie here, I volunteered to be in charge of the Elite Force. That gives Father the ability to roam between each pack and go to Realm meetings when he's needed."

"That's pretty cool. How long have you been in charge?"

"I've lost track of time. Time doesn't mean much to us after we've Changed."

"If you had to guess?"

"More than one hundred years," Xander says, looking at me apprehensively.

"How many times have the Elite Force been called to action?"

Cocking his head to the left, Xander shakes his head and says, "Only once since I've been in charge, when we were called to the school, when Vanessa, Chris, and the Rifts attacked."

"That's pretty good. How many attacks at a homebase have you guys had?"

"Not too many. The Rifts will try but with our Senses, it's hard to get too close to us without us either hearing or smelling someone coming."

"When did you guys Sense me?"

"Well, that's a funny story... we didn't. We didn't even know you were there until you were at the gate. That's why I put you in Holding. You startled us and we don't like to be startled, it's unsettling."

"I had put a Non-Tracking glamour on me but I would have figured you'd have been able to smell me. Do I not have a smell?"

"No, you do."

I laugh, "Well, that's good."

"No, no, it's a good smell. The only way I can describe it is the way it smells after it rains, but when the sun comes out, with a hint of floral and citrus. It's very unique and not something we are used to."

"Why is that?"

"All Inepties smell like copper. Depending on their nature, it's a stronger to lighter smell. The kinder and good natured have a lighter copper smell. Demi's smell like their Talents. Healers smell clean, kind of like soap. Mentalists, they have an almost inky smell, like a pen or paper right out of a printer. Telepathic Demi's smell the same. Protectors smell like metal or steal. It all really depends on their dominant Talent."

"Have you come across all of the Talents? To know what they all smell like?"

"Me personally? No, but Father has and so therefore, we know by his knowledge and by him telling us."

"That's cool."

"Yes."

"So why do you think the person or people that set Ondrei's homebase on fire, weren't detected?"

"That is something we are trying to find out. There was nothing except for the hole in the fence and the fires. We should have smelt them before they even got within a mile of his place and at the very least, we should have gotten some type of left-over smell from them, but there was nothing."

"How's that possible?"

"We aren't sure, which is why it's so concerning."

"Could it have been a demon?"

"Possibly but they don't typically just set fires and go about their business. And they leave a stink that's hard to miss. They smell like sulfur and rotten eggs."

"I wish I would have been thinking before we left. I could have tried to see if I could Sense anything."

"You did more than enough. Getting the women and children here was more important. We'll figure out what happened."

I hear the door out in the living room open and close, which makes me jump. My heart starts to pick up

Calm down. Nothing can hurt you. I take a calming breath. Xander looks at me with concern in his eyes

Ondrei comes through my bedroom door and says, "It's all clear out there. A and B Force are out on continual sweeps until morning. If something is going down tonight, we'll be ready."

I look at my watch and I'm shocked to see it's 10:46pm.

"Do you think you can sleep?" Xander asks.

"I can try," I say and then yawn.

"We'll leave you to it," Ondrei says, nods once, and salutes again before he leaves.

"We'll figure this out in the morning. Hopefully Father will return our call by then," Xander says as he heads for the door.

"Thank you, Xander."

"I'll be out in the hall, holler if you need me, I'll hear you," he says as he points to his ears. He smiles, nods once, salutes me, and then leaves my room, closing the door behind him.

I pull the throw blanket around me tighter and lie back down on my bed and close my eyes and try to go back to sleep but all I see is the mystery man from my dream... no, nightmare. I give up trying to sleep and get out of bed, leaving the blanket behind.

I walk out into the living room and find a decent size bookshelf I'd missed seeing when we first came in here. Most, if not all, are all nature books. I pull one off the shelf and take it to the couch.

I spend the next few minutes, maybe it's an hour, looking through books. Time is a weird thing to keep track of when I read. There's a knock at the door.

"Who is it?" I ask.

"Xander."

"Oh, come on in."

The door opens and Xander walks in, "I saw your light on and thought I'd check on you. Are you okay?"

"Yeah, I can't sleep. I thought I'd check out some of these books," I say, holding up the book I'd just finished reading. It was about all the natural springs and waterfalls in the area. "I'd really like to visit some of these places if I have the chance someday. They look beautiful."

"Pictures don't do them justice."

"Out of all the homebases, which is your favorite?" I ask him, gesturing for him to sit down. I pull my knees up to my chest and hug them.

"They each have something unique to offer but Father and Mother's place in Montana and this one, are probably tied for first."

"Why is that?"

"Father and Mother's will always be home and Ireland has forests and plenty of water. And Lexie is always very welcoming and always asking when I'll be visiting again. So, I enjoy down time here when I'm not at home."

"I can see how that could make them your top favorites."

"What about you? Have you traveled much?"

I look down at my knees, unexpectedly sad.

"No. The first time I traveled anywhere was to Greece, when all this—" I say as I wave at myself and around me "—started."

"And that's when you found out about Vanessa?"

"No, when I was in Greece, for the not even 24 hours, I thought she was still my mom. When we were in the 'accident'—" I do air quotes "—I thought they had killed her. It wasn't until after Ty and the guys saved me and the meeting with the Leaders, that I found out about Vanessa."

"I bet that was hard."

"I was devastated when I thought my mom had been murdered, the grief was unbearable at times. When I found out she wasn't my mom but my aunt, and she and her husband, Chris—" I refuse to call them 'Aunt' and 'Uncle' "—had murdered my actual parents, I was in disbelief, shock almost. And then I was angry and I guess I still am, or maybe even more. More because of what I've found out about them and their Rifts. About what they did before I was born and everything after, and even more so after the Battle, the massacre at the Elder's in Greece. They need to be stopped."

"Do you have a plan?"

"Not exactly. I need to find our Leaders. They've been missing for too long now. Too long without some kind of communication."

"So other than Greece, you haven't traveled anywhere?" Xander asks. I can tell he's trying to change the subject to something less depressing.

"Not until recently," I say. I then add, "Vanessa never let me do much other than go to school and come home. I was allowed to go swimming at the local pool but only by myself. Looking back on my life and comparing it to the last few months, I lived a very sad and secluded existence."

"Well, if you'd like, if we have time while you're here, I can show you around Ireland. How long do you plan on staying?"

"I'd appreciate that but I'm not sure how long I'll be here. I'll hopefully know my next move after I talk to Bane and Maisie."

"Which is what?"

I laugh a little and say, "I'm not a hundred percent sure. I just know I need to visit each Realm."

"And how do you know that's what you need to do?"

I decide to tell him about my dream or my out of body experience or whatever it was, when I met the Big Three.

"You think that was real?" Xander asks, after a minute of silence.

I laugh out loud in a short burst.

"I'm sorry, I don't mean to laugh," I say and try to catch my breath. "Had you asked that question six months ago, I would have said no. I would have said that I must have eaten something bad before going to bed but with everything I've seen these last few months, I believe everything until it's proven to be fake or false. You're a Werewolf, one hundred plus years old, can you really believe there isn't something bigger, more magical, out there than us?"

"Honestly, and I've never told anyone this before and I don't know why I'm telling you, but... I've always felt like I was cursed."

"What!?" I half shout, half choke out. "How can

you say that?"

"All my siblings and their children and their children... all the way down to the last of the children that have come of age, have paired up. If I haven't met my Mate by now, then I probably won't. Don't get me wrong, I'm honored to serve in my position, but it does get lonely."

"Have you never been close to finding your Mate? Do Werewolves date?" I ask.

"No, we don't date. Some of us might get feelings for someone but it's nothing like when we see our Mate, when our hearts call to each other. And yes, at one point I did think I had found my Mate. Her name was Ellarey McDaniels. Turns out she was a Rift and was using me for information on our sub-packs and my parents whereabouts. I was with her when Vanessa had first started her uprising. I found out she was a Rift because of how Vanessa knew Father and Mother would be in Paris, Ellarey had told her. We had been seeing each other for over a year. I thought the feelings I was having were how one feels when they have found their mate. I was wrong."

"I can imagine how heartbreaking that would be. Not only to be seeing someone, thinking they're your Mate, and then finding out they aren't but also that they were lying to you the entire time. It would be devastating."

"It was and it's one of the reasons why we

encourage young ones not to date."

"But on the other hand, that must be very lonely and frustrating. How are you supposed to find your Mate when you don't go out and look?"

"It's very frustrating," Xander says as he runs a big hand across his face. "When it's time for us to be with our Mate, it just happens. They come into our lives and then, that's it."

I get a warm, tugging, feeling in my chest. I get a Sense that Xander is supposed to stay with me.

"This is going to sound crazy but with everything I've learned, I'll just go with it," I turn and look at Xander square in the eyes. I say, "I have a feeling I'm the key to finding your mate. Just now, talking to you about all of this, I just had a feeling to keep you close to me. I know I said it before, but now, I really do think you're meant to come along with me, wherever this journey of mine takes me. If you're still willing to come along?"

"I am," he states.

"Are you guys still on patrol?" I ask after we're quiet for a few minutes.

"More like stationed."

"I honestly think we're okay. I don't think there will be an attack. If my dream was more than just a dream, I think it was targeted at me more than you guys."

"We'll stand guard just to be safe."

"Do you need to get back to your position?"

"I'm outside your room."

"Oh."

"If you wish for me to leave, and stand watch out in the hall, I will."

"No, this is good. I like having the company."

"If you're sure…"

"I am."

CHAPTER 23 -
WELL THAT'S NOT GOOD

I'm not sure when I fell asleep, but I wake up to the sound of my front door shutting. I look down and see Xander has put a blanket over the top of me. I wiggle down into the couch and fall back into a dreamless sleep.

◆ ◆ ◆

I wake up to a soft knock on the door. I look at my watch and see it's 9:21am.

"Who's there?" I ask.

"Lexie."

"Oh, please come in," I say as I sit up on the couch, wrapping the blanket around me.

Lexie walks in, dressed in a beautiful purple silk shirt and jeans, with her hair pinned to the top of her head.

"Good morning," she says, smiling at me. "I hope

you slept well, or at least better the second part of the night."

I laugh, "I had a dreamless sleep, which was very restful. Thank you. I can't believe I slept this long though."

"It sounds like you've been all over the globe, your internal clock must have been confused. You needed the rest."

"It was definitely confused."

"I wanted to invite you down for breakfast. My brothers, Shalien, Lorcan, who is my mate, and I waited to eat with you, so you weren't eating alone."

"You guys didn't have to do that," I say.

"We know we didn't have to, we wanted to," she smiles kindly.

"I'll hurry and change," I say, getting up and running to my room. I take my long sleeve shirt off and put on a bra and a short sleeve sky blue t-shirt. I grab a pair of undies, socks and jeans from my bag and hurriedly put them on. I put my tennis shoes on and run to the bathroom and glance at myself in the mirror. My hair doesn't look like I slept on it at all. *I must not have moved a muscle once I was out.*

I walk out of the bathroom, through the bedroom, and back into the living room.

"That color of shirt is lovely with your eyes," Lexie says.

"Oh," I say shyly. "Thank you."

"Shall we?" she asks as she opens the front door.

"Yes please," I say as I walk out. I'm expecting to see Xander but he must be down in the kitchen.

"So, how did you sleep? Was your bed comfortable enough for you?" Lexie asks as we start walking down the hall.

"It's wonderful. The couch is as well," I laugh.

"You slept on the couch?" she asks a little shocked.

"After my nightmare, I couldn't fall right back to sleep, so I went to the couch and read some books. Xander came in and we talked for a bit. I don't remember falling asleep, but I woke up on the couch," I laugh.

"You were exhausted," she laughs too.

"Yes," I laugh in agreement. And then ask, "I get to meet your husband... err, Mate?"

"Husband and Mate go hand in hand," she reassures me. "Yes, Lorcan was out when you got here yesterday. He was sorry to have missed you."

"It'll be nice to meet him," I smile up at her.

We walk in silence for a little bit. Walking down a couple flights of stairs.

"Can I just say," Lexie stops suddenly and turns to me, taking a couple steps down from where I've stopped. "There's a connection between you and Xander."

"Yes, there is, but not how you think," I say frankly. "I have met my Anima Gemella and I have told Xander this as well. We both agree we have a connection but it's not what I feel for Ty. We've agreed that he will come along with me on my journey until we figure out what this connection means. He also mentioned you'd told him to accompany me as well."

"I did," she says smiling. "He told me you didn't take that too kindly."

"I appreciate the suggestion because I don't think I would have invited him to come along, even with this connection we share. But this is a journey I'm meant to do myself, and that includes who I invite to come along with me," I say nicely but also as sternly as I can while this beautiful Werewoman looks at me.

"I understand and I apologize for stepping over the line. You are a strong, confident, woman and you are correct, this is your journey, and your decisions are the only ones that matter," she says, saluting me.

"Thank you," I say, taking a step down, hopefully implying we can get moving again. Even though she thinks I'm confident, speaking up for myself isn't something I'm used to doing yet, and it leaves me feeling slightly awkward.

Thankfully she turns and starts down the rest of the stairs. We turn and walk towards the kitchen. Ondrei and Shalien are leaning towards each other at the island, having a conversation. Xander is talking to a handsome man across the island from him, I'm guessing that it's Lorcan.

Shalien looks up and smiles, "Good morning, Miss Emma!"

"Good morning," I say back and look around at the others, smiling and nodding to them in greeting.

Lexie walks us over to the side by Xander and I sit next to him. She continues walking over to the other Wereman.

"Miss Emma, this is my Mate, Lorcan. Lorcan, this is the Miss Emma," Lexie says, smiling from me to Lorcan.

"It's nice to meet you," Lorcan says with a heavy Irish accent.

"It's nice to meet you as well," I say.

"I hope you're hungry," he says, now smiling over at Lexie. "She had a breakfast feast prepared."

"Oh, you exaggerate," Lexie says as she playfully slaps his shoulder.

"Does he?" Xander asks sarcastically. "So, every known breakfast food from the States, plus all the fruits that could be found at the Market, and all the pastries you could think of, is an exaggeration?"

"You hush," Lexie says, pretending to glare at Xander.

"You don't need to go through all this trouble," I say, feeling embarrassed that so much food was made just for me. "I'm really okay with just whatever you guys normally have for breakfast."

"So raw meat from an old deer dying in the woods

would be okay?" Lorcan asks me.

My eyes go big and I swallow back the little bit of vomit that had tried to escape my stomach. I clear my throat and say, "Mmmmm, yeah, that'd be fine."

They all bust out laughing hysterically.

"He's kidding," Xander says, laughing and then pats my back in a soothing way. "We don't eat that unless we're in our Wolf form. We eat normal food just like Inepties, just like Demi's."

I let out an over dramatic sigh and wipe my forehead, "I'm not saying I would have eaten it, but if that's what you would have placed in front of me, I would have at least attempted to put a piece on my fork."

They all laugh again.

"And don't feel like you're inconveniencing anyone," Xander says. "Lexie doesn't cook."

"Neither do you," she says, glaring at him for real this time.

"Who says I don't?" he asks, indignantly.

"Sophia," she says. She gets up and starts putting pan after pan of food on the table. Shalien goes to the fridge and grabs the platters of prepared fruit. Lexie grabs a couple baking sheets that have pastries on them.

"Sophia is just jealous that I cook better than her," he states. "I cook more than any of you guys. I'm not saying your cooking is bad, it's just a fact. I don't have a pack at my actual home, so I don't have young ones that need to complete their acts of service."

"Acts of service?" I ask, confused. I take the plate Lexie gives me and she gestures for me to take what I want. I grab a couple scoops of fruit, a muffin, some scrambled eggs, hashbrowns, and some bacon.

"You remember meeting Father and Mother at The Pit," Lexie states.

"Yes," I agree.

"Did they tell you our history?" she asks.

"Yes, but..." I say but can't recall them saying anything about acts of service for young ones.

"You don't remember anything specific?" Ondrei assumes.

"No, I remember what your parents told me but they didn't say anything about acts of service and anything about young ones. Just that your children Change at 12 years old once they hit puberty. And for the most part—" I side eye Xander "—you guys find your Mates by 18."

"Father doesn't know how old he is because when he was born, made into a Demi, they didn't measure time like we do now," Ondrei says.

My mouth pops open for a second but then I realize I remember the same reaction when Bane told me the same thing at the meeting, "Oh that's right. He met your mom in 1826. How old was she?"

"She was 17 and born in 1809," Lexie smiles. "You

have a great memory."

I don't tell them it's a Talent.

"They got married a year later after their first meeting, right?" I ask. My eyes go big as I look at Xander, Ondrei, and Lexie. "They said they found out real quick they could conceive. You were born in 1827?"

Lexie smiles and says, "Yes, yes I was."

I look at Ondrei and then at Xander, "And you two? The youngest were eight years later. So, 1835?"

Ondrei and Xander nod. Ondrei starts laughing at the look on my face. Xander looks concerned, like he's waiting for me to freak out.

"Well damn," I laugh. "You guys have great genes. You seriously don't look over 25."

They all throw their heads back and laugh loudly, except Xander, he's still looking at me strangely.

After I swallow a bite of food, I look at Shalien and say, "And you must be about the same age then? If Ondrei got married shortly after his 18th birthday."

"Yes, I'm just a few months younger than Ondrei," she says, smiling over at him.

"We all got married but one..." he kicks Xander's feet. "Someone hasn't found his Mate yet."

Xander grumbles and rolls his eyes but is otherwise unperturbed. He must hear this a lot from his siblings.

"We've talked about it," I say. "I can imagine how

lonely it can feel."

"Yes and no," Xander says. "Remember I travel between my siblings' homebases frequently. But I do spend most of my time protecting my parents Region if they get called out unless there is a need for me to go with them or my help is needed elsewhere. As you saw, Bronson is capable of running the homebase."

"So, what is this act of service you just talked about?" I ask. As they go into explaining what they meant, I continue to eat my delicious food.

"When our children are between the ages of 5-12, they go to school. They learn basic lessons, like math, reading, writing, and our laws. 10-12 years, along with their basic lessons, they learn our Regions. Once they hit 12-18 years of age, once they've Changed, they learn their Werewolf traits, learn to fight, and about the other Realms," Lexie says.

"18-25 years of age, they are in their acts of serve years. They serve as 'help'—" Ondrei says with air quotes "—to learn how to serve others. Their Mates also join them in acts of service. Their Mates also take night classes to learn about their Werewolf traits and our history. That way by the time they're 25, they know everything there is to know about their new lives."

"You'll see cooking staff before and after meals. Wait staff serve meals. House cleaning and all the other various duties. When you see these young ones, they truly are between the ages of 18-25. Once they turn 25, they can do as they wish. They can move away with their families to become pack members in a different Region. They also continue with their combat training. If they excel at combat, they can join the Force. They can travel. They can do whatever they want as long as if the call comes to join against something or someone, they get to the nearest sub-pack homebase," Lexie says.

"So, they can start having their babies while they're in the act of service years?" I ask.

"No, we changed that rule a while ago. They can get married at any time after they turn 18 but they must serve their seven years of service before starting a family. They are so loyal to Father and Mother, not one member has ever disobeyed that order, not any of the rules," Ondrei says.

"We argue and fight like any family but when it comes to our rules, our laws, there is no hesitation about them. We are one hundred percent loyal," Shalien says.

"How was it for you two?" I ask Shalien and Lorcan. "Going from human to Werewolf? If you don't mind me asking."

"I don't mind at all," they say at the same time. Lorcan nods at Shalien to go first.

"When I met Ondrei, I knew from that first moment, he was meant for me, and I was meant for him. I was a little shocked when he told me he was a Werewolf and then even more shocked when he showed me. But it wasn't a scared shock, I was in awe. He told me he would Change me after we got married and that I would become a Werewolf as well. My Change hurt. It's not as bad to go through it if you're born a Werewolf because it's in your DNA. But if you're an Inepti made into one, it has to change your entire bodily make up. Brain, bones, tissue, muscles... every molecule in and outside of your body has to be changed. That being said, I'd do it all over again. To go through two days of pain to spend Eternity with the love of my life, it's worth it," Shalien states, smiling warmly at Ondrei who looks at her with the most loving look on his face.

"My Change was the same and I concur, I would go through the Change 100 times over to get to be with my Lexie," Lorcan says, grabbing Lexie's hand and kissing it gently.

"You seem to be taking this all so well," Xander says, drawing my attention over to him. "Are you not freaked out?"

"No, not at all," I half laugh out.

"Really?" he asks, semi shocked.

"No, should I be?" I ask in return.

"Like I've said before, you're just a young one, new to the Demi world. I would think at some point it would all be too much," Xander says, tilting his head to his left side.

"I guess I'm good with compartmentalizing but nothing you guys have told me is so terrifying I'm going to freak out. Is it weird to think that I'm sitting here talking to people that are close to 200 years old? Sure, but it's not scary weird. I've changed and seen so much in the last few months, I don't think anything will surprise me to the point of hysterics," I laugh and so do the others, except Xander. "I'm serious, I'm fine."

"I know but, it doesn't seem natural, or normal," he says slightly confused.

"I'm not normal," I say matter-of-factly

"That's not a bad thing, ignore my baby brother," Lexie says smiling at me and then shooting a glare at Xander.

"I think being almost 185 means the baby brother stuff can stop," Xander shoots back at her.

"Like I told Ondrei, you and him, will always be my baby brother's," she gives them a smoochy face but in an endearing way. Ondrei laughs light heartedly.

I yawn unexpectedly as I push my empty plate away from me.

"Are you still tired?" Xander asks. "Did you get enough to eat?"

"I'm full for now, thanks," I say. I then laugh and add, "I honestly don't know if I'm tired."

"I could show you around Lexie's homebase, see if moving makes you feel better?" Xander says.

"I think that'd be good," I say. I turn to Lexie, "Have you heard when your parents will be getting here?"

"We haven't heard for sure," Lexie says. "We know they got word you're here and their response was that they'd be here as soon as possible."

"Okay," I say a little sad. "If they end up coming while we're out, will you let Xander know? I'd really like to talk to them as soon as they get here."

"I can do that," Lexie smiles.

I stand and take my plate to the sink and rinse it off. I then put it in the same dishwasher I put yesterday's breakfast plate. I turn and see Xander behind me and he does the same.

I walk over to Lexie and thank her.

"You are so welcome. If you find that you're hungry and it's not quite lunch time, please help yourself to anything you find in here or if you can't find something you want, Katy, our head kitchen service, will be in here at 11 o'clock," Lexie says. "Oh one more thing. If you'd like, I have a cabin set up for you if you wish to move out to your own space. You are more than welcome to stay in your room but guests tend to like to have their own, separate location."

"Oh wow, umm, I think the room will be fine, if that's okay," I say.

"It's totally up to you," she smiles.

"Thank you," I say again. They all nod and salute me, I salute back.

Xander nods at them all and then motions for me to go first. I head to the front door, but he opens it for me before I can get there.

"Thank you."

He just nods in response. We walk down the steps, and he turns to the left and walks for a bit, not saying anything. I look around and see that the little houses do look more like cabins rather than the houses at Ondrei's.

It's a little chilly but not terrible, it's actually perfect. The sun is shining bright, and the sky is a beautiful blue, no clouds in sight. The colors on the foliage are the wonderful colors of fall. So many different shades of green sprinkled throughout the trees. The air smells crisp and clean, like it does just before it gets cold.

"You don't want a place to yourself?" Xander asks suddenly.

"Not really," I say. "Save it for a family that needs it. I'm okay with a room in the house."

"You really are something," he says earnestly. "Not at all what I expected."

"How do you mean?"

"You're selfless and understanding," he starts. "You're kind, funny, smart, compassionate, thoughtful, and show gratitude for even the smallest of things."

"Have you met many Demi's who are the opposite of me?"

"The only Demi's I've been around are the Rifts."

"Oh, well then, I don't think you can assume that all Demi's are like that, because they aren't. The majority are all those things you described me as," I say.

"Fair point."

I look around again and I'm just so awestruck by how pretty it is here.

"It's absolutely beautiful here," I say, looking up into the canopy of trees we're walking under.

"Yeah, this is why it's one of my favorite places to visit."

"So, I know why you don't have your own place, but do you really not want one?"

"I have my own home just not a homebase. My home is in Canada but it's close enough I can get to Montana when I'm needed. My house is just big enough for me. And I'm the only one that has a place to themselves. I guess being the Roamer, has led me to like my isolation every so often."

"So… you're a lone wolf," I say jokingly and when Xander looks at me, I wink at him. Which makes him laugh and in turn, I start laughing too.

I'm looking at all the different colors on the ground around us that I don't notice where we've stopped. When I look up, I see we're standing in front of one of the clearest lakes I've ever seen. I can see the bottom as far as my eyes can see and I know it must get deep. I step to the shoreline and look down at the colorful rocks below the water.

"This is amazing," I say.

"It is," Xander agrees.

I bend down and run my hands through the water, letting it cool my fingers. It's not as cold as I was expecting it to be in October but it's still pretty cool. It would be refreshing to swim in it, that's for sure.

I stand and wipe my hands off on my jeans and beam up at Xander.

"Thank you! A walk was definitely needed," I say and then I yawn.

"I think a nap is needed as well," he laughs. "You really exhausted yourself, didn't you?"

I just shrug, which makes him glare at me a little.

"Let's get you back so you can rest," he says as he turns and starts heading back down the trail that I hadn't noticed we were on until now.

We walk in silence all the way back to the main house. We're met at the front steps by Ondrei. He waves at us as we get closer.

"What's up?" Xander asks.

"Are you parents here?"

"No, they're not here yet," Ondrei says to me with an apologetic look on his face. He turns to Xander and says, "We need to go check in with the Force here and make sure they're doing their patrols continuously to make sure there aren't any mishaps."

"Has there been signs of someone tampering with anything here?" I ask.

"No, this is all precautionary," he says, smiling.

"Can you find your way to your room or do you want me to show you?" Xander asks.

"I can find it, thanks," I say, smiling up at him and Ondrei. "Have fun."

They nod, salute, and then walk away. I turn and head up the steps and into the house. Finding my way to my room isn't hard. Once I get inside, I head to my bed and see my phone sitting on my table.

Crap. I need to do better at remembering this thing.

I turn it over and see I have some missed calls and texts waiting for me. I check my missed calls and I have three from Shae, one from Ty, one from Libby, and six from Zack. *Ugh.* I also have six voice mails from Zack, and three from Shae, and one each from Libby and Ty. I open my texts and have one from each of them. I open Zack's first because he was the last to text me.

Zack- *Where are you?* 8:01am Thursday

Annoyed, I text him back.

Me- *Zack, it's none of your business where I am. Just know I'm looking for your sister.* 11:05am Thursday

I close out of his thread and go to my next text, which is from Shae.

Shae- *Call me ASAP!!!* 10:01am Thursday
Me- *I'll call in a second. What's up?* 11:05am Thursday

I close out of her thread and go to Ty's.

Ty- *Please call me?!! ASAP!!!* 9:59:am Thursday
Me- *What's going on?* 11:05am Thursday

I close out of my text message app and go to my phone app again. Before calling them, I check my voicemail.

The automated voice states first, "*Wednesday, 11:01pm,*" and then Zack's frantic voice, "*Hey, Em, it's me, Zack. Will you please call me when you get this?*"

I got to the next voice mail.

"*Thursday, 12:07am... Emma, I really need to talk to you. Please. This is Zack.*"

"*Thursday, 1:01am... Emma **sniff** pllllease.*" Zack's voice cracks and I can hear him crying.

From his frantic voice and now his sad voice, I'm

starting to feel bad for ignoring him and being so short in my text replies. Even though I don't know him, he feels connected to me. I thought leaving him at the Estate would be best for him, which it is. He's safest there but I hadn't thought about how he'd feel.

I got on to the next voicemails.

"*Thursday, 2:10am… Emma I need you to call me. Tell me where you are.*" Zack's voice again, but he doesn't sound sad, he sounds urgent.

"*Thursday, 4:07am… If you don't call me back, I'm leaving here and I'll try to find you myself.*" Zack sounds desperate.

"*Thursday, 6:12am… Emma, I'm done waiting. I'm coming.*" Zack again but now sounds pissed.

"What the hell?" I ask myself out loud.

I go on to the next voicemail.

"*Thursday, 6:14am… Emma this is Shae, somethings happened. You need to call me as soon as you get this.*"

Panic starts to rise from my stomach into my chest. I hurry and listen to the next voicemails.

"*Thursday, 7:45am… Em, you need to get better about keeping your phone on you. Call me back, this is Shae.*"

"*Thursday, 8:50am… Emma, it's Libby. **sniff**. Call me.*"

"Oh, my gods, what?" I say out loud.

Two more voicemails.

"Thursday, 9:57 am… We really need to get our Link going, this is Shae. Call. Me."

"Thursday, 9:58am… Emma, love, it's Ty. Call me when you get this, please."

I don't know what I was expecting but hearing Ty's voice makes my panic simmer down a little.

I click on Shae's name and call her. As much as I want to talk to Ty, I need to make contact with Shae so we can get our Link connected, if possible. I'm not sure it can be done over the phone.

The phone only rings once when Shae answers.

"Good gods, girl!" Shae hollers into the phone. *"Took you long enough to call us back!"*

"I'm sorry," I say. "I slept until after 9 o'clock and then went and had breakfast and took a walk to help wake up. I'll do better about taking my phone with me. What the heck is going on and why are you awake at 1am?"

"Hold on, I'm texting everyone to tell them I have you on the line," she says. I here tapping and then she's back on the line with me. *"We're up still because shit has hit the fan around here. But we'll talk about that when they all get here. Before they do, I want to try to Link up."*

"How do we do that over the phone?" I ask.

"I don't think it has to do with it being on the phone, just us hearing each others voices and only our own. This long of a distance I think our minds need to have no distractions. Close your eyes and only think of my voice

and my mind," Shae says. I close my eyes and just focus on her mind and her voice. Within a second I feel like I'm with her.

"I've got you, do you have me?" I ask.

"I can feel a faint Essence," she says. *"Try to say something through the Link, don't say anything out loud."*

Shae, can you hear me?

I... I... her mental voice sounds weak and far away.

Shae, focus on my voice. Just follow my voice. I'm here. I'm right here.

I found you! Shae's mental voice hollers, making me jump a little.

"Oh shit!" I hear Shae exclaim into my ear.

"What happened?" I ask.

"Charlie just Jumped the guys here to my room," Shae says. From away from the phone, I hear her ask the room, *"Where's Libby?"*

"I'm here," I hear her faint voice and then a door shut.

"I'm putting you on speaker," Shae says.

Are you still there? Shae's mental voice asks.

Yes, but I can't talk to you and them at the same time.

Fair enough.

"What's going on?" I ask, getting my focus out of my head and back on what's going on with them.

It's silent on the other end. So silent, I look at my phone, thinking the call was dropped. But I see it's still connected. "Hello? What's happened? Does it have to do with Zack?"

"Have you heard from him?" Ty asks, hurriedly.

"He called me quite a few times early this morning, but I was sleeping. He left voicemails, progressively getting more frantic until he turned angry and said he was leaving and coming to find me. What's going on?" I ask again, but more sternly.

"He's escaped," Ty says flatly.

"Escaped?" I ask, unsure I heard correctly.

"Yes, and not just from the Estate, the island also," Ty says, sounding pissed now.

"How? We don't have any boats, do we?" I ask.

"No," Ty answers.

"Airplane?" I ask.

"We have them but he didn't take one," Charlie answers this time.

"Then how?" I ask, frantic.

"We don't know. The only other possibility is that he..." Libby starts to say. She takes a breath and then says, *"That he Jumped."*

"I'm sorry, what? You think he Jumped? No way, he wasn't a Demi," I say but then I'm hit with uncertainty. "Right? He wasn't a Demi?"

"We think he was," Ty states.

"More like a Rift," Charlie growls.

"What?" I say, confused. I sit on my bed because my head is spinning. "We would have been able to Sense it, right? That's one of the things about us, is that we can Sense another Demi. It's the way we can Track one another if we're looking for those who have been in hiding, right? Unless they put a... a Non-Trackable glamour on..."

"*We think that's what he did,*" Ty says. "*There's no other way for him to get off this island. And, he...*"

"He what?" I ask. I hear the room go silent again. I raise my voice out of anxiety of not knowing what's going on, "He what?"

"*He broke Frank out,*" Ty growls. "*They're both gone.*"

My brain goes numb for a second.

"How? How can this be?" I whisper out.

"*He had help,*" Shae says. "*Zack must of have had Vanessa help him hide who he was, she did it for nearly 18 years without us being able to Track her.*"

"ARRRGH!" I yell into the phone. "I can't believe I felt bad for him! I can't believe I let him trick me! I can't believe I fell for... his... story... His story! Was it even true?"

"*I sent Braylynn and Drew to do some investigating around the neighborhood last night,*" Ty says. "*We just came from debriefing them. The neighbors said the Brackets, the couple that lived there, didn't even have kids. Something about trying and not being able to, so they just decided to travel and see the World. Zack's story was a total lie."*

"Oh my gods," I whisper, realizing the truth. I put my hand to my mouth but a small sob escapes, "He killed them, he killed Mr. and Mrs. Bracket. And now that I know their real name, the name does sound familiar. We'd gotten their mail sometimes. He staged the house to look like someone broke in and there wasn't a little girl. There weren't any people there that looked like Meredith, Doc, or Billy, he made that up because he must have known we were looking for them."

"That's what we thought too," Libby says, sounding sad.

"I brought him into our home," I growl out.

"But the good thing is," Libby says, trying to find a silver lining. *"He can't tell anyone where it's at. It might have been his whole mission, to trick us into bringing him back to our new place so that he could report back to Vanessa. Even though he succeeded in getting there, he failed because he can't tell her where the Estate is located."*

"We're going to find him," Ty says firmly. *"We're going to find him and Frank. You don't have to worry."*

"I'm not worried about myself," I state. "I'm worried about what those two psychopaths are going to do to innocent people, especially Frank."

"We're going to find them," Max chimes in with

confidence.

"He was in that room, whether he put a Non-Trackable glamour on himself or not, his essence is all over that room," Ty says. "We'll figure out a way to find him."

"Track Frank!" I yell. "I doubt he's smart enough to have put a Non-Trackable on himself."

"Shit! Why didn't we think of that?" Charlie groans out.

"Because we were focused on Zack's lying ass," Clay growls.

"Max, go down and have them start doing a Track on Frank, see if we can get anything on him. I'll be down to help once I'm done talking to Emma," Ty says.

"Got it," Max says. I hear the door to Shae's room open and close.

"Am I on a wild goose chase?" I ask.

"What do you mean?" Libby answers first.

"I only decided to go looking for answers for our missing Leaders, after Zack mentioned them saying something about Montana. After talking to Tally, that's when I decided to go to Montana," I grumble out.

"I think it's important that you bond with the Beings from all the Realms," Shae states. "I think in the long run, it's what you're supposed to be doing. Don't worry about what's going on here, we're trained for this. All of us Beings need to be brought together, all the Realms joined together as one united front, and only you can do that."

"I just hope I'm not doing this, over here, when something bigger is going on somewhere else," I say.

"*No one knows where you are and that's probably how it should stay,*" Ty says a little sadly. "*As much as I want to know where you are and be with you to keep you safe, I think not knowing is actually keeping you safer. Zack knew you weren't here at the Estate, but he has no idea where you are, so he won't be able to find you. He won't be able to give Vanessa any useful information. She won't like that, although, she will be thankful to have Frank back, I'm sure.*"

"I'm going to keep my phone on me, from now on, and I'll have it set to vibrate when I get a call or text so that I can get back to you guys quicker," I say. "I'm hoping Bane will be back today and I'll be able to talk to him. Now that I know Zack's details about what happened were a lie, I doubt Bane has any information for us about our Leaders."

"*Whether you get that information or not,*" Libby says. "*Building a relationship with the Werewolves is priceless. You have a way about you that makes people want to be your friend. Want to be a part of your life. Shae's right, you're the only one that can bring the Realms closer together.*"

"*I'm not going to lie,*" Ty says. "*The bond between the Beings of the Realms haven't been as strong as they used to be. I was in on a meeting with Bill and Meredith once. There was some strife going on between the Realms. They all felt like not everyone was pulling their weight when it came to dealing with demons, whether they were minor or major demons. Some thought we Demi-gods were focused too much on finding Vanessa and protecting our own, that we forgot about our core code. Protecting the Inepties and the innocent against the evil in the World. Meredith tried to convince all the Leaders, that Vanessa was a bigger threat than they realized. Some of the Demi Leaders from different countries stopped coming to our Leader Conferences because they felt attacked by the other Beings. They felt like they were doing all they could to protect themselves as well as Inepties and the World from demons, almost stretching their resources thin. I, too, believe you are the one to join us back together, Emma."*

"I don't mean to change the subject, but you're talk about evil reminded me. I need tell you guys about a nightmare I had last night. Maybe you guys can help me figure it out," I say. I go right into my nightmare about the mystery man. Luckily it wasn't a long nightmare, but they stay quiet until I'm finished. "So, what do you think?"

"You mentioned, he said he was the king of gods?" Libby asks, sounding scared.

"Yes," I say timidly. "Why?"

"Oh gods, Ty... do you think it could be..." Libby starts to say. *"It couldn't be though."*

"What?" I ask, my voice shaking.

"*Kronos…*" Libby whispers. I hear all of them gasp.

"*It can't be,*" Ty says, sounding scared too.

"Kronos, as in the father to the gods? Father to Zeus, Poseidon, Hades, Demeter, Hera, Hestia, and Chiron?" I ask shocked.

"*Yes,*" Libby whispers.

"No, he's still in pieces, scattered down in Tartarus. I read about it in one of the books," I say. "One of the books there at the Estate."

"*He said Vanessa figured out how to communicate with him,*" Ty says.

"*Oh, my gods,*" Libby gasps again. "*He's how she's so powerful. He's taught her everything she's learned. How to steal Talents. I bet she's also behind the demons being harder to send back to the Underworld. He's told her how to do it all.*"

"*If the demons are getting stronger, that could be a sign that so is Kronos,*" Tally says. I hadn't realized she was there. "*If he's getting stronger, that could be why he was able to talk to Emma while she slept and project his image into her mind. He's not strong enough to do it while she's awake, which for now, is a good sign.*"

"Great, so not only do we have to worry about Vanessa and Chris, the Rifts, all demons being stronger, finding our missing Leaders, making the bond between all the Beings in all the Realms stronger for a better united front… now I have to worry about some beyond old, father of the gods, man creeping into my dreams and trying to seduce me into vowing myself to him?" I ask rhetorically. "Sure... no problem."

"Only two of those things you really have to do yourself," Shae says in a lighter tone. *"I know it'll be hard, but you'll have to practice putting up your Mental Shield before bed. I have no doubt you'll keep denying his attempts but who wants some random person creeping into their dreams at night. I know I don't. And yes, you are the only one that can bring us all together. But—"*

"But we're looking for our Leaders on this end as well, so you have help with that one," Ty interjects. *"Don't worry about Vanessa and the Rifts. You just keep doing what you're doing. Make sure all your defenses are up when you're out of the homebases of your Wolf friend... our Wolf friends. Demons don't stand a chance against you. If you do come across one, just hit it with your Pure Light Talent and it'll be instantly banished back to its fire hell of a home."*

"My Pure Light Talent?" I ask.

"That's what we've been calling the light that comes out of your hands," Libby says. *"It looks like the purest light I've ever seen. It's like sunlight, moonlight, starlight, firelight, all the natural light in the World, all balled up into one beautiful light."*

"I like that," I say, I look at my hand and let my Pure Light shine through just a little, so that it can comfort me. I hear someone yawn on the other side.

"You guys should all get some rest, it's so late there. There's not much more we can do right now. I'm going to take a nap myself and hope Bane and Maisie get here soon."

"Will you call me when you wake up?" Ty asks.

"Why don't you call me when you wake up?" I counter ask. "I know you're going to be going down to see if you can help Track Frank, but you can't be much help if you exhaust yourself. And if you guys do Track him, you can't just go out and get him. You all need rest to recharge your batteries. Promise me you'll get some rest."

There's silence for a second and then Ty says, *"I promise."*

"I'm going to turn my notifications to vibrate and I'll keep my phone in my pocket. Call or text if you find anything or need me," I say not only to Ty but for everyone.

"You do the same," Libby says.

"I will," I say.

"Good night," they say sporadically.

"Night," I say back.

"Talk to you soon," Shae says with a little implication in her voice. *I hope I'm the only one that caught that and no one becomes suspicious.*

"Bye," I say. She hangs up and I immediately go to my settings and turn on my notifications to vibrate. I put my phone in my pocket and lie down.

You okay? Shae's voice says in my head. I was expecting her, so it doesn't startle me.

Yes and no. It's nice to have an idea of what's going on but at the same time, why does it have to be Kronos behind Vanessa's crap? I ask.

Luckily, he's still not super strong. If he was, he'd be able to talk to you while you are awake. I was serious when I said to make sure your Mental Shield is always up. I know you got used to having it down around us but now more than ever, you need to protect your precious mind.

Won't that affect our Link.

Maybe but I'd rather have to talk to you over the phone or through text than leave your mind open for him to attack. But our Link might not be affected by your Shield. Like I said before, I think we've connected in a way no Seer and Demi have ever been connected.

Okay, I'll make sure my Shield is in place, good and tight.

Good, get some rest. I'm about to pass out myself.

Night. I say

Night.

Before I close my eyes to take a nap, I test my Mental Shield. I think about it wrapping around my brain. I decide to maybe see if it'll stretch around my entire body, to protect from anything Kronos might throw at me. Once I feel like everything is snug tight, I try to pull it away, and feel it protest around my brain and my skin. It's even protesting around my heart.

Interesting.

Feeling content that I've protected myself, I close my eyes and let myself fall into the darkness of sleep.

CHAPTER 24 -
ANOTHER ATTACK

I wake up with a start, sitting up quickly and looking around the room.

What was that? I look at my watch, it's 2:13pm. I'd slept for a good couple of hours. I try to listen harder. My Super Hearing takes over and I can hear running. So many people running around and their heartbeats are frantically beating, not just from the running, but in the way one's heart beats when their scared or upset.

*BANG*BANG*BANG*

"AWW!" I yell, covering my ears. I turn my Super Hearing off and hear the banging again, this time it's a normal sound coming from the door out in the living room.

I jump out of bed and Run to my door, I open it and see Xander standing in front of me. He looks pissed.

"What's wrong?" I ask, I move aside and motion for him to come into the room.

"There's been another attack," he growls.

"What?" I exclaim. "Here?"

"No, at Ondrei's again. Whoever it was, went back and completely burned the entire place down. Luckily none of us were killed but some of the men were hurt pretty bad. My sister, Helia, in New Zealand, sent her Force there to help gather all the men and they're taking them back to her homebase."

"What do we need to do?" I ask.

"Ondrei is taking a jet there this afternoon. He's going to go talk to Wassily and the other men and get whatever information from them he can get. We are doubling down security around all the homebases just to be ready for another attack. We don't understand why they've only attacked Ondrei's place though. There hasn't been even the tiniest blip of Rift or demon radar anywhere else."

"Before Ondrei goes, I want to talk to you guys. I talked to my friends back home earlier and what I found out might be useful information," I say.

"Let's go," Xander says, turning towards the door. "Ondrei was in his suite, packing. I'll text Lexie to meet us there."

Without another word, we walk out of the room. He pulls out his phone and sends a message. I follow him around the huge house until we're standing outside a huge oak door. Xander knocks once and then opens the door, walking inside.

"Ondrei, it's Emma and me," he hollers.

Ondrei comes from a room off to the left. The door behind us opens and hits me in the back. I hurriedly move out of the way. Lexie walks in followed by Lorcan.

"Oh sorry," Lexie says, patting my shoulder.

"What's going on?" Ondrei states. Shalien comes out of the room, rolling a small suitcase. "We're about done packing. Our jet will be ready to take off in 30 minutes."

"Emma talked to her friends back home and they told her something she thinks we should know," Xander says. They all look at me.

I tell them about Zack being a total fraud.

"So not only did Zack escape, but he also broke Frank out of his cell, so now they're both gone," I say.

"Sorry, who's Frank?" Lexie asks.

"He was one of my tormentors back when the Rifts had me," I answer.

"What?" Xander growls. "The Rifts had you?"

"Did you guys not know that?" I ask.

"No," Lexie says with her hand over her heart.

"You said that your parents told you guys about what Vanessa did to me and my parents," I say, looking at Ondrei.

"They told us how they'd murdered your parents

and kept you. She raised you like you were her daughter," he states.

"She did not raise me as a daughter or at least how I feel a daughter should be raised," I say. I shake my head, this is not the time for my emotional baggage. "I told you guys about how we went to Greece but it just turned out as a way for her to try to get me to Change quicker, right?"

"Yes," Ondrei and Xander say.

"No," Lexie says.

"Do you have time for a quick story?" I ask Ondrei.

"The jet won't take off without us and the damage has been done at home," he says sadly.

"I'm so sorry about that," I say.

"We can rebuild. I'm just so thankful we didn't lose anyone," he says, reaching out for Shalien's hand. She motions for all of us to have a seat.

I sit down and Xander sits beside me. Lexie and Lorcan sit across from us. Ondrei and Shalien sit in the loveseat to my right.

"Okay, so as a graduation gift, my mother... Vanessa... sorry, I slip up sometimes when I tell this story. I do not still think of her as my mother, just in this particular part of the story, I still thought she was," I say, clarifying my slip up.

"We understand," Lexie says. "Please continue."

"Okay, so I had been gifted a trip to Greece after I graduated high school, from Vanessa. I was so excited.

I had never traveled anywhere, not even out of New York City. We got to Greece, and we were in a taxi, heading to our hotel. We were hit by two black SUV's. Two men grabbed me and dragged me away. I saw two men stop Vanessa from coming after me, she was on the other side of the taxi. It looked like they were beating her up. Then they shot her," I pause as Shalien gasps.

"Oh my," Shalien says. Ondrei puts his arm around her.

"I started freaking out so one of the guys holding me hit me so hard I blacked out," this time Xander, well he doesn't gasp, he growls.

"He hit you?" he says through clinched teeth.

"Oh, just wait," I say. "I woke up in a room with dirt floors. I was there for three weeks. There were four men and one woman that would come into the room. She never spoke and I could barely see, I found out later it was Vanessa. The men would ask about the Mark, at the time I had no idea what they were talking about. The men would beat me until I was unconscious."

They all hiss and I feel Xander stiffen beside me. I see his hands are clenched into fists. I look over at him and his eyes are shut tight.

"It's okay," I say, patting his leg. "Look, I'm here. I'm fine."

"Nothing about this story is fine," he says between

his clenched teeth.

"Frank used to be one of my tormentors. I didn't know who he was at the time, I only knew him by his mint smell, which is why I called him Mint Man. He and another man, Tim, but I referred to him as Tobacco Man, were sent in as spies for Bill and the Guardians before I was taken. Tim would only slap me around and looking back, it didn't really hurt. I think he was only going through the motions to appease the others. He was also the one who brought me a dinner roll and water," I take a minute before I continue, giving them all time to process. "I've wondered if Vanessa knew who they were and that's why she had chosen them to torture me, to see how far they'd go. Either way, no one knew how far-gone Frank was and how messed up he became. He crossed over to her side and gave her the information she needed, and she told him he could be the one to end my life. Alcohol Man almost succeeded the last time he visited me, but Ty and his friends saved me sometime after that and I woke up in the Hospital Wing at The Pit."

"When did you find out about Frank?" Ondrei asks.

"Bill had called the Guardian's back for a debriefing. Frank returned, Tim didn't. We still haven't seen or heard anything from Tim. Bill and Ty think Vanessa did something to him. The debriefing happened to be on the day of my birthday. Everyone at

The Pit was throwing me a party. Frank showed up to it. I saw him from afar, I had never seen his face at the Rifts hideout, my eyes were always swollen shut or it was too dark to see anything. A friend, Charlie, who at the time, thought he had feelings for me, Jumped me to a different room for some privacy. He kissed me and I got mad. I told him to leave and go back to the party. I should have gone with him because Frank showed up but before I saw him, I could smell him. When I turned, I put a face to the man. He attacked me, but Ty showed up and saved me, again. And that's when I started to Change," I say.

I look around the room. Shalien and Lexie have tears in their eyes. The Weremen look as if they could rip a tree out of the ground right now.

"I have no words," Lexie says. "You've been through so much in the last couple of months. More than I thought, more than one person should have to endure."

"And for a young one and so small," Shalien says. She smiles and adds, "I don't mean to offend you. You are just so much smaller than any Demi-god, or Ineptie, for that matter."

"No offense taken," I say. I laugh a little and say, "I've been called small or tiny my entire life. Kids at school made fun of me because of it until they realized they couldn't get a rise out of me and then they just ignored me all together."

"And yet you are so selfless and kind," Lexie says. "It's astonishing that you are not bitter or hardened by the things that have happened to you."

"That's just it, they are just things that have happened to me, they aren't who I am. I chose to ignore the things kids said to me in school. I mean they weren't wrong, I was, and am, small. But I chose to ignore the mean things that were said or done to me. I choose, or try, to be a good person because that's who I want to be. I don't let the things that have happened to me, harden me, I just embrace the fact they're a part of my story and carry on with who I want to be," I say and then shrug because there's not much more to say.

Xander puts his arm around me and for the first time, gives me a hug. It warms my heart and makes me smile.

"I want to be like you when I grow up," he says and then laughs. We all laugh.

"We should all strive to be more like Miss Emma," Lexie says, as a tear falls down her face.

"So, we shouldn't hunt down the scum who calls himself Frank and send him down to Hades where he belongs?" Lorcan asks.

"No, I think that's the opposite of being like Miss Emma," Lexie says, chuckling as she taps her husband's knee. "However, we can still hunt him down and, with permission from Miss Emma, we can send him to the Stronghold."

"What's the Stronghold?" I ask.

"Hmmm—" Xander says, thinking "—think of the biggest prison you've ever seen or heard of, but times it by one hundred. That's the Stronghold. We run it down in Antarctica. It's so cold, not a lot of Beings can handle being there. The Stronghold is underground, it helps protect the occupants inside, from the frigid cold. Werewolves are the only ones who can survive outside for more than an hour. Demi's, Rifts, other Beings... they will literally freeze within 10 minutes of being outside, no matter how much clothing they put on. Even inside, prisoners have to wear specially made jumpsuits so they aren't freezing."

"Wow," I say, surprised. "I had no idea there was a place like that, but I did always wonder where all the Rifts would go if they got caught. I imagine it's mainly for Rifts?"

"There have been some other Beings that have gotten sent there," Ondrei says. "Werewolves are the only Beings that are completely loyal to their Leader. Jenna has a strong loyalty base from her family, but there are some that have defected from her. But that is her story to tell. So yes, the Stronghold has mostly Rifts there but there are a few Vampires and even Fae who have done such horrible crimes, their Leaders have sent them there."

"Once someone gets sent there, there's no

leaving," Lorcan adds. "I'm sure you were told we do not take someone's life just because, even with my joke about hunting Frank down, it would not have happened. When someone has done something and they do not get a second or third chance to make things right, they get sent to the Stronghold."

"When Vanessa and Chris get caught, they'll be sent there?" I ask.

They all look at each other and then back at me.

"That is one of their options," Lexie says. "It is for the Leaders of the Realms to decide their fate."

"Okay, so back to your original information. You said this person, Zack, escaped and took Frank with him?" Ondrei asks, getting us back on track. I see him look at his watch.

"Yes, sorry. My story telling sometimes makes me long winded," I smile sheepishly at him. "My friends are trying to Track Frank down. We believe Zack had put a Non-Trackable glamour on himself because we couldn't Sense he was a Demi. We could tell he was hiding something and that something didn't feel right about him, but none of us could put a finger on what was bothering us. Since finding out his true nature, I wonder if I would have spent more time with him, if I would have been able to figure him out. I was just so uncomfortable around him, I didn't like staying with him for very long."

"Do you believe he's connected to the attack at my

home?" Ondrei asks.

"Honestly, I don't know," I say. "I don't believe in coincidences but all I have are ideas or a feeling."

"Like what?" Shalien asks.

"I feel like he knew or at least guessed at where I was going. No one knew I was going to Montana. No one knew I was going to Jump to Australia just shortly after getting to Montana. And no one knows I'm here in Ireland. But I have a feeling something or someone saw me..." I trail off, suddenly remembering the man the night I got to Brisbane. My eyes go wide and I put my hand to my mouth.

"What is it?" Xander says, putting his arm back around my shoulder.

"I've just remembered. When I landed in Brisbane, it was dark. I walked through the square and when I got to the dock, I felt someone watching. When I turned, I saw a man standing back in the square. I pretended I was looking at a map and walked the opposite direction of where I was looking. He started following me, but I hid and put my Invisibility on—"

Lorcan interrupts me and says, "Your what?"

"It's one of my Talents, I can make myself invisible," I answer him. I continue with my story. "He walked past me. I kept my Invisibility on and went back to the dock. I Jumped myself to the lane leading up to your place."

"Did you recognize him?" Ondrei asks.

"No, not at all," I say.

"You say it was dark, how could you be sure?" Shalien asks.

"I have Night Vision," I say. And before anyone can ask, I add, "It's another one of my Talents"

"How many do you have?" Lorcan asks, impressed.

"I honestly have no idea," I laugh sheepishly.

"So, you got a good look at him?" Ondrei says again, getting us back on track.

"Yes, and I've never seen him before in my life," I answer. "But he could have been a Rift. I wasn't expecting to see anyone, so I didn't have my Senses scanning the area. I would have picked up that another Demi was within my vicinity had I been looking for one. I was so shocked at seeing him, I just wanted to get away. I didn't scan his Essence, just his mind quickly to see what he was thinking."

"I'll have the Force go into Brisbane and see if they can find anything," Ondrei states. He stands and says, "Thank you, Emma. This has been helpful."

"I'm sorry," I choke out. I've been holding back my tears since I realized the man in the square could have been a Rift and sent information to Vanessa, now the tears are rolling down my face. Xander's arm is around me again, holding me tight.

"For what, sweet girl?" Shalien asks, coming over to me. Ondrei right beside her. They kneel so their closer to eye level with me.

"I led that... man to you," I say between breaths. "Or led someone... to you guys."

"Absolutely not," Ondrei says, shaking his head. "This is not your fault. Whether that man is a Rift or not, you did not lead them to our home. They chose to go and they chose to set fire to it. Not you."

"How would he have known you were coming to North Stradebroke?" Shalien asks.

"You guys are the only Beings in the area, aren't you?" I ask.

"Jenna has her posts around Brisbane as well," Xander states, rubbing his hand up and down my back, trying to calm me.

"Oh gods," I exclaim. "They haven't attacked her have they?"

"We'll find out, but if they have, it's not on you," Ondrei says. "I'll send word to Jenna and ask how things are going on her end."

"Do you believe us, that none of this is your fault?" Shalien asks.

"It's hard to believe it when I feel like they did it because of me. They're looking for me, and if he told Vanessa he saw me on that dock, she would do anything to find me, to get to me," I say.

"Again, none of that is your fault," Shalien says. "Please believe me when I say it."

I nod but I don't really believe her. I didn't send

the person or people who set fire to their home, but I feel it down in my bones that it was because they thought I was there.

"Wait," I say. Having another thought. "Do you think they were still there? When I was putting the fire out? When I Jumped everyone here?"

"If they were, they were far away because we couldn't Sense anyone," Ondrei says. "We were on high alert. We would have been able to Sense them."

"But would you really? No one knew they were there to begin with, when they were starting the fire. If they had a Non-Trackable glamour or something to hide their scent, because they know how well your sense of smell is, they could have been undetectable," I say.

"She's not wrong," Xander says, reluctantly. "They could have watched her. They could have set the fires to see if she was there and if she'd show herself to put the fires out. She did just that and then she disappeared with us and the women and children. Whoever it was wouldn't have known where we went but this second attack could have been another way to draw her out but this time to ambush and take her. You need to get to Wassily and talk to him. Find out exactly what happened."

"Let's go," Ondrei says, standing up. He reaches his hand out for Shalien but before she takes his hand, she leans into me.

"You're safe here," she whispers into my ear as she hugs me.

"It's not me I'm worried about," I whisper back. She chuckles in my ear.

"Why does that not surprise me," she says as she stands.

"Ondrei," Xander says as he stands up, I stand with him. "Don't tell anyone that Emma is here. The longer her where abouts are unknown, the safer she'll be."

"I agree," Lexie says.

"My safety is the least of my worries. I don't want anyone to know where I am, so that I can keep the local Beings safe," I say. I look at Lexie, "Keep your family safe."

"My dear young one, you are part of this family now," she says, coming to me and hugging me. "Whatever this bond is you have made with my baby brother, it is a bond we all share. Our homes, are your homes."

"Well then, I'd like to keep the rest of these homes intact and not in ashes," I say. "And it sounds like keeping my whereabouts a secret will keep everyone, not just myself, safe."

"We must go," Ondrei says

Shalien hugs everyone goodbye, Ondrei does a forearm shake with the Weremen, and they head towards the door. Before leaving, they turn and salute me. I nod and salute them back

"I need to go to my room and make a couple phone calls. I need to let my friends know that I don't think Frank or Zack leaked information that I was visiting Werewolves. And maybe they'll know of any Rift activity in the Brisbane area," I say to Lexie, Lorcan, and Xander.

"I'll walk you to your room," Xander offers

"Lunch was served while you were resting, please go get something to eat before you make your calls," Lexie says. "I fear you aren't getting enough to eat, dear one.

"Thank you," I say. Now that she's drawn attention to my stomach, I can feel how hungry I am

"Katy will still be down in the kitchen," Xander states. "Let's get you some lunch and we can take it back to your room."

"Sounds good," I say. "I'd like you to stay for the calls though, if you don't mind. I want to introduce you to my friends. I think it would make Ty feel better knowing I have you to watch my back, even if he might be jealous he's not here to do it himself."

"Will he be jealous?" Xander smirks as we walk down the hall to the staircase.

"Don't all men get a little jealous when their girl is around another man?" I counter ask.

"Only if the man is insecure about himself and his relationship. If he doesn't trust the strength of the tie he has with his mate... his girl, then, yes I'm sure he would be jealous. Is Ty such a man?"

"No, I don't think so. I believe he knows what we have is the real deal. We are each other's Anima Gemella. But I think he might feel a touch of jealousy about him not being the one to be here to 'protect'—" I use air quotes "—me from whatever might come at me."

"You do not need protecting," Xander laughs.

"He knows that, but it's his instinct to want to protect me," I say.

"I can understand that," Xander concedes. "I feel the same way. It could be your small stature or the pureness of your essence that makes us feel this way. Even though you may look like you need protecting, in reality though, I pity the person or Being that comes up against you."

I hit my shoulder into him, which is his ribcage, and say, "Whatever."

Xander laughs so loud, that people turn and stare at us as we walk into the kitchen.

"Hi Katy," Xander says, still laughing. "Miss Emma here would like something to eat."

"If it's not too much trouble and nothing too fancy," I say hurriedly. "I don't want to be a bother."

"Not a bother at all," Katy says. She's got a beautifully thick Irish accent. She smiles at me and then her smile gets bigger as she looks at Xander.

"Uncle, you seem happy."

Xander just shakes his head but continues to smile. I look at Katy and see that she looks the same age as Xander and the other older Werewolves but from what Lexie said, she really is about 25 years old. She's beautiful. She has dark red hair, freckles across her nose, and really pretty green eyes. And like all the Beings, she's tall. I watch in silence as she makes me a sandwich

"Would you like pickles?" she asks

"Oh, on the side would be great," I say. I haven't had pickles in a while, my mouth starts to water just thinking about them

She puts a couple pickle spears to the side of my sandwich and then pulls out a fruit salad and adds a couple scoops to the plate. She then pulls out a box of chips. I reach in and grab the first blue bag I see.

"What would you like to drink? We have water, juice, soda-pop, sports drinks... pretty much anything you can think of," Katy says, walking over to another fridge on the other side of the kitchen.

"A soda-pop would be great, I haven't had one in a long time," I say. "Any brown flavor will be good."

She pulls out a blue can and walks it over to me, grabbing the plate from the counter, and hands both to me.

"If you need anything else, just let me know. I'll be down here all afternoon, preparing things for dinner," she says as she salutes me.

"Thank you," I say. I salute her back and turn to walk. Xander leads the way through the people that have gathered in the main room.

They say hi to us and wave. I nod and wave back. When we get to the stairs, I turn back and see everyone watching us.

"Why are they staring?" I ask.

"They're just curious about you."

I pull the plate to my face and pull a pickle into my mouth using my teeth.

Laughing, Xander says, "Can I hold something for you so you can eat?"

"You wouldn't mind?" I ask, as I let the pickle fall back down to the pate.

"Not at all," he says. "I'll hold the soda-pop, you eat."

"Thank you," I say as I hand him my blue can. I pick up the pickle and take a bite. "Sooo good."

"They are too sour for me," he says, making a face.

"These?" I ask, shocked. I hold the spear up in my hand. "They're one of my favorite foods."

"They get me right here—" he points to his jaw muscles and flexes them for emphasis "—every time I eat one. And even just thinking about it…"

I laugh and then slurp the pickle into my mouth. He grimaces and then laughs too. We get to my room and he opens the door for me. I go and sit on the couch, putting my plate with my sandwich on the table. He places the can by my plate and sits down on one of the comfy chairs.

I grab my sandwich and take a bite. While I chew, I get my phone out and look at the time

"If it's 3:57pm here, then it would be—" I do the math "—it's almost 6am at home, right?" I ask Xander

"Yes," he says

"I hope he got some sleep," I say more to myself than Xander.

CHAPTER 25 -
UNEXPECTED MATCH

I go to my phone app and tap on Ty's name. It starts to ring. I see Xander pull out his phone and he starts to type something into it.

It rings twice before I hear Ty's voice on the other end.

"Hello?" he says sleepily.

"Oh no, did I wake you?" I ask, putting my hand to my forehead. "I should have texted you first."

"Emma?" he asks, confused. With more alertness in his tone, he asks, *"Is everything okay?"*

"Yes, everything is fine," I answer. "When did you go to sleep?"

There's a muffled sound on his end, like he pulled the phone away from his face, and then the muffled sound again. Then Ty says, *"After we talked last night. You were right, getting some sleep was the best plan of action. So, I got about four hours of sleep."*

"I'm sorry," I say. "Go back to sleep and call me back in another couple of hours."

"Not a chance," he says, I can hear the smile in his

voice. *"I've missed hearing your voice. What are you up to?"*

"Having lunch right now. But I just got done having a talk with Xander and his siblings. I think we might have figured something out. Do you think you could round everyone up for an update?" I ask.

"Give me 10 minutes and I'll have everyone meet down in one of the Con-Rooms. Who all do you want to talk to?" he asks. I hear the muffled sound and then when he talks again, he sounds further away. *"I put you on speaker so I can send a group text."*

"Have the same group but make sure Malory and Alysa are there too," I say.

At Malory and Alysa's names, out of the corner of my eye, I see Xander look up at me. I look at him and see he has a confused look on his face. *What?* I mouth at him, but he just shakes his head and looks back down at his phone.

"Okay, done," Ty says in my ear. I hear the sound of blankets moving. The yearning to be there with him is so strong, I feel tears in my eyes.

"I miss you," I say and my voice cracks. I again see Xander look up at me but this time I ignore him. I don't need him to see how close I am to crying.

Ty stops moving on his end, I can tell because it goes quiet.

"Em, I miss you too," he says in a soft voice. *"We'll be back together before you know it."*

"Will we though?" I ask.

"It's your journey, Em. It's your rules, no one else's. You decide when you go and when you come home," Ty states.

"I hadn't thought about it that way," I say, laughing a little. I wipe a tear away. "In that case, I'll be coming home before I go on to the next Realm."

"Good because it's hard for me to sleep without you here," Ty says, softly again. *"I've gotten so used to you being in my arms at night, I've had to start cuddling around a pillow."*

"No, you haven't?" I laugh.

"I have too," he says, laughing also. *"I've missed your laugh too."*

There's a sound that comes through my phone, like a buzz. I look at my phone and see I have a text notification from Ty.

"Did you text me?" I ask, laughing harder.

"Just look at it," he laughs out.

I open the text app and tap on Ty's name. There's an icon for an image trying to come through. I click on it and it pops up of him lying on his bed, holding a pillow to his chest. The smile on his face makes me smile.

"Aww you look so cute," I say. "Lucky pillow."

"It's just a place holder for you and a poor place holder at that," he grumbles. *"It's not warm like you and doesn't cuddle me back. Doesn't kiss me or curl around me*

when I pull it close."

"I'm glad it doesn't, then I'd be fully replaced," I say sarcastically and laugh.

"You, Emma Hart, are irreplaceable," Ty says so sincerely, I can feel it in my heart that he truly means those words.

"I love you," I say, not caring that Xander hears me.

"I love you too," Ty says and I hear him moving around again.

I hear his phone being put down somewhere and then the sound of a drawer being opened. It sounds like he's pulling clothes out and then I hear a zipper. My face heats up a little as I know it's turning pink and I chuckle. *Why does that embarrass me so much? He's just putting on pants.*

"I'm going to go to the Con-Room and see who's all there," Ty states. I hear his bedroom door open and close. Then I hear wind for a couple seconds and then the wind stops, and I hear the ding of an elevator. *"Did you end up having a good nap?"*

He must of Ran to the Elevator

"Yeah, it was uneventful. My Shield worked or he didn't try to talk to me again," I say.

"That's good," Ty says. *"I'm sure it was your Shield. It's extremely strong."*

I hear the ding of the elevator door again. As he walks, he says good morning to unknown Demi's and then he says good morning to Phil. From there, I hear wind again.

"Did you Run?" I ask.

"I did," he says, surprise in his tone.

"I could hear the wind from it," I laugh.

"I'm the first one here," he says. *"I'll send another text and tell everyone I'm here. That might hurry them along."*

"Excuse my chomping, I'm going to finish my sandwich before everyone gets in there," I say as I take a bite of my sandwich.

"What chomping?" Ty asks. He chuckles and then says, *"You are the quietest eater I've ever been around."*

"It sounds loud in my head," I laugh. I look over at Xander and see him smirking and I have a thought, "Actually, Ty, I want to introduce you to Xander before everyone gets in there."

"Oh," Ty says, surprised. *"Okay."*

"Xander come here," I say, waving at him to come sit by me. "Ty, I'm going to switch to video call, okay?"

"Yup, sure," he says.

Xander comes over and sits beside me. I take a big bite of my sandwich, trying to get it finished and introduce these two before the group gets to the room. I don't know why, but I feel like I need to introduce them to each other before introducing him to the group.

I click the little video camera icon under Ty's

name and it starts making a dial sound. There's a weird sound and then it says connecting. Then Ty's face fills my screen.

"Hey, you," I say beaming at him. I hold the phone up and out from me, so my face isn't filling up the whole screen.

"Hey to you too," he smiles. *"It's good to see your face. Maybe we need to have all our personal phone calls like this from now on?"*

"I think I'd prefer that," I laugh. Xander clears his throat beside me. "Sorry, Xander."

"Just reminding you I'm in the room," he laughs.

I shake my head and turn the phone so it shows Xander and me.

"Ty, this is Xander Woods. Xander, this is Ty Conner," I say.

"Nice to finally meet you and put a face to your name," Xander says, he lifts a hand and waves. "I've heard a lot about you."

"It's nice to meet you as well. You're Bane's son, right?" Ty asks, cordially.

"I am. I'm the 6th born, 3rd son to Bane and Maisie," Xander says. I've come to realize that when they introduce themselves or other 2nd and 3rd generation Werewolves to someone, they add in their lineage proudly.

"I wanted you to see that I'm not completely alone or doing this all by myself. That I have backup if I need it," I say. I don't know why I feel nervous all of a sudden. I don't doubt my feelings or Ty's feelings for me, but I don't know how he'll react to Xander accompanying me from here on out. I don't know how he'll react to finding out we have a weird connection. *Here goes nothing*, "We have found that we have some kind of connection and he will be with me until we figure out what this connection means."

I brace myself for a look of outrage or something awful to cross Ty's face. Or for him to get outright angry, but he just smiles and says, *"Only you would connect with a Werewolf."*

"What does that mean?" I ask, stunned.

"I don't mean anything bad. Just that Werewolves are tough and great warriors. I should have guessed you'd become close with them," Ty says, shrugging. He looks at Xander and asks, *"She's easy to like, isn't she?"*

"Like breathing," Xander says, looking at Ty and then at me.

Ty laughs and says, *"Exactly."*

"So, you're okay knowing he'll be with me from here on out?" I ask.

"It makes me feel so much better, Em. To know you have a second-generation Werewolf as your backup man, I can breathe so much easier now," Ty says, once again, so sincerely, I feel it deep inside my heart.

In the background I see Charlie walk in, holding Shae in his arms.

"Is she okay?" I ask, suddenly worried.

"She had a Vision so she's pretty tired," Charlie says. *"She insisted on coming even though I told her I'd fill her in."*

"I'm not missing an Emma meeting," Shae says tiredly.

I don't have time to respond to her because everyone else starts filing into the room.

"Ty, is there a way to put me on one of the TV screens?" I ask. "I don't think everyone will be able to huddle around your phone."

"Sure can," he says. He walks over to a computer and puts the phone down. I hear typing as he looks back behind where his phone is sitting. For a second my screen goes black and then I'm viewing the room from a different angle. Everyone turns and looks at me.

"Hi," I say, waving and smiling at everyone.

Libby runs up and I see Shae tapping Charlie's shoulder, motioning to put her down. Once on the floor, she walks up to the screen as well.

"Emma!" Libby says, smiling and waving too.

"Em! Hi!" Shae says, excitedly.

"Sup, Em!" Charlie says, coming and standing behind Shae.

"Hi everyone," I say. "I've missed seeing you all."

"Why don't we all have a seat and then Emma can tell us what they've found out?" Ty suggests.

The girls wave and walk back to the tables but pick the closest seats to the screen. I smile at them and see Alysa and Malory walk in through the door. Xander sits up and leans in, his head tilts to the right. He squints and his head tilts back to the left side.

"You okay?" I ask him. He looks at me and then back at my phone. He looks around our room and then back at the phone. "Hey, are you okay?"

He looks at me and then shakes his head a little, and clears his throat, and whispers, "Yeah, I think so."

"Emma, why don't you introduce everyone to your new friend?" Ty draws my attention from Xander's strange behavior back to my phone.

"Umm, yeah... Let's start with that... Everyone, this is Xander Woods, 6th born, 3rd son to Bane and Maisie," he smiles at me as I introduce him as if I were one of them. "Xander this is everyone."

They all wave and say hi.

"Hello," he says. I'm watching the screen when he says this so I see Alysa look up immediately from the table.

"When I say your name, just wave so that he can put a name to your face, okay?" I ask. They all nod. "You met Ty a few minutes ago. This is Libby and Max, Shae and Charlie, Tate and his sister Tally, Clay and Malory, and Alysa."

I turn to watch Xander's reaction when I say Alysa's name. His eyes go big, his pupils dilate to the

EMMA HART AND THE WEREWOLVES

point his brown irises disappear, and his nostrils flare enough for me to notice

I hear him whisper her name, "Alysa.

Dude, Alysa is about to hyperventilate over here. I hear Shae through our Link.

I look at the screen and see Malory looking at her, touching her shoulder. Alysa shakes her head. I look back at Xander and his eyes and nostrils are back to normal. He looks more relaxed. Well, actually, he looks at peace.

"Are you okay?" I whisper.

"We can talk about it later," he whispers back and smiles.

"Oookay," I say. *No freaking way.*

"Em?" Ty gets my attention again.

"Right, the information," I stammer out. "I had forgotten that when I arrived in Brisbane, I had walked through a town square to get to the dock and there was a man. It was dark since it was really late at night, or early in the morning, however you want to look at it. Anyways, I didn't know he was there until I felt like someone was watching. I had turned and saw him. So, I acted like I was following a map and went a different direction. He followed, but I had already gotten to where I could hide and use my Invisibility. After he'd gone past me, I Jumped to Ondrei's place. We feel like he might have been a Rift and might have leaked, to Vanessa, that I was in the area. They tried to burn down the place while I was there. I think they were watching and set the fires to draw me out, to see if I was there. Today, they attacked again but succeeded in burning it all."

Libby gasps and puts her hands over her mouth, *"Did anyone get hurt? Are you okay? Oh, all the kids!"*

"Some of the Weremen got hurt but they'll be okay. I'm fine because—" I look over at Xander and then back at my phone "—I haven't been there since the first fires. I put the fires out with my Water Talent. Then I Jumped the Werewomen and children…"

"Don't tell us," Ty hollers. *"We can know everything except for where you are, I think it's safer that way."*

"I trust all of you," I say.

"And we appreciate that," Shae says. *"But your location should only be known to us if there's an emergency."*

"Okay, well, I Jumped them somewhere else, and I've been here ever since," I say. "I think the second attack was to draw me out again or to see if I was still there because I think this time they were going to ambush and try to take me, again."

"Good luck to those who try," Max says, giving me a head nod.

I laugh and say, "I'm not worried about myself, but I don't want any more homebases being destroyed because of me. Ty, is there any way to find out if the Vampires have had any attacks on their places there in, or around, Brisbane?"

"*Yes, why?*" he asks.

"I can't believe the Rifts would just immediately assume I was there to go visit the Werewolves if there were other Beings around as well. Xander says that Jenna has posts in Brisbane, I very well could have been going to visit them. I'd like to find out if anything has happened with them as well," I say.

"*I'll get a message out to Jenna now,*" Ty says, he takes his phone off the table and starts typing something on it.

"*What can we do?*" Max asks.

"Get in touch with all the Searchers and Guardians out on missions. See if they've heard or seen anything out of the ordinary. If Rifts have been flooding areas they normally aren't known to congregate, we need to know. Also, if they're packing up a known hangout and leaving, we need to know where they're going," I say. "Have you guys found anything on Frank's whereabouts yet?"

"*We've been able to pick up a Track, we're just waiting for him to stop and stay in one place for more than a couple of hours,*" Ty says. He puts his phone down and looks up at the screen. "*I'll let you know as soon as we have something.*"

"I'm guessing we have no Trace on Zack?" I ask, already knowing the answer.

"*None,*" Ty says frustrated.

"I can get some of the sub-packs in the States to be on the lookout for him. If you can get me a picture of him, I can share it with them," Xander states. Alysa's head snaps up as soon as Xander starts talking but as soon as he's done, she looks back down at her hands.

"How will you share it with them?" Shae asks.

"I will Shift and use our Mind link, they will see everything I want to share with them, whoever has Shifted. We always have a couple in Wolf form in all the sub-packs for situations like this, getting into contact will not be difficult," he says. Again, Alysa looks up as he talks.

"So, it doesn't necessarily have to be a picture, I could share an image of him from my thoughts to you Telepathically and it would serve the same purpose, right?" I ask.

"Yes, that would work," Xander says.

"Is there anything else we can do on this end of things?" Charlie asks.

"I don't think so, but if I think of something, I'll send a group text," I say. "You guys do the same."

"We will," Ty says.

"Thanks, guys," I say earnestly.

RINGRING**RING**RING**

Ty looks down at his phone and says, *"Phil's calling me. Emma, if that's all for now, I'll call you later?"*

"Yeah, I think we're finished for now," I say.

"*Bye, Em,*" Libby says. "*It's so good to see your face.*"

"*Yeah, we need to call like this more often,*" Shae says, smiling.

"From now on, this is how we'll debrief, sound good?" I suggest.

"*Sounds good!*" Shae and Libby say at the same time.

The guys all wave and say bye, Ty sends me a wink, Malory waves bye as well. Alysa though, she hasn't stood up yet and she's staring at the screen, at Xander. Xander is staring back also.

"Bye guys," I say. I turn to Xander and watch his expression as I hit the end button to end the call. He lets out a huge breath and closes his eyes. I put my hand on his forearm and ask, "What's going on?"

"It's her," he breathes out in a whisper.

"Alysa?" I ask in a question even though I know that's who he's talking about.

"Yes, Alysa," he says her name as if he's caressing her with his voice.

"Xander," I say his name as gently as I can because I want to jump up and start clapping my hands in an excited gesture.

"Mmmm," is all he says.

"Look at me," I say. Xander turns slowly, breathing in and out slowly. When he opens his eyes, I can see that the color has lightened from the color of chocolate to a dark honey color. I ask, keeping my excitement reeled in, "She's your Anima Gemella, isn't she?"

A smile so big, one I've never seen on his face, slowly spreads across his face, he looks down shyly and then up at me, "Yes, I believe she is my Mate. Even from far and through the phone, our hearts called to each other."

"EEEEK!" I squeal and then I jump up and start clapping. "I could tell something was going on between you too. I can't believe you could tell over the phone. But wait, when I mentioned her name, before you even saw her, you had a reaction, didn't you?"

"Yes," he states. "Something inside of me recognized that name, or maybe the person in which you were referring. Something woke up inside of me and told me she was who I had been waiting for, for all these years."

"We have to get you to her," I say, walking around the room.

"Emma," Xander says as he shakes his head. "If I was meant to be with her right now, I would be. I now realize my journey to my Mate is through you, but we have a different journey to finish before I'm finally united with my Alysa."

He says her name again with so much love wrapped around it, I can almost feel it in the air.

"Maybe this is the reason for our connection, I am

your contact that leads you to your Anima Gemella!" I say excitedly.

"Perhaps we should go see if Lexie or Ondrei have heard from Father or Mother," Xander says "Maybe the sooner we speak with them, the sooner we can be on with our journey."

"Let's go," I say, heading to the door. I open it and wait for Xander to stand and walk towards me.

Xander chuckles as he walks past me and I hurriedly follow him down the hall. Our pace is a little quicker than it has been before. I've been thinking about going home since Ty reminded me that I make the rules when it comes to my journey but now that I know Xander and Alysa are each other's Anima Gemella's, I want to get home to properly introduce them. I want to see how this will change Alysa, hopefully for the better.

Shae, you there? I send out to Shae in our Link.

Yup, I'm here. What's up?

You might want to check on Alysa. Xander just said she's his Anima Gemella. Well, actually, he said she's his Mate but it's the same thing. Don't say anything to her, I'd hate to be there for her being impatient on meeting him in person. He and I will be coming home once this first part of my journey is over.

Are you serious? I can hear the shock and excitement in Shae's mental voice.

I could see something happening to them and I asked

him after I hung up because his reaction was weird when the phone call ended. He said what he said and he looks different, more at peace kind of, I don't know how to explain it. Even his eyes are a lighter color.

Okay, I'll check on her. What do I say if she asks about him?

As much of the truth as you think she can handle. It's up to you, I guess, if you tell her what he said. You can tell her we'll be coming home at some point. But that might also make her unbearable... not knowing exactly when that will be.

I'll think of something to tell her if she asks.

Sounds good. Let me know if anything comes up about Frank and Zack.

You, too.

I will. I'm about to say bye but then I remember she had been carried into the meeting by Charlie because she was tired from having a Vision. *Oh, hey, what was your Vision about?*

Honestly, I don't know. It was so jumbled and confusing. I couldn't make sense of any of it. I can feel another one coming on. Charlie is taking me back to my room right now. I'll keep you posted.

Okay. Get some rest too. Bye, Shae.

Bye, Em.

After my mental conversation with Shae, I turn my attention to where Xander and I have arrived, a door I haven't been to yet.

"What's this?" I ask.

"Lexie's office," Xander answers as he knocks on the door once and opens it. He steps inside and holds the door open for me.

I look around and see floor to ceiling bookshelves on three of four walls, the wall behind Lexie's desk is one huge window. She has a desk that looks as if it would take ten of the strongest Werewolves to move. In the corner, is another desk much smaller than Lexie's. It has a large map of the World spread out acrossed it.

"Well, hello there," Lexie says, standing from her desk as she closes her laptop. "What can I do for you two?"

"Have you heard from Father yet?" Xander asks.

"Not yet," Lexie says. "Why?"

Xander looks at me and I smile widely at him, nodding at him.

"It's just we would... I... the journey... our journey... Emma..." Xander sounds confused.

"Xander, breathe," I say, chuckling and smiling warmly at him.

"What's going on, brother?" Lexie asks, coming to stand in front of him. She puts her hands on his massive upper arms and looks up into his eyes. "What has you so tongue tied? And what is up with your eyes?"

"I've found her," he blurts out.

"Found who?" Lexie asks confused, looking between me and Xander. I smile and put my hands to my mouth.

"My Mate, sister. I have finally found my Mate," Xander breathes out, not quite in a whisper but not shouting it like I want to for him.

"You've... you've found your Mate?" Lexie asks slowly and then ends excitedly. She runs to me and hugs me. "I knew you were something special to him."

"Nooo," I say hurriedly. "Not me."

Lexie slowly pulls away from me and looks between Xander and me, again confused. She asks, "Then who?"

"Emma just called home and I saw her. Even over the video call, I could feel our hearts calling each other," Xander says, running his hands through his hair. He sits in one of the large chairs in front of Lexie's desk.

"She's a Demi?" Lexi asks, shocked.

"Yes, Alysa," Xander whispers and that same feeling of love is wrapped around her name. He looks up at his sister and they stare at each other for a minute that feels like it drags on when they don't say anything else.

"Is that a bad thing?" I ask, not able to handle the quiet anymore. I was so excited that Xander had found his Mate, that Alysa's Anima Gemella has been found, I didn't think of the complications it might cause for two different Beings to be Mated. Lexie and Xander look at each other and then at me.

"We're not sure," Lexie says. "Father is the last Demi-god to have been Changed and he was changed by the original demon beast. Our spouses have all been Inepties. There has never been an attempt to change a Demi-god because no one has ever been Mated to one."

"I would guess it would be the same as when your father was changed, wouldn't it?" I ask. They share another look and then just shrug. "So, another reason to find Bane and Maisie and talk to them. They might have an answer."

"I'm going to go Shift and see if anyone has been in touch with them. Maybe they are in their Wolf form also and I can talk to them directly," Xander states. "Would you like to see me Shift?"

"Oh, can I?" I ask, excitedly.

"Let's go," Xander says, standing and walking towards the door. "I need to do something, or I might go crazy."

"I'll make some phone calls and see what I can find," Lexie says as we get to the door.

"Thank you," Xander and I say at the same time.

"Xander?" Lexie calls, making us both stop and turn towards her. She beams at Xander and says, "I truly am happy for you. No matter what Father and Mother say, you and Alysa will have your happy life."

"Thank you," Xander says sincerely. He turns and walks out the door, I follow him and shut the door behind us.

"Does Alysa being a Demi-god, mean you guys can't be together?" I ask.

"No, not at all," Xander says, slightly shocked. "It just means she might not be able to Change. If she can't be Changed, I don't know if we can have children. It just has never been done, so there are just some unanswered questions."

"I'm sorry," I say. "I didn't even think about any complications that might come between two Beings."

"It's okay, it's not your fault. And even if we can't have children, we can have a happy life together, that I am sure of," Xander says with so much assurance, I smile at him.

"I just can't believe your Anima Gemella is Alysa," I say, sounding more shocked now than excited.

"Why is that? Can you tell me about her?" Xander asks as we get to the front door and he leads us outside.

"Oh… ummm," I stammer out. "I'm not really the right person to ask about her.

"Why is that?"

"We haven't gotten along very well until recently."

"I'm confused, how could someone not get along with you?"

"It's a long story," I say. "One that I think Alysa should tell you."

"Okay," Xander says a little confused.

We walk down a different trail, not the same as the one that led to the lake. We only walk a little bit before we walk into a smaller clearing. There aren't any houses or buildings or anything here.

"What's this place?"

"It's where we bring the young ones to teach them how to Shift and use their Wolf traits."

"Oh, okay."

"Stand here, and watch," Xander says. I stop walking as he continues a little further into the clearing. "Don't be scared when I Shift. I'm still me inside my Wolf form."

"Okay," I say with a little choking sound. *Why am I nervous?*

Xander stops and turns towards me. I watch as he puts his head back and opens his arms out wide beside him. I was expecting him to shake, morph grotesquely, and for it to look and sound painful and take a long time, but what I see is the opposite.

One second Xander the Wereman is standing in front of me and then the next second a huge Wolf is walking towards me. At first, I want to say his Wolf form is as tall as an elephant, but it's not that big, maybe as tall as a large Clydesdale horse. It is, however, a lot bigger than any wolf I've seen in books or movies or tv documentaries. I watch as Xander walks towards me and when he's about ten feet away, he sits on his haunches and then lies down. When he lies down, and puts his head down, I can see his eyes are still the same dark honey color they changed into after seeing Alysa. His fur coat is the color of his hair, dark brown.

Xander, you're a handsome Wereman but your Wolf form is beautiful.

He jumps a little when I start to talk to him Telepathically.

How can you do that? he asks.

I tap my temple with my right hand, and I say, *One of my Talents. I thought I'd share that image of Frank and Zack with you since you'll be communicating with the others–* As soon as I say it, I can hear other voices in his head. *–I can hear them.*

You can? he sounds surprised.

I do not recognize this voice. A male voice says, confused.

They can hear me through you, apparently. I say, astonished.

Uncle Xander, what's going on? A female voice asks.

Emma Hart is here, somehow, in my mind. She is here in person with me, at Lexie's. We are needing you all to spread the word that we are looking for these two Rift's. They were captured and being held at the North American Demi-gods' new homebase, but they escaped.

As Xander is explaining that Zack and Frank escaped, I share a mental picture of them with Xander. His Wolf form tilts his head to the side as he's looking at me. *We are wanting to know if Father and Mother are in any of your Region's as well. We need to speak to them immediately. One more thing, keep an eye out for the North American Demi-gods' Leaders, Meredith, Doc, and Guardian Commander, Bill. They have been missing for a couple of months now and we all need to help locate them.*

As he started talking about our Leader's, I shared a mental picture of them with him as well.

There is a resounding echo of 'yes, sir's' and 'you got it, sir's'.

Get into contact with me via cellphone, or Lexie, as soon as possible if anything is found about any of these people that I have shared with you. Make sure the images are shared throughout your packs and pack leaders. That is all. Emma, I'm going to Shift back now.

I pull myself from Xander's mind and take a step back.

"That was interesting," I say and smile at him.

He grunts out a half laugh, half bark. Realizing he's about to Shift back, I close my eyes and turn from him. I didn't see his cloths shred into pieces but I sure as heck don't want to see him standing in front of me naked.

"Are you alright?" Xander says from behind me. His Shift is so quiet. I'm sure it makes their ability to sneak up on someone effortless.

"Yes, just wondering if you have a stash of clothes in the clearing?" I ask, embarrassed.

Xander chuckles and I can hear him walking around to stand in front of me, thankfully my eyes are still closed. He says, "Why would I need a stash of clothes?"

"Are you not naked?" I ask.

"Not at all," he laughs.

I open my right eye a tiny bit and see him standing in the clothes he had on before he Shifted. I open my eyes all the way and look at him questioningly.

"So, your clothes disappear when you Shift and reappear when you Shift back?" I ask, looking him up and down.

"Yes," he says. "Something about the magic in the Talent of Shifting. What did you expect?"

"Well, I thought your clothes would explode into smithereens, from your massive Wolf size compared to your Wereman size," I answer honestly.

"I guess I can see how that would be your assumption, but no, luckily our clothes do not explode," he laughs. "Whatever we are wearing when we Shift, is what we Shift back into. Sometimes, it's no big deal, other times, it can be a slight inconvenience."

"Like how?"

"Say we're here swimming in the lake and we get called to action and we Shift, we Run and Run and end up in, say, Greenland, when we Shift back, we'll be in a much colder area in swimsuits," he laughs. "Lexie once Shifted wearing a gown from a gala party she was at and ended up in South America before she was able to have time to Shift back. It was quite comical to see her standing in the desert in a gown meant for a ball."

"You guys must be able to Run and swim faster in Wolf form?"

"Yes, much faster," he says and then chuckles. "But not near as fast as you are able to Jump us."

I laugh and I'm about to say something when his phone starts to ring in his pocket.

CHAPTER 26 -
FIGHTING ALONGSIDE WEREWOLVES

Xander is chuckling when he pulls his phone out of his pocket and without looking at the caller, he answers, "Hello?"

His face goes from carefree and laughing to, shocked and panic within a single blink of my eye.

"What?" I ask him as I step up to him, my hand on his arm.

He puts his finger up for me to wait a minute. His nostrils flare and he looks ready to kill, "We'll be right there. Call all the Force's and have them standby and ready to leave in 30 minutes."

Xander is walking before he hangs up without saying anything else.

"What is it?" I ask, running to keep up with his long strides.

"Another attack," he says between clenched teeth.

"Where?" I cry out.

Xander turns to me, "Montana, Father and Mother's homebase. That was Bronson that called.

They're holding the attack off at the perimeter of the clearing, but the attacker's attempts are getting fiercer. He says it's a force he's never fought against before. We must hurry. I need to get the Elite Force assembled."

"Can I Jump us to Lexie's office?"

"Yes," Xander skids to a halt. He sticks his hand out and I grab it and Jump us immediately to her office.

"What in the world?" Lexie says, startled.

"Bronson just called, someone is attacking Father's homebase," Xander says hurriedly. "I'm going to get the Elite Force assembled and head there. You should get your Force Unit's B and C out on perimeter sweeps now and keep the boundary on lock down," Xander says, reaching for his phone.

"I should go with you," Lexie says.

"You need to stay here and make sure you're Region is taken care of and protected," Xander says, putting his hand on her shoulder. "Follow protocol. I know our homebases have never been attacked so much in our history, but we have protocol for this, follow it."

She takes a calming breath and says, "You're right. What can I do to help?"

"Help me call the Regions and tell them to have their Force Unit A ready. Elite Force is going into combat," Xander says. "I'll have the jet up and running in half an hour."

"We don't have that kind of time," I say. "We need to get the Elite Force and get to Montana now. Tell them to be ready in 5 minutes. I'll Jump us around and pick them all up along the way."

"No," Xander exclaims. "There are over 200 members of the Elite Force. That is far too many for you to Jump. Especially the long distances between Jumps."

"Xander, I can do this. I can get us to Montana quicker than any jet. We need to get there now, to stop whatever is attacking and to save your people... your family! I will not be told what I can and can't do. I know I can do this, tell them to be ready in 5 minutes, I'm going to go pack my things," I don't wait for his reply. I Jump myself to my room and Run around packing as fast as I can. I see my clothes that I wore here, are folded on the coffee table. I grab them and can smell that they've been washed. I grab my phone and call Ty.

As it starts to ring, I check the time. It's 4:43pm. The phone only rings twice before Ty answers.

"Hello?" he says, sounding out of breath.

"Ty, Bane's homebase is under attack—"

Ty interrupts and says, *"I know, we Tracked Frank to just a mile outside of where Tate showed us on a map where Bane's place is and Frank hasn't moved from there since early this morning. That's what Phil was calling to tell me.*"

"I'm going to Jump the Elite Force there and stop whatever is happening. If you guys can get there, I think it would be a good thing," I say, pulling the bottoms of my battle gear out of my bag and grab my battle gear top off the coffee table. I grab my Magikida out of my bag before I put the rest of the clothes back inside it. I put it in my backstrap on my battle gear top before I put my backpack on. I put my tennis shoes in my duffle bag and pull on my boots. I sling my duffle bag across my body and head out of my room, talking to Ty as I go. "Bring as many Guardians as you can. I don't know what the Rifts are trying to do or prove, but we need to help the Werewolves stop them. We need to show the Werewolves and the other Beings from different Realms, that we have their backs."

"*I'll bring everyone I can,*" Ty says. He sounds like he's running. "*Emma, promise me something?*"

"I'll try…" I say. "You know I can't promise anything when it comes to fighting the Rifts and Vanessa."

I hear him laugh slightly, "*Just promise me you'll be careful.*"

"I'll try my best," I say. "You be careful too."

"*I'll try my best,*" he repeats my words back to me.

I get back downstairs, I see Werewolves running around everywhere. "I have to go, I need to find Xander."

"*I love you,*" Ty says.

"I love you too," I say.

"*Bye, Em.*"

"Bye, Ty."

I don't bother hanging up, I sling my backpack to my side and slide my phone into the side pocket and zip it up. I'm just readjusting my backpack when I find Xander by the front door.

"Ready?" I ask him.

"Nearly," he says. He's changed into all black clothes. It must be their version of battle gear because as I look around, I see all the Werewolves that are starting to gather around, are wearing the same type of clothes. I'm happy to not only see Weremen, but Werewomen as well. Xander is looking around the crowd and shouts, "Miles?"

A Wereman comes up and salutes us as he stands in front of Xander.

"Yes, sir," Miles says.

"Do a head count. Make sure everyone is here, I want it done quickly," Xander commands. Miles doesn't reply with anything more than a nod. He blurs away as he Runs through the assembling crowd.

"All accounted for," Mile says, he wasn't gone more than 3 seconds.

"Fall in!" Xander yells. All the Werewolves fall into lines immediately. "Miss Emma is going to Jump us to each Region to pick up the rest of the Elite Force.

Stay in contact with your neighbor or you will be left behind, along with everyone behind you. Do not make that mistake, I will not be happy if we have to come back for you. Am I understood?"

"Understood, sir," the whole Unit replies together.

"Very well, take the hand of the person beside you. Those of you on the ends, listen up. Front row right, put your hand behind you, second row right, reach forward and take the hand in front of you. Second row left, put your hand behind you, third row left, reach in front of you. Do you see what I'm wanting accomplished? Let's get it done, you have 10 seconds," Xander commands.

I move to the left of the Unit with Xander. He stands with his hand on the shoulder of the first Werewolf. I reach my hand out for Xander's and he takes it.

"What do you need from me?" Xander asks.

"Just think of where we need to go each time, and I'll see it in your head," I say. "Think of exactly where we need to Jump into, hopefully near the Unit we're picking up but not close enough that we'll land on them."

"They have their instructions, we won't have that problem," Xander states.

"Okay then, just think of the first place and we can get going," I say.

"Everyone got a hold of a neighbor?" Xander yells.

"Yes, sir," another unison response.

Xander looks at me and nods. I let my mind search for Xander's mind and I see our first location. I act like I'm going to take a step and then we're there. It looks like a desert.

Xander lets go of my hand and I stand in my spot. I let him instruct the new Unit on what to do. It doesn't take more than a minute and then we're ready to go again. The next location is the same as this one

We repeat all of this until we're at the last place, which is in a deep, dark, green forest. I feel like I'm breathing water. I wipe the moisture off my forehead. This humid heat is getting to me, I feel lightheaded. I sway but Xander is back to me and puts a hand to my back.

"This is becoming too much," he says sternly.

"No, I need a snack and a drink," I say. I turn to grab my backpack but sway again. I turn so my backpack is facing Xander and say, "In my backpack, I have water and a granola bar, will you grab one for me please. If you need something, take what you want."

"I'm fine but I'm worried you're pushing yourself too much," he says, but I feel him unzip my bag and rummage around. He hands me a bottle of water over my shoulder and I take it. I down it in three gulps. I hand him my empty bottle as he's handing me the granola bar.

"I'll be fine," I say around a bite of the bar, I

practically inhale it.

"Would you tell me if you weren't?" he asks.

"Probably not," I say and smile.

Xander doesn't smile back, "What good will you be to us if you pass out? Or worse, hurt or killed?"

"Xander, I'm fine," I say sternly. "My body and mind push until it knows the danger is over and then that's when I crash. I just need rest after, nothing is going to happen. I feel pretty good and I'm Jumping what, over 200 Werewolves right now?"

"Give or take," Xander says, eyeing me.

"I'm fine," I say again. I turn away from him as I put the wrapper of my granola bar into my pocket. "Let's get going. This was our last stop, right?"

"Yes, we'll be to Montana in record time," he grumbles out.

"Why don't we Jump into Bane's area and grab the Force Unit there, first? Then, if there's somewhere else we can Jump to, that's nearby, maybe we can draw the Rifts away from homebase, keep the kids and nonfighters safe," I suggest.

"That's not a bad idea," Xander says after he's checked to see if everyone is in contact with someone. "There's a clearing not too far from Father's. It's close enough the Rifts should be able to Sense us and if they don't, we can sneak up on the ones in the area."

"I meant to tell you before we left Lexie's, Ty is bringing all the Guardian's that are left at home. They might already be there, since our home isn't too far from Montana. Well, closer than we are," I laugh.

"Do they have someone that can Jump them to Montana?" he asks.

"As far as I know, Charlie can only do four, maybe six tops, at a time," I say. "I know he's been practicing doing more but it might be better for them to fly in and then Run."

"We'll appreciate the help," Xander says. He turns and tells the group that there will be Demi-gods there fighting alongside us and to make sure to only fight the Rifts.

"How will they know the difference?" I ask.

"The Rifts put off a funky smell, not quite rotten but something not right," Xander says as he takes my hand.

"Yuck," I say.

"Makes it easy to identify a friendly from a hostile," he says, shrugging.

"I guess that's true," I say. Then, holding on tight to his hand, I ask, "Ready?"

"Are you?" he counter asks.

"Yes," I say. I don't need to look into his mind for Bane's homebase, but I look anyways to see if there's a specific place, he's wanting me to Jump to. He's picturing the furthest end of the clearing, away from the entrance.

I close my eyes this time and can feel the

difference as soon as we've arrived. The air is so much cooler, I can feel goosebumps popping up all over my skin. I open my eyes and see that a small layer of snow has fallen in the last hour or so. I turn to Xander and see him instructing the Force Unit here to join the ranks.

"Hey stranger," someone says behind me, I recognize Bronson's voice.

I turn and see him smiling at me, but the smile doesn't reach his eyes. He looks pissed.

"Hey, Bronson," I say. I gesture out into the trees where I can hear sound of screeching and yelling, "Any idea on what's out there?"

"No idea," he says, glaring in the direction ahead of us. "They backed off as soon as we started to Shift, so they haven't really shown themselves yet."

"Are Bane and Maisie back?" I ask, looking around.

"No, but they're on their way," he states.

"I wish I would have known where they were, we could have picked them up along the way," I say, looking around at the Elite Force as Xander talks to them.

"Sounds like you've done plenty," Bronson says.

I'm about to say something back to Bronson, but Xander walks up to us.

"Ready to Jump to the clearing?" he asks as he turns to me.

"Yes," I say, I can feel myself becoming dizzy, but I

force it away. *Now is not the time.* I take Bronson's hand and Xander's hand. I look into Xander's mind and see the clearing. Taking a mental step, we arrive as soon as I think about being here.

"That was awesome," Bronson says.

"Do you smell that?" the Werewolf next to Xander asks.

I take a deep breath and feel like my nose is instantly on fire, my eyes start to water. I ask, "What is that?"

"You can smell it too?" Xander asks surprised.

"Yes, what is that?" I ask again.

"Something evil," Bronson states. "Demi-gods can't usually smell demon stench."

"I'm not your normal Demi-god, remember?" I say while forcing a laugh and breathing through my mouth.

"That you aren't," Xander says. "Your senses will get used to it here in a second and it'll stop burning."

I wipe the tears away from my eyes and put my hand to my nose, trying to ease the burn. *I need a breeze please.* I send out and as soon as I think it, a breeze comes. It pushes the stinky stench away from us.

"That's better," I say.

"Let me guess, that breeze was from you?" Xander asks.

I smile and shrug.

"How long will we have to wait to see if they've taken the bait to come to us?" I ask.

"Not long," Xander says.

I hurriedly grab my phone out of my backpack and open the Map app, I put a pin in our location. I quickly make a group text and share our location with my friends.

Me- *We made it to Montana. Here is where we'll be fighting whatever is attacking. We're hoping we can draw them away from the homebase.* 10:10am Thursday

I put my phone back in my bag and then take my bags off and lay them on the ground. I turn around and look at all the Werewolves. They're scanning the trees as they spread out into a circle, me in the middle with Xander and Bronson.

"Will you guys Shift into your Wolf forms?" I ask.

"Some of us will," Xander answers. "It just depends on how each Wolf is more comfortable fighting. I tend to Shift in and out of my Wolf, rather than stay in one form for the majority of the time. I feel like it throws who, or whatever, I'm fighting off balance."

"That makes sense," I say. "I can see how that could be a huge advantage."

"Have you ever tried Shifting?" Bronson asks. "With all the Talents you have, I'm just curious if

Shifting is one of them."

"I haven't tried but I think it would be fun to test it out, not today, I don't want to get stuck as a slug and not be able to Shift back in time to fight," I say.

Bronson and Xander both throw their heads back and laugh out really loud.

"The first thing you think to Shift to is a slug?" Bronson says, trying to catch his breath.

"No, but wouldn't that suck that out of everything in the World I could Shift into, the slug IS the only thing?" I ask.

"I highly doubt a slug is the only thing you could Shift into, knowing what I know about you and what I've learned, I doubt there's anything you can't Shift into," Xander says.

"I don't—" I'm interrupted by the loudest, creepiest, ear-piercing screech I've ever heard in my life. I turn around to look behind me and see people walking out of the trees and dark grayish, misshapen beings walking amongst them.

"I don't believe it," Xander says from beside me.

"What?" I ask.

"They're Morfopeases," Xander says. He looks down at me and sees my confused look. He explains a little more by saying, "Major Demons, they can morph into whatever they think will get them closest to you. You must keep your mind and heart clear of anything other than fighting them."

"Do demons usually fight alongside Demi's?" I ask, as I watch the horde of demons and Rifts flood out of the trees.

"No, never," Xander says. "Something awful has happened."

I see Werewolves starting to Shift and Wolves are mixed amongst the Weremen. The Rifts stop walking when they see the size of the Wolves. The demons also stop, neither of them having seen the Werewolves in their Wolf forms before.

"I will try to stay close to you," Xander says. "But if we get separated, stay safe, and fight strong."

"How do we vanquish the demons and send them back to where they came from?" I ask, my heart pounding the longer I look around at the Morfopeases.

"With all demons, we, Werewolves, just have to get our teeth into them and our venom does the rest. Father explained it's the mixture of the demon beast venom that changed him and his Demi-god blood," Xander explains.

"Okay, so basically I just have to figure it out as I go?" I ask.

"Yes, but if you have trouble, just join me or another Wolf and we'll help send it back to Tartarus," he says, snarling, as we watch a Rift take a couple steps out into the space between where the Wolves are and the Rifts and demons.

"Send out the Demi-god that hides amongst you

and we will leave in peace," the man says. "None of you need to be harmed, just give us the girl."

Xander steps away from me and when I go to walk with him, he puts his hand back, in a gesture for me to stay. Ignoring my urge to go with him, I stop and Bronson comes and stands beside me. Xander weaves between Wolves and Weremen until he's standing on the outside of our circle.

"There is no Demi-god hiding amongst us," Xander says.

"You deny she is here?" the Rift laughs out. "They can smell her."

The Morfopease closest to him lifts it's snout like nose into the air and breaths in a rattling breath. It's long, split tongues slither out of its mouth, and its beady black eyes look in my direction. A chill runs down my spine as its eyes lock on mine.

"Clear your mind. Be strong. Be Brave," Bronson says beside me, I feel him move closer to me and his warmth gives me the reassurance that I need to straighten my back and stare back at the creature.

"No, I'm not denying that she is here. But she is not hiding. She is here because she is family. Members of our family don't need to hide," Xander says. "What business do you have with her?"

"That's not your concern, give us the girl, and we'll leave," the man says. "No bloodshed needs to happen today. A Demi is meant to be with her kind, she is to be with us."

"She is closer to my kind than yours," Xander says. "The only bloodshed that will happen today will be those that you lose, so I suggest you leave and take your demons with you."

"That's not going to happen," the man says. He turns towards his group and gives a small nod. They take the steps needed to get to where he's standing. He looks back at Xander and with an evil sneer, he says, "Let the fun begin."

The demons start morphing into different things and beings, none of them able to pick one form. The Rifts yell and start running towards Xander and his Werewolves. Xander throws his hands in the air and yells something, but from the yelling Rifts, screeching demons, and now bellowing Werewolves, I can't hear what he says but it must have been the signal for the Werewolves to attack because now they're running towards the horde coming at them.

I take a second to center myself. Having never fought against demons before, I let my instincts take over, doing so has never steered me wrong before, and I doubt it'll start now. I feel my body start to warm and a serene feeling fills me. Closing my eyes, I let the warm and calm feeling flow through from my heart to my head, and then out to my limbs.

"What the–?" Bronson says beside me. I open my eyes and look up at him. He's looking down at me in astonishment. I look down at myself and see my hands are glowing with a white light.

"One of my Talents," I say and shrug, he looks at me with wide eyes.

I look out at the scene unfolding in front of us and see the two sides collide with each other. The Rifts pulling out their Magikidas or using Talents to try to bring down the Werewolves, but they are too fast and can move and twist like I've never seen before. They dodge the Magikidas, and the Talents being used on them don't seem to be fazing them. I see the Morfopeases now morphing into people, causing the Werewolves to faulter for a second, the pause giving the Rifts time to land a hit with their hands or feet, or a slice from their swords.

"The Morfopease are morphing into loved ones, aren't they?" I ask for confirmation from Bronson.

"Yes, they tend to choose those forms during a fight, at least that's what we have learned. This is the first time we've ever faced a Morfopease, let alone multiple," he says in disgust.

I watch as a Wolf is brought down by two large Rifts on its back and it howls in pain. Without thinking, I race over to the wrestling trio just as a Morfopease gets to them, it's about to sink its yellow teeth into the Wolf's neck when I throw my hands out and let my Light stream out. The Morfopease looks up and just before the light touches it, it's eyes actually bulge out of its head in surprise

When my Light hits it, it screams a high-pitched sound and then it explodes into ashes. The Rifts on the Wolf's back look up at me. For a split second, I see terror on their faces. Then, they're jumping off the injured Wolf, and are stalking towards me

One flings his hand out towards me and I swipe my hand in front of me like I'm swatting a fly away. I feel a tiny prickle on my palm as whatever he shot at me, hits me. It doesn't really hurt, it just feels like when you poke yourself on something. He throws something at me again and I swipe it away. He looks at his partner and back at me, and whispers something at him

The other Rift, the bigger of the two, smiles at me and rubs his hands together and then cracks his knuckles. They're close enough to me now that I can hear each crack

"This will be fun," the bigger Rift snarls

He charges me and I spin out of the way. He skids to a stop and turns back around, running at me again. Just as he's about to me, I hear running from behind me. I look quickly and see the other Rift coming up. I dive and roll to the side and the two Rifts smash into each other, their head making a sickening sound as they hit. I roll to my feet and prepare for another charge. The bigger one pushes the smaller Rift off of himself and looks down at his partner

"Paul?" he says, shaking him. Paul doesn't move, he's knocked out cold. The big Rift looks up at me and says, "You'll pay for this."

"I didn't do anything," I say, innocently. "You're the one who ran into him.

He snarls at me and charges. Just as he's getting to me, he bends down like he's going to tackle me. As I jump up, I put my hands on his shoulders and throw myself up into the air, flipping over his back. He spins quicker this time and catches my ankle, slamming me onto the ground

Before I have time to catch my breath, he pulls me up with my back against his chest, his arms wrap around my waist. He lifts me up and squeezes. If my breath hadn't been knocked out from landing on the ground so hard, he'd be squeezing the breath out of me know

Shit! I start to panic in my head

Emma? I hear Shae in my head. I can feel her searching my mind through our Link, so I let her see what's going on. *Shit! We're close. Stay calm, if you panic, you'll waste the air you have in your system. Remember your training*

With that thought, I throw my head back and connect with the Rifts nose. He grunts in pain and loosens his grip just enough that I can finally take a breath in, not the deep breath I want, but enough to get air into my lungs

Fire! I think in my head, willing it to form on my hands. I can feel my hands instantly get warm, so I put them on his arms that are wrapped around me. He screams in pain and I look down as I see my hands burning his skin. He drops me and takes a step away, looking down at his burnt skin

I roll away from him and stand in a crouched position, catching my breath. I shoot out a Stunning Ray at him and he crumples into a heap on the ground. I run to the Wolf as it's still lying on the ground

Are you okay? I ask. Its eyes open wide and it looks at me.

He stabbed me and slashed me on my left side. I hear a gravely male voice in my head. I'm not familiar with it so I must not have met this Werewolf yet. He tries to move to show me where he's hurt.

Lay still, I'll Heal you. I say. Again, his eyes go wide. I place my hands on his massive shoulder and his back. *Just watch around us and tell me if someone is coming. This won't hurt and it won't take long but I don't want anyone catching us off guard.*

Yes, ma'am. He says, even his mind voice sounds like he's in pain

With my hand on his shoulder and his back, I let my Healing Talent flow out. I can feel where he's hurt badly and I send my current to those spots first. I can also feel little nicks, and shallows cuts, around his legs, so I Heal those as well

I feel him shiver and then I pull my hands away, standing up. The huge Wolf stands and he shakes out his fur.

Thank you, Miss Emma. He says sincerely, he bows his head and pushes it into my chest. I scratch between his big ears and then pat him kindly.

Shall we? I ask as I step away and motion to join back into the fight.

Absolutely. I hear him say and then he growls. He runs away from me and jumps right back into the fight.

I turn just in time to see a Morfopease creeping up to me. I steady my heart and mind, not letting myself give away anything it could use against me. It starts to twitch but can't make a form. It stays in its awful original form. It starts making a clicking sound and sticks it's tongues out at me. The tongues get about a foot out before they stop and start wiggling in the air.

"That's gross," I say. I let my Light feel my hands again and start to move my hands in a circle, forming a ball. Before I throw it at it, I say, "You really shouldn't stick your tongues out at people."

I throw my ball of Light at it and it does the same as the last Morfopease. It screams and then explodes into ashes. I turn and look for where I can help, when I see new people appearing out of thin air.

CHAPTER
27- NO! NO!

I see Charlie appear with Ty, Max, and Clay. Then Charlie disappears but is back in less than a second with Tate, Tally, and Ret. I watch a couple more times as Charlie Jumps three people at a time into the clearing. My eyes search for Ty and find him shouting at his Guardians.

He must Sense me because he stops talking and looks around. Our eyes meet and we stare at each other. He smiles his devastatingly beautiful smile at me, and I can't help but smile back, even though we're literally in the middle of one hell of a fight.

The love I feel for this man makes my whole body come alive. This love gives me strength I didn't know I needed, I can feel my back get straighter and my nerves calm. But before I can go to him, my attention is pulled away by a cry of pain that reaches me through the other sounds going on around me.

I look away and see a Werewomen fighting three Rifts. One has his hand above his head like he's swinging an imaginary rope. When he brings it down repeatedly, the Werewoman screams in pain with each swipe he sends, I see blood spray into the air. *He must have some kind of Whip Talent.* I Run to her side and fling a protective glamour around her. I send my Healing current out to her and let it Heal her. I turn my eyes to the Rift with the Whip Talent and send out a blow that knocks him back on his ass and he rolls backwards like he's being pushed by something.

I send out a Stunning Ray and he lays motionless on the ground. The other two Rifts look down at him and then back up at me. They take two steps towards me and the Werewoman, who I can feel is Healed, I shake my head at them, making them stop in their tracks.

I turn to the Werewoman quickly, and ask, "Are you okay?"

"I am now, thank you, Miss Emma," she says.

"I've got these two, go help someone else," I say, nodding at her, my eyes on the two Rifts.

"Thank you," she whispers and runs away.

When she leaves, the two Rifts take a step towards me, and I shake my head again. "I wouldn't come any closer, if I were you."

My words have them freezing again. They look at each other and then back at the Rift lying on the ground. They look back at me and glare. They start walking at the same time again.

"I warned you," I say as I send Stunning Rays at both of them with my hands. They fall to the ground immediately and don't move.

I turn to find Ty again but see he has joined the fight. I also see he's brought almost all the Guardian's from home, if not all of them. I honestly can't say for sure if they're all here because I haven't met all of them yet. But there are at least 50 Demi-gods fighting alongside the Werewolves.

I look around and find myself in the center of the fighting but there's a good 20 yard perimeter of space between me and the fights going on around me. Whether the Werewolves are keeping the Rifts and Morfopease from getting to close to me or if it's just a coincidence, I'm not sure. I'm about to run to help a group of Wolves when I'm stopped in my tracks by a voice in my head. His voice.

You still refuse to bow to me? His voice says.

Kronos... I say with as much hatred as I can muster in my mind. A Morfopease close to me turns its head to me and stalks towards me. It starts shaking and its body starts to twist and change grotesquely. Soon, Kronos is standing in front of me.

"NO!" I shout.

You wish to see me, my love. He hisses in my mind.

"No, I don't," I say, I put my hand up and make the Morfopease stop. "Don't you dare call me your love."

He would not morph into my form if you didn't want

me. He croons softly and lovingly me in my head. *I will call you what I wish, my love, for you are mine, and mine alone.*

"I am not," I say, letting the truth in my words sink into my mind, making him feel the words.

You will see, I will make you mine. He says threateningly.

I let my Light get bright in my hands and then I throw it at the Morfopease as it takes a step towards me again. It explodes into ash.

"I will never be yours," I say. Without meaning to, I think of Ty and our last embrace.

You shouldn't test me, my love. He snarls.

I calm myself down and breath in some deep breaths.

"No matter what you say, I will never be yours. You've picked the wrong girl," I say sincerely.

You are my son's chosen daughter. YOU! ARE! MINE! He bellows. I wince at how loud his voice is in my head. When he speaks again, it's quieter and more sinister. *And mine alone.*

"If they are my fathers, or a part of me, then that makes me kind of your granddaughter, you sick freak," I say.

That does not matter to me. You are mine. He snarls again.

"No," I say bluntly. "Again, I am not. Not now. Not ever. You will never touch me."

So be it, I shall show you how far my reach is, even from this hole I am in. I am close, my love, to getting out and when I do, I will find you. I warned you. He says and then he's gone

I check my Mental Defense and find it's been weakened. *Maybe from Jumping, literally, around the World and all the use of my Talents. I can't let it weaken again.* I think to myself as I force my Defense to tighten back up and pull it tight.

I turn around to see where I'm needed and see two little kids advancing on a Werewoman, who's backing away from them with her hands out in front of her. Tears are running down her face.

I Run to her side.

"What's wrong?" I ask her, keeping my eyes on the kids. As I look, I see the beady eyes that I've come to know are the eyes of the Morfopease.

"My children," she cries out in a whisper.

"They aren't your children," I say, but even as I look at her and back at them Morfopease, I can't bring myself to vanquish them in these forms. *Evil geniuses to choose children forms, her children's forms.*

I feel my hands tingle and look down at them. My Light has changed from the pure white to a yellow like the sun. My instincts are telling me to hit them with this Light. So, I shoot it out at them. They instantly change from children to their original form.

I roll my hands into balls and let the Pure Light

fill my hands and then I throw it at the Morfopease. As they turn to ash, I turn to the Werewoman.

"See, not your children," I say, putting my hand on her shoulder. She's trembling. "Maybe you should try to fight in your Wolf form. Use the strength of your connected minds to help keep your family members images out of your head, that way the Morfopeases can't use it against you."

"Thank you, Miss Emma, that's a good idea," she says. She nods and then Shifts quickly. She shakes her fur out and stretches before she bounds away.

As I'm looking around to see where I'm needed next, I see the Rifts being taking down quicker by Demi's and the Werewolves taking out the Morfopeases. And I see combination of the two Beings working together to take down whatever they're fighting against.

From across the clearing, I see Vanessa. My feet feel stuck to the ground. *When did she get here?* I ask myself. Beside her, I see Chris. They've brought more Rifts and Morfopease with them and he's shouting at them and waving in every direction, motioning for them to join the fight.

All around me I see Magikidas being drawn and Demi's and Rifts fighting each other with them as well as their Talents. Werewolves are being attacked by more than one Morfopease but holding their own, for now.

I have to do something! I shout at myself. *Get moving!*

I run around, joining fights left and right. Vanquishing Morfopease and Stunning Rifts. Just as I feel like we're getting the upper hand again, I feel someone beside me.

I look and see Ty.

"Hey," he says out of breath, looking down at me.

"Hey," I say back. He pulls me away from the throng of people we're surrounded by and pulls me into his arms. I wait for the thrill of electricity that comes from his touch but it doesn't come. *Weird. Must be from my adrenalin already being so high from fighting.*

"Let's get out of here," he says, putting his hands on my shoulders. "I can't bear the thought of losing you."

"We can't leave," I say, shocked by his words. "We have to stay and fight."

"I know, but—" he takes a breath "—the possibility of losing you is distracting me."

"Well, I'll be fine," I say. "Focus on getting this battle over so we can go home."

He's about to say something when I hear another howl of pain. I turn and see another Wolf being swarmed by Morfopease.

"Go, do your thing," he says. He bends down and kisses me deeply. It feels wrong. I pull back and look him in the eyes. His beautiful eyes stare back at me and a smirk crosses his face. "I've been waiting forever to do that."

I shake my head and as I turn to help the Wolf, I reach out for its mind.

Get off of me you stinkin' piece of– before she can finish her thought, the Morfopease on her back, digs a dagger like claw into her side. She howls in pain again, "ARRRRRROOOOOO!"

I Run to her and as I get to her, I throw my hands out and throw the Morfopease off of her. Using one hand, I throw out my Pure light and start turning the Morfopease to ash. With the other, I pace it on the Wolf's shoulder and Heal her quickly. Once the demons are gone, I look around to make sure we're in the clear for a minute, and then place both hands on the Wolf.

"Easy," I say to her. I can feel her panting. "I'll have you healed in a minute."

Thank you. She thinks with anguish soaking thoughts. It takes another couple of minutes to heal her completely, the Morfopease did a number on her.

"You are one tough Wolf," I say to her as I feel she's fully healed. I pat her shoulder and push her up and away from me. "Get back out there."

She barks out a laugh and runs away.

I turn just in time to see Ty fighting two Rifts and a Morfopease. He's holding his own. I turn and see Charlie and Max fighting four Rifts, one goes down a hole that Charlie must have opened up with his Earth Talent. Max whips his hand around his head and the Rift directly in front of him starts spinning and floating in the air like a tornado has a hold of him. It's the first time I've seen Max use his Wind Talent.

Clay and Tate are fighting a Morfopease each. The demons keep changing from different people and back to their original forms at an alarming rate. Clay and Tate must be having to really focus on not thinking of their loved ones and concentrating on the fight, to keep the Morfopeases from morphing.

I see Tally fighting alongside a Demi I don't recognize, and she takes down a Rift with a swipe of her Magikida. I look around the fray, to see if I can find Libby or Shae, or Malory and Alysa, but I don't see them anywhere. They must be wherever the Guardians were Jumped from.

Good, I don't think they've had enough training for this, this is some intense stuff. I think as I watch a Wereman fighting a Morfopease that keeps turning from a child back to its awful form. When it's back to its disgusting self, the Wereman jumps at it and sinks his teeth into its neck. The demon starts to shake and almost curls in on it's self and then it bursts into ash.

I look back over at where Ty is fighting and see that Vanessa has joined in, and is throwing something at Ty. It feels like time slows down. I see Ty batting away whatever she's throwing at him. He swipes his

Magikida out and the Morfopease he hits vanquishes immediately.

Oh! Our swords work too? I errantly think to myself. I force myself to move my feet, to get my body moving. I can see Ty's facing turning red and his chest is heaving. He's getting tired. *I need to get to him.* But before I can Run or Jump myself to him, I see Vanessa evil smile come across her face as she throws a black ball of something at Ty and as he tries to deflect it, it goes right past his hand, and hits him square in the chest.

For a split second, my world stops. Everyone stops moving. All sound is snuffed out. I watch as Ty falls in slow motion, backwards and lands on the ground, his body bouncing a little until he doesn't move again.

As fast as my word stopped and the sound went away, it comes back faster and louder. I hear someone screaming. I realize it's me.

"NOOOOOOOOO!" I yell out. I see red. Everything around me has a tint of red. Rifts rush me, I bat them away, Stunning them as they take a step towards me. All the Morfopease leave who their fighting and all converge on me.

I let my Pure Light fill me and I throw my arms up and out wide in front of me, letting the Light explode out towards all the Morfopease. As they all scream and erupt into ash at the same time, my feet start to move.

As my eyes are locked on Ty's body, I see out of my

peripheral vision, Rifts now leaving who they were fighting and surge towards me. I take step after step, willing myself to Run.

Get to Ty. You have to— My thought is cut off as I see Ty's silver light leaving his body.

"No… no…" I whisper out, my feet stumbling over themselves. I feel the first wave of Rifts getting closer. I feel a pain like nothing I've ever felt rip through me. I also feel an anger I've never felt before either. I throw out my hands, blasting all the Rifts coming towards me with Stunning Rays. They go flying backwards and fall into each other, not moving.

I have an open path to Ty. I see Vanessa through my red haze of fury. She looks around at all her men and women lying in piles around me. She surprises me with a smile. She looks down at Ty and smiles again. She winks at me and then vanishes into thin air, only to reappear twenty yards away, where Chris and some of the last Rifts are standing. Even the thought of Vanessa's new ability to Jump, doesn't take my focus away from Ty's light.

I finally Run to him but I'm too late. His sliver of bright white is fading. I raise my hand and will it to come back to me. I use whatever Talents I can think of to bring it back. Wind doesn't touch it. Nothing works. As I watch it drift farther up, I place my hand on Ty's chest. He's still warm but I can't feel his essence anymore. His heart doesn't beat. I put my hand up towards his silver light and beg the gods to help me.

"Please, Fathers, help me save him. I can't lose him," I say as tears run down my face. But as I beg, I see his light slowly disappear as the sunlight hits it. I shout, "NO!"

Out of the corner of my eyes, I see Demi-gods walking closer to me. I see them look down at Ty and then up at me, and then over at where I know Vanessa and Chris are standing.

I thought I was angry before but now, this anger I feel, is nothing I've ever felt.

"ARRRGH!" I scream out. I jump to my feet and turn towards Vanessa.

Yes, embrace this feeling. Use it to destroy your enemy. I hear Kronos' voice in my head. *Embrace this rage. I can help you defeat her and her followers.*

I'm shocked for a second to hear him speaking of helping me that the ringing in my ears fades enough that I can hear someone calling my name.

"Emma!" Tally yells. I don't take my eyes off of Vanessa, her smile is turning into a frown.

"YOU!" I scream.

Yes, take her out! Kronos says encouragingly in my head. *Hurry. Take her out before she disappears again. Revenge your Anima Gemella's death.*

I take a step towards Vanessa, my hands balling into fists.

"Emma!" I hear his voice and I jolt to a stop.

CHAPTER 28 -
SOME FEELINGS WILL STICK WITH YOU FOREVER

I *t can't be.* I look down at Ty's body on the ground. His eyes are closed and he's still motionless.

"Emma," I hear his voice again. I turn in a circle, trying to find where it's coming from.

I freeze in my second turn around. Ty is standing in front of me. I stumble back. My eyes going down to the body on the ground. I quickly look up to the Ty standing in front of me. I turn my head and look behind me where Vanessa is standing. She looks pissed.

I turn back to the Ty standing and my left hand goes to my chest, where I can feel my heart trying to escape. My right hand goes to my mouth to stifle the sob that's coming.

"Ty?" I breathe out.

"Yes, it's me," he says, taking a step towards me tentatively. "I don't know who that is but it's not me."

I see Tally and Tate standing behind Ty, their eyes going from the Ty on the ground to the Ty in front of them. They look as shocked as I feel. Charlie, Clay, and Max walk up behind Ty as well, looking just as confused.

"I... I..." I say.

He's lying. Your Ty is dead. Kronos says frantically. I throw my Defenses back up now that I can think clearly.

"That's it," the Ty standing says. "Take a breath and try to calm down. Look at me, trust me."

I look Ty in the eyes and even without touching him, I feel the zing of electricity zip around me. I look down at the Ty on the ground and feel confused. I feel the warmth in my hands return and I look down, seeing them glowing with the Yellow Light. I lift my right hand and with my palm out, I shoot it out at the Ty on the ground. He shines for a second and then I see Zack lying on the ground.

I stumble away, startled.

"What in the hell?" I hear Charlie say.

I feel an arm on my shoulder and I jump. I turn and see Ty, my Ty, looking at me with concern.

"Emma, I don't know how to explain that yet—" he points at Zack "—but I'm right here. I'm alive. I'm fine."

"Ty," I cry out. He pulls me into his arms and holds me while I bawl. I can feel something trying to pull at my thoughts, but I push it way with as much force as I can and it instantly stops and disappears.

"AHHH!" I hear someone scream. I turn in Ty's arms and see Vanessa writhing in pain from where they're standing. "No! It's not my fault!"

I see Chris holding her up, he says something to one of the Rifts behind them who hurriedly touches Chris and Vanessa's shoulders. They disappear before I can tell someone to get to them. The other Rifts turn to each other and Jump away as well.

I hear cheering and turn in Ty's arm again and see all the Wolves have Shifted back into their Werewolf forms. They are pumping their fists in the air and clapping each other on the shoulder. I look around and see only Rifts lying on the ground. I scan the crowd and see Xander and Bronson walking towards us.

When they get close enough, I don't move from Ty's arms, but I reach my hand out for Xander. He takes it and squeezes.

"You fought well, young one," he smiles at me. "Everywhere I looked, you were there, kicking demon ass."

"I'm so relieved to see you're okay," I say, looking at Bronson. "You too, and everyone else.

I look closer and see that Xander has a cut on his shoulder but it's not bleeding too bad, he'll be able to heal it himself with his Werewolf traits. Bronson has what looks like the start of a black eye. I look around my friends and see they all have cuts and bruises but all of those will be healed soon too.

"What happened here?" Xander says, looking down at Zack. "Isn't this the kid that escaped?"

"Yes," I say, pointedly.

"He looked like him and then you changed him into this," Bronson says, confused.

"Did you come up to me during the fight?" I ask Ty, looking up at him.

"No, I only saw you from across the way when we first got here, and then we joined the fight," he answers.

"It was him," I say, piecing it all together as I talk. "I think he must have had someone Shift him into looking like Ty to get closer to me. He came to me, disguised as you, and asked me to leave with him. It didn't feel right... something inside me didn't feel right but I thought it was just from being in the middle of the fight. And when he touched me and kissed me, I didn't feel the same either."

Zack's comment after he kissed me makes sense now.

"He kissed you?" Ty says between clenched teeth.

"Yeah," I say. Feeling ashamed, I add, "I'm sorry."

"I'm not mad at you, he duped you," Ty says. "If he weren't dead, I'd like to throat punch him."

"No reason to be upset about it," Tate says, patting Ty's shoulder. "Because he is, in fact, dead."

"I know, I just don't like the thought of someone

doing that to Em," Ty says, running his hand through his hair. He looks at me and says, "I was worried about you, there for a second. The look on your face... I've never seen that look before."

"When?" I ask.

"Right before I got your attention," he says as he rubs his hands on my arms. His touch is slowly warming me up. I hadn't realized I'd gotten so cold. "Your eyes turned dark, like the light behind them had gone out. You looked like you could kill. And your hands..."

"What about my hands?" I ask, looking down at them.

"They had a black mist twirling around them," Tally says.

"Did they?" I ask, picking each hand up and looking at them closely.

"Yeah," Ty said.

"I was seeing red. I was feeling a pain I've never felt before and hope to never feel again," I say, stepping closer to Ty and turning so my back's against him. "When I saw Vanessa, the pain turned to an anger I can't explain in words. And then... Kronos was in my head, encouraging me to take Vanessa out."

"Would you have?" Ty asks.

"With how I was feeling, I'm afraid I would have," I say, bowing my head. "I... I wanted the pain to stop, and I wanted Vanessa to stop taking away the people that mean the most to me. You were dead... I thought you were dead. When Kronos started egging me on, I felt like killing Vanessa would be the only way to stop all of it, the pain and her taking everyone from me."

Ty's arms tighten around me.

"You know that killing her wouldn't make the pain go away, right?" Ty says softly. "Nothing can take that pain away. Not even time, I don't care what anyone says. When someone is truly taken from us, nothing can make it feel better. We just have to learn how to live with the pain. We have to come to terms with the loss and continue living the way we know we should."

"I know," I say. "At least, I know that when I'm thinking clearly. I now know that if I ever feel like that again, I'll have to really focus on not letting the pain take over. I can't let the anger it caused take over. I truly believe that someone being sentenced to death should be a last resort. I also believe that Vanessa can't be reformed to a decent Demi, but does she deserve to die? That's not my decision to make. I have to learn how to control my anger towards her. I don't know how to practice that but the feeling of losing you will stay with me forever, so maybe I can recall it enough to practice."

"We both need to practice that," Ty says. "I too, still have the feeling of losing you burned into my brain."

"I hear meditation helps," Tally suggests.

"I think we could all benefit from learning how to control our feelings from when we thought we lost someone," Charlie says with a grim look on his face.

"Not to change the subject but—" Tate starts to say "—what do we do with all these Rifts?"

"The Stronghold?" I ask, turning from Ty to Xander.

"That's what I was thinking," Xander says. "There's plenty of room and no chance of escape, unless they chose death over imprisonment."

"The Stronghold is the best place," Ty says. "It's where we should have taken Frank. But we weren't done questioning him."

"Speaking of Frank," Clay says as he pulls his phone out. "I wonder if the other Unit got to him."

I look up at Ty questioningly.

"I sent a small Unit to finish Tracking down Frank. I'll check in with them here in a minute," he says.

"Are we taking him back to the Estate?" I ask.

"No," Ty says firmly. "We've been interrogating Frank long enough. He hasn't given us any useful information. It's the Stronghold for him as well."

"I'll get the jet's up and running, and we can take care of transferring the Rifts to the Stronghold," Xander says.

"Why don't I take care of that?" I hear a faintly

familiar voice from behind us. I turn and see Bane and Maisie standing there, looking around in shock.

"Father," Xander says, standing at attention.

"Grandfather," Bronson says, following Xander's example.

"Bane!" I shout. I walk to him and hug him. I turn to Maisie and hug her too, "Maisie!"

"Hello, Miss Emma," she says as she pats my back. I step out of our hug and back to Ty. "It looks as if things have been taken care of here. We went straight to the house and we were told by Miss Libby that you all were here."

"What happened?" Bane asks, looking around.

"I'll fill you in when we're back at the house," Xander says. "I'll have the Elite Force bind the Rifts so if one or some wake up, they can't escape."

"Sounds good," Bane says.

"Wait," I say. "I'll make it so if one, some, or all wake up, they won't be able to Jump if one of them has that Talent."

"How—" Tally starts to ask, but Charlie cuts her off.

"Haven't you learned, there's not much Emma can't do," Charlie says. "If she suggests something, just assume it's a Talent."

"Good point," Tally says, laughing.

I step away from Ty and spread my hands out in front of me and put a glamour on all the Rifts so that they can't Jump or disappear from this clearing using any type of Talent.

"It's done," I say. "I'd still bind them so if they do wake up, they can't run away. I only made it so they can't escape by a Talent from this clearing."

Xander salutes me and then nods at his father. He says, "Excuse me, I'll meet you back at the house."

"So, Miss Emma, I hear you've been needing a word with me," Bane says. Maisie leaves him and starts walking around the Werewolves. She checks their wounds and hugs them tightly. I pull my attention back to Bane and get my train of thought back to him.

"Yes, I have. I was trying to track you down to see if you've seen or heard from our Leaders. Meredith, Doc, and Bill have been missing for months," I say.

"Are you sure they're missing?" Bane asks.

I look at Ty who looks at me with his brow furrowed, and then he looks back at Bane.

"Pretty sure," Ty says. "We haven't seen or heard from them since before the battle at the Elders."

"But does that mean they're missing?" Bane asks again.

"I can't imagine them leaving on a mission without telling us. Or the very least, getting into contact with us," Ty says but he sounds unsure.

"Was there a sign of a struggle when they first went missing?" Bane asks.

"No," Ty says slowly.

"Perhaps they aren't missing. Maybe they're on their own journey," Bane says.

"Do you know something?" I ask. "Have you spoken with them?"

Bane looks at me and then at Ty, then around at the others. He finally answers with, "I haven't spoken to them in a month or so but that is all I will say."

"They're okay, though?" I ask.

"Yes, as of the last time I talked to them, they were okay," he answers as he pats my arm reassuringly. "Now, if you'll excuse me, I need to go talk with the Elite Force and my son."

"Excuse me, Bane," Tate says as he steps up beside me. "I'm Tate Conner. My sister and I are here in the States looking for one of our lead Guardians, Arthur Blanc. Have you by chance seen him or heard anything about him?"

"He is with the other Leaders," Bane says. "Now, I must go check on my men."

"Thank you, Bane," I say. He salutes me, nods to the others, and then walks away.

"I can't believe they left without saying anything," Ty says.

"I'm confused, too," Tate says as Tally comes up and puts a hand on his shoulder..

"I'm sure they had their reasons," Tally says positively.

"Should we go back to the main house?" I ask. "I'm starving."

"How are you feeling?" Ty asks, taking my hand as we start walking back to Bane's house.

"Not too bad actually," I say. "I feel tired but not like I'm going to pass out like I have before. But I feel hungry, really hungry."

"Let's go get you some food," Ty says.

"Hang on," I say. I let go of Ty's hand for a second and Jump myself over to where my bags are still lying. I grab them up and then Jump myself back over to Ty and my friends. Ty laughs as he reaches for my bags.

"Let me carry these for you," he says. "You've carried enough of a burden for today."

"Thanks," I say. I reach up on my tiptoes and kiss his cheek. He turns quickly and kisses me on the lips.

"Hold off on making out until we get somewhere where you can get a room, okay?" Tally says from beside us.

I step away from Ty but we both laugh. Some alone time with Ty is exactly what I need right now. We start walking back down the trail, heading to Bane's house.

"Hold up," I hear Xander's voice from behind us.

I stop and turn, Xander catches up quickly.

"I'll walk with you, Father's going to take some time checking in with the Elite, to make sure they're all good," Xander says. "He told me he'd be to the main house shortly to hear what happened."

"Sounds good," I say.

We start walking, everyone silent for the first half of the walk back.

Charlie breaks the silence by saying, "I can't believe Vanessa and Chris got away again."

"I was thinking the same thing," Max says.

"Let's make a rule right now. The next time we are in a battle and they show up, we all try our hardest to get to them before they can disappear. No matter what's going on around us, our number one priority is to get to them and make sure they can't get away again," I state.

"Agreed," they all say together.

"Did you see how she Jumped?" I ask.

"Yes, where did that come from?" Clay asks.

"She must have it the way she and the others have been able to use Talents that aren't their natural Talents," Charlie answers.

"We've got to figure out how their doing that," Max says.

"I think it has to do with Kronos," I say. "I don't think he can give them Talents but I think he might be able to tell them how or who to use to learn how to take Talents from someone else."

"Now that we know Vanessa has been in contact with him too, I think you're right," Ty says.

"Did you also see how she was in pain right before

they Jumped her away?" Tally asks.

"Yeah, that was weird," Tate replies.

"I have a feeling Kronos was punishing her. He must have more power over her because she's vowed herself to him, so he has an actual connection with her," I say, only guessing at what was happening to her. "She might not have even been in physical pain, he was only making her think she was in pain, like attacking her mentally."

"You might be right," Ty says. "Which is another reason for you to keep your Defenses up."

"I'm not going to argue with you on that," I say, cringing inward at the thought at how close I was to letting Kronos talk me into doing something dark and unforgiving.

As we walk into the clearing, we hear yells of relief.

"Clay!" Malory says.

"Charlie!" Shae yells.

"Max!" Libby hollers.

They were all sitting on the front porch and are now running towards us. Their three men run towards them and scoop them up into tight embraces, kissing them enthusiastically.

I feel Xander freeze beside me. I stop and look back at him, he's just a couple steps behind us.

"What's wrong?" I ask.

His eyes are looking all over the clearing,

bouncing from all the little cabins and then up to the main house. They search the entire front porch and then they look like they're looking into every window. I hear the front door open and close and then the loudest gasp I think I've ever heard. I look back at the porch and see Alysa standing at the top of the stairs.

"Alysa," Xander whispers out.

"What's going on?" Ty asks from beside me.

I smile hugely at him and says, "Watch and see."

"Alysa," Xander breathes out again. I look up at him and see his pupils have dilated again.

"Come on, I'll introduce you to Alysa properly," I say, grabbing his arm and pulling him with me. Ty looks at me confused.

As we get closer, Alysa walks down the stairs slowly. Not in her dramatic way she would have normally but as if she's in a trance. Her eyes are stuck on Xander's eyes. He's breathing heavily but not in a creepy way. I laugh a little to myself and pull him along. We pass the trio of couples and they stop kissing.

"Emma!" Shae and Libby exclaim at the same time.

"Hi!" I say excitedly, momentarily sidetracked from Xander's introduction. The girls dislodge themselves from their men and come hug me. "I've missed you!"

"We've missed you too," they say in unison again.

"Emma, please," Xander whispers out impatiently.

"Sorry, sorry," I say, looking up at him. He looks as if he's in physical pain.

"What's going on?" Libby asks.

"Come and watch," I say. I look at Shae and nod towards her sister. She smiles and goes to Charlie to walk with him.

We don't have far to walk before Alysa meets us. I stop Ty and I from walking but Xander takes another couple steps forward. Ty looks at me and then at Xander.

"Xander Woods, this is Alysa Shae," I say. "Alysa, this is Xander."

"Xander," she whispers out.

"Alysa," he counter whispers.

They extend their hands to shake and when their skin touches, you can see their bodies shake from the shock.

"My mate," Xander says with so much feeling behind his words, my eyes tear up.

"My Anima Gemella," Alysa says in a whisper.

"What?" everyone else says in a gasp of disbelief.

I laugh and grab Ty's upper arm with my hand and hug him to me.

Alysa and Xander close the distance between each other and Xander drops his head so his forehead is against Alysa's.

"You have no idea how long I've been waiting for you," Xander says softly.

"I'd love for you to tell me," Alysa says sweetly. "Please, I want to know everything about you."

Xander pulls his head away from Alysa and starts to walk past Bane's home and leads Alysa away from us.

"Umm, what just happened?" Libby asks as she laughs.

"Alysa finally found her Anima Gemella!" Shae cheers.

"A Werewolf?" Charlie breathes out.

"I mean, it's pretty fitting. Her Anima Gemella needs to have a tough skin so to speak," Clay says, laughing. Malory slaps his shoulder, but she can't hide her giggle. "Am I wrong? We can all agree she's not the easiest to get along with at times."

"I think this is going to change her in a way you'll all be surprised," I say, watching Xander lead Alysa up the steps and into what I guess is his cabin. "I think part of her... issue... was that she wanted her Anima Gemella so badly it started to make her bitter and spiteful."

"You're not wrong," Shae says, laughing.

"A Werewolf though?" Charlie says again.

"They have their complications that they'll have to work out, but Xander is an amazing man, not just Wereman, but man. He'll be good for her," I say.

"Miss Emma," a young girl says from the main house door. "My name is Nelly. My granddaddy, Bane, called and said you'd be coming back to the house. I've prepared some food for you all, if you'd like to come in and get something to eat."

"Oh, thank you, Nelly," I say. "That would be wonderful."

We walk up the steps and follow her into the house. She leads us to the dining room table and gestures for us to sit.

"We'll bring out the food," she says, saluting as she leaves the room. We don't have to wait long before she's coming in with two plates full of food, and a couple more servers are behind her.

Once they've given us our plates, Nelly says, "We'll bring in some drinks and just let us know if you'd like more food. We have plenty if you need more."

"Thank you, Nelly. This looks great," I say.

As she leaves, Charlie says, "Bane has a waitstaff?"

"It's part of their act of service years," I say before I take a bite of food. It tastes so good. It's chicken fettuccini alfredo, a green salad, and garlic toast. I look at my watch and see it's just after noon. *The battle only lasted a little more than two hours?*

"What do you mean by their act of service years?" Libby asks, leaning forward.

I explain to them the stages of learning for Werewolves and answer questions the best I can. I'm just finishing my second helping of the alfredo when Xander and Alysa walk into the room, holding hands.

"Hey there," Shae says. She stands and hugs her sister. I think it's the first genuinely loving hug I've seen them give each other. Shae turns to Xander, "Hi brother-in-law, I'm Shae, well my name is Malysa but I go by Shae."

Xander laughs and gives Shae a hug, "It's nice to meet you, Shae."

Xander gestures for Alysa to sit where she likes and as soon as their both seated, Nelly brings food out for them. Alysa thanks her graciously and I look wide eyed at Ty. There's already a huge difference in Alysa. I don't think I've ever heard her say thank you to someone she feels is lesser than her.

"What did we miss?" Xander asks.

"Not much. Emma was just filling us in on your stages of learning for your younger crowd," Libby says. "I love the idea of act of service and for multiple years. I think it's a wonderful way to teach people how to be selfless."

"Emma is a quick learner, I'm sure there isn't anything she doesn't know about my family," Xander says fondly.

"Oh, I'm still learning things. I don't know it all," I laugh.

"May we join you," Maisie's voice comes from the other side of the room. I look up and see her and Bane walking towards us with Bronson.

"Please," I say excitedly.

I watch as Maisie and Bane walk down and sit across from Xander and Alysa. Maisie cocks her head to the side and then her hand goes to her mouth.

"Xander," she says his name in a loud but lovingly way.

Xander gets up and asks Alysa for her hand, they walk around the table and Bane and Maisie stand up slowly. I hear Xander introduce Alysa and when he's finished telling his parents who she is, I hear Maisie squeal in delight.

"Mother-in-law to be doesn't have a problem with a Demi-god as a daughter-in-law," Charlie says from beside me. I elbow him but hide my laugh with my hand.

"I think she's relieved and happy that Xander has finally found his other half, can you imagine waiting almost 200 years to find Shae?" I ask him. "I know I'd be over the moon excited after waiting that long."

Charlie looks down at Shae, who's head is leaning up against his shoulder. He kisses the top of her head and then looks back at me.

"I wasted too much time without her, so no, I don't want to even think about what it would be like to have to wait 200 years," he breathes out, the humor he had just a minute ago, is gone.

I put my head on Ty's shoulder and watch

the happy parents embrace their, soon to be, newest daughter-in-law and then they sit and eat. Conversation breaks out along the table. The guys telling their parts of the story of the battle. Who they fought, how many Morfopeases they vanquished. How many Rifts they took down. How much fun it was to fight alongside the Werewolves and how they hope they'll get another chance to do it again.

"Emma, is this true?" I hear Bane ask. I open my eyes, I hadn't realized I'd closed them.

"I'm sorry, Bane, is what true?" I ask.

"What Xander has just told me?" he counter asks.

"I'm sorry, I didn't hear what he was saying," I say, confused.

"He said you Jumped around the World gathering the Elite Force to get them here quickly," Bane says.

"Oh, yeah, that's true," I say.

Bane and Maisie look at each other along with everyone else.

"You did?" Ty asks.

"How else were we going to get here as fast as possible?" I ask him back.

"I thought they were already assembled. Not that you had to Jump around to gather them all up," Ty says in shock.

"Oh, no. They were all at their homebases," I say as I take another bite of my food.

Ty looks down at his food, looking more shocked

than before.

"How are you not passed out?" Max asks from across the table.

"I had snacks," I say, shrugging.

"The key to you not passing out is eating a snack?" Libby asks doubtfully.

"Yeah, I think so, it keeps my energy up, doesn't it?" I say.

"We'll have to make sure we carry snacks everywhere we go," Ty says.

"I'm not saying I'm not tired, because I am, but it's not the complete exhaustion that I feel after I've Jumped a bunch of people," I admit. "I feel like I could sleep for a couple of hours, but not days. Does that make sense?"

"It does," Ty says. He kisses my head and adds, "We'll go take a nap as soon as we're done with lunch."

I look down at Bane and see that he's back to listening to Xander. Maisie's hand is to her mouth and she looks shocked. Occasionally, Bane's expression turns to surprise as well and he looks at me in astonishment.

"No way, did she really?" I hear Bane say. I look back down at him and he looks at me. "Emma, did you vanquish an entire legion of Morfopease?"

"Yes, not all, but a good portion of them at the end," I say, uncertain at why his tone is so stern.

"And knock out the group of Rifts that I saw

laying out in the clearing?" he asks.

"I didn't do all of that, the others helped," I say quickly. "Everyone helped and did their part."

Bane stands and walks down to me. He squats down and gets eye level with me.

"You, dear young one, are something else," he says and then a huge smile crosses his face. "You are truly magnificent, and I can't be prouder to welcome you into our family. You and your friends."

"We are just so grateful for what you've done for our family," Maisie says, coming to stand behind her husband.

Bane stands and steps beside her, grabbing her hand. "You all fought a battle that wasn't yours to fight. You all stood as true Demi-gods today. As someone who was once in those shoes, I am proud of you all, young ones."

"Thank you," Maisie says wholeheartedly

"For coming to the aid of my family, please know that you have my family's loyalty, Emma. You have brought back our faith in the Demi-gods. With you leading the way, I know we can right the World again," Bane says, saluting me

A chorus of cheers and agreement erupts around the table from my friends and new... family. There's no other way to explain the feeling I have for the Werewolves, other than family. It's how I feel about my Demi friends and everyone back home at the

Estate.

"Thank you, Bane and Maisie," I say, as a tear rolls down my face. "That truly means the world to me."

The table quiets back down and conversation picks back up. Bane and Maisie, with Xander and Alysa, excuse themselves from the table and head back outside, it looks as if they're continuing their talk out there.

I settle myself back in my chair and put my head back on Ty's shoulder. We're listening to the stories the guys are still telling. I lean into Ty and just enjoy the comfort of the happiness that's coming off everyone's essence in this moment.

I know I'll have to start planning my journey to the next Realm, but for now, I can enjoy my friends, my family.

Once again, a special thank you to my Beta readers. I want you all to know how much I appreciate all the time and support you have given me through this process of writing "Emma Hart and the Werewolves". It's been a long road, but with all your encouragement and enthusiasm when I would bring up an idea I had or that I had **finally** finished another chapter, I can honestly say this wouldn't have gotten finished if it weren't for you seven wonderful people. So, thank you! THANK YOU! THANK YOU!

Melissa Kendall
Danielle Martin
Jane Wisdom
Lacey Wisdom
Stephanie Mays
Mike Wisdom
Logan Nedrow

www.ingramcontent.com/pod-product-compliance
Lightning Source LLC
Chambersburg PA
CBHW032246020726
47497CB00014B/943